FROM BELOVED AND BESTSELLING
AUTHOR
ROSANNE BITTNER
COMES THE LONG-AWAITED
SEQUEL TO THE
SAVAGE DESTINY SERIES

Share in the love and laughter, tears and triumph, and the
exciting story of the Monroe family. The years have been
long but joyous, and now it's time for Abigail Monroe to
gather her family around and share their story with us one
last time . . .

* *

They heard the cry then, and all laughter and talking
ended for the moment as all eyes turned upward. The
cry came again, a familiar sound anyone who'd grown up
in this land knew, except that such things were usually
heard closer to the mountains.

An eagle was circling overhead. Abbie's heart nearly
stopped beating, and she felt Swift Arrow's grip tighten
around her. Even the youngest grandchildren fell silent,
as the eagle circled for several minutes.

"Father," Wolf's Blood said softly.

The big bird swooped down, gliding over their heads
and flying off toward the mountain peaks on the western
horizon.

"Dear God," Margaret muttered.

Abbie could not find her voice. There had been another time when an eagle flew near her, when she had
gone to the top of the mountain on which Zeke was buried. She had needed to know Lone Eagle was still with
her, and he had come, in the form of an eagle, circling
close enough for its wing tip to touch her cheek . . . and
she had not been afraid. She had only been comforted.

ROSANNE BITTNER

SAVAGE DESTINY
Eagle's Song

ZEBRA BOOKS
KENSINGTON PUBLISHING CORP.

ZEBRA BOOKS are published by

Kensington Publishing Corp.
850 Third Avenue
New York, NY 10022

First Printing: June, 1996
10 9 8 7 6 5 4 3 2 1

Printed in the United States of America

A dedication . . .

There are many people to thank for the publication of this book, most of all Walter Zacharias and Kensington Publishing. I am deeply grateful that they have agreed to reissue my entire SAVAGE DESTINY series so that new readers can now enjoy this wonderful family saga. My thanks also to two different editors who spent time on this book, Jennifer Sawyer and Kate Duffy; and my deep gratitude to my agent, Denise Marcil, without whose perseverance and support the reprint of this series and publication of a seventh book might never have happened.

Still, there is one person who deserves the biggest thanks of all, my very first editor, who bought that very first book back in 1982, Pesha Rubinstein. Pesha is an agent herself now, but it was she who worked with me on my very first sale, she who urged me to turn that first book into a series. One book turned into four, then six, and now here is the seventh. After forty books, I still have readers who say the SAVAGE DESTINY books are their favorite, and that Zeke and Abigail Monroe will live in their hearts forever. They will most certainly live in mine forever.

Thank you, Pesha, for believing in that first book and in my writing potential. This one is for you.

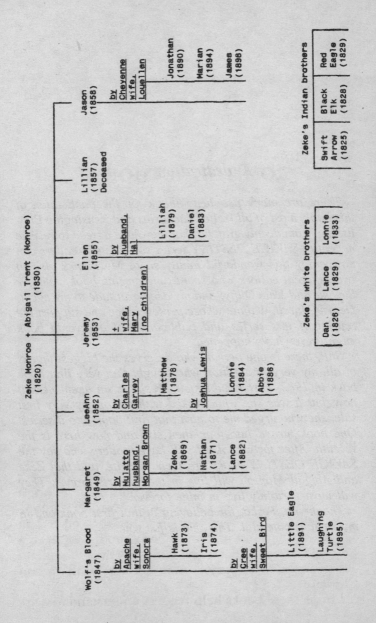

Zeke Monroe + Abigail Trent (Monroe)
(1820)   (1830)

Wolf's Blood (1847)

by Apache wife, Sonora
- Hawk (1873)
- Iris (1874)

by Cree wife, Sweet Bird
- Little Eagle (1891)
- Laughing Turtle (1895)

Margaret (1849)

by Mulatto husband, Morgan Brown
- Zeke (1869)
- Nathan (1871)
- Lance (1882)

LeeAnn (1852)

by Charles Garvey
- Matthew (1878)

by Joshua Lewis
- Lonnie (1884)
- Abbie (1886)

Jeremy (1853)

by wife, Mary (no children)

Ellen (1855)

by husband, Hal
- Lillian (1879)
- Daniel (1883)

Lillian (1857)
Deceased

Jason (1858)

by Cheyenne wife, Louellen
- Jonathan (1890)
- Marian (1894)
- James (1898)

Zeke's white brothers

Dan (1828)	Lance (1829)	Lonnie (1833)

Zeke's Indian brothers

Swift Arrow (1825)	Black Elk (1828)	Red Eagle (1829)

FROM THE AUTHOR . . .

Eagle's Song is the continuing saga of the Monroe family, book #7 in my *Savage Destiny* series. When I wrote and sold the first book of this series, *Sweet Prairie Passion*, I had no idea the story of the half-breed, Zeke Monroe, and the sixteen-year-old girl he married, Abigail Trent, would lead into such an epic family saga as had emerged by the time I wrote book #6, *Meet the New Dawn*. By then the characters in this dramatic unfolding of the settling of the West and its effect on the American Indian had become as real to me as my own relatives. I "lived" with them through forty-five years of tragedy and triumph.

Those of you who have followed this series know these characters well, but for those who are not familiar with them, I assure you that you can enjoy *Eagle's Song* with no confusion. As each character emerges, you will learn enough about him or her to go forward, moving into two new love stories involving two of Zeke Monroe's grandsons. *Eagle's Song* will carry both new and past readers into a new era for the Monroe family, continuing their quest to carry on the pride they all feel in being the sons and daughters and grandchildren of a man and woman who risked their very lives to settle in a new land and to preserve the heritage of the proud Cheyenne.

I hope these books help readers understand and appreciate America's dramatic history, the strength of those who settled this land, not just physically, but their strength of character, their willingness to die for what is right. For the Monroe family, that strength is carried on through the children and grandchildren of one man who was a legend among the Cheyenne to whom he was related through his mother, and also in the white man's world. Zeke Monroe, Lone Eagle to the Cheyenne, lived in a time when a man could mete out his own justice, and when a man, especially a half-breed, had to fight his way through life in order to survive and protect his own. Zeke, more Indian than white, lived in two worlds, but finally chose to live as a white man because of his magnificent love for a young white woman he met when he scouted for a wagon train in 1845 . . . his Abbie-girl.

It was this love that carried Zeke and Abbie through thirty years of watching a changing West, through having seven children and many grandchildren.

At the end of book #6, Abbie, living and teaching on a Cheyenne reservation in Montana, was planning a family reunion, to be held at the old homestead, a ranch in southeast Colorado along the Arkansas River, now run by Zeke and Abbie's daughter, Margaret, and her husband, Morgan Brown. This will be the first time for all of Zeke's children and grandchildren to be together in many years. Because so many readers wanted me to write about this reunion, I decided that was how I must begin this continuing family saga. Abbie hopes and prays that her "prodigal son," Jeremy, will come. For seventeen years Jeremy has lived apart from the family, denied his Indian blood; and now he is afraid to see them all again, not sure how, or if, he will be welcomed . . . especially by his older brother, Wolf's Blood, the firstborn, the son closest to their father, the very "Indian" son who will not easily forgive Jeremy for deserting the family and breaking his father's heart.

Come with me now and meet the Monroes. Come into Abbie's heart and live with this woman, still strong and lovely in spite of her years; feel her pride and great love for her family . . . and feel Zeke's presence as the family comes together and walks forward into new challenges, new loves, new beginnings; their spirits lifted by the winged eagle to new tomorrows.

He comes, in the spirit of the eagle,
Floating on heaven's breath,
Circling over loved ones,
Watching,
Guiding,
Waiting . . .
Waiting for his Abbie-girl . . .

One

A tingle went through fifteen-year-old Arianne Wilder's whole body. Did Hawk have any idea how she felt when she was near him? She hated it when school was dismissed for the summer, because that meant she could not see the Indian boy every day. At least school gave her an excuse to be near him.

She watched him now from a distance, peeking around the back side of a barn to see him exercising a horse, a handsome Appaloosa, one of many fine horses raised by his father, Wolf's Blood. "These Cheyenne are good at breeding fine horses," her brother had told her. Drake Wilder was an agent here at the Northern Cheyenne Indian Reservation, and after their parents had drowned a year ago when a passenger ship sank on Lake Michigan, Drake had brought her here to live with him and his wife. Arianne's heartache over losing her parents had been soothed somewhat by the diversion of coming to live on a reservation, seeing a people totally foreign to her, so mysterious and fascinating.

Every day had been an adventure, a source of wonder, of learning not to be afraid of the Indians, who, she had discovered, were just as human as her own people. Somehow she had thought they would be savages, ready to scalp her at any moment. Some did have that look in their eyes, some of the older ones, like Hawk's father, Wolf's Blood, who had lived through the days of making war. Wolf's Blood's uncle, Swift Arrow, had even been a part of the Custer massacre.

Swift Arrow was a half brother to Hawk's now-deceased grandfather, Zeke Monroe, called Lone Eagle by the Cheyenne. Some white men had called him Cheyenne Zeke. Swift Arrow was now married to Zeke's widow, Abbie Monroe, Hawk's beloved grandmother. It seemed strange to Arianne that an ageing white woman would marry a full-blood Indian man like Swift Arrow, let alone keep her first husband's last name; but then Swift Arrow had no Christian last name, so Abbie continued to call herself Abbie Monroe. Besides, people said Abbie's only true love was Zeke Monroe.

There was so much more Arianne wanted to know about Hawk's fascinating family . . . so much she wanted to know about Hawk himself, surely the most handsome young Indian man on the reservation! Did she dare walk over there and talk to him? They were friends. He probably wouldn't care. But then she'd never gone to visit him alone like this, and her brother would be furious if he knew she was here. He'd given her strict orders to stay away from the young Indian boys. He would be sending her away soon to a school of higher learning, though she didn't want to go. She didn't want to ever be far away from Hawk. She was glad he was not one of those who'd been sent away to special vocational schools in other parts of the country, where Indian children were forced to cut their hair and wear white people's clothing and were forbidden to speak their own tongue. Her brother said Wolf's Blood would not allow any of his children to be taken from him, and because of their white blood, which they got from their grandmother, Abbie, they were allowed to stay.

She looked around to be sure Wolf's Blood was not about. He was tall and rather fierce looking. She'd heard Abbie Monroe mention once that her oldest son looked exactly like his father, Zeke. The stories she'd heard about Cheyenne Zeke gave her the chills, and she wondered if they were really true, especially about how skilled the man had been with a big hunting knife he'd always carried.

Whenever Hawk's grandmother spoke about the man, a wonderful glow came into her eyes. From stories she'd heard from Hawk's younger sister, Iris, whom she had befriended so she could be closer to Hawk, Zeke and Abigail Monroe had shared a great love, the kind of love Arianne sometimes fantasized about having with Hawk. Hawk's father was part Cheyenne, his mother a full-blood Apache. She had been dead several years, killed by soldiers back when Hawk and Iris lived with the Apache in Arizona. Hawk's father had been imprisoned in Florida, but Abbie had gone there to fight the authorities and get her son out of that awful place and bring him and her grandchildren to the reservation here in Montana. Iris said if it were not for Abbie, their father might have died in that prison, and she and Hawk would still be on an Apache reservation, or maybe both sent to the special Indian school in Pennsylvania, never to see their father or Grandmother Abbie again.

Arianne thought what a wonderful, brave, strong woman Abbie Monroe must be. She taught here at the reservation now, but before school was finished for the summer, the woman had talked about a family reunion she was planning. She had permission to take Wolf's Blood and his family to Colorado with her, to meet with the rest of the family on a ranch there where Hawk's father had grown up.

He was going away! Maybe for the whole summer! Maybe her brother would send her to school back East before Hawk returned to Montana. She had to talk to Hawk, tell him that even if she went away, she would never forget him and she wanted to write to him and to come back to Montana someday.

She felt her heart would burst with love at the sight of him, so tall and strong for fourteen, looking more like seventeen. His black hair was brushed out clean and long, hanging over the blue calico shirt he wore, under which she was sure were strong arms. She watched him work the horse, recognizing it as his favorite, one he called Lone Eagle, after his grandfather Zeke's Indian name. He had a rope around the horse's neck and was trotting it in a circle inside a corral. She watched him run up to the horse then and leap onto its bare back without the aid of stirrups. Astride the horse, his long hair dancing in the wind, he looked every bit the warrior. She could see him in buckskins, his face painted, a lance in his hand. It was obvious many of the Indians on the reservation still longed for those days, especially Hawk's father. Many of the men drank too much. Her brother said it was their way of drowning their sorrows. Suicide was common, and her brother fretted over what to do about it.

She watched Hawk do some trick riding. He stood up on Lone Eagle's back, jumped back down and hung off the side of the horse, jumped from one side to the other. She'd watched the Cheyenne men race and do tricks like that, knew part of it was from days of making war, when they would duck soldiers' bullets by falling to the sides of their horses. It seemed that to the Cheyenne a horse was just an extension of man, a part of his own body.

Hawk jumped down from the horse and took the rope from its neck, petting the animal as he spoke to it in the Cheyenne tongue. His father had insisted his children remember and use both the Cheyenne and Apache tongue as often as possible. He did not want them to forget, had made them promise to teach their children and grandchildren the Indian language and customs.

She could see Hawk was preparing to leave the corral. This might be her last chance to talk to him before he went into the simple white frame house where he lived, although behind the house was a tipi where his father often went to sleep, or to sit for days and pray the Cheyenne way. People said Wolf's Blood didn't like the frame house, but he'd had it built for his white wife, Hawk's stepmother, Jennifer. She wondered why a man so Indian as Wolf's Blood had married a white woman with red hair, and it gave her hope that perhaps Hawk would consider doing the same . . . marry a white girl. Her brother would be angry if he knew her secret thoughts, but she didn't care.

She took a deep breath, drawing on all of her courage, and walked from behind the barn, pretending she had just now reached the ranch and was casually passing the time of day. "Hello, Hawk!" she called out.

He turned as he was reaching for a bridle. For one quick moment Arianne thought she saw pleasure in his dark eyes. "Arianne," he said in a casual greeting. He turned and shoved the bridle bit into Lone Eagle's mouth, reached up and fit the straps around the horse's ears. "What brings you here?"

Arianne rubbed her arms nervously. "I just . . . I wanted to know if you're still going to Colorado for a family reunion."

"Sure. When my grandmother speaks, everybody listens, even my father, in spite of how ornery he can be sometimes." He grinned, turning to face her, the reins in his hands. "Father says that my grandfather, Zeke, could be really mean sometimes, that he killed a lot of men protecting his family back in the old days, and was as wild at times as any warrior. But when it came to my grandma, Abbie, he had no power at all. Whatever she said, that was the rule."

He laughed lightly, and Arianne smiled in return, feeling tingly all over. "He must have loved your grandmother very much."

The boy nodded. "I wish I could have known my grandfather better. I was only seven when he died, and he had already been gone several months before that, scouting for the army." Hawk then turned and patted his horse's neck, wondering if pretty Arianne Wilder realized the feelings she stirred in him. He'd never thought about girls as being anything more than a nuisance until the last year or so, and in spite of his grandmother being white and his stepmother being white, he knew that for the most part white girls, especially a sister of the reservation agent, were off limits to Indian men. But this one . . . Damn, she was pretty . . . But then so were most Indian girls. With secret pride he knew several of them had an eye for him.

"How did your grandfather die, Hawk? I've heard so many stories."

He turned to adjust the bridle. "He had a disease, arthritis. It was crippling him. He was a proud man and did not want to die in bed. He helped the army bring some Cheyenne to Fort Robinson, but there they were mistreated and my grandfather took their side, helped them in an attempted escape. He was shot down." His voice lowered, full of emotion. "My father still comes close to weeping when he talks about it. He was there. Grandfather Zeke died in his arms. They were very close. Only my father and Grandmother Abbie know where my grandfather is buried, high in the

Rockies." He took a deep breath. "Sometimes I worry about my own father deciding to die like that. He hates the reservation life. It is hard for him to live this way. And I have seen signs . . ."

Arianne was surprised he was talking so much, and she felt privileged that she was his sounding board. "Signs?"

"Of that same disease, in my father. He is almost forty. That is not so terribly old, but in winter I can tell he is sometimes in pain, and the joints in his hands swell."

"Your father seems very strong and agile yet. How old was your grandfather when he died?"

He faced her. "I think he was almost sixty years."

"Oh, then surely your own father has many years left."

He nodded and looked around. "Your brother would not want you to be here. You will get me in trouble."

Arianne shrugged. "I have a feeling you and your father are used to trouble." She tossed her strawberry blond hair back behind her shoulders, dropping her arms and hoping he would notice her budding bosom. "Besides, I can do whatever I want and have whatever friends I want. I'm here because I like your sister, and I like you, and I . . . I just wondered how long you'll be gone. I wanted to say good-bye, because my brother is sending me back East to school in a couple of months. I might not be here when you get back. I wanted to know if . . . if I wrote you letters . . . if you'd answer them."

He studied her blue eyes, the smattering of freckles across her nose. How many stories had he heard from his father about how white women can get an Indian man in trouble without even trying? Wolf's Blood had married a white woman himself, Jennifer, but she was actually a half cousin to him, the daughter of one of his grandfather Zeke's white brothers, Dan Monroe, who used to be an officer in the Western army. Dan was retired now, married to his third wife, Rebecca. His first two wives had died, and Jennifer was a daughter by the first wife. She was a widow when she met Wolf's Blood, and cousins or not, they had fallen very much in love.

"I suppose I would answer your letters if it would not get you in trouble. Besides, it would just be as friends. Where is the harm in that?"

I wish we could be more than friends, Arianne thought, but surely boys Hawk's age gave little thought to anything romantic. "I see no harm in it," she answered. Why was it so hard to tear her gaze from his? What was he thinking? "I . . . guess I should go to the house to see Iris. She's the real reason I came over here, to say good-bye to her," she lied.

Hawk nodded. Did she know he'd noticed her for months now, noticed how her breasts had changed, how much prettier she'd become in the few months she'd been here? Did she know he wondered how she felt to the touch? What her lips tasted like? "Thanks for wanting to write," he told her. He turned and petted Lone Eagle again. "Do you like my horse? He is one of father's finest."

"He's beautiful," she answered, touching the horse's nose. Lone Eagle whinnied and tossed his head proudly, as though he understood the compliment.

"Would you like to ride him around the corral?"

"Oh, could I? Is he gentle?"

"He is as wild or as gentle as I want him to be."

Arianne walked around to the side of the horse. "Do you have a saddle?"

He laughed. "Only whites need saddles. The best way to ride a horse is bareback, to feel every muscle and movement. You have to let go of your own spirit, let it melt in with the horse's. Feel him beneath you, grab his mane and ride with the wind."

"But I'd fall off without—" Arianne let out a little scream when strong hands grasped her about the waist and hoisted her up. In an instant she was plunked on Lone Eagle's back.

"Get your leg over and hold his mane," Hawk ordered with a grin.

Red-faced, Arianne swung her right leg over the horse's neck and straddled the animal, her stockinged calves showing beneath the hem of her dress. "Hawk, I'm not wearing riding britches."

"So?" He kept hold of the reins. "Grab his mane and hang on. Father says white women are always too concerned about what is proper. They do not know how to be free and natural like Indian women." He began walking Lone Eagle around in a circle, and now that she was atop the muscular, powerful mount, Arianne could not imagine how Hawk did the kind of trick riding he did. She'd always been a little bit afraid of horses, had only ridden sidesaddle a few times. Mostly she rode in buggies with someone else driving.

Hawk said something to the animal in the Cheyenne tongue, and Lone Eagle began trotting a little faster.

"Be careful!" Arianne warned. "I'll fall!"

"No you won't." Quickly Hawk tossed the reins over the horse's neck, as he ran alongside the animal, then he leapt onto its back behind Arianne, reaching around her to take the reins. Suddenly he felt the hidden man inside emerging, wanting to show off. He planted an arm around Arianne's middle to hang on to her, keeping the reins in his right hand and kicking the horse's sides to lead it through a gate.

Arianne screamed and laughed as they rode off at a gallop, and her heart pounded with glorious joy at the feel of his strong arm around her, at being pressed so close against him. She was terribly frightened by the wild ride, but too excited about the chance to be near Hawk to care.

They rode for nearly a mile before Hawk stopped the horse and turned him. "Now, that was not so bad, was it?" What was that smell to her beautiful, light hair? A sweet scent. Soap? Perfume? She turned to face him . . . so close that he could look deep into those blue eyes.

"It was wonderful," she said, her cheeks rosy from the wind in her face, her breath coming in little pants from excitement.

"See what I mean about riding bareback?"

Arianne thought he was even better looking up close. Never before had any boy given her feelings like this. "Yes. Thank you, Hawk."

Suddenly Hawk found himself doing the unthinkable, unable to stop it from happening. He leaned closer and pressed his lips against her full mouth, feeling a strange, new fire rip through his blood at the touch. The fire roared hotter when she returned the kiss with surprising fervor. He had thought she might object, be offended; but she threw her arms around his neck and let out a little whimper. He could not resist taking his arm from about her waist and moving his hand over her ribs, carefully inching up to touch, with great curiosity one of those breasts he'd noticed. Again she made no objection. She only whimpered again and kissed him even harder. He squeezed the breast, could feel her nipple through the material. He heard a whistle then and quickly let go of her, turning to see his father at a distance, riding toward them.

"We'd better go back," he told Arianne, meeting her eyes again.

"I don't want you to go away, Hawk."

"This is a very important thing to my whole family.

I have no choice. We will see each other again. We will write, and you will come back."

"I think I love you, Hawk. Is that a silly thing to say? Does it make you angry?"

He grinned nervously, looking down at her breasts. He never dreamed it could feel so good to touch and kiss a girl. He wanted to do more, but wasn't sure how to go about it. He'd been around a few older girls, white and Indian, who seemed willing enough to teach him things. But he'd never been interested, until now. Maybe he'd accept one of their offers and learn a few things. Then, when Arianne was a full woman . . .

"No, it doesn't make me angry," he answered. "I thought *you'd* be upset, for my . . . touching you."

She reddened deeply, turning around. "I hope you don't think less of me."

He reached around her waist again, kissing her hair, smelling it again. "I would never think less of you for anything." He turned the horse, and realized his father was coming closer. He must have seen him ride off with her, had come out to make sure his son didn't do something foolish . . . which Hawk already had done. He turned Lone Eagle and headed back toward the ranch, and Arianne kept her eyes averted when Wolf's Blood caught up with them.

"There are many chores to be done before we leave in the morning," the man told his son.

"Yes, Father."

"Arianne can go and visit with Iris. We will be gone at least two months."

Hawk met his father's dark eyes, wondering if he would ever be as strong and honorable as this man who had once ridden with Cheyenne Dog Soldiers. He could see a warning look in his father's dark eyes, felt embarrassed that the man surely knew what he'd been up to, probably had seen him kiss Arianne. They said little as they rode back, and Hawk held on to Arianne when she slid off the horse, his hand trailing over her breasts as she did so. She turned and looked up at him, tears in her eyes.

"Good-bye, Hawk." She turned and ran toward the house.

Hawk jumped down from his horse, and just as quickly his father was dismounted and facing him. Hawk looked up into the man's dark eyes, still standing a few inches shorter than his father. "I know. I should not have ridden off with her."

Wolf's Blood grinned. "Believe it or not, I was your age once, my son. I remember the feeling. But it was only Indian girls I looked at."

Hawk knew the story about his father's first love, a Cheyenne girl. He'd been only seventeen, and she was sixteen. She was killed at Sand Creek back in '64, when Colorado volunteers had massacred several hundred peaceful Indians there, including women and little children. That was what had turned his father toward making war and riding with the Sioux and Northern Cheyenne. His first wife, Hawk's Apache mother, So-nora, had been a slave to a white trader. His father and grandfather had both fought in vicious wrestling contests to win her through money bet on them, because Wolf's Blood had felt sorry for the poor young girl and had wanted to take her home with him. They had fallen in love, and from that love had come Hawk and Iris. Now Sonora, too, was dead.

"You've married a white woman yourself now," Hawk reminded his father. "So did your uncle, Swift Arrow. If we are going to be forced to adapt to the white man's world, then sometimes that will include marrying their women, just as for a hundred years their men have been marrying *our* women."

Wolf's Blood nodded, a glittering warning in his

eyes. "Such things will not happen overnight without much trouble, my son. Jennifer has brought me no problems, because my father's white brother, Dan, loved me like his own and did not mind that his daughter also loved me. She can have no more children, so it was not so wrong for us to marry. But *some* white women can bring much trouble, especially when they are the sister of the reservation agent and have been forbidden to get too friendly with any of the Indians."

Hawk lifted his chin proudly "No man can order the heart," he told his father.

Wolf's Blood stiffened, pain in his dark eyes. "My father and mother suffered so much, son, as have I. I do not wish to see my children also suffer. It is time for new beginnings, as my mother would say. That is why we are all going to be together in Colorado. Be careful of your heart, my son. You are still very young."

Hawk turned away. "It doesn't matter. Agent Wilder is sending Arianne away to school in the East anyway. She might already be gone by the time we get back. We only promised to write."

"Mmmm-hmmm." Wolf's Blood put a hand on his son's shoulder. "I saw you kiss her."

Hawk frowned and met his eyes again. "She was right there close to me, and she *wanted* the kiss. Would you not have kissed her if you were me?"

Wolf's Blood grinned, and Hawk thought how handsome his father still was. Today he wore leather boots, denim pants and a red shirt, a red bandana tied around his forehead, his long, black hair hanging loose. But often he wore Indian regalia, buckskins and moccasins. Like his own father and uncle, Wolf's Blood preferred to dress and live as an Indian. "I think I probably would have had to kiss her," he answered, ". . . if I were you." He squeezed his son's shoulder. "I just want you to be careful, son. Very few whites have yet accepted us as being human, let alone equal to them. It is wrong, but it is a cold, hard fact. Come now. Let's get things ready for our journey. I have friends who will tend the horses while we are gone."

"Yes, Father."

Wolf's Blood left him, and Hawk turned away and licked his lips, still tasting that kiss, thinking he would probably never forget it, or how pleasurable it was to touch Arianne Wilder's breast. Yes, he would answer her letters.

Two

"Do you think he'll come?" Abbie nestled into her husband's shoulder.

"You have asked me that at least a hundred times, woman." Swift Arrow turned to kiss her hair. He knew she was referring to her wayward son, Jeremy, who had left the family nest seventeen years ago and never returned. Abbie had learned over the years that the man had found work with the railroad, and was quite wealthy and successful now, married and living in Denver. Other Monroe children had been through times of trial and doubt because of their Indian blood; and some had also denied that blood. But all who did had regretted it and had learned to be proud of their Indian heritage, even Zeke and Abbie's daughter, LeeAnn, who did not look Indian at all with her blond hair and blue eyes.

Jeremy was the only child who had never returned and had stopped writing years ago. He seemed to have no regrets, or if he did, he had told no one.

"I think perhaps if he does not come to the reunion, it will be out of shame. I cannot believe my nephew is not full of sorrow over the fact that he never saw his father again before Zeke died."

Abbie sighed with worry, so glad she had this man to turn to for comfort and strength. Being with Swift Arrow was so like being with Zeke, for they were one in spirit. "Wolf's Blood told me he and Zeke did see

Jeremy once, back when he and Zeke were working for the army rooting out whiskey traders. They were somewhere in Kansas, I think. They saw him unexpectedly, and it broke Zeke's heart when Jeremy pretended he didn't even know him. Wolf's Blood has always been so angry with his brother for never coming home, and for denying his Indian blood. I worry a little about a confrontation between the two if Jeremy does come to the reunion, yet I am praying so hard to see him again. After Wolf's Blood took me to the mountains to see Zeke's burial place, we stopped in Denver to try to see Jeremy at the Union Pacific offices, but he was on vacation in Europe." She ran her fingers along Swift Arrow's arm, the muscles still hard in spite of his sixty-two years. "I have a son who has been to Europe, but he can't travel a couple of hundred miles from Denver to the ranch to see his own mother." She blinked back quiet tears. "He's thirty-four years old now, Swift Arrow. It seems impossible. I've never even met his wife and don't even know if he has any children . . . grandchildren I've never known. I so dearly treasure my grandchildren."

Swift Arrow felt her tears against his bare skin, and he moved to wrap his arms around her. For many years he had secretly loved this white woman who all that time belonged to his half brother, Zeke. She had lived among his people in those early years, Zeke's new bride, wanting to learn the way of the Cheyenne because they were Zeke's family through the Cheyenne mother he and Zeke shared.

He hated to see this woman hurting. Abigail Monroe had garnered a great deal of respect from the Cheyenne when Zeke first brought her to their village, back in the days of freedom for his people. She had proven herself to be a woman of great courage and resourcefulness, a woman utterly devoted to her husband, willing to live an entirely different way just for Zeke. At fifteen, she had lost her entire family on a wagon train headed West, and on that same journey she had met Zeke Monroe, who scouted for the emigrants. It had been a fateful journey, their meeting had bound two people together in a love beyond measure, and it had taken Abbie many years to overcome her husband's death back in '79.

He smiled at the memory of how Abbie came into the mountains to find him years later, announcing he should come to the reservation and teach the young children the Cheyenne ways, help them carry on their customs and language. But he'd seen in her gentle brown eyes the real reason she'd come looking for him, after he'd lived alone all that time refusing reservation life. He'd taken her into his arms that day, admitted he had loved her since she first came to live among the Cheyenne, and they had made love right there in the grass, both knowing in their hearts it was right, neither caring how much the other had aged. She saw beyond the slightly softened muscles and the ageing skin; and he saw beyond a waist that was getting a little thicker, the lines about her eyes, the smattering of gray in her dark hair. What did those things matter when two people loved each other and needed to be held? Abigail had aged beautifully. She was one of those women who only seemed to get better, more elegant with age, a woman whose spirit remained forever young.

"I think he will come," he assured her. "I have prayed for it to my gods, and you have prayed to your Jesus. There is another reason I am even more sure he will come."

Abbie moved back slightly to meet his eyes in a shaft of moonlight cast through a window. "What is that?"

"Zeke will bring him."

She frowned. "How do you mean?"

"He will be there. You know that his spirit will be

with us all, and somehow that spirit will reach into Jeremy's heart and make him come. Zeke knows how much it means to you. Jeremy will be there."

She sighed, leaning up and kissing his cheek. "It's a wonderful thought."

"*Ai*, it is good." He moved on top of her, a man who always slept naked. "Tomorrow we leave, and it will be a long journey by horseback and train, with little or no chance to make love. I think perhaps it would be wise to share our bodies now, before tomorrow comes."

Abbie smiled. "Wise?" She laughed lightly. "I would hope you want to make love for more reasons than just because it is wise, my husband." She watched his handsome face break into a smile.

He nuzzled her breasts, breasts that had nurtured seven children, one of whom had died at a young age, little Lillian, buried in Colorado many years ago. There was something about a woman's breasts that comforted a man, and in his mind and heart Abbie was still the sixteen-year-old beauty Zeke Monroe had brought to his Cheyenne village and sometimes left in Swift Arrow's care when he had to be gone. Now, at last, he could mate with her, be inside her, give her pleasure and take his own pleasure in return. She made it easy for him to feel as young as he was in those early days, when he was an honored Dog Soldier, a great warrior . . . in those early days when the Cheyenne roamed free, masters of a land that stretched from Canada to southern Colorado.

What glorious, wonderful days of freedom those times were! But they were gone now. All that was left was this small reservation in Montana, another for the Southern Cheyenne, clear down in Indian Territory, miserable country. It seemed incredible that the once-proud, strong Cheyenne Nation could be brought to this, but he had learned to accept his fate. It was Abbie who gave him the strength to carry on, Abbie who had made him understand he must help teach the young ones to keep the tradition alive.

Abbie welcomed him inside herself, and he gladly shared her body, eager to do what he could to ease her pain over Jeremy and to help her not worry over the son she had not seen for seventeen years.

LeeAnn finished packing another bag, happy at the prospect of the whole family being together at the old ranch. She turned to look in a mirror, using a hair pin to catch a stray piece of blond hair and put it back in place. She studied her face, her blue eyes, her light skin. Who would ever believe she carried any Indian blood? She would never quite forgive herself for denying that blood for years when she went to school back East . . . nor for unwittingly marrying a man she later learned was a deadly enemy to her own family. Thank God she was out of that awful marriage, and her son Matthew, nine, who looked very Indian, was happy, loved by his new stepfather, Joshua Lewis.

What an ironic twist of fate it was that had brought her and Joshua together. Joshua was the product of a Cheyenne woman's rape by a wealthy businessman named Winston Garvey, a man who later tried to find the boy to kill him just because he didn't want a half-breed son. It was Zeke Monroe who had rescued the boy and his mother, who had taken Joshua to missionaries after Joshua's mother died. He'd been born with a club foot and needed many operations, care Zeke knew the Cheyenne could not give him. He'd been raised by missionaries, Bonnie and Rodney Lewis, who'd adopted and loved him, and now he walked almost perfectly, but he still wore a brace on his right leg, from his knee down past his ankle. After Rodney Lewis died, Bonnie had married Dan Monroe, Zeke's white brother. She was Dan's second wife, and she had died a few years ago. She had never had children of her own.

Dan was remarried now, and Joshua was a successful journalist in Cheyenne, Wyoming. Were it not for the help he'd given her back in Washington, D.C., when she was married to Winston Garvey's son, Charles, she could be dead now. She shivered at the memory of how he'd beaten her and threatened to kill her and their son. Matthew's features were so Indian that she'd had to admit her Indian blood to Charles. Charles hated Indians, had been taught to hate them by his evil father. He had even tried to kill both her and Matthew, just like his own father had tried to kill Joshua.

That was many years ago, and better forgotten. Matthew would never know what had happened to his real father, how he had died. It was a family secret, and the boy had long ago accepted and learned to love Joshua as his father; truly the man was the only father he even remembered. Now she and Joshua had two more children, Lonnie, who was three, and little Abigail, one, named after her grandmother.

"I wonder what will happen if Jeremy comes?" she said, raising her voice so that Joshua would hear her out in the hallway where he'd carried part of their luggage.

"Wolf's Blood will probably beat him bloody," Joshua answered jokingly, coming back into the bedroom.

LeeAnn turned to face him. "That isn't funny, Josh. He just might really do it. Jeremy might not come just because he's afraid of his brother. They were so different."

Joshua sighed, coming over to put his hands on her shoulders. "What will be will be. They're brothers, LeeAnn, and Abbie will be there. Wolf's Blood wouldn't do something to spoil this reunion for her. Anyway, you

know your mother. She'd never allow it. She'd step in
and throw a few punches herself if she had to."

LeeAnn slid her arms about his waist. Joshua was a
good man. He loved Matthew like his own, and through
Joshua she had learned that lovemaking could be gentle
and beautiful, not ugly and humiliating. Charles Garvey
had brought her nothing but pain and terror.

"You're probably right," she said, resting her head
against his chest. "My mother has a way of taking control. She could even control my father, most of the
time, anyway. That was not an easy thing to do."

"From what I remember about Zeke, I can understand that." Joshua pulled away. "I have to get down
to the newspaper office and get things in order. Cheyenne can't go without a daily paper just because the
man who owns it isn't here."

"Are you sure you can be away a month or more?"

"Thomas Handy has been my right-hand man for a
year now. He can handle things while I'm gone. I have
complete confidence in him. And I can keep in touch
by wire from Pueblo." He turned and picked up his
hat. "It won't be long before all cities out in this big
country are connected by telephone, like Sheridan
and Cheyenne are now. Can you imagine it? Being able
to call all the way up here to Sheridan from Pueblo,
Colorado? Maybe even from the ranch?"

LeeAnn felt a little pain at the memory of times
when her father had had to leave home for weeks at
a time, sometimes months, to help the Cheyenne or a
family member . . . the time he'd had to come and
rescue her after she'd been abducted by Comancheros.
How he'd fought to save her! Could any man ever
match her father's courage and skill? How wonderful
it would have been back then if he could have picked
up a telephone and called home to let her mother
know they were all right. All those times poor Abbie

had had to wait and wonder and pray, not knowing if her husband or a family member was dead or alive.

"I can't imagine there would be a phone line all the way out to the ranch," she told Joshua. "What a wonderful thing that would have been for Mother."

Joshua grinned. "It sure would have, for all of us. Dan and my mother could have called from Fort Laramie to see how Zeke and Abbie were doing, Jeremy could have called from Denver . . ." His smile faded. "If he would have."

Little Abigail began to cry. "Time for another feeding," LeeAnn said. "I'll finish packing while you're gone. Mother will be arriving within a couple of days from the reservation with Wolf's Blood and Jennifer and the whole crew. I hope the reservation can get by without my brother Jason for a month or two."

"Well, the last letter from your mother said another doctor had come to work there, so there shouldn't be any problem with Jason having to leave for a while."

LeeAnn went into an adjoining bedroom, where she picked up little one-year-old Abigail and held her in her arms to stop the child's crying. "I wish Father could see how all the children turned out . . . Wolf's Blood having his own ranch on the reservation, Margaret and her husband running the old ranch down in Colorado, Ellen and her family also ranching near the old place." She met her husband's soft brown eyes. "And you, Joshua, the little half-breed boy Zeke and Abbie both risked their lives to protect. Now you're the owner of a daily newspaper in one of the biggest towns in Wyoming. Jason is a doctor on a Cheyenne Indian reservation. Father would be so proud of that, proud of Mother's living up there, teaching the Indian children. Now all we need to make it all complete is to see Jeremy again."

Joshua walked over and kissed little Abigail's cheek.

"He'll be there." He gave her a wink and walked out, met at the doorway by Lonnie. He picked up the sleepy boy and gave him a quick hug and kiss.

"Come on, Pa!" Matthew called from the downstairs entrance to their two-story, frame home. "You said I could help at the newspaper office today."

"Coming!" Joshua called to him. He put Lonnie down and headed down the stairs. Lonnie rubbed his eyes and walked over to his mother, who stood at a front window to watch Matthew and Joshua walk out and across their tidy, green front lawn, on through the gate of the picket fence that surrounded that yard.

She thought about Margaret. It would be so nice to see her older sister. Margaret was a true Monroe, tough, a fighter. She'd married Morgan Brown, a big, strong mulatto man who had brought love and peace to her during a time when she was lost and confused because she looked so Indian and had been terribly hurt by a white man she'd thought loved her. Yes, Margaret also had strayed for a while, hating her Indian blood. She had turned to prostitution, but inside she was a good and loving woman. What child raised by Abbie Monroe would *not* be good and loving? It was just that they had all grown up during a period when most whites hated Indians . . . many still did. That hatred had deeply affected some of the Monroe children, those like Margaret and Wolf's Blood, who looked very Indian, as well as those who showed no sign of their Indian blood . . . like herself . . . and Jeremy.

They had all learned to adjust and accept who they were, to be proud of that side of themselves, because their father had been proud and because their mother was proudest of all. "Please make Jeremy come to the reunion," she quietly prayed.

* * *

"I hate getting on this thing," Wolf's Blood grumbled. He watched his mother and Swift Arrow prepare to board the train. "I know that my uncle also hates the trains. They are just another sign of how the white man has destroyed the old ways."

Jennifer placed a hand on her husband's arm. She had adored Wolf's Blood since she'd first met him as a child. She smiled at the thought of what a grand mixture the Monroe family was, how "Indian" some of them could be, like Wolf's Blood and Swift Arrow, how "white" others were, like LeeAnn. "You grumble too much, dear husband. Life goes on, and the world is constantly changing. Sometimes the changes hurt, but they can't be stopped, as you well know."

He sighed, waited, watching each family member board. They had come south with one covered wagon for all the luggage, most of them riding horseback while the children rode in the wagon. Abbie herself had driven the team of horses that pulled it. They had met LeeAnn and Joshua here in Cheyenne, now a thriving city, another sign of white progress. Wolf's Blood hated cities, hated crowds, hated the idea of riding this train all the way down to Pueblo, where his brother-in-law, Morgan, would meet them with another wagon. Their own wagon and horses would be boarded here in Cheyenne until they returned.

Abbie and Swift Arrow climbed onto the train's platform, followed by LeeAnn, Joshua and their three children; then Jason, his youngest brother, of whom he was very proud. Jason didn't look Indian, but he was a handsome young man at twenty-eight, with an Indian's heart and spirit, a caring man who worked as a doctor on the Cheyenne reservation. He herded his own onto the train then: his seven-year-old stepdaughter, Emily; his fourteen-year-old son, Hawk; his thirteen-year-old daughter, Iris; his beautiful wife, Jennifer, who pleased him greatly.

Dan and his wife, Rebecca, boarded behind him, and Wolf's Blood took a seat beside Jennifer, thinking how Zeke would love to see the family together like this. Wolf's Blood felt his father's presence almost constantly, and the picture of the burial platform high in the Rockies, where he'd placed his father's body, was still as vivid in his mind as on the day he'd taken the man there eight years ago. The pain of the loss was sometimes as intense now as it was then.

He glanced at some of the other passengers, well aware that many were staring at the "Indians" who had dared to take seats. *Let them stare,* he thought. Maybe they would begin to understand what they had done to the Cheyenne, the Sioux, the Comanche, the Apache, the Arapaho, the Navajo, the Nez Perce—all of them. Even the old enemies of the Cheyenne, the Crow and Pawnee, were on reservations. It was too bad that old hatreds had kept the various tribes separated during a time when uniting might have helped their cause. He often wondered how it might have been if all Indians had come together in one mighty force against white encroachment. Man for man, any Indian warrior far outmatched almost any white soldier. It had taken thousands of soldiers to round up a mere thirty-five Apache under Geronimo; and again, thousands of soldiers to catch up with and capture a couple of hundred Nez Perce trying to flee to Canada. If all Indians had fought as a force, this land would still belong to them.

He looked out the window as several long screams burst from the engine's steam whistle and the locomotive began chugging away from the station . . . toward home . . . toward Colorado . . . the old ranch. Again thoughts of his father returned . . . how he'd died like a warrior, how he'd fought his crippling arthritis and refused to die in bed. He flexed his own hands. Yes, much as he'd tried to ignore it, he knew without seeing Jason or any other doctor that he was going to gradually develop the same disease, and like his father, he was, by God, not going to die a crippled old man. He'd lived the warrior's life for many years, and he'd die that way.

He glanced at his mother, caught her watching him. Damn. There was not a more discerning woman on the face of the earth than Abigail Monroe. He'd wanted to keep this from her, just like his father had tried to do. He especially wanted to keep it from Jennifer. He watched his mother's all-knowing eyes, tried to tell her silently not to say anything. He saw the pain there. No one would better understand what was going through his mind than Abbie. Wolf's Blood was so like his father. He looked exactly like Zeke, and it seemed the man's very spirit dwelled in his own soul.

He turned to look back out the window, unable to bear the pain in his mother's eyes. It was nothing to worry about now. After all, it was just a minor ailment for the present. His father had carried the disease for years before it began to truly cripple him. Wolf's Blood knew he had a lot of good years left. He had a ranch of his own, where he bred beautiful horses, just as his father had done. He had a beautiful, loving wife, three beautiful children, a son as proud of his Indian blood as he was and his father had been. Hawk was a good boy, smart, handsome; a young man who would learn to live in the white man's world without losing his identity. He just hoped the boy would be careful about being seen with that agent's sister. It was a good thing they would be apart for a while. Maybe Arianne Wilder would be gone by the time they got back. It would be best for Hawk if she was.

The train rumbled south. It would go right through Denver. Denver! How he hated that city, where he'd gotten into trouble more than once, where he'd gotten into his first fight with a young Charles Garvey, the Indian hater his sister had ended up marrying.

Denver . . . where his sister Margaret had gone and got mixed up in prostitution, after she had been so hurt by a white man that she felt worthless. There she had met and married Morgan Brown, a mulatto who had taught her about love.

Denver . . . where Jeremy lived now . . . the one family member no one had seen since he first left the ranch seventeen years ago . . . no one but himself and Zeke . . . once . . . in Kansas. Jeremy had hurt his father so badly that night, still denying his Indian blood, ashamed to admit in public that Zeke and Wolf's Blood were his father and brother. Would he come to the reunion? Had his mother's letter to the Union Pacific offices in Denver even reached Jeremy?

Wolf's Blood's hands curled into fists at the thought of his brother's desertion. If Jeremy came, it would be difficult not to light into him and give him what he deserved. Still he knew what joy it would bring to his mother if Jeremy showed up.

The family would be complete then. At the ranch they would meet up with his sister Margaret and her husband Morgan and their children: Zeke, eighteen, named after his grandfather; Nathan, sixteen, and Lance, five. His sister Ellen lived not far away with her husband, Hal, and their children, eight-year-old Lillian and four-year-old Daniel.

So many brothers and sisters, nieces and nephews. Young Zeke and his own son Hawk would have much to talk about, since they were nearly the same age. Yes, it would be a happy time for all of them, and one thing he knew for certain . . . someone else would be there. They wouldn't see him, but he'd, by God, be there in spirit, laughing with them, crying with them, holding them, silently guiding and protecting them. Lone Eagle would be with them.

He glanced at his mother again, smiled for her. He had a feeling she knew what he was thinking. She smiled in return, but there were tears in her eyes. There would always be tears in her eyes for her Zeke, until the day came when she could walk *Ekutsihimmiyo,* the golden road that led to the place of beauty where all go in death, where there are no trains, no dirty, noisy cities, no soldiers or settlers . . . where the grass is green and the prairies are alive with buffalo . . . where a man can be as free as the wind . . .

Three

Mary walked into her husband's study, a large room that smelled of pipe smoke, its walls lined with books. Jeremy Monroe had built a good deal of wealth through his work with the railroad, and Mary was proud of him, proud of the beautiful brick mansion in which they lived in the wealthiest section of Denver. Jeremy was on the board of both the Kansas-Pacific and the Denver & Rio Grande, had started with the railroad as a baggage boy and moved up at an amazing pace because of his intelligence and loyalty, and because of innovative ideas he'd presented to make rail travel more attractive and lucrative, like suggesting better eating establishments at rail stops.

They had been happy, in spite of the hurt she carried because she could not have children. She had thought that was the only pain they would ever have to bear, one they had learned to live with; but eight years ago, when Jeremy had received the letter from his mother telling him his father had died . . . Never had she seen such alarming depression in her husband. For weeks she had hardly let him out of her sight, terrified he might commit suicide. He still suffered from the fact that his father had died without his ever having gone back home, died thinking his son was ashamed to call him father, ashamed of his Indian blood.

Only when Jeremy had received that letter had Mary

learned the truth about her husband. He'd been afraid to tell her, afraid she wouldn't love him if she knew he was part Indian. How ridiculous! She loved Jeremy for himself, the good man, loving husband, wonderful provider he was. Mary had urged him ever since to go back home, see his mother. What if she, too, died without his seeing her again?

Now she had caught him staring again at this latest letter from his mother. He'd been invited to go back to the ranch this summer for a family reunion. If ever there was a perfect time to be with his family again, this was it. The letter was an open invitation, love and forgiveness evident between the lines.

"Have you decided yet?"

Jeremy raised his eyes to look at her, unable to hide the fact that he'd been crying. He took a deep breath. "I have to. It would kill my mother if I didn't show up. God knows I've done enough to hurt her."

Mary felt a lump forming in her own throat. "We had better start packing, then. We can take the train to Pueblo. I suppose we'll have to hire someone to drive us from there to the ranch. You do remember how to get there, don't you?"

Jeremy smiled sadly. "I remember." He thought of how he should go riding in on a horse, but then, there was no father to prove anything to anymore. He had never cared about horses and riding the way Zeke and Wolf's Blood had, and he remembered his father being upset with him once or twice for being afraid of horses when he was little. By the time he was six or seven, Wolf's Blood was riding as though he was a part of the horse, and riding bareback to boot.

Jeremy knew damn well Zeke Monroe loved him just as much as any of his children, but there had always been a wall between them, and he'd never been able to get close to the man like Wolf's Blood had. At thirty-four years of age it seemed silly to care anymore about Wolf's Blood being the "favorite son," but he couldn't help it, even though Zeke would never have wanted any of the children to feel that way.

"It will take us four or five days to get there. The rest of them have probably already left." He sighed, tossing his mother's letter onto the desk. "I'll have to finish up some loose ends at the office." He stood up and rubbed at his eyes.

"I know this will be hard for you, Jeremy," Mary told him, walking closer. She wished she could have known Zeke Monroe, imagined what a contrast he must have been to this son. The way Jeremy described his father, he could look as wild and mean as any painted warrior. To look at Jeremy, it was difficult to believe such a man could have been his father. Her husband was handsome, but in a gentler way, his eyes a soft blue, his hair medium brown, still thick and wavy. He was not "big and tall" in the way he'd described his father and his oldest brother, but he was a well-built man, just the right height as far as she was concerned, and the arms that held her in the night were strong. "You'll be glad you did this," she finished, placing her arms around his waist. Her heart ached at the lingering trace of tears in his eyes.

"You think so, do you?" Again came a rather bitter smile. "When you see Wolf's Blood you'll know what my father looked like. God only knows what he'll do or say, what *any* of them will do or say."

"They're family, Jeremy. They won't beat you and they won't turn you away, and I highly doubt any of them truly hates you, not even Wolf's Blood. If he was as close to your father as you say, then he'll do what he knows his father would want done and will welcome you with open arms."

He scowled. "Oh, my dear wife, you have not met

my wild-spirited brother. You'll see. But thank you for
your support. And thank you most of all for understanding my past and my feelings." He kissed her forehead. He'd met Mary Foster at a dance held for high
officials with the railroad; her banker father had been
a big investor in the Denver & Rio Grande. She had
a simple beauty, her sandy hair thick and lustrous, her
eyes a gentle brown, her complexion flawless. She'd
been somewhat self-conscious at the dance because she
was taller than all the other unmarried young women,
but to him that only made her more elegant. She was
not a snob, even though her upbringing could have
made her so; and it broke his heart that the one thing
she wanted most was something money could not buy.
She could not have children. They had considered
adopting, but she'd wanted a child of her own.

"How should I dress?" she asked.

He shrugged, letting go of her. "However you want,
but you don't need anything fancy where we're going.
Take one of your riding outfits. Hell, you ride better
than I do, and all my sisters ride. They'd probably like
to go off with you for some good gossip. That's what
women like to do, isn't it?" He laughed lightly. "You'll
like my sisters. And you will be shocked at how different we all look, from savage Indian to sweet LeeAnn
with her blond hair and blue eyes." He took his suit
jacket from the back of his chair. "Say, maybe you can
show Wolf's Blood how you can ride, do some of that
jumping you do at the riding club here in Denver.
He'd be impressed with that."

"You need a special horse for that, you know," she
answered, folding her arms authoritatively.

Jeremy pulled on his jacket. "Mary, believe me, what-
ever kind of horse you need, you'll find it on the ranch.
My father raised the most beautiful horses in Colorado;
I'm sure Margaret and Morgan have kept up the family

tradition. And if I know Wolf's Blood, he'll be more than happy to show off some of his own trick riding. I've never met his children, but in this latest letter Mother sent me, she gave me a list of all the grandchildren. Wolf's Blood has two by an Apache woman. The oldest is a boy named Hawk, and my bet is he's as good on a horse as his father is. Wolf's Blood wouldn't have it any other way." He straightened his lapels. "And Margaret named her oldest boy Zeke. Hawk is fourteen; Zeke is eighteen. He was just a little baby when I . . ." His smile faded. "When I left." He walked over to a hat rack and put a silk tophat on his head. "I've got to get back to the office."

Mary nodded. "I'm glad we're going. I'm just sorry . . . sorry you don't have children of your own to take along and brag about. Your mother is probably expecting to meet a few more grandchildren."

He ached at seeing the pain in her eyes. "Mary, I am taking a wife who makes me very proud. I don't need to present children to my mother as if they were trophies. She'll understand. It just about broke her heart when she had to have an operation to keep her from having any more children. That was right here in Denver, after Jason was born. You'll really like my mother, and I have no doubt whatsoever that she'll like you. You're a lot alike in strength and character."

"I have a feeling that is a wonderful compliment."

His eyes teared again. "If you knew my mother, you'd know it is. Abbie Monroe is . . . well, there's no one like her. She's a very special woman." He walked to the door. "And no matter what kind of welcome I get, it will be quite an experience seeing the ranch again, being in that house." He closed his eyes and turned away. "My God, the memories . . ." He walked out into the hallway. "I'll be back in two or three hours. Go ahead and finish packing."

Mary watched after him, thinking how good this was going to be for his soul. She wondered if his mother had somehow suspected he needed this.

Young Zeke Brown raced his sturdy Appaloosa gelding against Georgeanne Temple's sleek roan mare, the animals neck and neck until Zeke's horse finally inched ahead just before they reached the creek, which was their finish line.

"One more yard and I'd have had you!" Georgeanne yelled, pulling up her mount and patting its sweaty neck. "Poor Princess ran her heart out."

She slid off the saddle, and Zeke did not miss the roundness of the hips that filled out her green velvet riding skirt. Georgeanne Temple was the prettiest girl in Colorado, as far as he was concerned. It was too bad she was Carson Temple's daughter. Her father was doing what he could to make life miserable for his parents; how a man like that could produce such a sweet person, he couldn't understand. He and Georgeanne had met two months ago, after she had returned home from a year of finishing school in New York, where she'd lived with her maternal grandmother. Georgeanne had been out riding, and Zeke had been rounding up stray horses. He would never forget that first meeting, the instant attraction he'd felt, the same attraction he'd seen in her own eyes.

Georgeanne walked up to him and held out her arms as he jumped down from his own horse. "You always have an excuse for losing," he teased. He embraced her, loving the delicious feel of her full breasts against his own broad chest. Although his parents had instilled in him a sense of honor and humility, he was not unaware of his good looks, a mixture of one-quarter Negro, one-quarter Indian and the rest white, giving him

handsome dark eyes, high cheekbones, what Georgeanne called "perfect" lips and nearly black hair that
hung in a cascade of careless waves just past his shirt
collar. He couldn't help being glad for his appearance
and the tall, strong build he'd gotten from both his
mulatto father and his half-Indian grandfather Zeke . . .
glad because Georgeanne Temple thought he was "the
finest-looking man west of the Mississippi. At eighteen,
to be considered a man by someone as educated and
well traveled as Georgeanne filled him with great pride.

She kissed his cheek. "I just let you win because it
isn't ladylike to beat a man in a horse race," she told
him. Georgeanne studied his handsome grin. She'd
never met anyone like Zeke Brown, so sure and solid,
a man who knew responsibility far beyond the young
men she'd met back East. She could not help being
attracted to him, and she didn't care that he had Negro and Indian blood in his veins. He was magnifi-
cently strong yet gentle, a soft-spoken man who could
take care of himself and knew what he wanted in life,
yet didn't brag and bluster his way through life like
her father. Carson Temple seldom spoke without yell-
ing, and he liked to make sure everyone understood
how important he was.

She loved her father, but he was a man so full of
himself that he seldom took the time to wonder or ask
how anyone else felt about anything. As far as she was
concerned, her father had killed her gentle, submissive
mother with his constant orders and demands. In her
growing-up years she remembered her mother always
crying, remembered her father berating the woman for
being "weak and stupid" . . . remembered a gunshot . . . whispers . . . a funeral . . . her mother gone.
It was not until she was older that she understood about
the suicide.

"Don't let go of me, Zeke."

Zeke studied the sincere love in her brown eyes, pulled her close again, kissing her hair, her eyes; meeting her mouth when she turned her face up to capture a kiss. He most certainly loved kissing her, and when she sometimes suddenly turned fearful and possessive like this, he found himself wanting to comfort her, hold her forever. He wanted to undo the tumble of curls into which her auburn hair was bound, wanted to get rid of the clothes that kept him from seeing and touching her naked skin, yearned to taste the fruits of her breasts, ached to be inside of her. He wanted to claim Georgeanne Temple as his own, but he had his family to think about . . . and the trouble he could bring upon them by loving this woman.

He hated this age of being in between, having all the feelings and needs of a man but unable to be a man in every way for her. This young woman lived in a stone mansion, on the estate that adjoined his parents' property, land that had once belonged to an Englishman named Sir Edwin Tynes . . . a man from his grandma Abbie's past, one who'd gone back to England many years ago. If only he had not sold his land to Carson Temple! And yet . . . if he hadn't, Zeke would never have met Temple's daughter.

He couldn't resist the urge to have Georgeanne lie down in the grass, the manly need to move on top of her. He moved a hand to a full breast that lay fetchingly beneath a bolero jacket and white, ruffled blouse. Maybe today she'd let him open that blouse, unlace her camisole, reach inside and feel her breast, touch the nipple, taste it. Maybe today . . .

"Zeke, we can't do this!" Georgeanne spoke the words between a barrage of hot, hungry kisses. "I want you so much but we know we can't do this yet," she whispered.

"Why not? Who will know?"

"We will! What if I got pregnant?"

Pregnant? She thought he wanted to go that far with her, which could only mean she was *willing* to go that far, if not for their unique situation. Manly desires fought wildly against an upbringing that had taught him responsibility. He had to think about his parents, what a man like Carson Temple could do to them if he knew about this, the rage the man would inflict on the Monroe/Brown ranch if Zeke Brown got his daughter pregnant. Temple hated Morgan Brown simply because he was part Negro, hated Margaret because she was part Indian and looked *all* Indian. He was a prejudiced, pompous bastard, and sometimes Zeke wanted to shoot him.

He raised up on one elbow, still fondling the breast, running a thumb over the hard nipple he could feel through her blouse. "I'd love to get you pregnant, if you were my wife," he answered. "I want you to have my babies, Georgeanne. I want you to help me run my own ranch someday. Somehow we'll make that happen."

Her eyes teared. "What can we do about my father? I'm so afraid of what he'd do to your parents, your ranch. I don't want to be responsible for that, and I know you don't either."

Zeke closed his eyes and sighed, calling on all his strength and notions of honor to sit up and turn away from her. She was right. They couldn't do this . . . yet. "Of course I don't." He sighed deeply, getting up and walking away from her. "I don't know what the hell to do, Georgie. I'm afraid to tell my folks. They wouldn't have any problem with you if they knew you, but they understand the trouble this could bring to the family—and to me. They'd tell me I should try to forget about you, but that would be impossible."

He turned to face her, and Georgeanne noticed the

lingering swelling at the crotch of his denim pants, had felt that hardness against her thigh just moments ago, had wanted to feel him inside of her. She'd lived on a ranch long enough to know about mating, and she wasn't afraid of it, not with someone as sweet and gentle as Zeke Brown. He was a year younger than she, but seemed older. He had awakened natural womanly desires she had given little thought to before meeting him. She quickly got to her feet, knowing that if he came back and lay down beside her again, she would not be able to turn him away. Their love had grown too fast, had become too strong, their need to mate almost unbearably painful.

"We both know why I can't tell my father." She walked over to her horse. "Maybe we should try to stay away from each other for a while, give ourselves time to think. There has to be a way for us to be together, Zeke."

He walked up behind her, wisely not touching her. "My grandmother Abbie will be here in a week or so. Mother says she's a very wise woman, and from what I've known of her, I think she is, too. She's been through some bad times with my grandfather Zeke over the years, big challenges like what we're facing. I have a feeling my grandfather would know exactly what to do about this, but he lived in a time when a man could deal out his own justice and make threats and defend himself however he chose. We can't live that way anymore."

She turned to face him, her eyes misty. "Men like my father can. Men with that kind of wealth seem to still be able to set all the rules. I love him, Zeke, but I don't honor him. I'm not proud of how he behaves. I'll never forgive him for killing my mother's spirit. As far as I'm concerned he might as well have shot her himself. He's different with me. He babies me, holds me up on a pedestal. If he knew . . ." She shivered.

"I know what he can be like, and it frightens me to think what he'd do to you if we told him we wanted to marry. Maybe I should just leave the ranch, and we could find a way to be together someplace else, in Denver or Colorado Springs. I don't know."

He dared to put a hand on her shoulder. "Don't do anything yet. Let me talk to my grandmother when she comes. Let's try to get through the summer. I might go to college at Fort Collins. I was going to just stay here and take over the ranch someday, but if I'm going to marry someone like you, I'll need an education, need to know other ways of expanding, making more money."

She shook her head, turning to look up at him with a sad smile. "I don't need a rich man, Zeke. You know that. Riches didn't bring my poor mother any happiness, and my grandmother, sweet old woman that she is, always taught me that money means nothing. It's love that counts, Zeke, and we have plenty of that."

He took hold of her hand. "My grandmother would probably say that in a situation like this we have to be practical. That's a favorite term of hers. She says Grandfather Zeke taught her that. Sometimes being practical means doing something that hurts."

A tear slipped down her cheek. "I don't want to be practical, Zeke, because that would mean we should end this and go our separate ways."

They both felt an aching love, both knew they did not want to end this beautiful friendship that was turning into something much deeper. "Let me talk to my grandmother. We'll take some time to be alone and think. No more riding together for now. When I want to meet again, I'll leave a note for you, nailed to the tree here, like always. By then, if you've changed your mind—"

"I'll never change my mind!"

His own eyes began to brim with tears. He leaned down and kissed her lightly. "I won't either." He turned away and leapt into his saddle without using a stirrup. "I love you, Georgeanne Temple. We'll figure this out. I just don't want to cause a ruckus right before my grandmother's family reunion. This is real important to her. We'll have to lay low at least until everybody has gone back home. You understand that much, don't you?"

She mounted her own horse. "I understand." She turned the horse to face him. "I wish I could be there. I'd love to meet your grandmother and your cousins and aunts and uncles."

"I would love for them all to meet you. We'll see how things go. Maybe you could sneak away and come meet them. The problem is, my folks don't even know about us yet. Give me some time to decide how to tell them and my grandmother."

She nodded. "I'll be thinking about you, Zeke."

"I'll sure as hell be thinking about you." *In my bed at night, embracing a pillow instead of the woman I want to make love to.* "Thanks for understanding."

She rode closer, leaned over to kiss him one last time. They reached out and embraced once more in a hot, hungry kiss before Georgeanne quickly pulled away and turned her horse, riding off in the direction of the Temple ranch. Zeke watched her until she was out of sight, feeling a frustration inside at not being able to have her.

Four

Margaret and Morgan met Abbie and the rest of the family with two wagons. Abbie's heart swelled with love at her being surrounded by all these descendants of the precious love she had shared with Zeke Monroe. She sat amid luggage and straw in the back of a buckboard, holding LeeAnn's youngest, her namesake, little Abbie, on her lap. Abbie's brother, Lonnie, sat curled next to his grandma at her left, and on her right was Lance, Margaret's youngest. Matthew sat across from her beside Wolf's Blood's stepdaughter, Emily. The two were nearly the same age, and they chattered about silly things, the way children do. Abbie studied Matthew, nine, a very dark child who did not at all look as though he belonged to his blond-haired mother.

The grandson of Winston Garvey, Abbie thought. How chillingly strange. She was grandmother to a boy whose grandfather had violated her in the worst way . . . yet she could find only love in her heart for Matthew. He could not be blamed for his paternal heritage. He would never know that Joshua, the man he now called father, was really his own uncle, a half brother to Charles Garvey, fathered by Winston Garvey and a Cheyenne woman the man had raped. What ironic twists life could take.

LeeAnn and Joshua rode in the same wagon with Abbie, and when she glanced at LeeAnn, she realized her daughter had noticed her staring at Matthew. She saw the lingering pain in LeeAnn's eyes. The woman would never quite forgive herself for abandoning the family and marrying a man who was a hated enemy of her own father. Nor would she forget the hell she suffered as Charles Garvey's wife.

In the other wagon rode Jennifer, with Wolf's Blood's Apache daughter, Iris, and Wolf's Blood's sister, Ellen, who with her husband Hal had accompanied Margaret and Morgan to Pueblo to greet the family at the train. Two more grandchildren, Ellen's eight-year-old Lillian and four-year-old Daniel rode with their mother in the second wagon. Ellen and Hal owned a small ranch next to the old Monroe spread.

Margaret and Morgan's son Zeke had brought extra horses, which thrilled young Hawk. He rode with Zeke and with Zeke's younger brother Nathan. Jason and Swift Arrow also rode with them, and Margaret and Morgan each drove a wagon. Dan rode in the seat beside Morgan, and beside Margaret sat Dan's wife, Rebecca.

So . . . here they all were. Abbie's eyes teared at watching them, and she felt a tug at her heart at the sight of eighteen-year-old Zeke, sixteen-year-old Nathan and fourteen-year-old Hawk, all dark, handsome young men, all big and strong like their grandfather Zeke, good riders, boys turning into men. If only they could have had their grandfather with them longer.

This was not going to be easy, coming back to this place with the whole family in tow. So many years away . . . so many memories. She could almost see Zeke himself riding with his grandsons, laughing with them, racing against the wind. How could the memory of him still be so vivid, after eight years? How could the ache in her heart still be so fierce?

"Come out of that wagon, white woman!"

Abbie turned around to see Swift Arrow riding beside her. "What on earth do you mean?" She let out
a quick scream when Swift Arrow reached over the side
of the wagon and thrust one arm around her bosom,
lifting her onto his horse with a strength that surprised
her, considering his age. All the children and grandchildren laughed when he kicked the fine Appaloosa
gelding Morgan had brought for him from the ranch
and headed away from the rest of them at a gallop.
Abbie swung a leg over the horse's neck and perched
herself in front of Swift Arrow, clinging to her husband's arm as he held her fast. She thought how age
had not changed him so much. He was still solid, had
always been a strong, vital man.

"You are embarrassing me, Swift Arrow!" she
shouted. "I'm fifty-seven years old!"

He only laughed. "Does it not feel good to ride free
this way? You are not so old, woman, that you cannot
still do these things."

"I didn't mean that I was too old for riding. But
we're acting like children!"

He slowed the horse, waiting for the others to catch
up. Abbie looked at him, and they kissed. It was then
she saw his eyes were wet. "What is it, my husband?"

He took a deep breath, made a sweep with his arm.
"All this land, such big country, but not big enough
for Indian and white man to share. It has been so many
years since I was last here, Abbie. Do you remember?
Once the Cheyenne roamed all this land, from down
along the Arkansas almost up to Canada, and now we
are confined to that little piece of land in Montana,
while the Southern Cheyenne are living on an even
smaller parcel of land in that hot, dry Indian Territory." He met her eyes, studying her lovingly. "But it
was not just white settlement and soldiers that drove
me to the north. Do you remember?"

She studied his handsome face. "I do. But at the time I truly was not aware of the real reason you left and never returned, never rejoined the Southern Cheyenne. I never realized how deeply you cared."

He touched her cheek with the back of his hand. "I have loved you since only a few weeks after Zeke first brought you to our Cheyenne village, when you were only sixteen summers. He was a lucky man, and I, too, am lucky to have you for whatever years we have left in this life. Do you know why I pulled you out of that wagon and decided to remind you whose woman you are now?"

She turned back around and leaned against his chest. "Why?"

He settled both arms around her, and his horse dropped its head to graze quietly. "Because here, in this land called Colorado, here you were Zeke's woman. Here you will feel the memories, feel his presence. Here you will be surrounded by Zeke Monroe, my brother, who loved you as much as it is possible for any man to love a woman. For the next few weeks I will lose you to that memory, but I do not mind so much. I know that you need this."

She ran her hands along his powerful forearms. "I also need you, Swift Arrow. When the memories become too painful, I will need you to hold me like this, remind me that I am still alive, still a woman with needs, still loved, that I am not alone after all."

He turned the horse. "Look at those two wagons full of children and grandchildren. Look at those fine grandsons who ride near to us now, so handsome and proud. I have no children or grandchildren of my own blood, and that is a loneliness that will never leave me. I know that your heart will always belong to Zeke, but I am grateful that I can relieve some of my own loneliness through his children and grandchildren, and in your arms. I am grateful to have this much. I love you and yours as much as Zeke would have. I would die for any of you, as he would have."

"I know that, Swift Arrow. And I am grateful in turn to have a little bit of Zeke with me, through you; yet I love you only for who you are. And there were times all those years ago when I knew I *could* have loved you as a wife, if I had not already loved and belonged to another."

He leaned around to see her face, frowning. "This is true?"

She kissed him again. "This is true."

His eyebrows arched, and a teasing look came into his eyes. "Then it is a good thing you never said so to me or to Zeke. Just think of how we might have fought over you. Oh, that would have been a bad one! And Zeke with that knife of his . . . I think perhaps I would have been scattered all over Colorado."

Abbie laughed. "I think perhaps you are right."

The rest of the Monroe brood caught up with them then, and they began teasing the two about behaving like young lovers.

"I think our uncle is feeling like a young warrior again," Margaret called out to Swift Arrow.

"I *am* still a warrior!" Swift Arrow reminded her, raising a fist.

"Grandma, are you all right?" Matthew called to Abbie.

"Of course I am," Abbie answered with a smile.

"But you are too *old* to be riding off like that," Wolf's Blood teased.

Abbie's mouth dropped open, and she faced her son. "Too *old?* I can do anything now that I could do forty years ago! I've been riding horses since I was a little girl, and I'll have you know I've shot three Crow Indians, had an arrow dug out of me and given birth to seven children out here with only your father to help. I've fought outlaws, dug a bullet out of your father, come out here on a wagon train, lost my entire family on the way. I've lived with Indians, cleaned and dressed buffalo hides, made pemmican—"

"Wait! Wait!" Joshua protested. "Save all of that for when I can write it all down! You're supposed to start at the beginning and give me all the details, remember? I'm going to make you famous, Abbie."

Joshua had told her on the train that he wanted to write a book about her. Abbie waved him off and the others laughed.

"She *should* be famous," Dan added. He, too, was smiling, and Abbie thought how, in spite of his blond hair and blue eyes, when he smiled, he seemed so very much like his half brother, Zeke; his mannerisms, the sound of his voice. "I like Josh's idea of writing a book about your life."

"Mother is made of the stuff it took to settle and tame this land," Margaret said. "I wish I had her strength."

"Now you're all beginning to embarrass me," Abbie told them. She wondered at the hint of trouble she'd detected in Margaret's last statement. There had been something there in her daughter's dark eyes. Something was wrong. She would have a talk with Margaret as soon as they were settled in at the ranch.

The ranch. They would all sleep under the stars tonight, and by tomorrow noon they should be there. She could only hope Jeremy would come too, before some of them had to leave again.

They heard the cry then, and all laughter and talking ended for the moment as all eyes turned upward. The cry came again, a familiar sound anyone who'd grown up in this land knew, except that such things were usually heard closer to the mountains.

An eagle was circling overhead. Abbie's heart nearly

stopped beating, and she felt Swift Arrow's grip tighten around her. Even the youngest grandchildren fell silent.

"Father," Wolf's Blood said softly.

The eagle swooped down, gliding over their heads and flying off toward the mountain peaks on the western horizon.

"Dear God," Margaret muttered.

Abbie could not find her voice. There had been another time when an eagle flew near her, when she had gone to the top of the mountain on which Zeke was buried. She had needed to know Lone Eagle was still with her, and he had come, in the form of an eagle, circling close enough for its wing tip to touch her cheek . . . and she had not been afraid. She had only been comforted.

It was nearly noon the next day when the family procession crested a low hill below which lay the main ranch house, the original log cabin Zeke had built for his Abbie-girl thirty-five years ago. This was where he had agreed to settle into ranching, to lead a white man's life because it was best for his white wife, who had already given him two children and had lived in Indian camps until then, never complaining. Abbie could not help the quick squeeze she felt in her heart, the lump in her throat. She asked Margaret to stop the wagon, told them all to go ahead of her. She wanted to take her time and walk in, alone.

They all left her, and she stood staring at the cabin for a long time, noticing that Margaret and Morgan had added a couple of rooms. How many times had she waited down there, watching this very hill, looking for Zeke to come back to her after being out scouting, or rescuing a child or helping the Cheyenne in some way. And he had always—always—come back . . . until that

one time when he already knew he was dying . . . She
glanced to a stand of trees several hundred yards behind the house, where a creek meandered across the
property, where she knew the grass was green and purple irises grew. How many times had she and Zeke gone
there to be alone, to make love in that soft grass, to say
good-bye. Their last moments together had been spent
there.

She walked down the hill, watching a herd of Appa-
loosas grazing in the distance, seeing more horses in a
corral near the biggest barn. She remembered when
the original barn burned down. Zeke had worked so
hard to build this one. The horses outside were so beautiful, and those in the corral looked like thoroughbreds,
a sleek black one especially beautiful. Morgan had done
a wonderful job of continuing to breed fine horses,
strengthening the herd Zeke had had to rebuild after
the Comancheros who stole LeeAnn away also stole
most of his horses.

What a day that was. She had seen Zeke Monroe in
many battles, but never had he fought so viciously, or
managed to keep fighting in spite of severe injuries,
as on that day. It had devastated him not to be able
to keep them from taking LeeAnn, and it had taken
him months of searching to find her. He'd risked his
life yet again to save her.

That was Zeke, and that fierce fighting pride was in
all his children and grandchildren. Already young Zeke,
Nathan, Hawk, Wolf's Blood, Swift Arrow and Jason
were at the corral admiring the thoroughbreds. The
younger children were climbing out of wagons and running everywhere, Lonnie chasing chickens, his strong,
chunky little legs making the boy too quick for LeeAnn,
who held Abbie on one hip. Emily and Matthew were
heading into the barn to go exploring, and Lillian and
Danny went chasing after them. Jennifer and Rebecca

followed Margaret into the house, and Morgan, Dan and Joshua began carrying in luggage.

Abbie drew in her breath, praying for strength. It would not be easy going inside the house, seeing the mantel clock Zeke had bought her over thirty years ago still sitting above the fireplace, his mandolin resting in a corner of the main room. She could still hear him playing it, could hear his deep singing voice as he entertained her and the children with Tennessee mountain songs. In the main bedroom sat a brass bed, another gift from Zeke. He'd been so proud and happy to bring it to her. After years of sleeping together Indian-style on a bed of robes, he had decided his white woman deserved something better. It had never been easy for him to live the white man's way, but he'd done it . . . for his Abbie.

She took another deep breath and headed toward the house. She was determined not to spoil this reunion by constantly crying and talking about the past, but her awareness of Zeke's presence was almost overwhelming. Ever since seeing the eagle yesterday, she had felt him with her. How could he *not* be here? His heart lay in this land, and his blood ran in the veins of practically every person running about the barn and corral.

Young Zeke headed her way then, on a horse. "You want to ride the rest of the way, Grandma?"

"I'd rather walk. Will you walk with me?"

"Sure." The young man jumped down from his horse, dwarfing Abbie with his fine physique. "Were you always this little, Grandma, or are you shrinking?"

Abbie laughed. "No, I am not shrinking! Five feet two inches is not all that little, but I always did have trouble keeping enough meat on my bones. Besides, when I'm surrounded by men the size of you and your father, I can't help but seem shorter than I really am. Your grandfather and I used to draw stares whenever we were together in public. It wasn't just that I looked so white and he looked so Indian, it was the difference in size. I am sure we made quite a comical couple."

Zeke grinned, but he felt a pain in his heart. What would people think if they saw him and Georgeanne together? He needed to talk to his grandma about that, but he would give her time to get settled in and to rest. She stopped walking and looked up at him.

"You are so handsome, Zeke! How I wish your grandfather could see you now."

He shrugged. "Thanks, Grandma. I wish he could see *you*. Mother says you're fifty-seven now. But you sure don't look it. She says grandpa was always proud of how pretty you are, made you use creams and such to keep your skin soft. I guess it worked. You're a really pretty woman."

"My goodness!" Abbie laughed lightly. She placed an arm around the young man's waist, and they walked down the hill together. "Tell me something, have your parents decided where on earth everyone's going to sleep?"

Zeke laughed. "Yes. The women and youngest children in the house, the men and older boys in the barn. We have an area all cleaned out, with clean straw and quilts and all that. It's plenty warm this time of year, so we'll survive."

"Oh, yes. Believe me, the Monroes have survived conditions much worse! Which reminds me, your mother made a strange remark on the way here. She said she wished she had my strength. There's nothing so strange about that, but it was the way she said it, as though something was troubling her. Is there something going on I don't know about?"

"No. Everything is fine," he answered, too quickly.

Abbie stopped walking and faced him again. "Zeke Brown, I'll have you know that your grandfather could not hide it from me when something troubled him. Your mother is exactly like him in that way. Something *is* wrong, and I want to know what it is!"

Zeke sighed and looked down at the house. "She told me not to say anything." He met his grandmother's eyes again, and he knew she was not going to walk one more step without learning about the problem. He rolled his eyes in exasperation. "Mother will hang me for this."

"No she won't. I won't let her."

Zeke smiled sadly and dropped the reins of his horse to let the animal graze. He folded his arms, and it struck Abbie that this first grandchild of hers was already a man, going on nineteen years old, with the build and countenance of someone much older. Wolf's Blood had always been that way, and Hawk was fast following. "We've got some problems with an adjoining landowner, the man who bought all the property that Englishman owned for so many years."

Another pain stabbed at Abbie's heart. She and the children once stayed with Sir Tynes for protection while Zeke went searching for LeeAnn. During that time her little daughter Lillian had died. She still lay buried on Tynes's property. That had been one of the roughest periods for her and Zeke . . . And Sir Edwin Tynes had fallen in love with her. He had offered her the chance to live in his stone castle, the chance to be wealthy and to travel, to lead a life most women dreamed about. But she had only wanted her Zeke, a simple life here on this ranch. Sir Tynes had returned to England, taking his broken heart with him. "I didn't know the property had finally been sold. It sat unused for so many years."

"Well, I guess the Englishman died, so the family could finally sell off—" He frowned. "What's wrong, Grandma?"

Abbie had paled and turned away. Edwin was dead!

Another person from her past gone. So many! *Too* many! And there would surely be more before she breathed her last breath. "Sir Tynes was a wonderful friend," she told him. "I didn't know he'd died." Had he thought about her in his last hours? She felt almost guilty for not being able to be with him, tell him good-bye.

"I'm sorry, Grandma. I didn't know you knew him that well."

She took a deep breath and faced him again. "So, there is trouble with this new owner?"

Zeke nodded. "His name is Carson Temple. He's a blustery, bigoted, bragging loudmouth." *And I'm in love with his daughter, Grandma. I don't know what to do.* "He wants the ranch because so much of it borders the river. The man owns eight thousand acres of prime grazing land, some of it also bordering the Arkansas. He doesn't need this measly eight hundred acres, but some men want all or nothing. He's one of them."

Abbie held her chin proudly. "Well, he can't have it, and that's that. I own this property, legally. I have the papers to prove it, and I came here with the intention of signing it all over to Margaret and Morgan. So, there is no problem, is there?"

Zeke picked up the reins of his horse. "I wish it was that easy, but the man has been harassing us, making threats of what can happen if we don't sell out to him, that kind of thing. He's the kind who has enough money and influence to do whatever the hell he wants and get away with it. It keeps my folks constantly on edge and on guard." *And if they knew I've been seeing Temple's daughter, they would be furious. And that doesn't even come close to the rage Temple would feel if he knew.* It all seemed so damn hopeless. Already he ached for Georgeanne, missed her. He'd come so close at that last meeting, so close to having her totally, to branding her as his own; and she'd wanted it as much as he had.

Abbie frowned with concern. If Zeke Monroe were alive, he'd know what to do about this. Carson Temple would lose some of that bluster if he had to face Cheyenne Zeke. The trouble was, Zeke had lived in a time when a man could deal his own justice, which in Zeke's case meant killing a man if necessary. Men couldn't do such things so easily now and get away with them. There were laws in this land now, white man's laws. Margaret was half Indian, and Morgan half Negro—two strikes against them. However, the *real* owner of this ranch was Abigail Monroe, a white woman who still had a lot of fight left in her!

"We'll talk about this in a few days, Zeke. And don't you worry. We'll get it settled. Maybe I'll pay a personal visit to Mr. Carson Temple. Believe me, after all the years I lived with your grandfather, one thing I learned was not to be afraid of anything or anyone. Carson Temple is nothing. He's just another human being, no better than anyone else for all his money." She placed a reassuring arm around his waist again, and Zeke in turn put an arm around her shoulders, thinking how small they were physically, but how big they were emotionally. She was probably the only person who would understand his love for Georgeanne.

"You're some woman, Grandma. I can see why Grandpa Zeke loved you."

Her eyes teared. "That's the best compliment I've ever received from a grandchild."

"I wish you lived closer. I hope you'll stay all summer."

She patted his back. "I'll stay a good long time, Zeke. I promise."

Five

Abbie set an apple pie on the long picnic table Morgan had built by hand. The table was spread out under a cottonwood tree in front of the house, a tree that had grown considerably since Abbie was last there and which shed a good deal of shade over the table. There would not be enough room for everyone at the table, so some would sit in chairs on the porch or on the steps, with plates on their laps.

They had all been here two days and up to now had eaten in shifts. Today they would all eat together, one royal feast the women had worked hard to prepare, except for the meat, a side of beef that Morgan and the other men had cooked over hot coals for nearly twenty-four hours. The air was rich with the wonderful smell of sizzling meat, hot biscuits and pies. Everyone gathered, children laughing, the older boys joking and teasing each other. Last night Wolf's Blood and Swift Arrow had performed the Cheyenne war dance for the children, told stories about the "old days" of freedom for the Cheyenne, stories that had made Abbie cry as she remembered. She knew it felt good to Swift Arrow and Wolf's Blood to be all Indian again, to remind the children of their heritage. At the reservation, both of them often came to the school to teach, to make sure the Indian children did not forget their ancient customs and language.

The family made a circle around the table, all twenty-four of them. A few feet away stood three hired hands who worked for Morgan, waiting for the family to say a prayer before they, too, joined in on the feast.

"Father in Heaven," Abbie said, "some of us call You Jehovah and pray to You through Christ, some of us call You *Maheo,* but all of us know You are the same God who watches over all of us. You have brought us here together, carried us through tears and heartache, and we thank You for this moment of happiness we are able to share, thank You for the family members we still have with us. We pray for the loved ones who have"—*Zeke! It still seemed unreal that such a man could be dead. And Lillian . . . little seven-year-old Lillian . . . always so frail*—"for loved ones who have gone before us. We know they are with us still . . . in spirit." Swift Arrow squeezed her hand. "We also pray for loved ones who live but who are not with us, namely our son, brother, uncle . . . Jeremy. May he feel our love, know that he will always be welcome if he . . ."

She hesitated, hearing a rattling noise in the distance. She glanced toward the hill, where she had often watched for Zeke. A buggy was approaching. She could not see who was in it, but somehow she knew. "Jeremy," she said softly, her heart pounding harder, tears welling in her eyes. She gazed across the table at Wolf's Blood, who also had turned to look. "Thank You, Jesus," she finished. "Amen." She glanced around at the others. "All of you, stay here. And please, this is a very special day. If that's Jeremy coming, then God Himself brought him. I don't want anyone saying anything that might make him want to leave. We have a royal feast set out here. Let's enjoy it, and enjoy the fact that the entire family is together at last."

Wolf's Blood turned back around to meet her gaze. She could see the smoldering anger in his dark eyes.

"Please, Wolf's Blood. Do this for me, and for your father. He would welcome Jeremy, in spite of how badly the boy hurt him. You know that."

Wolf's Blood sighed deeply. "You forgive so easily." He shook his long, black hair behind his shoulders. "Do not worry. I will not spoil things. I will have a talk with Jeremy later—alone."

Abbie gave him a warning look before leaving the circle. She ran toward the buggy. A stranger drove it, someone Jeremy had hired in Pueblo to bring him here, she supposed. The woman was a stranger, but she had no doubt who the other man was, even though he'd only been seventeen when she'd seen him last. He was heavier, in the way any man fills out beyond his teen years, but there was no mistaking the blue eyes, the wavy, sandy-colored hair. He said something to the driver, and the man drew the buggy to a halt.

Jeremy stared at his mother, then slowly climbed out of the buggy. He was astounded at how she looked, still beautiful for her age, truly hardly any different than when he'd left all those years ago. What was it he saw in her eyes? Shouldn't she be angry? Unforgiving? She was just a little heavier than he remembered but still well shaped, looking tidy as she always did, standing stiff and straight in a yellow calico dress, very proper . . . and oh, so strong, a woman of true pioneer spirit. *My God, what she has suffered,* he thought. He had not forgotten the hard times of those early years. Yet she'd been so devoted to his father. He had no doubts about how deeply Zeke Monroe's death must have affected her, but Abbie, being Abbie, had made it through, stood here now as strong as ever . . . and he could swear she seemed happy to see him.

Abbie reached out to him. "Jeremy! You came! Thank God you came! Come and let me hold you, son."

He could hardly make his legs move. Why had he

stayed away so long? Why had he waited so long to explain his heritage to Mary? He'd been so sure she would leave him. He had let that fear, and his shame in his Indian blood keep him away from his precious mother all these years. He had allowed it to take him away from the ranch at a time when his father dearly needed his help, and now he would never have the chance to tell his father he loved him, never be able to feel the man's strong arms around him. But sometimes a mother's arms could be just as comforting.

He walked toward her, and in a moment she was in his arms, weeping against his chest, and he, too, was crying. *"Na-hko-eehe,"* he said, surprised he'd remembered the Cheyenne word for Mother. Abbie wept harder, clinging tightly to him.

"You were so loved, Jeremy," she told him. "So much more . . . than you ever knew. He's . . . here, Jeremy. Zeke is here. I feel his spirit everywhere, and I . . . I know he's holding you at this very moment, just as I am."

The words cut like a knife, and Jeremy broke down, unable to control his own emotions. "I love you, Mother," he finally managed to say. "Not a day has gone by . . . that I haven't thought about you . . . and that's the God's truth. The same goes for . . . my father. I'll never forgive myself . . . for deserting him like I did. I never . . . I just never imagined a man like Zeke Monroe could die."

"We all meet death, son. No one is immune from it, not even men like Zeke. I was so afraid . . . I, too, would die without seeing you again."

She pulled away, wiping at her eyes, and Jeremy handed her a clean handkerchief from a pocket of his tweed suit jacket. By then his wife was there, handing him a handkerchief from her handbag. "I'm Mary," she told Abbie, "Jeremy's wife. And I must say, you're

even lovelier than Jeremy's description of you. But
you're so much tinier than I had pictured."

Abbie smiled through her tears. "And what had you
pictured?"

"I'm not sure. I guess, from the way Jeremy described what a strong, resilient woman you are, how
you've lived with Indians and all . . . I pictured a big,
stout woman who would be rather frightening and
overbearing."

Abbie laughed lightly, glancing at Jeremy. "What on
earth have you told her about me?"

He watched her lovingly. "Only the truth, that you're
one in a million. There probably isn't another woman
in this country who could have put up with Zeke Monroe and survived what you've been through."

Abbie shook her head, wiping at her nose and eyes
again before her vision cleared enough that she could
take a good look at Mary. She was lovely, with an air
of elegance about her that spoke of someone who'd
grown up in wealth, Abbie decided. Her soft green
dress was simple in design, but obviously of fine quality
material, and it fit as though specially made for her.
Her straw hat was trimmed with dried flowers and a
green ribbon that matched her dress. She was slender,
her ivory-skinned face showing rouge in just the right
places, her gentle brown eyes sparkling with sincerity
and love—and wet with her own tears.

"Thank you for welcoming Jeremy as you have," Mary
told her. "This was not easy for him. He didn't stay away
out of meanness or because he didn't care. It was because of me, Mrs. Monroe. He was afraid to tell me,
afraid he'd lose me because I come from a wealthy family in Denver and he figured they would—"

"You needn't explain," Abbie interrupted. "I understand these things far better than you could ever imagine." She looked up at Jeremy. "After a while you were

afraid to come back simply because you'd been gone so long and were ashamed."

Jeremy's eyes teared anew. "I didn't know if I was wanted."

Abbie closed her eyes. "Jeremy, how could you think such a thing? I wrote so many letters."

He sighed deeply. "I know. I couldn't keep them because I was afraid Mary would find them. I just . . . I couldn't bear the pain in Father's eyes, and the rest of the family, I figured they'd rather not see me again, especially Wolf's Blood. I saw them, Wolf's Blood and Father both, back in seventy-three in Dodge City. It was by accident. I got off a train there, and I was in a saloon with a couple of other railroad men who were bragging about chasing off some Indians." His eyes showed his pain. "Then I looked across the room, and there sat Father and Wolf's Blood, watching me. I've never been so devastated or ashamed. We went outside and talked, and the hatred in Wolf's Blood's eyes . . . the pain in Father's—those looks have haunted me for years. Then I met Mary, and she was so sweet and gracious, and I loved her. I didn't want to lose her."

Abbie watched him lovingly. "Surely you knew you could have had children who looked Indian. How did you expect to explain that?"

Mary turned away.

"Mary can't have children, Mother, although we didn't know that when we married. I guess I was just too much in love to think that far ahead."

Abbie remembered how it had hurt after Jason was born and she'd had surgery to ensure she could have no more children. "I'm sorry, Mary. Thank you for loving my son as you do."

The woman took a deep breath. "Jeremy has suffered more than you know, Mrs. Monroe. You don't realize how much it means to him for the family to welcome him."

Abbie took hold of her hand. "You are family, too, Mary, so you certainly must call me Abbie." She looked up at Jeremy. "We were just sitting down to a royal feast, a side of beef, apple pies. We were saying grace, and I was praying for you and"—new tears formed in her eyes—"and there you were!" She looked him over. "You look well, strong." She put her hands on her hips. "And successful. You're still a railroad executive?"

He nodded, wiping at his eyes again. "I am."

"And I suppose you have a beautiful home in Denver."

He shrugged. "Yes, it's quite nice. I'd like to show it to you. You're part of the reason I've accomplished what I have, you know. You taught me well, gave me as good an education as I could have gotten in any regular school."

Abbie smiled. "I tried my best. Of course, some of you didn't care much about learning."

Jeremy lost his smile. "You mean Wolf's Blood. Is he here?"

"Oh, yes, he's here."

Jeremy sighed. "He's hated me ever since Dodge City. He wanted to light into me then, but Dad wouldn't let him."

"He does not hate you, Jeremy. And if he wants to have it out with you, he'll have to go through me first!"

Jeremy could not hold back a chuckle. "Now, there's a picture. You stopping Wolf's Blood from whatever he wants to do—*anybody* stopping him."

"Come, both of you. Come down and join us. Even your uncle Dan is here with his wife Rebecca. I want to introduce each and every family member to Mary." She met Mary's eyes. "No fancy living here, Mary."

"I don't mind. It might be rather fun bunking with all the women—Jeremy told me what the accommodations might be. I am sure everyone will be full of conversation, and much more interesting than the pampered fluff of Denver. I get so bored at some of the parties there. Maybe after learning everything about the family and your past, I can curl somebody's ears with the stories *I'll* have to tell when I go back."

Abbie smiled. She liked this wife Jeremy had chosen. In spite of an apparently wealthy upbringing, the woman had grit. Abbie looked at her son, holding her chin proudly. "You have chosen a woman not so different from one you'd have needed if you had stayed here to run the ranch, Jeremy. In spite of making a far different life from the rest of us, deep inside you are not so different. You've fought to be the best at what you do, and it's your inborn strength and determination that helped you. You got that from Zeke. He hated the railroad. You know that. But he knew it couldn't be stopped, and he'd be proud to see what you've made of yourself. It was only the fact that you were ashamed of your Indian blood that saddened him. It made him think you were ashamed of having him for a father."

Jeremy shook his head. "Never. I just . . . I saw so much prejudice, Mother, saw what the Cheyenne suffered, what you suffered for being married to an Indian. I figured it was impossible for me to make something of myself if people knew I had Indian blood. After a while it just got easier to say nothing at all, until I saw Father that night in Dodge City, saw the way he looked at me." He blinked back more tears. "The terrible disappointment."

"That is in the past, and he understood better than you know, Jeremy. Now let's go. The biscuits will get cold." She turned and headed down the hill.

Jeremy paid the buggy driver, asking him to take the

rig below and unload the luggage, then drew a deep breath and headed down the hill with Mary, watching the family, feeling their stares. He realized he didn't even know any of the children. When he'd left, Margaret's baby, Zeke, had only been a year old. His grip on Mary's hand tightened as they drew closer, and some of his nervousness eased when Margaret and LeeAnn left the others and came to greet him with hugs and kisses and a shower of questions. They welcomed Mary with open arms. Then came Ellen, then his little brother Jason.

Jeremy was astonished at their ages, had always pictured them as they were when he left. Jason had only been eleven. Now he was twenty-eight, and a doctor! His uncles, Dan and Swift Arrow, so much older! Abbie lined them all up, introducing them all to Mary.

Through all the introductions, Wolf's Blood remained standing quietly at a distance. Mary was taken aback by the sight of the man Jeremy had told her looked so much like his father. If that was the case, then Zeke Monroe truly had been very Indian. In all her years here in Colorado, she had never even met a real Indian. How strange! Jeremy said the Cheyenne once roamed all over Colorado. Now there were none left.

"And this is Jennifer, Wolf's Blood's new wife," Abbie was saying, introducing a beautiful young woman with red hair and green eyes. "These are Wolf's Blood's children by his Apache wife who was killed several years ago, Hawk and Iris, fourteen and thirteen. And this is Emily, Jennifer's daughter by her first husband."

So, she had met them all . . . all but Wolf's Blood. Mary had felt his eyes on them, knew Jeremy felt the gaze too, and that he probably wanted to avoid this final introduction. Wolf's Blood remained a few feet away, waiting his turn. Abbie led them up to where he stood proudly, arms folded. He wore buckskin pants and just a vest because of the hot day. His bare chest and arms showed hard muscle, very dark skin. He was a handsome specimen of a man, who looked every bit the warrior, and Mary couldn't help but wonder how safe she'd be if this were twenty years ago and Wolf's Blood and Swift Arrow still rode with the infamous Dog Soldiers of the Cheyenne.

"My God," Jeremy muttered, staring at Wolf's Blood. "You look . . ." He turned to his mother, unable to keep more tears from coming to his eyes. "It's like looking at Father," he said in a voice gruff from emotion.

Abbie turned to look at Wolf's Blood. "Yes," she answered. "Anyone who wants to have known Zeke, has only to meet his firstborn son to see that Zeke Monroe most certainly still lives."

Mary just stared as Abbie introduced them. Wolf's Blood looked her over, and she could see why Jeremy was nervous about his older brother's reaction. Here was a man who had raided and killed at one time, a man who was obviously very proud to be Cheyenne and who probably could not understand why anyone would want to hide his Indian blood.

"Welcome to the family," he told Mary.

"Thank you. I am proud to be a part of it," she answered wisely. She saw a flicker of appreciation and acceptance in Wolf's Blood's eyes, dark eyes that he then turned to his brother. They simply looked at each other for several silent seconds before Wolf's Blood finally spoke.

"So, my brother, you have finally come home. You have made our *mother's* heart glad."

Jeremy nodded, again feeling the sickening sense of shame as Wolf's Blood's eyes drilled into him. He knew the remark was meant to hurt, that behind the statement Wolf's Blood was saying he had broken their father's heart. No two people could be closer than Wolf's Blood and Zeke had been.

Mary spoke up. "*I* am the reason Jeremy didn't come back sooner. He loved and missed his family very much, but he was afraid to tell me the truth, afraid I would stop loving him. For a while I was all he had, or so he thought."

"You don't need to speak for me, Mary." Jeremy stepped closer. "We have a lot to talk about, Wolf's Blood. Now isn't the time, but if you want to get it out of your system and take a swing at me, go ahead and do it. I don't blame you."

Wolf's Blood lowered his arms, and Mary waited with a pounding heart. "We *do* have much to talk about," he answered. "I would very much like to hit you, my brother, but I will not do it. Father would not want me to." He put out his hand. "In his memory, and in honor of my mother's wishes, I give you my hand."

Jeremy could so easily picture this brother wielding a tomahawk, or the big knife their father had given him years ago. How could brothers be so utterly different? He took hold of Wolf's Blood's hand, and they exchanged a handshake full of brotherly challenge. Then Jeremy turned away, walking with Abbie back to the others, but Mary continued to stare at Wolf's Blood a moment longer.

"I hope you know your brother respects and admires you more than anyone else in this family, except perhaps your mother. He wanted to be like you, but it just wasn't in him. Perhaps there was too much gentleness in him, which he got from Abbie. Is that such a terrible thing, Wolf's Blood? He's a good man who took a different path in life, and he is as honorable and respected in his own circle as you are in yours. In that way he is as much a Monroe as any of you."

Wolf's Blood's eyes narrowed as he studied her intently. "I think my brother picked a good woman. You are wise in your words."

Mary stepped closer. "I am asking you not to hurt him, not just physically but emotionally. No more piling on the blame. He considered suicide once. I can have no children, Wolf's Blood. Jeremy is all I have, and I do not intend to lose him anytime soon."

Some of the animosity left Wolf's Blood's eyes, and he glanced over at Jeremy before meeting Mary's gaze again. "I had no intention of hurting him physically, although landing my fist in his face is something I have often dreamed of doing. Still, he is my brother. No son or daughter of Zeke Monroe ever touched each other that way, and neither my mother nor my father ever once had to hit us. Pride and obedience and respect were simply understood. I will not bring him harm, in any form."

Mary prayed he meant what he said. Wolf's Blood took her arm and led her to the table, where the feasting had begun. Now there were twenty-six of them, plus the hired hands, and the surrounding air was filled with talking and laughter.

Through it all Jeremy studied each sister and brother, each niece and nephew he'd never known. It struck him then that even though he had no children of his own, he most certainly did still have family. Perhaps some of his nieces and nephews could visit them during the summers in Denver. He would like to know all of them better.

They ate their way through several courses, most of them hardly noticing that Wolf's Blood had left. They were eating dessert when he returned, riding bareback on a painted Appaloosa, looking every bit the warrior. He'd brought along a roan gelding, saddled and ready to ride. "For you, my brother," he announced. "You *do* still ride, don't you? Perhaps in Denver you only ride in carriages."

Everyone around the table quieted as Jeremy rose. "I can ride." He remembered their younger days, when Wolf's Blood could ride circles around him. Every morning Wolf's Blood and Zeke would ride off together, racing, Wolf's Blood practicing tricks. Jeremy never had been able to do some of the things Wolf's Blood could do on a horse, and most of the time, when Wolf's Blood would be out riding the wind, Jeremy preferred to be inside studying his lessons.

"It *has* been a while," he told Wolf's Blood as he mounted up, a stark contrast to his brother. Jeremy sat astride, in a suit, on a full-saddled mount while his brother sat bare-chested on a painted horse with only a blanket on its back. "I suppose you can still do all those fancy riding tricks," Jeremy said.

Wolf's Blood grinned. "We all begin to get a little old for some of that," he said. "I leave most of that to young Hawk. He is a very good rider."

"How could he not be?" Jeremy answered. "He's your son."

Wolf's Blood grinned proudly. "Still, I am not *that* old," he answered. He turned his horse and charged off, letting out a chilling war whoop, grabbing the horse's neck and falling to the side, jumping off and touching his feet to the ground while the horse ran, then leaping up onto its back again.

Jeremy just shook his head. "Good Lord," he muttered. He rode off to catch up with him.

Mary looked at Abbie with worry in her eyes, and Abbie only smiled. "He'll be all right. They need to do this, Mary."

Mary nodded. "Yes, I suppose they do."

The whole family watched them disappear over a rise.

Six

Jeremy rode hard to catch up to his brother, not an easy feat even for an experienced rider, but he had not been in the saddle for quite some time. He remembered there was talk lately of some kind of gasoline-powered carriage having been invented and people really believed that someday everyone would be using them. He smiled at the thought of how someone like Wolf's Blood would hate such a contraption.

Wolf's Blood finally slowed down, turning his horse and riding back to meet him. They were entirely alone, in the middle of wide, rolling hills with not a tree or animal in sight. "This is all part of the old ranch," Wolf's Blood told his brother. "I went riding yesterday, and I saw barbed-wire fencing around the northern and eastern borders. Whoever bought the Tynes property has put it up. We should talk to Margaret about that. I think there is some kind of problem with the new owners."

Sweat glistened on his dark skin and on his horse's neck. The animal tossed its head and shook its mane, and Wolf's Blood himself shook his hair behind his shoulders as though imitating the horse. "I remember another time, when Father and I came across that ugly wire. Do you remember that day? One of Father's Indian brothers' horses was badly injured on the wire."

"I remember a little bit about it," Jeremy answered.

"We were all headed north, I think. You were going to your first sun dance."

Wolf's Blood nodded. "I got in a fight with Charles Garvey that day. He was with some men who tried to keep us from going across their land. Do you know that I killed Charles Garvey a few years ago?"

Jeremy studied the man who had made the statement as though it were nothing. He scrambled to think, and it all began to make sense. "I'll be damned," he said quietly. "At one point Mother wrote me that LeeAnn had been married to Garvey, that she never realized what a hated enemy of the family he was. She said LeeAnn was back home and getting a divorce, that Charles Garvey had been found murdered by highwaymen . . ." He frowned. *"You?"*

Wolf's Blood swung a leg over to sit sideways on his mount. "You do not know the whole story about the Garveys, because you were gone when it was all revealed. We kept it quiet because, if you remember, Garvey's father disappeared one night after an Indian raid on his estate outside of Denver. We never wanted our name linked to any of that. In truth, Father and I killed him. He had captured our mother, beaten and raped her, trying to make her tell him who his Indian son was, where he was. Mother would not tell him it was Joshua, because she knew he would find and kill him. When Father came back from the Civil War and found out Mother had been taken, he managed to find out the truth, and he and I went after Winston Garvey."

Jeremy felt sick at learning what had happened to his mother. "I remember when she was taken away, but when you and Father brought her home, you never said what had really happened."

"It was best no one knew, not even the rest of the family. They were all told many years later, after LeeAnn came home with her son, Matthew. Josuha is the one who helped her get away from Charles. Charles was furious with her when their baby son looked Indian. She had to admit to him she was part Indian, and he beat her and said he would kill her."

Jeremy ran a hand through his hair, trying to get it all straight in his mind. "How do you know all this?"

The look of bitterness and hatred that came into Wolf's Blood's eyes would frighten anyone who did not know him. "Because I came across him on the road from Bent's Fort to the ranch. He did not realize who I was. He offered to pay me to murder his white wife and their little boy."

Jeremy's eyes widened with horror. "I can't believe that!"

"Believe it! Would I lie about such a thing?"

Jeremy closed his eyes and looked away. "My God."

"I killed him that night. LeeAnn knows, as do Joshua and Mother. I think Margaret and Morgan know, too, but no one else. LeeAnn does not want Matthew to ever find out. He thinks his father was killed by outlaws. He does not know the whole truth about his father and grandfather, or that Joshua is really his uncle, half brother to Charles Garvey. I thought that you should know because you never realized the extent of what our mother suffered. Your desertion of the family only added to the other heartaches she had to bear over the years. I knew it, and that was why I resented you even more. I could not stand to see how her heart was breaking. It was hard on Father, too. When we saw you in Dodge City, he already knew he intended to die because of the arthritis, but he would not tell you. He was too proud. He wanted to die like a warrior, and so he helped the Cheyenne escape from Fort Robinson, knowing the soldiers would shoot most of them down, *hoping* they would shoot him. He died proudly, but I know that deep in his heart he was thinking of you and LeeAnn, the two children he never got to see again."

Jeremy's throat ached with a renewed need to weep, and his fingers tightened around the reins he held. "Damn it, Wolf's Blood, I loved him as much as any of you! I just . . . I never was able to show him that love. You knew all the right ways, did all the right things. You and Father were like one person. I realized I could never be to him what you were."

The words caught in his throat, and he stopped to swallow and wipe at his eyes.

"Damn it," he muttered. He took a deep breath before continuing. "I tried to show him, did my chores, forced myself to learn to ride better, even though I hated it. But I was never *you!* I just wanted him to love me for *me,* not try to make me something I could never be. Do you know how much I envied you? Do you have any idea how much I would have loved to go with you on those morning rides? I didn't go because I knew I wouldn't be able to keep up, and because I suspected neither of you wanted me along!"

He turned his horse and trotted a few feet away, angry at himself for breaking down in front of this brother who was always so strong. He could not remember ever seeing him cry, but he could just imagine what it had been like for Wolf's Blood to hold his dying father in his arms, to bury him alone. "I wish I could have been there with you . . . when Father died . . . could have helped you bury him. It must have been . . . awful for you." He took the handkerchief Mary had given him from his pocket and blew his nose, then felt a hand on his shoulder.

"Get down, Jeremy."

Jeremy dismounted without looking at his brother. "Sit here in the grass."

Jeremy sat down beside Wolf's Blood, and they let the horses graze loose.

Wolf's Blood sighed. "I did not realize how much of this is my fault," he told Jeremy. "When I think back, I realize I was very possessive of Father. I *wanted* to be the favored one. I was proud to be Indian, and I treasured our morning rides. I could have urged you to come with us, but I liked being alone with Father. Deep inside I suppose I knew you felt left out, but I thought it didn't matter that much to you. You liked your books, and you never liked horses so much."

He quickly wiped at his eyes, and Jeremy was surprised to realize Wolf's Blood was also fighting an urge to weep.

"I will tell you one thing, Jeremy, one thing I know is the truth. Zeke Monroe—Lone Eagle—he loved every child equally, each one for different reasons. Perhaps he was even more proud of certain ones than others, but that had nothing to do with how much he loved each of us. The love itself was always the same. You remember what he went through trying to keep the Comancheros from taking LeeAnn. I was not there, but Mother told me, and I have no trouble picturing it."

Jeremy bent his legs and rested his elbows on his knees. "I don't think any other man could have kept fighting in spite of such awful injuries," Jeremy told him. "It was so vicious. He was beaten and cut everywhere, but in spite of all that and most likely a concussion, he went after them anyway. It was a bad time for all of us, especially Mother. She had to worry about what was happening to LeeAnn, wonder if Father was dead or alive; and then Lillian died of pneumonia and Margaret ran off to Denver, ending up a prostitute." He shook his head. "I remember Sir Tynes had an eye for Mother. I think he actually offered to make her his wife, let her live like a queen. After all she'd been through, what woman wouldn't be tempted to take a man up on such an offer?" He smiled through his tears. "But not our mother. No, sir. Zeke Monroe was her man, and the devil himself could not have made her an offer that would have made her leave him. Father came back, bringing LeeAnn with him safe and sound. He went to Denver and brought Margaret home. Of course, by then she had met and married Morgan. She was okay. Down deep inside she had that Monroe pride and spirit, and that got her through."

Wolf's Blood pulled at a blade of bunch grass and stuck it in his mouth. "Father would have done what he did for any of us. If it was you the Comancheros had taken, he would have done exactly the same thing. I don't think you ever understood how much he loved you. And I know he held nothing against you or LeeAnn when he died. He is with us now, you know. Do you feel him?"

Jeremy watched the horses graze. "Sometimes."

Wolf's Blood got to his feet. "Do you remember some years back, when Mother and I came to Denver and tried to see you? You were gone to Europe with your wife. We left you a note."

Pain pierced Jeremy's heart at the memory—a note he'd never answered, the note that told him his precious father was dead. "I remember."

"We came because we were on our way back from the mountains. I took Mother there to see where our father was buried. She insisted on going higher up the mountain alone. She spent the night there. When she came back down she told me an eagle had come to her, floating on the wind. It came so close it brushed her cheek. She knew then that it was Father touching her through the eagle spirit. And just a few days ago, when we were on our way here to the ranch, an eagle circled overhead and swooped down close to us before flying off. Do you know how rare it is to see an eagle this far east? There are no high trees here, no mountains, no place where an eagle would nest. There is only one explanation for the eagle's presence. It was our father. I know it in my heart. I also know that he is aware that you are here, and that if he could be here, he would tell you how much he . . . loves you."

Jeremy rose to face Wolf's Blood. "I'm sorry, Wolf's Blood, that you went through all that alone."

Wolf's Blood nodded, his lips pressed tight, tears running down his face. "I do love you, Jeremy. If someone were to try to harm you, I would kill him, just as I killed Charles Garvey to keep him from hurting LeeAnn."

Jeremy's head ached from a continued struggle not to break down. "And in that respect, you truly are our father's son," he answered. He could not control the urge to walk up and embrace his brother. Only at that moment did they both realize that in their entire lives they had never embraced. They clung to each other, allowing the tears to come, tears too long buried. For several minutes they wept, letting go of all the hurt and all the sorrow. Wolf's Blood finally released his brother and turned away, walking to his horse and wiping his nose and eyes with the blanket, the only material available.

Jeremy managed to find enough left of his handkerchief to use for himself. "Mother probably thinks you're beating the hell out of me right now," he joked, looking for a way to brighten the moment. "God knows I wouldn't have a chance if you tried it."

Wolf's Blood grinned. "Father would see. He would be very angry with me."

Jeremy walked over to his own horse, removing his suit jacket because of the heat. "I can't help wondering now why I was always a little bit afraid of him, considering the fact that he never once laid a hand on any of us. He was just so damn big and fierce looking. But then, when he was around mother . . ." He laughed lightly. "Our mother sure did have a way with Zeke Monroe, didn't she?"

Wolf's Blood leapt onto the back of his horse in one swift movement. "She has a way with all of us."

Jeremy grunted as he mounted his own horse, using a stirrup. "She's an incredible woman."

"Do not mention to her that I told you about the rape. She probably would not want you to know, and she does not like anyone mentioning it. It took her many years to get over it."

Jeremy nodded. "I won't even tell my wife."

"Your wife is a good woman. I see it in her eyes. I am sorry you have no children. Children are the best thing that can happen to a man."

Jeremy sighed. "It's been hard for her. I'd like to at least get to know my nieces and nephews better, if you'll ever let any of your children come to Denver. I want to help, Wolf's Blood—make up for my absence somehow, if that's possible."

Wolf's Blood walked his horse closer. "I will tell you something, my brother. It is not bad yet, but I am suffering from the same disease that began to cripple our father."

Jeremy looked him over in surprise. "What? You appear so strong."

"I am. For my age . . . and for the moment. Like father, it comes and goes. Some days are worse than others, especially in winter. I want your promise to do what you can for my children if things get worse and I should die. Hawk is a fine young man, and both he and Iris have enough white blood that they are not legally required to stay on the reservation. I want Hawk to have a good education. I want him to learn how to live in the white man's world, to fight his battles the

legal way, not the old way, like father and me. I want
him to learn the new way, but I want him to always
remember his Cheyenne blood and to be proud of it.
Now that I know you are as proud and strong as any
of us, and now that I can already see what a fine
woman your wife is, I am thinking of sending Hawk
to school in Denver, where he could perhaps live with
you. He would be with family and not thrown into the
cold white man's world with no one close by who loves
him. What do you think of this?"

"I'm a little surprised. I didn't know you had any
such thoughts or plans. But I would be thrilled to have
him, and so would Mary."

Wolf's Blood nodded. "Hawk wants to go to college.
I trust him, in that I know education will not change
him. I thank you, my brother, for any way you can help
him. Iris, too, although she has a beautiful, educated
stepmother who will love and guide her."

Jeremy frowned. "And how did you end up marrying
Jennifer, a woman with such light skin and red hair
and green eyes?"

Wolf's Blood grinned. "A woman does not have to
be Indian in looks for me to love her. She only needs
to have the Indian spirit, a loving, loyal heart. Jennifer
is that way. We have only been married six months.
She pleases me greatly."

The words were spoken matter-of-factly, in the way
Jeremy remembered most Indians had of being openly
honest and blunt. "And Mary pleases me," he answered. Then he sobered. "What happened to Hawk
and Iris's mother, Wolf's Blood? Her name was Sonora,
I think."

Wolf's Blood felt the old ache in his heart. He nodded. "After I killed Charles Garvey I took her to live
among the Apache. I knew it was best to go away, and
she had always wanted to go back to her people. We

became involved in Geronimo's flight from the soldiers. She was killed. My children were kept at Bosque Redondo, that hated reservation. I, and others who surrendered, were sent to prison in Florida. Mother and Dan went there and got me released, and she got permission to take the children from the reservation. You know Mother. She will not take no for an answer."

Jeremy nodded. "I'm sorry about Sonora."

Longing shone in Wolf's Blood's dark eyes. "It was another time, in the days of freedom. Things changed so quickly. It is hard for ones like me, and for our uncle, Swift Arrow. But Hawk is young enough to learn the new ways. I do not like it, but I know that, for my children to survive, it must be done. The old ways are no more. It is good that our father died when he did, before he saw the worst of it. It is not over yet for the Sioux, I fear. There is still much trouble, much unrest, on the reservations in the Dakotas. Hawk wishes to study law. He thinks he can use that knowledge to help keep the government from tricking the Sioux and Cheyenne out of even more land."

"Maybe he will. I'll help him however I can. He'll have a place to stay if he comes to Denver. I'll look after him."

Wolf's Blood nodded. *"Ha-ho, nis'is."*

"And thank *you,* my brother, for understanding my side, for taking me back into your heart."

Their gazes held. "You never left my heart, *Ohkum-hkakit.*"

Jeremy felt a rush of pride at the use of his Indian name, Little Wolf. It had been so many years since he had even given thought to it, and for a long time he did not think he would feel pride when he heard someone address him that way. "You remembered."

Wolf's Blood smiled. "I know *all* the children's Indian names. I was first called *Hohanino-o,* Little Rock.

Margaret was *Moheya.* Blue Sky. LeeAnn, *Ksee,* Young
Girl. Then there was you, then Ellen, called *Ishiomiists,*
Rising Sun, little Lillian, *Meane-ese,* Summer Moon, and
then Jason, *Eo-ve-ano,* Yellow Hawk."

Jeremy nodded. "I had forgotten some of them."
He straightened in his saddle. "We'd better get back
before Mother sends the whole bunch of them to find
us."

Wolf's Blood laughed. "It would not surprise me."
He rode off ahead of his brother, and Jeremy followed,
beginning to feel free of all the guilt that had plagued
him for so many years. How sad that only now were
he and his brother feeling close, after all those years
of growing up here on the ranch together. It hurt to
think of all the lost time, all the things they could have
shared. He decided he had also better have a good
talk with young Jason, another brother he hardly knew.

He rode off after Wolf's Blood, who had already disappeared over a hill. Just as he crested the hill, his
brother charged back over the top, letting out a war
whoop and coming close enough that if he'd had a
tomahawk he could have whacked it across Jeremy's
neck and killed him in an instant. The sudden appearance nearly scared Jeremy out of his saddle, and Wolf's
Blood rode past him laughing, then turned and rode
up beside him.

"You see how easy it is? An Indian can hide from
soldiers without even using trees and rocks. Our uncle,
Swift Arrow, says that is how it was for Custer. Thousands of Sioux and Cheyenne were camped just beyond the hills, and Custer did not even know it! They
swooped down on him before he had a chance to run.
How I wish I had been there!"

He rode ahead again. "I'll bet you do," Jeremy muttered. The Custer massacre had been only eleven years
ago, and now all Indians were confined to reservations.

How quickly their lives had changed. No wonder so many of them drank and committed suicide, or so he'd heard. He did not doubt it. He hadn't asked Wolf's Blood about it because he knew it would upset him. Thank God Wolf's Blood had remained strong, had stayed away from whiskey, as their father had always warned them to do.

He watched his brother ride down to the ranch, thinking how true it was that a whole way of life was over for the Cheyenne and a new one was beginning. He felt an odd ache in his heart. For all his joy at being close to his brother at last, he could not help but wonder if he would see him again after this reunion. He decided he would stay as long as possible. To hell with the responsibilities awaiting him in Denver.

Seven

The entire family sat around a campfire, little Abbie sleeping in her mother's lap. It was a time of perfect togetherness Abbie knew they might never again see. It warmed her heart to know Wolf's Blood and Jeremy were at last close. There seemed to be only one problem to master now, and that was Carson Temple.

"We are all here for you, Margaret," Abbie spoke up. "And you, too, Morgan. I already know you're having problems with the man who bought the Tynes property. I think the whole family should know what is going on. Maybe we can help."

Margaret frowned. "How do you know about it?"

"Zeke told me, and he was right to do so. I can read you like a book, daughter of mine, so I asked Zeke what was troubling you."

Margaret cast her son a scolding frown. "I didn't want to dampen the reunion or worry you. Morgan and I will find a way to handle Carson Temple."

"Temple is a sonofabitch, to put it bluntly," Morgan put in, bitterness in his deep voice. "He hates Indians and Negroes. I have a feeling he's part of that group of men who call themselves the Ku Klux Klan. They've created a lot of havoc for Negroes in the South since the war, what with murders and hangings. I don't understand everything about it, but enough to know it's pretty bad. I think Carson Temple is one of them. Although whether he is or not, he hates people with dark skin, and he wants this land, wants the riverfront property we own, wants the good grassland. Most of all he's just a man who can never own enough land, a man who is never satisfied with what he already has. He enjoys showing how important he is, enjoys threatening people, trying to make them shake in their shoes."

"I would like to stand face to face with this man," Wolf's Blood spoke up, his face rigid, his dark eyes blazing.

"No," Margaret told him. "You go back to Montana and stay out of it, Wolf's Blood. You would get yourself in grave trouble if you tried to bring Temple any harm. He is a very powerful man, with many men to protect him. He has money and influence, and he literally owns the law in Pueblo. To bring him harm would mean your certain death."

"What exactly has he done?" Dan asked.

"He knocks down fences," Zeke answered. "He poisoned one of the windmill troughs. We lost six good horses. We couldn't prove who did it, but even if we could, nothing would have been done. He's set fire to grassland, and sometimes he just rides in here with an army of men and threatens us, says we'd better leave or we'll regret it. He's also been putting up his own fences, barbed wire. One of my horses was badly maimed by it."

"Does he have any legal rights this property?" Jeremy asked.

"Of course not!" Abbie answered. "I have the legal deed to this land." She looked across the campfire at Margaret. "You should have told me about this. I could have brought the deed with me."

"Temple would only find a way to work his way

around it. The land agent is paid out of Temple's pockets."

"Well, I hate to say it, but Mother is going to have to go back to Montana and make a second trip down here," Jeremy answered. "She should bring that deed. I'll have an attorney in Denver write up a letter of some kind stating that this land belongs to Abigail Monroe. Maybe we could have Margaret and Morgan's names added to the deed. Morgan, you're the one who has stayed on and worked this ranch. God knows *I* don't deserve any claim to it. If Mother wants all the rest of the children's names added, we can do that. Temple would never be able to negate that."

Morgan nodded. "I suppose we can make sure the deed is neat and legal, but Temple has ways of trying to force people out. He can make life miserable for us if he wants, and there is no law to prevent him. If I try to stop him with guns, we all know where that would lead."

"I'll send out a U.S. Marshal when Mother returns with the deed," Jeremy said. "He can inform Mr. Carson Temple of the kind of trouble he'll be in if he continues to make problems for you."

Wolf's Blood turned to look at him. "Well, it seems my brother has a different kind of fighting power than I and our father had. We did our fighting physically. Now Jeremy fights with the law and the pen." He grinned. "He is a stubborn Monroe after all—ready to do battle a new way."

"In the courts if we have to," Jeremy added.

"Then so be it," Abbie said. "I'll come back with the deed, and Jeremy's attorney can update it and verify its legality. Zeke and I claimed this land back when all a man had to do was say, 'This is mine,' and that was that. To make it legal, we had William Bent draw up the original deed. The government at that time didn't care who took what, as long as the land was settled; and those who ran Colorado Territory didn't care either as long as the settlers weren't Indian, so the land is in my name. Negroes have land rights now, too. We'll add Morgan's name. Besides, he's half white."

"If it will help, put my name on it, too, then," Dan told them. "I want nothing from it, of course, but at least I'm all white, and I'm a Monroe besides. They can't do a damn thing about it."

Margaret blinked back tears. "Thank you, Uncle Dan. That's a wonderful suggestion."

"Then it's decided," Abbie said. "And I think Jason's name should also be on it. That way when Dan and I are gone, the Monroe name will still be a part of this land. And if for some reason Margaret and Morgan should ever *have* to sell out, I want it agreed that they are the ones who keep the money. They and their children. They're the ones who stayed here and worked the ranch."

"I have no problem with that," LeeAnn put in. "Lord knows I, too, deserve no claim to it."

"Ellen and Hal have helped us very much," Margaret told them, "but things are not going well on their own ranch. Carson Temple has cut off their water supply. He's after their land, too."

Abbie sighed in exasperation. "Ellen, why didn't you tell us?"

"Like Margaret, she didn't want to worry you," Hal answered for his wife. "In our case it's not so important. I'm not the best at this life. I've been thinking of moving to Pueblo. What I'd like to do is have our piece hooked onto the Monroe land under a new deed. Morgan can pay us for it as he can. I have a legal deed to that property. With it, Morgan would have even more land for grazing and such, and with more land comes more power. We don't want anything from Morgan if he should have to sell this place. All I'd want is something for the five hundred acres I'll add to it."

Abbie rose, folding her arms. "That gives Morgan thirteen hundred acres. Not much compared to Temple's eight thousand, but as long as it's all legal, he can't do anything about it."

"Ten thousand," Margaret answered. "We've heard Temple recently bought up more land than the Tynes property. He has ten thousand acres, and word is, he'll acquire twice that much before he's through, between harassment and help from the land agent. What makes me sick is, most of the land he's acquiring once belonged to the Cheyenne, part of the original Treaty of Fort Laramie, back in fifty-one."

The words brought back so many memories for Abbie, of days when Zeke and Swift Arrow were both young warriors. Thousands of Indians from many tribes had attended that council, games were played, horse races took place nearly every day for weeks. There was feasting, challenges between enemy tribes; but all knew it was a peace council. All believed the Treaty of 1851 was the last treaty they would have to agree to, that the vast lands granted to the Indians under that treaty would remain forever theirs.

How wrong they all were. The Great Smoke was the beginning of the end for the Cheyenne and so many other tribes. Countless promises had been broken since then. That original treaty took years for Congress to sign, and by then it had been altered so drastically that it barely resembled the original. The government continued to treat the Indians as though they had no importance whatsoever, and as though promises meant nothing. Could anyone blame them for their uprisings, their anger?

So, now men like Carson Temple would own much

of that land. Not one bit of it was left to the Cheyenne. She reached over and took hold of Swift Arrow's hand, realizing the memories that treaty stirred for him, too. "All we can do now is try to hang on to what we've managed to keep in the Monroe name," she told all of them. "I think we should pray about it, and then I think we should sing some of your father and grandfather's Tennessee mountain songs. I remember many of them."

Everyone seemed to relax a little, and they held hands and prayed. As soon as they were finished, Abbie noticed Zeke still looked very troubled. He left the circle as they sang and walked off into the darkness. After several songs Abbie made an excuse to also leave. She walked in the direction Zeke had gone and called out to him.

"Out here," he said, calling from near the corral.

Abbie allowed her eyes to adjust to the moonlight, then saw his silhouette near the corral gate. She walked in that direction, wishing when she reached her handsome grandson that she could see Zeke's eyes better. "You're still troubled, Zeke. Is there something more we don't know about?"

The young man sighed, turning to rest his elbows on the top rail of the fence. "You'll be angry."

"Now why on earth would I be angry?" Abbie folded her arms, frowning. "Listen, Zeke Brown, you can tell your grandma Abbie anything. What is it?"

He swallowed, taking several quiet seconds to answer. "Carson Temple has a daughter. She's nineteen, and beautiful. Her name is Georgeanne, and she's nothing like her father."

Abbie felt an ache in the pit of her stomach. "Dear God," she muttered. "You've been seeing her."

"Yeah." He remained turned away. "I love her. If you met her, you wouldn't believe Carson Temple was her father. The way she describes her mother, she must be a lot like her, sweet and gracious; except Georgie is a lot stronger than her mother. Her mother . . . shot herself."

"Dear Lord!"

Zeke finally turned to face her. "Georgie was pretty young, about eleven. She didn't realize at first what had really happened, how her mother had died. Her father told her a few years later, and he explained it as though it was her mother's fault for not being a strong person. Carson Temple has no patience with anyone who cries or who fails at something. Georgie remembers how he used to treat her mother, always ordering her around, berating her for the smallest mistake, always telling her a wife had no rights. Georgie blames her mother's death on her father. But what's strange is the man let her go to a finishing school back East, where she stayed with her maternal grandmother. He doesn't mind her getting a higher education, thinks she's like him. She says he always talks about how strong she is, how proud he is of her. She's feisty and independent, and he likes that." He stepped closer. "But she's also very warmhearted, very liberal in her thinking . . . for a wealthy white woman. She doesn't judge someone by their heritage, only by their character. She says when she went East, she learned how there were a lot of different kinds of people in this world, and she never did feel comfortable with her father's prejudice and his barbaric way of getting what he wants. It shames her. He's a narrow-minded bigot who thinks of nothing but his own power and importance."

"And he would have your hide if he knew you were seeing his daughter!" Abbie added, "Let alone what he might try to do to your parents and this ranch. You're walking a dangerous line, Zeke!"

He shoved his hands into his pockets. "What about you, when you married my grandfather? Everybody knows what you went through to be with him, but you loved him and you stuck it out."

Abbie touched his arm. "It was another time; and I didn't have to answer to a man like Carson Temple, nor was I putting Zeke at risk because of such a man. If I had thought it might cost him his life or the ruination of his family, I might have chosen differently, just because I loved him so much. I've always preached to my children to follow their hearts, Zeke, but that's often easier said than done. The way I loved Zeke, I might have stayed with him anyway, but I might also have loved him so much I would have given him up because it was best for him. In our situation, it was the other way around. *Zeke* fought the relationship because he thought it was best for *me* if we parted ways. He even almost left me a couple of times after we were married, just because he couldn't stand seeing the sacrifices I made to be with him. It's a terribly difficult choice, Zeke. I wish I knew what to tell you. Your grandfather was married before me, you know, back in Tennessee. Indian haters killed his white wife and their baby just because she dared to love an Indian. He was only about your age then. I wish he were here for you now."

Zeke rubbed at the back of his neck. "Yeah, so do I." He closed his eyes. "Damn it, Grandma, I can hardly stand being away from her."

"Then you had better tell your mother and father."

He threw up his hands and turned away again. "That's the hard part. They'll be furious. And they probably won't believe Georgeanne could be any different from her father. But she is. I wish you could know her."

"So do I, Zeke. All I can say is she must be quite

something if she can look beyond your heritage and see the fine young man you truly are. I already love her just because *you* do. Maybe if you are careful for a time, wait until we get things settled with the deed and make sure Temple can't rob this land from us, maybe then you can be together, maybe go away together. I know it's hard to be patient when you're young and in love, but you *have* to wait for a while, Zeke. You understand that, don't you?"

He shrugged. "I guess. I have to see her once more, though, just to tell her that much. There's a place where we meet and ride together. She goes there every day, hoping I'll show up."

Abbie sighed, feeling sorry for his tender heart. "Be very careful, Zeke, for your parents' sake."

He nodded. "I will. Thanks for understanding, Grandma."

She grasped his hands. "Young love is something I totally understand. I was only fifteen when I met your grandfather."

"Georgeanne is a full-grown, educated woman, old enough to know what she wants, but her father treats her like he owns her. He brags about her being well schooled and independent and all, 'like a real rancher's daughter,' she says he puts it; yet he seems to think she shouldn't have a mind of her own in some things. She only came home this past spring for a quick visit with him. She never intended to stay, until she met me."

Abbie's' heart ached for him. "I hope neither of you gets badly hurt from this, Zeke, but I don't see how it can be avoided. Please be very careful about meeting this girl. Her father sounds like a brutal man." *Very much like Winston Garvey,* she thought with a shiver. "Everyone will be going back in a couple of days. However, I'm going to stay a little longer, go and help Ellen do some packing for their move to Pueblo. I'll be here for a little while if you want to talk more about this. I just hope this Georgeanne is sincere and not leading you on, teasing you for some reason."

"She wouldn't do that. She's taking just as much of a risk as I am when we meet each other. And it's there in her eyes, Grandma. There isn't a mean bone in her body. She's got her pa's strength and determination, but in the right ways."

Abbie put an arm around him and walked him back toward the circle of family around the fire. "You be sure to write me and let me know what happens, Zeke; and you should tell your parents."

"I guess I will, after I see Georgie once more. Life sure can be hard, can't it?"

Abbie shook her head. "Oh, my dear grandson, I am the last person who needs to be told that. Life is much harder than you know. I just hope you don't learn all your lessons the difficult way."

It was the third week of July when everyone began packing to return. It was decided that Hawk and Iris would go first to Denver and see where their uncle Jeremy lived, get to know him better so that when they went there for school they would be more comfortable. LeeAnn and Joshua and their children would also go with Jeremy. LeeAnn wanted to see her brother's home. Wolf's Blood was curious, but he hated cities, especially Denver, which held bad memories for him. Thus he and Jennifer would head on home with Dan, Rebecca and Jennifer's daughter Emily. Jason would also go straight home. His doctoring services were needed at the reservation.

Abbie and Swift Arrow would return home a few days later. Abbie would then return, going to Denver first, with the deed to the property, so that Jeremy could have it updated by an attorney. Swift Arrow would not come with her. He had been away from the mountains and the land of the northern Cheyenne too long, and he had no desire to go to a city like Denver. Like Wolf's Blood, he hated such places. Dan agreed to accompany her, as he was retired from the army now and had decided he'd enjoy seeing Denver and Jeremy's home, which he did not doubt was nothing short of a mansion.

Abbie disliked good-byes. Leaving this old ranch would always be one of the hardest things she would ever do, but at least she had a few more days before she had to go.

Hugs, kisses, tears. This reunion had been the highlight of her life, except for the day Zeke Monroe asked her to marry him. That was at Fort Bridger, forty-two years ago. They had already made love, somewhere in the wilds of Wyoming, a love-struck girl and a lonely half-breed bent on branding her as his own. And he'd most certainly done just that.

Wagons were loaded, and Abbie laughed to see the ever-elegant Mary climb into a bed of straw in the back of one of the buckboards. She had taken to the family as though she'd always known them, and that was a credit to her character. Jeremy had chosen well, just as Wolf's Blood had said.

Abbie fought a growing dread she could not even name. So many memories, so many changes. How could forty-two years pass like a breath of wind? Soon it would be time for the old ones to pass away, and then these children of hers would be the old ones, then the grandchildren. It was a fact of life, one generation passing their wisdom and knowledge on to the next, the kind of change one simply had to accept. There was not one child or grandchild here of whom she was not proud, and that was what counted.

Swift Arrow moved beside her, putting a reassuring arm around her, as though he could read her thoughts. "We have lived through so much change, Abbie. These children, especially the grandchildren, they go on to something new. People like us belong to the past."

Her eyes teared as the wagons lumbered off, everyone waving, LeeAnn crying. "Don't take too long getting home, Mother. Stop and see us in Cheyenne on the way!"

"I will." Cheyenne. Now a white man's town, it was named for a tribe of Indians who no longer lived anywhere near it. Abbie watched the wagons until they disappeared over a hill . . . that same hill where she used to watch for Zeke's return.

Zeke rode to the northeast quarter of the Monroe property, his heartbeat quickening when he saw Georgeanne waiting for him. She'd found his note! He kicked his Appaloosa, Rain Dancer, into a gallop, jumping a fence to get to the other side where she waited. Georgeanne laughed and rode off with him, both of them heading for the stand of trees where they always met in secret. On the way, Zeke pulled her off her own horse and onto his, settling her in front of him.

"You are now my captive," he told her when they stopped.

Her eyes widened in mock terror. "And what do Indians do with women captives?" she asked.

Zeke felt a sudden, almost painful need for her. "They ravish them," he answered.

She placed her arms around his neck. "Is that what you intend to do to me?"

He met her mouth in a hot kiss, searching deep. He'd not yet mated with any woman but he had a

damn good idea how it was done and how good it
would feel. "I would like to," he finally answered, kissing her neck. "God, I've missed you Georgie."

"And I missed you. How was the reunion?"

"It was really nice." He told her about the family,
every member, how his two uncles had reconciled, how
rich his uncle Jeremy was. "Grandma Abbie is so pretty
for a woman her age, and so wise. I wish you could
meet her. I told her about you, Georgie."

"You did? What did she say?"

"She said to follow the heart, but that sometimes is
a hard thing to do. She said we must be careful and
wise. I have to think about my parents." He kissed her
again, moving a hand to feel her breast through her
blouse. The kiss lingered when she whimpered at the
touch.

"It feels so good to have you touching me again,"
she told him in a near whisper.

He leaned back and looked her over, studied the
auburn hair that she wore loose today, thick tresses
drifting over her shoulders and a few strands across
her face. "Have I ever told you how beautiful you are?"

"Not as beautiful as you are handsome."

He laughed. "Grandma has given us some hope,"
he told her. "She has a deed to our property. She is
going to get it and have a lawyer in Denver make sure
it is legal; then she will add my great-uncle Dan's name
to it. He is all white. Once everything is straightened
out with the deed, your father cannot take our property away. Then maybe you and I can be together. We
just have to be careful until then."

She frowned "I'm glad about the deed, but I hate
the waiting. Maybe we should just run off together."

"I would like to, but for the moment I would not
want to do that to my parents. They need my help on
the ranch. And if we ran off together, your father

might do terrible things to them and it would be my fault."

"I understand. In fact, I can't stay this time. Father thinks I am just out for a short ride and am coming back soon. A big landowner from Kansas is staying with us to talk business, so Father wants me there for lunch. The man owns land all the way from western Kansas into Colorado, and he might sell it to my father. Father would own even more land then. It seems he can never have enough. It's like whiskey to him. Land, land, land. I'm sick of it!"

"That's the way some white men are. Land means power, and it makes them drunk. That's what my parents say and what my grandfather Zeke used to say. It is the reason there is no land left for the Indians."

Georgeanne sighed. "I'm sorry I can't stay. Will you meet me here again tomorrow?"

"You know that I will."

"Good. You can tell me more about the reunion. And we'll talk about how we can be together. I love you, Zeke. I haven't really said it before."

His heart took a quick leap. "And I love you. You are a good woman, Georgeanne Temple, and God means for us to be together."

As they kissed once more, he wondered how much longer he could go on meeting her this way without invading her body and feeling himself inside her, claiming her, making sure she knew to whom she belonged. He was miserable with the want of her.

"Maybe tomorrow I will ravish you," he teased.

She traced slender fingers over his full lips. "And maybe I would let you. I want my first man to be you, Zeke, my only man. Is that too brazen of me?"

He drew in his breath from the sheer force of his desire. "Not at all. It is beautiful to hear. I will be back tomorrow."

Neither of them wanted to think about their promise to be careful. It was simply too hard. Their need was too strong.

"I love you, Zeke Brown," she repeated, her voice raspy from want.

"And I love you, Georgeanne Temple. Come hell or high water." He grasped her about the waist and hoisted her over onto her own horse. "We'll find a way," he repeated.

She reached out and touched the hard muscle of his forearm. "I'm glad you came. I was beginning to wonder if you would ever come back."

"I will always come for you." Reluctantly, he turned his horse and rode out of the trees, charging up to the fence and leaping it again.

Georgeanne watched, thinking what a fine specimen of man he was, how agile on a horse, what a good rider, a powerful young man. Yes, she was in love! She rode out of the trees and headed back toward the ranch house, hating the thought of having to sit through lunch with her father and Martin Jeffers from Kansas. It would be so boring. Her father would strut and brag and carry on in his booming voice about the importance of owning land. She could just hear him. *Someday all this land will be worth millions. Gathering land is like gathering gold.*

Perhaps. She really didn't care. She only cared about Zeke Brown. She kicked her horse into a faster trot, unaware that from a hillside behind the trees two men sat watching her.

"You see? I knew she was coming out here to meet someone. Even from this distance I know who that is. It's the Brown kid. We'd better tell Carson about this."

"You think he's stuck her?"

"Hell, yes. His pa's half colored, and his ma is part Indian. Coloreds and Indians both pant after white women. I don't know how he influenced her, but it's obvious Carson Temple's girl is lifting her skirts for him. Her pa's gonna be furious." The man grinned. The hired hands of Carson Temple turned their horses and headed for the main ranch, eager to tell the news, anxious to see Temple's reaction. This could be Temple's answer to getting his hands on the Monroe property, and a good excuse to hang an Indian.

Eight

It seemed forever to Zeke before he could ride back to the secret meeting place he and Georgeanne felt belonged only to them. When he first saw her, his heart pounded with anticipation, and he could see the look of eagerness on her face as they dismounted and tied their horses. He took her hand and led her deeper into the trees, where they spread out a blanket and sat down.

Zeke felt suddenly awkward, a little nervous. "So, did the man from Kansas leave yet?" he asked.

"This morning. He hasn't made up his mind for certain but he's pretty sure he wants to sell his land. Father will be one of the biggest landowners in Colorado if he does."

The thought sickened Zeke. "My grandmother says a lot of this land used to belong to the Cheyenne, under a treaty they signed in 1851. Now the Cheyenne are all gone, mostly because of men like your father, I'm afraid."

She lay back, resting on one elbow. "I do wish I could meet your grandmother."

"Maybe you can. I'm thinking of telling my parents about you while she's still here. Grandma Abbie understands how I feel. She'd help make my parents understand. They'll be pretty upset at first." He leaned down to face her, already feeling more relaxed. "Anyway, if I tell them, maybe you can ride over and meet them all. Or maybe we could tell them together."

"Maybe." She smiled, studying his dark eyes, always enraptured by his stunning looks. "I'll bet your mother is beautiful. Your father, too. I remember some of the mixed bloods back in Georgia were very good looking."

"You said your grandfather owned a plantation there."

She nodded, sobering. "A very big one. That's why my father is rich. My grandfather made a great deal of money from the plantation before the war, but when slavery was abolished, everything changed. The plantation was ruined, our home burned. I, of course, was not around to see all that. My grandfather wisely invested in businesses and land farther north. That's where my father met my mother. After my grandfather died, Father sold everything and came West. Owning a lot of land is in the family blood, I guess. With everything so changed in the South, father decided to come out here instead. He says the real money is now in cattle and land." She touched his hand. "I suppose his hatred of Negroes comes from when he grew up on the plantation. I remember hearing my grandfather talk about them. I could tell he must have been cruel to them. He and my father grew up in a time and place where Negroes were like cattle, plow horses, whatever. They did not see them as people."

Zeke felt a deep bitterness. He'd never seen anything of slavery, but his father had told him stories about it, stories that had made him shiver. He was glad such things could not take place any longer, but the lingering prejudice in people like Carson Temple gave him a good idea of what life must have been like for slaves, and it told him that the attitudes of some men had not been changed by the abolishment of slavery. When he looked in the mirror, he didn't see an In-

dian or a Negro. He just saw a man with dark eyes and
hair, a man with skin that tanned deeply in the sun.
Anyone who did not know him probably could not be
certain what strains of blood ran in his veins. Georgeanne had told him he was the most handsome man
she'd ever laid eyes on. He didn't meet enough people
to know if that was true, but if she believed it, that was
all right with him.

"My father has told me stories about slavery that I
can hardly believe," he told Georgeanne. "He and his
mother were slaves. He never even knew his father. His
mother was forced to"—he continued to study her
hand—"forced to go to bed with her owner. After she
got pregnant, she was sold to somebody else. She had
my father, and he, too, grew up a slave, until the war
ended all that. His mother was dead by then. My father
made his way West, learned to ride and break horses,
made a pretty good living, met my mother in Denver,
married her, then came to live at the ranch. He helped
my grandpa Zeke, learned a lot from him. Then when
Grandpa died and Grandma left, he and my mother
just kind of took over."

"What was your mother doing in Denver?"

Zeke met her eyes. "My mother is a fine person,
Georgeanne." God, she was pretty. Today she wore a
blue riding skirt, a white blouse that fit her generous,
firm bosom nicely, a matching blue vest over the
blouse. Her blue felt riding hat had a wide brim, and
her boots were made of a fine black leather.

"I am sure she is. What has that got to do with Denver?"

He sighed. "I was told her story only a couple of
years ago myself. A long time ago she was deeply hurt
by a white ranch hand who promised her the world,
talked her into his bed, said he'd marry her. Then he
told her white men don't marry Indian women. They

only sleep with them. She was pretty young. She thought maybe that was true, that she had no happiness in her future. She rebelled, ran away to Denver and . . . and got into prostitution. That's how my father met her."

"Your mother was a *prostitute?*"

He frowned. "Don't say it like that."

"Oh, I don't mean it in a bad way. I think it's kind of exciting."

"Exciting!"

"Oh, you know. Just that she's been through the worst and ended up a married lady with children, helping run a ranch. A person just doesn't expect that of a prostitute. I always figured most women like that have some reason for doing it, something terrible that happened to them when they were younger. And that's exactly the way it was with your mother."

"She's a good woman, strong and honest, like all the Monroes. My father saw that good in her, and he understood why she was leading that life, because he, too, was a man torn between two worlds, a man scorned and spit on just because he was half Negro. He could tell she did it to cover the hurt, to defy her Indian blood. It was his love that got her away from there and brought her back."

She leaned over and kissed his cheek. "It's so sad what hurt can do to people, so sad that such very good people can be brought to ruin by others just because of their heritage." She studied his muscular arms. Today he wore only denim pants and a vest, and the sight of his powerful chest and shoulders brought little surges of desire in her that told her there was a woman within, waiting to be awakened by the right man. She was convinced that right man was Zeke Brown. She'd been courted back East when she stayed there with her grandmother, but no young man had made her feel the way this one did.

"You're sure my background doesn't mean anything to you?" he asked her. "I mean, hell, Georgeanne, we're falling in love. We both know it. And we know what that could mean for both of us, the suffering, the name-calling—"

"Zeke Brown, anyone who looks at you would not even know what kind of people you come from, but I'm not saying that's why it doesn't matter. I'm saying most people will just see you as the fine man that you are. I will admit I never dreamed this could happen to me, not because I am like my father, but because it's just not accepted where I come from. It's something that never entered my mind."

He studied her blue eyes intently. "You sure you aren't doing this as a kind of rebellion against your father? An act of defiance? Don't use me that way, Georgeanne, even if it's not intentional. Think hard about it and ask yourself if that's what this is."

"Zeke! Why would you think that?"

"I don't know." He shrugged. "The way you talk about your father, I guess. You surely love him because he's your father, but you don't much like his views. You're always kind of defiant when you talk about him. Maybe you're just trying to prove something to him, that his hates can't dictate whom you choose to love."

She pouted, stretching out on her back. "I *don't* use people that way, Zeke Brown. You make me want to cry by talking like that."

He smiled, leaning over her, then moving on top of her, bracing himself with his elbows. "I wouldn't want to make you cry."

She studied him with misty eyes. "I love you, Zeke. You believe that, don't you?"

He watched her quietly for several seconds. "Yeah. I believe it. And I love you." He leaned closer and met her mouth in a sweet kiss that deepened into something more savage, as desire awakened in them both. They had never lain together this way, bodies pressing, each eager to see how it would feel to lie next to each other naked. He slipped his arms under her, lost in her, wanting to taste and see and touch much more. It felt good to press his hardness against her thigh, to rub against her everywhere. He longed to be inside her, wished they could be married right now. He pulled away for a moment, his eyes shining with desire. "I could never give you the kind of life you're used to, Georgie."

"We'd be all right. I don't need those fancy things, and you're a strong, smart man. I know you'd do fine at anything you try. Besides, I have an education. I could—"

Her words were cut off by the sound of a rifle being retracted. Another. *Click.* Another. "Get off my daughter, you stinking nigger!"

Both of them froze in place, Georgeanne's eyes widening in horror. Zeke slowly rolled away from her, and they sat up to see six men approaching out of the trees, one of them Carson Temple. Rage and pride began to consume Zeke as he rose to face the man. Temple was big, with a brutal look in his pale blue eyes. His rifle was aimed directly at Zeke's middle as he came closer, his whole body tense, his big belly protruding over the waist of his denim pants. Zeke stood six feet tall, but Temple matched him.

"Father, what are you doing here! How did you find us?"

The man's hate-filled gaze moved to his daughter, and softened just a little. "One of the men saw you meet this sonofabitch here yesterday. We watched for you today, from just over the hill to the south. When I saw this bastard ride here to you again, we came in on foot." He shook his head. "My God, Georgeanne, how could you shame me this way!" he roared in a deep voice. "You're an educated girl who knows coloreds and Indians are worthless filth. You know how *I* feel about them! And that I've been trying to get the land from this boy's folks! You've just given me good reason to kill the whole damn family and burn down every building on their ranch!"

"Don't you touch one person in my family!" Zeke growled, his fists clenched.

Without warning, Temple swiftly slammed the butt of his rifle across the side of Zeke's head, sending him sprawling. Georgeanne screamed and ran to Zeke, kneeling down beside him to see an ugly gash just above his temple.

"Dear God!" She looked up at her father. "How could you do this! I love him!"

The man leaned down and grabbed her arm, yanking her away from Zeke. "I don't ever want to hear such a thing out of your mouth again! Do you know what men are going to call you now? Do you have any idea how you've embarrassed and disappointed me!"

"I don't care!"

"He's got colored and Indian blood!" Temple boomed.

"And he's half *white! More* than half! You'd never know to look at him just *what* he is for sure! But I don't even care! He's a wonderful man, strong and smart and sensitive. *Sensitive!* You don't know the meaning of the word, or even how to love someone!"

He squeezed her arm tighter. "I know I love my *daughter,* and I know what's *best* for her! Someday, little girl, you'll thank me for this. You'll realize what a stupid thing you've done, and if we're lucky, we can avoid any real damage. These men here know they'd best keep their mouths shut! I can trust them. You go back to the ranch, and not a word will be said about this again, understand? I'm chalking this one up to your being too lonely out here and too young and naive. Like most women, you're easily duped by a handsome man."

She jerked her arm away. "Don't be so insulting! I'm nineteen years old, Father! I've been to school in the East! I've met *plenty* of handsome young men, but none of them was as wonderful and sweet as Zeke Brown!"

Zeke heard the slap, the scream, the tears. He struggled to get to his feet to help Georgeanne, but his body wouldn't move for him, and when he opened his eyes he saw only darkness.

"I'm sorry, Georgeanne, but you need some sense knocked into you," Temple told his daughter. "I'm sending you back East for a while, away from all this. And I'm telling you right now, if you really care what's best for this boy here—and his family—you'll never see him again. *Never!* I'll let them off light this time, but any more of this, and they'll *suffer!* I'll burn them out, shoot their horses, kill this kid's father, if I have to, kill him, too! If that's what it takes to keep you away from him, I'll do it. I'll not have any colored grandbabies, you understand, girl? I hope to hell you haven't let him stick himself inside you! That's all boys like this want, don't you know that? They all dream about getting inside white girls!"

"Stop it!" Georgeanne screamed, putting her hands to her ears. "Zeke's never touched me that way! He's always been honorable."

"Bullshit! Get on your horse and ride back with Luke."

"No! I won't leave Zeke! He's hurt, and you're going to hurt him more!"

"Don't you worry about him. I'll just take him back

to his folks and set them straight! But I *will* hurt him more if you don't leave, right now!"

"No, wait!"

Zeke heard Georgeanne struggling and protesting.

"Do like I say, girl, if you don't want him hurt any worse than he is."

"Promise me! Promise me, Father!"

"Just get on that horse and ride out of here!"

More tears, followed by the sound of a couple of horses riding off.

"Loop a rope around his boots," Zeke heard Temple order. "We'll take the boy back to his folks, but not on his horse."

Zeke felt the rope being tied around his ankles.

"Give me the other end. I'll tie it around my saddle. He won't be such a pretty boy by the time he gets home. Bring his horse along. We wouldn't want to be called horse thieves, now, would we, boys?"

Zeke heard laughter, felt a tug at his ankles. Horror engulfed him when he realized what Temple was going to do. It was close to two miles back to his place, and he'd be dragged through dry grass and over gravelly ground—some of it baked hard by summer sun—over rocks and anything else that might be in the way, but there was nothing he could do to stop it from happening. "Georgie," he whispered.

"Mother!" The word was screamed, in a way that told any mother her daughter was horribly upset. Abbie jumped up from where she had been sitting by the creek where the irises bloomed, the place she used to share with Zeke. She ran back toward the house, noticing several men out front sitting on horses. Even from this distance Abbie could tell there was a body on the ground behind one of the horses. Margaret was bent over it, screaming and wailing Zeke's name. Little five-year-old Lance stood beside her crying.

"My God," Abbie moaned. She ran toward the house, heading for the back door first. Morgan was over a mile away with the other ranch hands, singling out horses to take to Pueblo to sell. Swift Arrow and young Nathan had gone with him. She and Margaret were here alone. She ran to a wall and grabbed an old shotgun that once belonged to Zeke, hoping it was loaded, and hoping that if she had to use it, it would not blow up on her. She marched out the front door then, pointing the gun at the big man whose horse had dragged Zeke's body. "You must be that stinking, yellow bastard they call Carson Temple!" she said, taking a firm stance.

All the men looked at her in surprise. "Who the hell are you?" Temple asked.

Abbie had to agree the man was indeed intimidating, what with his size and his booming voice; the look in his icy blue eyes.

"I am Zeke Brown's grandmother, and believe me, mister, I've killed men before! I was out here fighting to settle this land before you ever ventured into this land! And if my husband were still alive, he'd have your hide ripped open right now. You'd be food for buzzards! What have you done to my grandson!"

The man shifted in his saddle. "You Abigail Monroe?"

"I asked the first question!"

"He's alive. All I've done is give him fair warning. He touches my daughter again, he's *dead!* Maybe his parents, too. This house burned, the barns burned, the horses run off. You understand that?"

Margaret looked up from Zeke's bloodied body. "What are you talking about?"

Temple cut the rope that held Zeke, then turned his horse. "You don't know?"

Margaret rose. "I only know you tried to kill my son!" she screamed. She ran up to the man and hit at him fruitlessly. Temple placed a foot against her chest and thrust her to the ground with it. The other men laughed.

Abbie fired the shotgun into the air, silencing all of them. "That will bring Zeke's father and his men, along with my husband, Swift Arrow, a full-blooded Cheyenne who was at the Custer massacre, a man who would dearly love to return to his warrior ways and kill more white men! I suggest all of you leave!" She aimed the shotgun at Temple. "Shoot me if you want, Mr. Temple. I am sure shooting a woman would mean nothing to a coward who beats and tortures young boys! But I'll tell you one thing. You'll go down, too! From this distance I could open a pretty big hole in your fat belly!"

The man looked at the others, who all grinned. He looked back at Abbie. "You tell your grandson to never see my daughter again. If he stays away from her, I'll leave his folks and this place alone . . . *if* they can prove legal title."

"It's legal all right! I'll be bringing back the proof in just a couple of weeks! The ranch is also in the name of my brother-in-law, a *white* man named Dan Monroe, who was an officer in the United States Army! And I am part owner—Abigail Trent Monroe. *I* am white! My half-Cheyenne husband was the finest man who ever walked! He built this ranch, and you could never hold a candle to him in courage, honor, skill— not in *any* way! Now get off our land!"

Temple turned to Margaret. "I've got plenty more men, and I own the law. You damn well know I can come back here and rip this place apart! I can make

things so bad for you, you'll *have* to sell! You tell your
son it's all up to *him!* All he has to do is never see my
daughter again! His family's fate is in his hands!" He
turned his horse and signaled the others to leave. They
rode off just as Morgan and Swift Arrow and the others
appeared at the top of a hill, in response to Abbie's
gunshot. They rode in fast when they saw Temple and
his men riding away.

Margaret walked back to Zeke, collapsing beside
him. "My God, Mother, look at him! He could die!"

Abbie gathered her courage and forced herself to
walk over to where the young man lay in a bloodied
heap. His vest hung in shreds, and his skin was ripped
and bleeding, bruised everywhere. He groaned, tried
to move.

"Lie still, Zeke," Abbie told him.

The men reached them, Morgan jumping down and
running up to his son. "God in heaven!" He looked
toward Temple and his men. "I'll *kill* him!"

"And you'd be hanged!" Abbie told him. She glanced
at Swift Arrow, saw murder in his eyes. "Please, my husband, keep your senses about you. I know what you want
to do, but right now Zeke needs us, and *I* need you,
just as Margaret needs Morgan. Remember we live under new laws now! Don't try to go after them."

Swift Arrow, fists clenched, looked down at her
proudly. "Men should be allowed to live the old way,
allowed to avenge such a thing!"

"What did he mean about Zeke and his daughter?"
Margaret wept.

"He was seeing Carson Temple's daughter," Abbie
told her.

"What!" Morgan bent down beside his son. "How
do you know? Why didn't you tell us?"

"He told me just two days ago. I warned him how
dangerous it was, and I made him promise to talk to

you before he saw her again. Apparently he did not heed my warning." She leaned down and gently touched her grandson's hair. "She must be a wonderful young woman, nothing like her father. He said he loves her."

"My God," Margaret wailed. "I could have told him! I know what happens in cases like that!"

"Not in all of them, Margaret! And it was not Georgeanne Temple who hurt him, it was her *father.* It's different from what happened to you, but there is no time to talk about any of it now. We've to get Zeke inside and do something for him."

"Help me pick him up," Morgan told Swift Arrow.

The two men carried Zeke inside, and sixteen-year-old Nathan, bitter hatred in his dark eyes, picked up Lance to try to stop his crying. Margaret hurried after Zeke and the men. "Take care of your little brother," Abbie told Nathan, who looked very much like his older brother, but was not built as big.

"Will he die?" he asked Abbie.

Abbie held up her chin "We won't let him. I nursed your grandfather back from worse injuries, and Zeke is young and healthy." She hurried inside, where Zeke lay in his own bedroom, shivering and groaning, moaning Georgeanne's name.

"He . . . hit her," he murmured. "I'll k-kill him! Kill him!"

Margaret began gently bathing Zeke's wounds, and Abbie looked across the room at Swift Arrow, who stood watching with arms folded, fierce anger in his eyes. He would dearly love to avenge this the Indian way. She begged him with her eyes not to try to do so. "Ride and get Ellen and Hal, will you?" she asked him.

He came close to her. "I will get them." He grasped her arms gently. "The white man lives by a strange law, one that is good only for the white man, but bad for all others."

She put her hands to his chest. "Remember that. I could not bear to lose another husband, not this soon."

Tears trickled down her cheeks, and Swift Arrow leaned down to kiss them. "I will remember."

He turned and left, and she hated the fact that men like Swift Arrow had to swallow their pride the way they did now. She knew how hard it was for such men. She looked at Morgan, such a big, handsome, gentle man, who was once a slave. He well knew what men like Carson Temple were capable of. Temple was probably right. The fate of this ranch and of Zeke's family lay in whatever decision Zeke made once he recovered . . . if he recovered.

Nine

The train rumbled into Cheyenne, and Wolf's Blood looked out at the crowds in the street. The banner that hung across it read COWBOY AND INDIAN FESTIVAL. Tables with food on them were set up all along the boardwalks, some with wares for sale, and just as the train passed that street he could see horses and riders dashing along a cross street, apparently in a race.

"Some kind of shindig going on, I see," Dan commented.

Wolf's Blood sneered. "Cowboy and Indian festival, so the banner reads. I wonder where they got the Indians. There sure aren't any to speak of anyplace close by."

"First they get rid of them, then they have festivals using the idea of Indians for excitement." Jason leaned over to look out the window himself.

"If they want to see a wild Indian in action, I could show them some *real* excitement," Wolf's Blood commented.

Jennifer squeezed his hand. "I think you had better stay away from the festivities," she told her husband with a soft smile.

Wolf's Blood snickered. "Don't worry. I have no interest. Dan and Jason and I will go and get our horses and the wagon."

"Are you sure your mother and Swift Arrow will be all right riding all the way back to Montana on horseback?" Rebecca asked. "I hate to take the wagon and make Abbie ride."

Wolf's Blood laughed a little harder. "I thought you knew my mother better than that by now."

Dan grinned, feeling a little tug at his heart. There was a time, after Zeke died, when he'd thought about asking Abbie to marry him; but the only man who could even come close to replacing Zeke was Swift Arrow. Rebecca was a sweet wife. She'd come to the Cheyenne reservation for missionary work, and she had been easy to love. He'd never told her about his feelings for Abbie. "Abbie used to ride horseback, and sometimes walk, for hundreds of miles, when she lived and migrated with the Cheyenne," he told Rebecca. "She might be older now, but the toughness is still there. She'll be just fine."

The train puffed to the station platform, where more crowds were gathered. Wolf's Blood dreaded having to get off amid so many people. He looked forward to getting home to the peace and quiet of his own ranch, even though he would again be confined to the reservation. He missed Hawk and Iris already, but was happy Jeremy would get to know them better. He felt good about his talk with Jeremy, had actually regretted having to leave him back in Denver.

He imagined Hawk and Iris had been quite mesmerized by Denver and their uncle Jeremy's mansion. That was all right. He wanted more for them than the confines of reservation life. Jeremy could give them that. The white man's world was here to stay. They might as well learn to live in it.

Jennifer leaned near him to look out the window, and he knew a twinge of guilt over his educated, refined wife having to live on a reservation. He could tell by her eyes that she missed Denver some, as she'd lived and taught there for years before her first husband died. Still, though she had given up the excitement of Denver to be with her Indian husband, she had not lost the glow of her love for him. Besides that, she was near her father, which meant a lot to her.

He leaned over to whisper in her ear. "I will be glad to get home and get you to bed," he told her. They had not been able to make love all this time, between traveling, sleeping together with other family members and men and women being separated between the barn and the house while at the ranch. He enjoyed watching her blush at the remark. She was so fair, the red only glowed even deeper. She laughed lightly, and Wolf's Blood gave her a quick kiss, not unaware that some of the passengers on the train were staring and whispering.

The train finally stopped, and they disembarked. "Let's get the horses and get out of here quick," Wolf's Blood commented, conscious of more stares.

"Is *he* one of the Indians in the show, Mother?" one young boy asked.

"I don't think so, dear. He just got off the train. Besides, the Indians in the show are just white men painted up to look like Indians. That man looks *real.*"

Wolf's Blood glanced at the woman, deliberately giving her a dark glare he might give someone he was about to attack and kill. He enjoyed seeing the sudden fear in her eyes. She grabbed her son's hand and hurried away. Wolf's Blood just shook his head and chuckled, but deep inside he felt a growing rage. White men painted up to be Indians? What a farce! If they wanted to put on a show with Indians, why not use real ones?

He waited with Dan for their baggage, and they all took some bags, carrying them to the end of the platform, where Rebecca and Jennifer would watch everything while the men went for the horses and wagon they'd left boarded here four weeks ago. Just as they prepared to step off the platform, four men who had apparently been drinking heavily charged toward the train station on horseback, whooping and yelping, shooting handguns into the air.

"Hey, there's one of them wild Indians!" one of them laughed, pointing his gun playfully at Wolf's Blood. "Maybe we ought to shoot him!"

A few women screamed and scrambled out of the way, dragging children with them.

"Put those guns away, you idiots!" Dan shouted. "Guns aren't allowed in Cheyenne any longer."

"You the law?" one of the men asked, a grin on his face.

"I just got off the train, but I can sure as hell go *get* the law!"

People backed away as the men pranced their horses around, waving their guns and laughing. The one who had spoken to Dan turned his eyes back to Wolf's Blood, who stood glaring at him, unflinching, obviously contemptuous of the drunken fool. The man noticed the fair-skinned, red-headed woman standing beside Wolf's Blood, clinging to his arm.

"Hey, lady, what you doin' hangin' on to that Indian buck? Decent white women don't let themselves be seen touchin' dirty Indians."

People whispered, and one woman told her husband to run and get the sheriff.

"This man is my husband," Jennifer replied boldly.

"And my nephew," Dan put in. "Now get the hell out of the street with those guns before someone gets hurt!"

The man actually cocked his gun, still waving it in Wolf's Blood's direction. "How's come you got an uncle with blond hair and blue eyes, and a wife with red hair and green eyes, huh? That don't make sense. You must be the product of some white woman bein' raped by some damn savage."

Wolf's Blood started forward, but Jennifer kept hold of his arm. "Wolf's Blood, don't! You aren't even armed!"

"Except for my knife"—he sneered—"and my father taught me to use it well!" He gave Jennifer a gentle push back, resting a hand on the handle of his wicked Bowie knife, the one his father had given him as a gift years ago.

"You thinkin' on takin' a scalp, Indian?"

"Maybe this is just one of the shows," a man in the background commented.

"I don't know. I don't like the looks of it," someone else replied.

"Hold up there! Guns aren't allowed in town," a man shouted from up the street. Wolf's Blood noticed he wore a badge.

"We're just havin' a little fun, Sheriff," one of the drunken cowboys told him.

Everything then happened in a brief few seconds. A young boy set off a firecracker, and the noise caused the horse of the man closest to Wolf's Blood to rear. The sudden motion and the startling sound of the fire-cracker made the drunken cowboy release the hammer of his handgun, and it fired. The stray bullet found a mark, and Wolf's Blood felt Jennifer's hold on him suddenly tighten as her body jerked. People screamed and scattered, hanging farther back to stare at Wolf's Blood as he hung on to Jennifer as she slumped, her forehead opened up from a bullet hole. He lowered her gently to the street, and he did not need his brother Jason, a doctor, to tell him his wife was dead.

So quickly! In one short breath the woman he'd kissed just minutes earlier, promised they'd make love when they got home, was no longer alive. His beautiful

Jennifer, whom he had had with him for only a few
months . . . innocent, sweet, loving . . . and some
drunken cowboy had killed her, just because he'd
wanted to show his oats to an Indian—an Indian. This
was his fault. Jennifer had married an Indian, and she
had died for it!

This was no time for reason. All that was wild and
vengeful in him surfaced, all the rage at what his people had suffered over the years, his frustration at being
confined to a reservation, at being considered less
than human just because of his looks—all exploded
into power and revenge, and the man who was once
an honored warrior, an esteemed Dog Soldier, whirled,
yanking out the Bowie knife. Before Dan or the
authorities or anyone could reach him, Wolf's Blood
threw the knife, landing it into the heart of the cowboy
who had shot Jennifer.

But that was not enough to quell the rage inside of
him. He ran up to the man, yanked out the knife and
deftly scalped him. There were more screams, and people backed farther away, even the sheriff.

"No, Wolf's Blood! Stop! Stop now before it's too
late!"

He recognized Dan's voice.

"Wolf's Blood, don't!"

That was Jason. He thought about Hawk and Iris,
his precious children. He would miss them dearly. And
poor young Emily, seeing her mother shot down before
her eyes, seeing her stepfather scalp a man. But there
was no stopping it. She would learn to understand. A
couple of bullets whizzed past him. The other men
were shooting at him, but they were too drunk to hit
their mark. Letting out a war whoop, he leaped at one
of them, ramming the knife into his side and pulling
him off his horse. He deftly mounted the horse,
ducked another bullet, vaguely aware that most people

in the crowd had flattened themselves on the ground
or ducked behind cover. He charged a third man, letting out another shrill cry of revenge. The man tried
to flee, but Wolf's Blood caught up to him and
rammed his knife into his back, startling people up
the street, people who were unaware of what had taken
place near the train depot. He reached over and sliced
off another piece of scalp.

People stared, unsure if this was real or an act. Those
who realized it was real ran for cover, terrified of the
"wild Indian" who had apparently gone mad.

Wolf's Blood rode hard then, felt a couple more bullets whiz past him. That must be the sheriff shooting
at him. He had no idea what he would do, where he
would go. He only knew he had to get out of town.
He was Indian. He'd killed some white men. Maybe
Jennifer's death was an accident, but that would not
matter. He'd killed two men besides the one who shot
her. It had been right, necessary. His heart screamed
with grief for his wife. When he reached the distant
mountains and was alone, he would cut his arms and
chest, let blood in his mourning. He would never hold
Jennifer again, never make love to her. He might never
see his children again, or Dan or his sisters and brothers . . . or his precious mother.

So be it. Somehow he'd known this was his destiny.
He'd wanted to die like a warrior. Now there would
be no choice. He forced back the tears. There would
be time later for crying. He had to get away or be
hanged, and no Indian wanted to die by hanging, for
hanging strangled the spirit and kept it from reaching
the land beyond, where buffalo were still plenty in
numbers . . . and where his precious father waited for
him.

* * *

A messenger brought the telegram to Jeremy's home. "What's this about?" Jeremy asked.

The man sighed. "It's from Cheyenne. You'd best just read the telegram, Mr. Monroe."

Jeremy took it with a frown, paying the man for bringing it before going to his study. He decided to read the message alone first, his heart beating faster with dread. He suspected it must be some kind of bad news, feared it could have something to do with Wolf's Blood, since he'd gone on up to Cheyenne yesterday after the rest of them got off in Denver.

He closed the door. Mary was downtown with LeeAnn and all the children, and Joshua was sitting on the back porch, enjoying the vast, manicured gardens behind the house. Jeremy opened the telegram, read it, felt as though the blood was flowing right out of his body. "No!" he groaned.

He read it again, tears coming to his eyes. He could hardly see as he left the room and made his way on shaky legs down the richly paneled hallway that led to the kitchen at the back of the house. One of the cooks said something to him, but he didn't even hear. He walked out the back door to find Joshua, who immediately rose in alarm at the look on his brother-in-law's face.

"Jeremy! What the hell is wrong!"

Jeremy handed Joshua the telegram and turned away, his shoulders shaking. "I'll never see him again," he groaned.

A bewildered Joshua read the letter. It was from Dan. SHOOTING ACCIDENT IN CHEYENNE. JENNIFER ACCIDENTALLY KILLED. WOLF'S BLOOD KILLED SHOOTIST AND TWO OTHERS. FLED ON STOLEN HORSE. LAW AFTER HIM. CATCH ABBIE AT STATION IN DENVER AND EXPLAIN. COME WITH HER. BRING IRIS AND HAWK. THIS IS TERRIBLE LOSS. JENNIFER MY ONLY CHILD. OUR HEARTS BROKEN AT WHAT WOLF'S BLOOD

MUST SUFFER. WILL EXPLAIN MORE WHEN YOU AR-
RIVE. DAN.

Joshua folded the telegram, finding it difficult to
believe what he had just read. "Dear God," he murmured.

"How could it all have happened?" Jeremy groaned.

"Maybe you should come to Cheyenne with us after
Abbie gets here and learn the details. I can just imagine what the headlines have been like in my newspaper.
I wonder if the man I left in charge realized Wolf's
Blood was my brother-in-law." A lump rose in his
throat at the words. Just days ago they had all been a
strong, unified family, closer than any of them had ever
been. He looked at Jeremy, could see he was still crying. This was a tragedy for him. No one knew what
had been said between him and Wolf's Blood at the
reunion, but they had obviously become much closer.
"How in God's name are we going to tell Hawk and
Iris?"

Jeremy shook his head. "I don't know." He sniffed.
"It's just like my brother, isn't it?" he tried to joke. "I
can just see him going after those men. And right in
town!" He broke down again, taking a moment to re-
cover. "If that isn't just like what our father would have
done! It was in him, Josh, you know? It was just . . . in
him. His wife was killed, and he . . . couldn't let that
go unavenged. He still lived in that . . . old world . . .
where a man could deal out his own justice."

Joshua walked over and put a hand on his arm. "It's
more important than ever now for you to teach Hawk
and Iris a new way, Jeremy. We have to teach Hawk
that the best revenge is to learn how to deal with things
like this the legal way."

Jeremy nodded. "Wolf's Blood must be in a living
hell right now, out there somewhere alone. But I know
him well enough to know they'll never catch him. Not

Wolf's Blood. He won't be found until he *wants* to be
and he'll die just like . . ." His voice broke again. "Just
like my father did. He'll die like a warrior." He took
a deep breath and swallowed, rubbing the back of his
neck. "Did you know he was beginning to get the same
disease Zeke had? Arthritis?"

Joshua frowned. "No. He told you that?"

Jeremy nodded. "That day we talked. He said that
was why . . . he wanted me to look out for Iris and
Hawk. I know deep down he'll find a better way to die
than lying in bed a cripple, just like Zeke did." He
threw back his head and sighed. "He and Jennifer have
only been married a few months. He hasn't even been
out of that Florida prison for a full year yet. Now
he'll . . . be living in another kind of prison."

Joshua turned away, feeling sick. It was going to be
just as hard to tell Abbie about this as to tell Hawk
and Iris. And he hated the thought of telling LeeAnn.
He wasn't sure whether to send a wire to Margaret's
or to wait until Abbie reached Denver. Either way, Margaret and Ellen had to be told about their brother.
Thank God the family had had that one last reunion.

He heard it then, the screeching call, almost a sound
of distress. He looked up. "My God. Look at that,
Jeremy."

Jeremy turned to him, then walked down the steps
and looked up. An eagle floated above the house.
Jeremy shivered, more tears coming. "Father," he whispered.

"His spirit is restless. His firstborn is in trouble,"
Joshua said quietly.

Abbie sat at the creek again, one last time before
she would leave. Young Zeke was still in a bad way, but
she had to get home and get that deed in order to

see that all the legalities were taken care of for Margaret and Morgan. That would help save the ranch, but something else was important. Poor young Zeke had a difficult decision to make.

It was a beautiful summer morning, birds singing, the water rippling past. She fingered a purple iris she had broken away from where others bloomed, studied its perfect shape and beauty, remembered a time when Zeke had surprised her here after he'd been away for many weeks. She'd seen some of the purple iris floating on top of the water and turned to see where they'd come from, and there he'd stood.

It was pretty here, peaceful. She thought how life could be so wonderful if it were not for people like Carson Temple. She smelled the fresh air, closed her eyes and let the warm breeze caress her face, felt the sun on her skin. She wished she could shake this sensation that something was terribly wrong and that it was something more than just the tragedy that her grandson had suffered.

"So, here you are." The words came from Swift Arrow, who dismounted a shiny black gelding, part of Morgan's huge herd of finely bred horses. "I thought I would find you here."

"I think better here. Zeke and I made a lot of decisions here, and this is where we spent our last . . ." She drew in her breath, getting up from the grass to face Swift Arrow as he walked closer, holding the reins to the horse. "Swift Arrow, something is wrong!"

"Of course. Young Zeke—"

"No! I felt it yesterday evening, but I didn't say anything."

"Felt what?"

She turned away. "A kind of pressure on my heart, a tingling in my blood." She folded her arms and rubbed the backs of them as though chilled, even though it was a very warm day. "I've felt this way before, Swift Arrow, at times when Zeke was in trouble." She shook her head. "I'm scared. Not just for Zeke, but for the rest of the family. Someone else needs me."

He walked up and put his hands on her shoulders. "We will leave in only a little while for home. Then you will know."

She turned to face him. "I hate leaving Zeke in this condition. I'm worried about what he'll do when he's stronger, worried about poor Margaret and Morgan."

"We will get the deed, and our grandson will simply have to do the wisest thing for the moment. I have spoken with him. I explained to him how once, when I was not so much older than he, I, too, fell in love with a woman I could not have. I had to ignore the pain in my heart and go far away from her to try to forget her, someplace where I knew I would not have to see her and want her. I explained that I lived without her love for many, many years."

She placed her hands on his shoulders. "And did you explain who it was?"

"That it was his own grandmother?"

She smiled through tears. "I never realized, Swift Arrow."

"It would not have mattered. Zeke was your whole world, and that was as it should be. Yes, I explained it to young Zeke, only because I wanted him to understand that sometimes we must give up the one we love, although his situation is very different. The woman he loves is not attached to another. But he has the family honor to think about, keeping this land in the family, keeping his parents from suffering, as well as his brothers. It is apparent men like Carson Temple cannot be stopped." His eyes beamed with hatred. "But I could stop him for you if you say the word."

She shook her head. "I am sure that you would. But

I don't want to live without you, Swift Arrow, and I fear something worse has happened. I might need you even more than I realize."

He kissed her lightly. "We will take one thing at a time. Since being forced onto a reservation, I have learned to take one day at a time and not think too far into the future. We will talk with Zeke once more, tell him how much he is loved by the others in the family. He is young. He will survive this, just as all the Monroes survive the challenges that come to them. We will then go and get the deed and make sure all is taken care of. If something more has happened, we will find out about it when we reach home, and together we will survive that, too."

Her eyes teared more. "I think it's Wolf's Blood." She shivered, resting her head against his broad chest. Swift Arrow circled his arms around her. "I heard a wolf howling last night," she told him. "I said something to Margaret about it, and she said there have been no wolves around here for the last couple of years. She never heard it. Only I did."

Swift Arrow kissed her hair. He fully believed in contact from the spirit world, and that the animal spirits could bring messages. He had always been very close to Wolf's Blood, had taught him the Cheyenne way, as any honored uncle would do under Indian custom. Wolf's Blood had lived with him for several years, warred with him. He did not doubt he'd been as close to the boy as his own father had been, and he, too, had a deep sense that something was wrong. He had not mentioned it to Abbie, for fear of upsetting her, and now here she was, having her own suspicions. That was part of what he loved about her. Her heart and spirit were Indian.

"I heard it also," he told her. He sat down, pulled her down into the soft grass, moved on top of her and studied her brown eyes, eyes full of surprise and even more worry. She knew there was almost certainly something wrong if he, too, heard the wolf. "Wolf's Blood and the real wolves are *taku-wakan,*" he told her, using the Sioux words for "kindred spirits." He had lived and made war with the Sioux for many years, knew their language as well as his own Cheyenne tongue.

"Swift Arrow—"

He cut off her words with another kiss, this one deeper, more demanding. "I will tell you how it is, my wife. Something is in the air, something tragic. It does not only involve Zeke and possibly losing this ranch. It involves your firstborn son. Whatever is to be, whatever lies waiting for us, we have only this moment. Perhaps our hearts will be too full of sorrow to think of desire, but for now we can pray we are wrong. For now we are here, together, alone, and I think you need the strength that comes from being one with your man. Perhaps soon I will lose you to some kind of sorrow that will take you away from me, so for now I want my woman, all of her, her heart, her spirit, her body. Let us take this moment to just be with each other and put all fears away, Abbie."

She studied his dark eyes, knew he was right. This could be their only moment of sweet peace, and this might be her last visit to this special place. "I wish to be buried here," she told him. "Remember that."

"I will remember." He kissed her again. "But for now we are both very much alive, and I remember a young girl of sixteen who looked so very pretty in an Indian tunic. Even then I loved her."

He pushed up her dress, and Abbie was lost in him, his every movement a gentle command, his long, black hair brushing against her face as he deftly removed her drawers. They did not need preliminaries, did not even need to fully undress. He unlaced his buckskin leggings and lowered them, untied his loincloth, and in a moment he was inside of her. Somehow they both knew they needed this. They drew strength from it, and perhaps they would need that strength over the next few days or weeks.

"*Ne-mehotatse,*" Swift Arrow groaned.

"And I love you," Abbie answered. She relished the feel of him inside of her, and as always, when he made love to her, she experienced brief flashes of another man . . . another time.

Swift Arrow nuzzled his face against her breasts, and she closed her eyes and grasped his hair, whispering his name. Above them an eagle circled . . . silently . . . so as not to disturb them.

Ten

"I'm going away. I don't know how far or where, but it's the only thing left to do."

Margaret and Morgan sat beside Zeke's bed, holding each other's hands, both feeling helpless to heal their son's broken heart and battered pride. "We love you, son, and we need you here," Morgan told him. "But God knows I understand the things a young man goes through when different bloods run in his veins. I'm your father, and I'm supposed to be the one to give you good advice. In this case I'm at a loss. I want to keep this place, out of pure stubbornness and pride, because it would break your grandmother's heart to let it go . . . and because it just isn't fair that men like Carson Temple should get away with brutalizing others and forcing them to do things against their wills. But I also want my son's happiness. I could have told you it doesn't lie in loving the daughter of a man like Temple. You don't think it's possible right now, but you *will* get over that girl. You're only eighteen and—"

"I'll *never* get over her!" Zeke blinked back tears. His upper torso was still covered with scabs and bruises, his face, still swollen in places, a mass of scratches and cuts. "But I'm determined to do the last thing that sonofabitch Temple expects. I'll let him think he's won, but actually *we* will win, because I'm strong enough to do it. I'm strong enough to do exactly what he asks and get out of Georgie's life. And you know why?"

"I think we already know, Zeke," Margaret answered. She could not help wishing she could kill Carson Temple. For the past ten days since Temple had dragged Zeke home, she had lived in agony for his physical and emotional pain, and she had begged and pleaded with an enraged Morgan every day not to try to avenge his son's beating. Besides hurting for her son, she hurt for Morgan, a man who had seen so much abuse himself, a proud, strong man who again had to swallow that pride; yet his ability to do so made him even more courageous in her eyes. Now it seemed Zeke was very much like his father that way.

Zeke's hands balled into fists. He had called his parents into his room to tell them his decision, and he was determined to be strong about it. "I'll leave because I love Georgie so much, I don't want *her* to suffer. I don't matter in this. She's white, wealthy, educated, beautiful . . . and she's got a heart of gold. Why should she have to put up with name-calling and ridicule? I love her *too much* to keep seeing her. After what happened with my uncle up in Cheyenne . . ." He shook his head. "I don't know. It just made me realize that things don't ever change much and probably won't for a long time, maybe never. Look what white settlement did to the Indians, and they got away with it, because for some reason government and the law allow Indians to be treated badly. There will always be men like Carson Temple, men who'll never accept us as worthy, and they'll keep getting away with what they do. It's got me all confused and torn inside, and it isn't fair to Georgie for me to become more serious about her until I really know myself, until I'm a full man and know how to deal with all this. By then she'll probably"—how he hated the thought of any other man taking Georgeanne to his bed!—"she'll probably have found somebody else, somebody more suited to her."

Margaret put a hand to her dark hair, feeling very tired, beaten. They had received the news about Wolf's Blood and now besides her son, she had her brother to worry about. "We don't know this girl, Zeke. I wish you would have told us about her, but then you probably would not have taken our advice to stop seeing her. For you to make a decision like this . . . it only shows us how mature you have become."

"It's hard for me to believe Carson Temple could have a daughter as sweet and accepting as you say this Georgeanne is," Morgan said, rising. "She sounds rather idealistic to me, and the dreams of idealists usually last only until something comes along to shatter them, like what happened here. This could be the best decision you ever made, because after a while this girl might have become disenchanted, doubting her decision." He walked to a window, folding his arms and looking outside. "By now her father has ranted and raved and filled her mind with falsities, preached at her about the folly of her ways. By now she, too, is probably thinking it's best you two forget each other. Maybe her father has already sent her away."

Zeke felt sick at the thought. If only he could see her once more, talk to her, explain his decision . . . tell her it had nothing to do with how much he loved her, for he did, and he always would. "You would have both liked her, I'm sure of it. She's every bit as wonderful as I already told you. She sees the brutality in her father, believes it's his fault her mother committed suicide. He apparently is capable of being cruel to Georgie, too. Although she told me he's always treated her well, that day he caught us together, he hit her." He shook his head, aching with a need to kill. "I'm not going to put her through any more hurt and humiliation, either from her father or other people. I'm going to get out of her life, save this ranch for Grandma Abbie and for you. I'm going to show Carson Temple just how strong I really am." He rested his head against a pillow. "Maybe if I get away from here, go to the mountains, I'll find some answers. I want what's best for you, for Grandma, for this ranch and for Georgeanne. If I try to keep seeing her, a lot of people will suffer, including her. This way makes it easier on everybody."

Morgan shook his head. "I hope you know how badly I want to avenge what that man did to you, Zeke. I don't want you to think me a coward."

Zeke ran a hand through his dark hair, wincing at the pain in his arm. "I'd never think that of you. I love you, Father. I don't *want* you to try to avenge this. That's just what Temple would like to see you do, and you can bet he's ready and waiting. If something happened to you, I'd never forgive myself. And Mother needs you, while Grandma Abbie doesn't need any more heartache right now. I know she feels she's needed here, and she has to bring back that deed, but now she's got the awful tragedy of Wolf's Blood and Jennifer to contend with. I don't know how she manages to put up with so much."

"My mother is one of the strongest women I know," Margaret answered, "but she isn't getting any younger and I do worry about how all this will affect her. Wolf's Blood was very, very special to her. He was like my father in so many ways, actions, beliefs, looks, temperament. And now there are Hawk and Iris to think about. How awful for them! And poor Emily has lost her mother." She closed her eyes. "None of us knew just how significant the reunion really would be, after all."

She worried about her mother, who was probably in Cheyenne now. Thank God she had LeeAnn and

Joshua and Swift Arrow. What a terrible thing this was for Iris and Hawk, but at least they, too, had their grandmother, and now Jeremy. Thank God Jeremy and Wolf's Blood had reconciled before this happened. At least each member of the family had someone to whom to turn for comfort. They weren't so scattered that any of them had to be completely alone. Still . . . Zeke! Her precious son! He *would* be alone if he left home as he'd said he'd do. "Where will you go, Zeke? You *must* keep in touch with us, let us know you're all right. I hate the thought of you being away from here, alone. You've never been away from this ranch. Life can be hard out there, Zeke. I know better than some."

Zeke saw the shame and hurt in his mother's eyes. She was such a good woman. The hurt she had suffered over the white man she thought loved her must have been terrible to have made her run off to Denver and turn to prostitution. He suddenly realized she well knew how he was hurting over Georgeanne. "I'll be all right. I'll find work somewhere, but I won't go to a big city like Denver. I'll go someplace more quiet, up in the mountains. I promise to write and let you know where I end up."

Morgan turned from the window, his eyes red from tears. "I'm so sorry, son. I feel like I've let you down somehow. I should go with you, but I can't leave your mother, the ranch, Nathan and Lance."

Zeke grimaced as he shifted, moving his legs over the side of the bed. "No. Even if you *could* leave, I wouldn't want you to go. I love you, but I need to be alone, to think about this whole thing and learn to live without Georgie, figure out who the hell I really am, what I want to do with my life. Grandma Abbie says there is a purpose in all things that happen in life. Maybe God has some kind of purpose in this.

Maybe there is something out there waiting for me
which I don't yet know about."

"You *will* come home again," Margaret said, plead-
ing in her voice. "Promise me."

Zeke studied her flawless complexion, and he could
easily see how beautiful she must have been when his
father met her in a brothel in Denver. He nodded. "I
promise. Heck, I couldn't stay away forever. I might
even come back here and take over the ranch someday.
This is just something I have to do for now. If I'm
going to forget about Georgeanne, I have to get far
away from here for a while."

Forget. How in hell was he going to forget? Already
he ached to hold her again, hear her voice, see her
smile, taste her lips . . . "I'll come back," he promised
again. He gritted his teeth against the pain as he tried
to rise, and instantly his parents were there, each taking an arm.

"You shouldn't get out of that bed," Margaret told
him. "You're still much too weak."

"I intend to get stronger as fast as I can. The sooner
I leave, the better. I want to walk around a little, and
I want to talk to Nathan and Lance, explain to my
brothers how much I love them and that I'll be back."

"They'll miss you, son," Morgan told him. "They
both look up to you."

Zeke swallowed against tears at the thought of leaving this place, the only home he'd ever known. In all
his eighteen years he had been no farther than Pueblo.
He refused to let his poor, worried parents know how
scared he was. He had been man enough to think he
could fall in love with Georgie, man enough to want
her in every way any man wanted a woman. He'd
thought somehow it would have been magical, easy.
Now he realized what a fool he'd been, what a terrible
risk he had taken. He might have cost his parents their

very lives, at the least the ranch, the beautiful horses
Morgan worked so hard to breed and raise . . . this
land that had meant so much to his grandpa and
grandma. He'd even hurt Georgeanne. He should have
listened to that little voice of warning the very first
time he'd set eyes on her, but she'd been so easy to
talk to, so pretty, so open and accepting.

He had to forget her. How he'd do it, he had no idea.
He just had to be strong. It would save a lot of people
a lot of suffering. One thing was sure, though, he'd
never forget or forgive Carson Temple, and he would
never stop praying that somehow, someday, that man
would get what was coming to him!

It rained lightly, uncommon for southern Wyoming
in early August; but the weather seemed to fit the
mood. Iris and Hawk stood at their stepmother's grave,
their spirits as gloomy as the weather. Abbie watched
them, unable to do anything to soothe their broken
hearts.

Her biggest worry was how Hawk would react to this.
Like grandfather, like father, like son. The bitterness in
his eyes was frightening, but what hurt most was the
terrific loneliness she saw in them as well. He'd been
so close to his father, and now Wolf's Blood was gone
from his life, Hawk's only consolation being the fact
that his father was, as far as they knew, still alive.

Dan had waited until they'd all arrived before holding Jennifer's funeral service, and now a preacher
spoke over her, but Abbie hardly heard him. How
many times over the years had she turned to the Bible
herself, her only consolation. Knowing that someday
she and all her loved ones would be in a better place,
where they would at last have only love and peace, was
the only thing that had held her up through all the

losses she'd suffered over the years—through the two
worst losses, her little Lillian . . . and Zeke.

In spite of her own loneliness and that of Hawk and
Iris—and poor Dan, losing his only child—the loneli-
est person of all had to be Wolf's Blood, out there . . .
somewhere . . . grieving for Jennifer . . . longing to be
with his children. He would hide as long as possible,
she was sure, because he would never allow himself to
die by hanging. That was the worst way for an Indian
to die. He could ride up to authorities and challenge
them, let himself be shot down. She knew her son well.
That day would probably come, but he would hold out
as long as possible because of the children. He would
wait until they were older, knowing that his death
would be too hard on them at such tender ages. And
he would want to know what they did with their lives.

That was her biggest hope. Wolf's Blood would
surely find a way to get in touch with her, because he
would want to know about his children. Oh, yes, she
would see her son again, and until that time he would
survive because he'd once lived off the land for years.

She held tightly to Swift Arrow's hand, knowing this
was equally hard on him, for Wolf's Blood was as much
his son as he'd been Zeke's. She glanced at him, seeing
the tears on his cheeks. Things like this, and like what
had happened to young Zeke, were hard on such men,
men who believed it right for them to avenge wrongs
committed against their own. She knew it took great
control on his part to stand and do nothing.

On her other side stood Jeremy. He'd come along
to be with her and with his niece and nephew. Jeremy,
wayward son, now as much a part of the family as if
he'd never left them, so much more loyal and loving
and concerned than she'd ever thought he would be.

He placed an arm around her, and she knew he was
feeling a deep loss. He'd had only those brief weeks

to truly get to know his oldest brother, and now . . . LeeAnn stood weeping in Joshua's arms, and Matthew stood next to them, holding little Abbie. Three-year-old Lonnie clung to his mother's skirts, sniffling, not sure just what was wrong but afraid because his mother was crying. Dan stood near the minister, devastation on his handsome but ageing face. At least he had Emily, who was being consoled by Rebecca. Jason stood alone, wiping at tears, and Abbie thought what a quiet, devoted son her youngest was, silently strong. In his entire life he had never caused her one bit of trouble or concern.

Hawk and Iris stood with their arms around each other, surely feeling alone against the world in spite of being surrounded by a loving, supportive family. The preacher finished his eulogy, and each family member threw a handful of dirt and some flowers on top of the wooden coffin. Abbie turned to Jeremy. "I'm worried about Hawk. At his age, he could turn this hurt into a rebellion that could make him choose all the wrong ways in life."

"You leave Hawk to me," he told her. "Wolf's Blood wanted them to live with me for a while. Now, with this happening, I intend to make their stay permanent. I never had children of my own, but as far as I am concerned, I now have a son and a daughter, and I intend to do right by them. I made some promises to my brother; I intend to keep them. It's the only way I can make up for . . ." He choked up and had to turn away. For the next few minutes all those present consoled each other, embracing, weeping, surviving another family tragedy only through the comfort of those family members left.

"I hate those men!" Hawk sobbed. "I hate them all! The people who stood and watched and didn't do anything! The people who think my father should be arrested and hanged! Those men all *deserved* to die, even if they didn't do the shooting. They all started the trouble!"

Abbie could just picture it. Dan had explained what had happened, and from his army days of fighting Indians, and certainly from knowing Zeke and Wolf's Blood, he well knew the viciousness and quick vengeance they were capable of rendering. He'd seen both of them in action; so had Abbie. She could just imagine how swiftly Wolf's Blood had killed the men who had started all of this. It would be a natural reflex for someone like him, still the warrior at heart. Soldiers were searching for him now, determined to bring in the "savage" who had killed three white men, scalped two of them; but Abbie knew they would not find him. Men like Wolf's Blood could hide forever in country like this.

"What you have to do now, Hawk, is use this experience the way your father would want you to use it," Jeremy told the boy.

Hawk shivered, wiping at his eyes. "What do you mean?"

"I think you already know. We've had some good talks. I know Denver is a strange, new world for you and Iris, and you've only just begun to get to know Mary and me, but your father asked you to come stay with us after the reunion for a reason." He grasped Hawk's shoulders, thinking how he looked older than his fourteen years. He was going to be a big, strong man, like his father and grandfather. "Wolf's Blood asked me to look after you and Iris if anything happened to him. Even if life had remained normal, he wanted you to come stay with me when you were a little older. He wanted you to go to college."

Hawk sniffed, his head hanging. "I know, but I'm

not sure why. A man doesn't need college to run a ranch on an Indian reservation."

"I'm not so sure that's true anymore, Hawk, as big as some ranches are getting. A man has to keep books, run a ranch intelligently, or he can lose everything. But that isn't what we're talking about here. You know we're talking about something much more important than ranching. After this, you know in your heart your father won't want you to just go back to the reservation and live the ordinary life of a reservation Indian. Nor does he want you to be full of hatred and do something foolish. You know what he really wants of you, Hawk, and it's very important for you to carry out his wishes."

The rest of the family gathered around the boy and his sister, wanting to lend their support in any way they could.

Hawk shook his head. "I don't really want to live in Denver. I like you and your wife, Uncle Jeremy, but I just want to be at the ranch for a while."

"That's fine. I understand that. Still, eventually you have to come to Denver and get some higher schooling."

"I'm not smart enough—"

"Oh, yes you are. You're plenty smart, Hawk, smart enough to understand why your father wants you to get an education. It's just another way to be a warrior, Hawk."

The boy blinked back more tears, meeting Jeremy's gaze. "A warrior? How?"

New hope shone in his dark eyes, and Abbie was proud of Jeremy for choosing just the right words to get the boy's attention.

"By fighting a different way," Jeremy told Hawk. "Your father and grandfather did their fighting under old rules, in a time when a man could do those things.

But your father's life has extended into a time when those ways don't work anymore. For fighting under the old rules, your father will have to spend his life in hiding. He wants his son to learn the way of the warrior, but the way that can truly help his people, a new way—with legal action and the courts, Hawk. There are several good law schools in this country, and I can afford to send you to any of them. There are good colleges right in Denver and in Fort Collins. From now on whatever happens to American Indians is going to be decided in courtrooms and Congress. Indians will need educated people from their own ranks to speak for them, people who know their way around the government bureaucracy, who know the law and how to use it to their benefit. *Education* is the new way for the warrior, Hawk, and that is what your father wants for you. He told me so. He asked me to make sure you learn this new way. He taught you the Cheyenne way, and your great-uncle, Swift Arrow, can continue to teach you Cheyenne customs and beliefs. Those you should always keep in your heart. But *I* can teach you another way to be a warrior!" He squeezed the boy's shoulders tighter. "Believe me, Hawk, a pen can be as mighty a weapon as your father's Bowie knife. A legal document can be as effective as a lance or tomahawk. *Education* can be your weapon, the same as a rifle. It can be your *fire*power!"

Hawk stood there shaking, and Abbie pulled Iris into her arms, watching her son and grandson.

"I . . . miss my father," Hawk said, his lips trembling.

"I damn well know that, Hawk. You have no idea—" Jeremy stopped, a sob engulfing him. He pulled the boy into his arms. "No idea how well I understand . . . what it's like to miss a father."

Abbie closed her eyes, pressing Iris tightly against her bosom.

"*I'll* be your father for a while," Jeremy told Hawk. "Yours and your sister's, and Mary will be your mother. She's waiting in Denver right now, hoping you'll both come back soon. She would dearly love to do some mothering, and what better children to take into your home than your own niece and nephew? I owe your father . . . so much, Hawk. Let me do this. And at the same time, you'll be doing what your father wants. You'll be a true warrior, in the only way left for a man to fight his battles."

Hawk pulled away, looking from Jeremy to his grandmother, then to Swift Arrow, a perfect example of a mighty warrior of old. Swift Arrow's eyes were bloodshot from tears, but he managed a smile of reassurance, nodding his head. "Your uncle Jeremy is right, *nexahe*. Be a Dog Soldier in this new way, and you will bring honor to your people. You will prove how smart and wily a Cheyenne warrior can be. You will count coup in the new way. The struggle is not yet over. There are many things still not settled, especially for the Sioux. Perhaps there is a way you can help not only the Cheyenne, but also other tribes. We must all stay together now, fight as one Nation. And you can help in situations like the one affecting your aunt Margaret and your cousin, Zeke. Such wrongs should not be allowed. It will take men like you to right them."

Hawk thought about it for several quiet seconds. He looked beyond the graveyard at the distant hills. His father was out there somewhere, running from the law when he shouldn't have to. His cousin Zeke was lying badly injured, just for loving a white girl; his grandma's ranch was in jeopardy because of a white man who thought he could defy the new laws. His father hated men like Carson Temple, and those who now sought to hang him. For a brief moment he thought he could hear war drums, singing, bells jingling, rhythmic dancing. He could feel his father standing near him, hear his whispered words. *Do this for me, my son, so that my vengeance will send a message and my loneliness will be relieved.*

"Do you think I'll ever see my father again?" he asked his grandma, Abbie.

She kept an arm around Iris. "Oh, yes, you will see him. He'll find a way. And he'll want to know you've done what he wants."

Hawk looked back at Jeremy. "I'll come to Denver. First I want to go home, though, see the ranch again, decide what to bring with me. There are horses to sell."

"I have stables," Jeremy told him. "Keep your own favorites for yourself and Iris, and bring them to Denver."

Hawk looked at his sister. "Will you go?"

The girl left her grandmother's arms and hugged her brother. "I want to go wherever you are, Hawk." She wept.

Hawk turned his gaze to Jeremy again. "We'll all go up to the reservation first. Grandma Abbie has to get the deed. Will you come? See my father's ranch? His horses?"

Jeremy nodded. "I would be honored."

Hawk kissed his sister's cheek and turned back to look at the grave, then walked over to Dan and Emily. "I'm sorry," he said, new tears forming. "It wasn't father's fault."

"I know that," Dan told him. "At least Emily and I have each other. You do what you have to do. Going to live with Jeremy is a wise decision."

They all paid their last respects and left the graveyard. Dan and Emily were the last to go. They laid wildflowers on top of the casket, and Dan thought back over the many years he'd lived in this land, sometimes fighting Indians, always respecting them. His first wife, Jennifer's mother, had been too fragile to bear up under army life, but Jennifer had been strong. She'd loved Wolf's Blood since she was a little girl. It wasn't fair that she'd been able to share only a few months with him as his wife.

Reluctantly he turned and left. They would all stay the night here in Cheyenne at LeeAnn and Joshua's home, then leave for the reservation.

No one saw the wolf. It hunkered down at a distance, hiding behind a gravestone . . . waiting. As soon as they were gone it came closer, sniffed around the fresh mound of dirt, then lay down across the grave, whining.

Eleven

"Son, you aren't well enough to go."

"Mother, I cannot put it off any longer. I've been two weeks healing, and I have no broken bones." Zeke looked into a mirror, setting a wide-brimmed hat on his dark hair. He was washed and shaved, wore a clean shirt, denim pants and boots. He'd packed only three changes of clothes, nothing fancy, one extra pair of boots and gear for shaving and washing. He would pack a blanket roll and his sheepskin jacket on his horse, and he would take along money he'd saved from over the years, mostly what Morgan felt he deserved to be paid for his part in tending the ranch. Morgan had given him more, and though he hated to take it, he knew he would need it until he found work somewhere. "I'll pay Father back just as fast as I can. I know you're hurting for money. If Carson Temple hadn't burned down the feed shed and all that hay we had stored in it last fall, you wouldn't have had to buy so much feed and oats for the winter."

"We'll make do, Zeke. I'll feel better knowing you can buy yourself decent meals and rooming."

"I won't need more than an open campfire and soft grass most of the time, till winter sets in at least." He turned to face his mother, hated the look of agony in her eyes. "Things will work out somehow, Mother. When Grandma Abbie gets back with that deed, and with me gone, this place will be saved. Once I decide what to do with my life, find a way to"—how could he ever forget Georgie?—"a way to get over Georgeanne, I'll come back." He pulled on a leather vest. "By then Georgeanne will have forgotten all about me, most likely. She'll probably go back East once she finds out I'm gone, end up marrying someone else."

"You won't try to see her first?"

He picked up his carpetbag from the bed, then reached over and took up his rifle. "It's best I don't, not just because her father would probably shoot me on sight, but because if I see her again. . . . I might not be able to leave after all, and the trouble will start all over again." He stepped closer, leaned down and kissed his mother's cheek. "I'm sorry, Mother, for putting you through this."

She straightened proudly. "You are not the one who should be sorry. We know whose fault this is, and someday he will pay. One thing is sure, he'll never touch Monroe land!"

Their eyes held, both hating having to part. Zeke was not about to admit how afraid he was, leaving home for the first time, how much he'd miss his parents and brothers. Reminding himself this was for them, he walked past his mother and went outside, tying his gear onto Indian and shoving his rifle into its boot. He knew how to use it well, and he could hunt, had camped under the stars many times. Hell, he was part Indian. His grandfather had lived like one for years. Even Grandma Abbie had. If they could do that, so could he.

Georgie! That was the hard part. He'd ride off and probably never see her again, and that was a hurt worse than any he'd ever known. It would probably even be a long time before he saw his grandma again. What if she died while he was gone? He couldn't think about that. He had to do this. Grandma Abbie would understand. She'd be with him in spirit.

Margaret came out of the house with a gunnysack. "Tie this on. It's full of food—potatoes, bread, things like that."

He fought the tears that wanted to come and tied the sack onto the horse. Morgan came from the barn, leading two of his finest horses, a sturdy roan gelding and an Appaloosa. Nathan and Lance hurried along beside him as he approached Zeke. He handed over the ends of the ropes tied around the horses' necks. "Take them with you, son. You can use them for pack horses if you need more gear later for something, and they're valuable. If you get to hurting for money, you can sell them. Or, Indian could go lame for some reason. If he does, you'll have another horse to ride."

Zeke felt stunned at the offer. The two horses were worth at least five hundred dollars. "Father, you've given me enough."

Morgan studied the lingering scabs on his son's face. "Not near enough, son." He handed out the ropes. "I love you, Zeke Brown, more than any man can love a son. I wish I could change all of this for you." His eyes teared. "It's not going to be the same around here without you."

Zeke swallowed, nodding. "I love you, too, Father. You know how much. It's because I love you so much that I'm going." He turned and tied the ropes to his saddle horn, then reached out to embrace his father. The two men hugged for several long seconds, neither wanting to let go. It was the same with Zeke and his mother. He turned to Nathan then. "You're the oldest now. Help our father. Keep the place going, Nathan. I'm sorry I've caused you to have to do more work."

"It's okay, Zeke. Please write, though. Let me know what it's like out there."

Zeke then picked up Lance, who did not fully understand why his brother was going away or that it would probably be for a very long time. "You help Mother and Father, Lance, and be a good boy for them. Promise me."

Lance nodded, his lips puckered, wanting to cry but not sure why. " 'Bye, Zeke. Bring me something when you come home."

You might be a man by the time I come home, Zeke thought. "I will," he answered. He set the boy down, took one more look at his parents and brothers, then turned and mounted up. He undid the ropes tied to his saddle horn and held them in one hand, taking the reins to Indian in the other. The memory of racing Indian against Georgeanne's Princess stabbed at his heart. He hadn't really known her all that long, just long enough to know he loved her.

It had to be done now. He'd made his decision. "God be with you."

"We'll be praying for you, Zeke," Margaret told him, shivering with the need to weep.

"I know you will." He looked at Morgan, but there was nothing left to say. It was all there in his father's eyes, and he hoped this parting was not such a strain on the man that he would take sick over it. Morgan Brown had never been anything but strong, robust; had never had a sick day in his life. But he was not getting any younger, and Zeke knew how much this hurt him. "Just remember the important thing is not to let Carson Temple win. He gave his word that if I left, and if you could prove ownership, he'd leave this place alone. I'm giving him time to prove he'll keep his word. Grandma Abbie said Grandpa Zeke always used to promise to come back when he had to leave her. His blood runs in my veins, and I'm telling you

I'll be back. Maybe I'll be a rich man when I come back, and we'll buy up all of Carson Temple's land."

He grinned, glad to see the remark had brought smiles to his parents' faces, although there was a great sadness behind the smiles. He turned his horse. He had to leave before he cried like a little boy. This was a time to put behind him all childish things, including a young love that was probably best forgotten. He rode off, heading up the road that meandered over the hill toward Pueblo. He would not look back. It would be too much to bear, seeing his parents still standing there. "Help me, Grandpa," he whispered. "Help me know what to do, where to go." A great temptation to see Georgeanne first ripped through him almost violently, but he knew that was the worst thing he could do. He had to let go. He had to forget. She'd hate him for leaving without a word, but it had to be done.

The tears came then, but he kept riding.

Wolf's Blood shivered. Even in summer the mountains were cold at night, and all he had was the horse he'd taken the day he fled Cheyenne, all his baggage left behind. He had no coat, and the only blanket on the horse he'd stolen was the saddle blanket. It was all he had now to keep him warm at night.

He considered the horse itself rather worthless. It could not compare to the beautiful, near-perfect ones he bred at his own ranch . . . but he would never be able to go home now. This horse would do until he reached Montana. Somehow he had to get back to the ranch to take a couple of his own best horses and get some supplies, if he could sneak in there without being caught. Soldiers stationed around the reservation would probably be watching the ranch with keen eyes, but then, many times he had snuck up on soldiers without being spotted, in the days of making war. He knew how to move without making a sound, how to make himself blend in with the brush and the rocks. He shared the spirit of the wolf, cunning, silent. He would find a way. Maybe he could even see Hawk and Iris once more.

He wrapped the blanket around his shoulders and leaned against a tree, afraid to build a fire because he might be spotted. He'd made his way north, keeping to the mountains, pretty sure he'd completely lost the soldiers who had been chasing him. He could not help feeling proud that at least he had not lost his old skills at fooling soldiers, tricking them, leading them on a wild-goose chase. He remembered he'd deliberately taunted a whole company of soldiers once, getting just close enough for them to shoot at him and take up the chase. He'd led them right into a trap, a canyon where Cheyenne and Sioux waited. Many soldiers had died that day!

He had wanted to be a warrior again—but not this way . . . not this way. Jenny! His beautiful, precious Jenny, smiling and kissing him at one moment, falling to the ground with an ugly bullet hole in her head the next. He was not even sure how many days had passed since that awful point in time. Three days ago he had vented his rage and sorrow, crying out to *Maheo* and cutting his arms and chest in his agony, wanting to feel the pain and to make a blood sacrifice. He had loved and lost two wives. There would be no more now, only loneliness . . . utter loneliness. Missing, wanting, needing Jennifer was a pain that would last a long, long time, as would the feelings of guilt, for he was sure her death was his fault. If she had not been with him that day, a white woman with an Indian, she would still be alive. Dan would still have his daughter. Emily would still have her mother.

Adding to his grief was the fact that he could never again be with Hawk and Iris. He prayed they would go with Jeremy, learn to live a new way, fight their battles the white man's way, much as he hated the ways of the whites. He prayed Hawk would not rebel and get himself in trouble. If only he had a chance to talk to him, hold both of his children just once more, tell them he loved them, urge them to get off the reservation and not waste their lives there. They were still young enough to need a father and mother. Maybe Jeremy and Mary could be that for them. He trusted Jeremy now, had no doubt that his brother would do all he could for the children, for Jeremy dearly wanted to make up for all the years he'd lost with his own father and the rest of the family. Believing Hawk and Iris would be taken care of was all that kept him going.

He heard a wolf howl not so far away, and he watched the dark shadows. He was not afraid, for he felt a close kinship with these creatures. He'd had two wolves as pets when he was younger, and he could not help wondering if now they felt his sorrow and loneliness and wanted to comfort him. He sat very still, not caring if a whole pack of them *did* come and tear him apart. There was really nothing left to live for, except to somehow see his family again, including his mother, whose heart must be shattered over this . . . and Swift Arrow. He sorely missed his uncle.

Bastard! Stupid, drunken, white bastards! Like so many of those who had come here and stolen Indian lands. Why should such worthless, bigoted people be allowed to take away so much? He was glad he'd killed them. It had felt good to kill them—and to fool the soldiers and trick them into losing his trail. Guards or not, he would find a way to get onto the reservation and see his children and his mother. If he could do that much, it would relieve his loneliness, at least a little.

If only he could hold Jennifer once more, tell her how he loved her . . . make love to her. He leaned his head back against the tree. He missed her so, missed the family, the warmth and happiness he'd experienced at the reunion . . . He missed his mother.

Now, because of one drunken white man, all of them were gone from his life. For the last few days he'd lived on berries, vegetables from a settler's garden he'd raided one night, and on raw squirrel. He'd killed it with a silent toss of his knife, but couldn't cook it for fear of making a fire. There were plenty of chipmunks and prairie dogs in these mountains. And of course there was still some big game in these parts, mountain goats, mountain lions, deer, elk, moose. Yes, he could survive physically, but he was not so sure how to manage his heart and emotions.

There came the howling again, this time from several wolves, still to his right and many yards away, from what he could tell. Closer, he heard a whining sound. His horse began to snort and whinny, and Wolf's Blood slowly rose, walking over to be sure the animal was tied tight enough so it could not get away. He reached up and grabbed the animal by the mane, talking softly to it, trying to calm it, but the terrified steed reared and yanked. Snapping the rope before Wolf's Blood could check the knot, it whirled and ran off into the darkness.

Wolf's Blood stood there alone, hoping the horse would not injure itself. If he could not find it in the morning, he would simply go on by foot until he found a camp or settlement where he could steal another mount as he made his way north. For now all that mattered was the fact that many wolves were nearby, either stalking him . . . or coming to join him. He stood very still, all senses alert. Without a fire, he could not even see their eyes.

He heard the whining sound again, even closer. At more of a distance he could hear soft yips, a growl, and even farther off another howl, then another and another. Rather than being afraid, the sounds filled him with hope and happiness. His old companions, the wolves, knew he was here! They sensed his loneliness and knew he was cold. Yes! His friends were coming.

He knelt down, keeping the blanket around himself. "Hello, my wolf friends," he said softly. "I am glad you have come. Please stay with me."

Bright moonlight burst forth as a cloud passed from the moon, and now he could see a little better. Four! He'd seen at least four of them. One came closer, whining again. It was a young one. It sniffed around him, and he moved not one muscle. "Welcome, *Ohkumhka-kit*," he whispered. He daringly and very slowly moved one hand out from under the blanket, and the little wolf began licking it.

Wolf's Blood grinned. Surely his father had sent the wolves to keep him company. The ground beneath him was packed soft with pine needles, for he was high in the mountains, amid a thick forest of spruce. He lay facedown into the needles, breathing deeply of their sweet scent . . . waiting. He would either be attacked and ripped apart, or these wolves would comfort him.

He felt them coming then, one . . . two . . . three. The little one was burrowing its nose into his neck, sniffing, whining, licking. A bigger one lay down on one side of him. Another lay across his legs. Another lay on the other side of him. More piled around him, until he was covered in furry warmth.

"Thank you *Maheo*," he prayed, "for taking away the cold." His heart felt a little lighter to know the wolf

spirit was still with him, to know he still had this kind
of power. Yes, he was still a warrior, still a part of the
wild things. And just as he was now comforted, he
knew it was a sign that his beloved children would also
be comforted. *Maheo* would see that they were taken
care of. And somehow his mother would know he was
all right.

He could sleep now. He closed his eyes in warmth
and comfort, utterly exhausted from days of riding and
hiding, shivering cold at night, hungry for a decent
meal, weary from many tears, worn out from sorrow.
Sleep suddenly came easily, and he welcomed it.

He had no idea what time it was when he'd drifted
off, how long he'd slept before a shaft of sunlight
broke through the treetops and shone down warmly
against his face. He opened his eyes, taking a moment
to gather his thoughts and to realize he was alone. He
quickly awakened then, looking around. The wolves
were gone . . . all but one. The young one that had
approached him the night before. He blinked, trying
to remember. If not for the little one still lying nearby,
he would have to wonder if they had really come at all.
Was it a dream? Surely not. Here was this *oh-kumhka-kit*,
watching him. The young wolf rolled onto its back as
though begging to have its belly rubbed.

Wolf's Blood grinned, reaching over and scratching
its stomach. "So, little one, you will stay with me. You
will be my companion. Your mother has given you to
me." He remembered another time, years ago, when
a small wolf had appeared to him after white men had
killed his first wolf pet. He and his brothers and sisters
had been out looking for a Christmas tree for their
mother. That was how it was for him. The wolves simply
came. They knew when he needed their spirit power.

He stood up, noticing the horse that had run off
the night before now stood grazing nearby. The spirits

were being good to him today! He rolled up his blanket and tied it onto the horse, using only rope, as he had discarded the saddle many days ago. He hated white men's saddles. He walked over and picked up the young wolf, which licked at his face. He plopped the wolf over the horse's back, and, amazingly, the horse did not protest, as though it understood it need not fear. Wolf's Blood leapt onto the horse, keeping the wolf in front of him as he took up the reins and left the magical spot where last night he'd slept warmly among a pack of wolves.

"Ha-ho, Maheo," he said, thanking the Great Spirit for bringing the wolves and helping ease his broken heart. He headed north, not even aware that an eagle winged its way behind him from treetop to treetop.

Margaret looked up from sweeping the porch to see a lone rider coming on a sleek, roan-colored horse, and even from a distance it was obvious the rider was a woman. She set the broom aside, calling for Morgan, who was in the house finishing his lunch. "Someone's coming—a woman."

Morgan left the table, coming out onto the porch, followed by Nathan and Lance, both eager to see who it might be. It was very unusual to see a woman riding alone in such big country.

"It's her," Margaret commented. "It must be."

"Who, Mother?" Nathan asked.

"That girl who got our Zeke in so much trouble. Carson Temple's daughter."

"If she's his daughter, she can't be very nice," Nathan said.

"Zeke loved her. Let's remember that and give her a chance," Morgan reminded them, studying the rider as she came closer. She reined her horse to a slow walk when she saw them all watching her, obviously hesitant to come closer. Morgan stepped down off the porch, nodding to her. "You're Georgeanne, aren't you?"

Georgie could not help feeling apprehensive. Surely these people hated her for what had happened to Zeke. Apparently her father had convinced Zeke not to see her, for she had not heard from him since her father had had her dragged away from that last liaison. The threats probably involved his family, and she hoped she was not bringing them terrible problems by coming here to see Zeke. She was determined to convince him they could find a way to be together.

She urged her horse closer, studying Morgan Brown. He was quite a handsome man, with more features about him that spoke of his Negro blood than Zeke had. She glanced at the woman who was now stepping off the porch. Indian! She looked pure Indian, and anyone could tell she'd been quite beautiful when she was younger. She was still attractive. This had to be Zeke's mother. She looked back at Morgan. "Yes, I am Georgeanne," she replied.

Morgan caught the hint of a lingering Southern accent. It brought back memories he would rather keep buried.

"I know that my father has hurt all of you deeply," Georgeanne continued, "and I have come to apologize and to . . . to see Zeke. Surely we can work something out—"

"Zeke is gone," Morgan interrupted. "And what your father did to him deserves much more than a simple apology." He could not keep back his anger. "How can you sit there and think words can make up for our son's almost dying! Or for the threats your father posed to us! Your *father* is the one who should be here apologizing! If he didn't own the law in Pueblo, I'd have him arrested for attempted murder!

As it is, if we have any more trouble from him, I have a brother-in-law in Denver who will send out a U.S. Marshal!"

Georgeanne felt sick inside. She struggled against tears, trying to comprehend this man's anger. Something much worse must have happened to Zeke. Her father had promised not to hurt him any more than the blow to the head. "I . . . I don't understand, Mr. Brown. I didn't know that hit on the head brought him close to death. Where is Zeke? Why isn't he here? I need to see him! I want to know he's all right!" Tears began spilling down her cheeks then.

Margaret had walked up beside Morgan, and she put a hand on his arm. "Calm down," she said. She looked up at Georgeanne, thinking how utterly beautiful this young woman was. And she sat her horse well, obviously an experienced rider. Her tan-colored, suede riding outfit—a split skirt, white blouse, short-waisted jacket—was set off by brown leather boots and a narrow-brimmed brown suede hat was perched atop auburn hair. "Miss Temple, don't you know what your father did to Zeke?"

Georgeanne shook her head, wiping at her tears with a gloved hand. "I'm not sure . . . what you mean."

"You don't know he was dragged home by the ankles, tied to your father's horse?" Morgan demanded. "He was a bloody mass of torn flesh by the time he got here, half dead."

Georgeanne paled visibly. "My God!" she cried. She doubled over then, grabbing Princess's mane and weeping against her neck. "Oh, God, Zeke . . . I didn't know! I only . . . stayed away for your protection. If I . . . had known . . . I would have found a way to come here . . . be with you."

Margaret reached up and grasped her about the

waist. "Climb down from there, Miss Temple. Come inside."

Georgeanne dismounted, remaining bent over and still weeping as Margaret kept a hand at her waist and led her into the house.

"You two stay out here," Morgan ordered Nathan and Lance. The two boys stood outside the screened door, watching and listening as Georgeanne was led to the kitchen table. She sat down on a chair, and Margaret told Morgan to find her a clean handkerchief. After he retrieved one from the bedroom chest, Georgeanne blew her nose and wiped her eyes, finally gaining control of herself.

"It can't be true," she sniffled. "My father promised he wouldn't hurt Zeke any more than he had. He promised!"

"Carson Temple isn't a man to keep promises," Morgan growled, taking a chair across the table from her. "Not if it involves Indians and Negroes. You ought to know your own father better than that. Zeke says he was conscious enough to know the man hit you—his own daughter! In my whole life I've never laid a hand on my children! To have some other man do that to my son was the same as sticking a knife in my belly! If I could get away with it, and if my family didn't need me like they do, I'd kill Carson Temple! I'm sorry to put it that way, but it's the truth, girl. And now because of him, my precious firstborn son is gone!"

Georgeanne shivered, meeting his dark eyes. "I didn't know about Zeke being hurt that bad. My father . . . had me taken away, but he promised not to do any more harm to Zeke. After that I stayed away long enough to let my father calm down . . . let him think I'd given up on Zeke. I didn't want him to do him more harm or to hurt either of you or the ranch." She looked at Margaret pleadingly. "Please don't

blame me for this. I love Zeke! I truly love him! I'm
not like my father. You have to believe that. My father
is a brutal man who hates those of different back-
grounds, and as far as I'm concerned, it's his fault my
mother . . ." She closed her eyes and hung her head.
"Maybe you don't know."

Margaret sat down next to her, putting her hand on
Georgeanne's shoulder. "Zeke told us about your
mother. I'm sorry."

Georgeanne wiped at her eyes again. "He drove her
to it. I'm sure of it. He tries to control people, tries
to control everything and everyone around him, does
whatever he has to do to get what he wants." She
turned to Margaret. "I came here to show you my own
feelings haven't changed. I wanted to meet you, to
prove to you that I'm not like my father. And I came
to see Zeke, to make sure he was all right, to tell him
I love him and that we can find a way to be together.
My father went away on business, so I came as soon as
he left." She looked around the simple log cabin, such
a far cry from the cold, stone mansion she lived in.
She had everything most people could ever want, but
she would trade it all to live here with Zeke—to be his
woman, sleep next to him. "Where has he gone? How
badly was he injured? And *why* did he go away? Why
didn't he talk to me first, at least send a letter to me?"

"Because he's determined to forget about you,"
Morgan answered. "He knew if he saw you again, he'd
not be able to leave. He figured it was best to end it,
Miss Temple, for your own sake. He was afraid that
even if you could be together, you'd suffer in other
ways for being married to someone of color. Besides
that, he didn't want any more trouble for us right now.
He figured your father was just waiting for him to try
to see you again. It would give the man an excuse to
come here and burn us out, which is exactly what he

threatened to do if Zeke kept seeing you. He's got the power and the men to do it, Zeke knows that. But I think his biggest fear was that your father would kill me, and he'd have blamed himself for that. I told him I'd find a way to handle all this, but he wouldn't listen. He was determined the best thing to do was to just go away, get out of your life, leave your father no excuse to come here and destroy us. His grandmother is coming back here in a few weeks with legal documents proving ownership, and that will be that. But there will be an awful emptiness in our lives as long as Zeke is gone."

New tears came to Georgeanne's eyes. "And in mine. He won't be able to forget me, Mr. Brown, any more than I can forget him. I'll *never* do that! And I'll never stop loving him! I want you to know this." She looked at Margaret. "My feelings are sincere. I have to find him. Please tell me where he is!"

Margaret shook her head. "We don't know. He said he would write, but that he would not be back for a long time. I'm sorry, Miss Temple, but our son is a wise, generous man willing to make sacrifices for his family. I love him, and I happen to agree this is probably best, in spite of the fact that I believe you truly do love him. We can't always have what we want in this life, child, and sometimes loving someone means giving that person up. He needs to let go of you, and for a while we must let go of Zeke. He's never been out on his own, away from the ranch, so maybe it's best he does some exploring. You were a part of that outside world, something different, beautiful, well traveled. You know about things he's never seen and done. Until he has had some of those experiences for himself, he could never be sure he truly loves you, could never be strong enough to face what you must if you choose to be together. I hope our son did not . . . take advantage of your love. I hope there is no danger that you . . . that he could have left you carrying his child. Please tell me it never went that far."

Georgeanne blushed deeply. *I wish it had,* she wanted to answer. "No. We both knew that was too dangerous. Zeke is very wise. He treated me with full respect, and was strong enough to . . ." How was she going to forget his delicious kisses, the touch of his hand on her breast, the feel of his powerful body pressing against her own? "Nothing like that happened."

Margaret breathed a sigh of relief. "I'm glad for that." She patted Georgeanne's shoulder. "You're a beautiful young woman, and I can feel your sincerity. It's amazing that Carson Temple could have a daughter like you. I can understand how easy it was for our son to love you, Miss Temple."

"Georgeanne. Please call me Georgeanne."

Margaret rose. "I am sure this is best for you both, Georgeanne. Time will help heal your heart. You're meant for a different life than what Zeke could have given you. If you're unhappy at the ranch, maybe you should go back East. Maybe there you'll find . . . someone else."

Georgeanne shook her head. "I'll never find anyone like Zeke." She wrung the handkerchief in her hands. "If only I knew where he's gone."

Margaret blinked back tears of her own, for Zeke and for this young woman who was apparently so in love with him. She moved around to kneel in front of her. "Let it go, Georgeanne. Go and find your own life, away from here. Let Zeke find *his.* The man inside him is trying to find his way in this world, learning, growing. The hurt will subside after a while, I promise. If God means for you to be together, you'll find each other again when the time is truly right. Search your own heart, child. Look at me. Take a good look, at me and at Morgan."

Georgeanne studied them both for a moment, seeing only a man and woman who were handsome to behold.

"Think about Zeke's heritage, child. I carry no bitterness, but I do know the hard, cold facts of life, and they are that most people think their own kind should stay with their own kind. *We* don't believe that has to be so, and neither did Zeke's grandma, Abbie, who married my father, a half-breed Cheyenne man. She would be the first to say that all that counts is love, but she also can attest to how a woman can suffer when she makes such a choice. You have to do your own soul-searching, child; give yourself time to know if you're strong enough to face the problems that would come to you from marrying someone like Zeke."

Georgeanne closed her eyes. "I don't care what you say. We could be apart for ten years and I'd love Zeke just as much the moment I set eyes on him again as I do now." She stood up and faced them. "I'll do as you say and try to go on with my life. I'll most certainly leave the ranch because I can't be around my father right now. But I'll never forget Zeke. I won't stop loving him, and I know I could handle any problems that would go with marrying him. That's what I came here to tell him, but now . . ." Zeke! Would she ever see him again? "How bad was it? Is he scarred?"

Morgan rose. "It's hard to say. He still had a lot of scrapes and bruises on him when he left. Some of the wounds were deep enough that they'll leave scars, mostly on his arms and back and chest. He kept his arms wrapped up around his face, he said, trying to protect his eyes, so his face didn't get scraped all that bad."

Georgeanne sniffed, struggling to hold back the tears. "I'm so sorry about all of this, sorry we had to meet this way. Please promise me you will get word to me if you hear from Zeke."

Morgan shook his head. "I don't think we should. This was Zeke's decision, Georgeanne, not ours. If this is the way he wants it, we will not interfere. If he decides to try to find you, there is nothing we can do about that either. This is between him and you."

She wanted to die. He was gone. Gone! Maybe he'd go all the way to California, or up to see some of his cousins in Montana and Wyoming. It could be weeks or months before anyone heard from him, for he was apparently determined to forget her, and that would take time. She could not stay at the ranch all that time, having to be near her father. She didn't want to hate him, but he was the reason for all of this, and she would never forgive him for that or for nearly killing Zeke after promising not to do him any more harm.

"I am glad to have finally met you both," she said sadly. "Zeke always had nothing but wonderful things to say about you. I wish I could brag about my own father the way he brags about his." She turned away and headed for the door.

"Georgeanne," Margaret called out. Georgeanne stopped. "We're sorry, too. Anyone who grows up under the thumb of Carson Temple and turns out like you must be unique, very wise and perceptive. There is obviously an inborn goodness in you, perhaps from your mother. I am glad to know our son chose such a woman to love. I'm just sorry it had to turn out this way."

"So am I," Georgeanne answered, her throat aching from a constant battle against tears. She stepped outside, glanced at Zeke's brothers, then walked to her horse, which Nathan had tied to a hitching post for her. She undid the reins and mounted the animal, remembering the joy she'd felt racing against Indian, laughing with Zeke, sharing friendship, sharing kisses—remembered how good it felt to have his strong arms around her. Somehow she was going to find him again. She was convinced God meant for them to be together.

Part of her felt totally defeated, but she refused to let it take over and destroy her, make her lose hope. She glanced at the doorway, where Margaret and Morgan stood watching her. "We will see each other again, I promise," she told them. She turned and rode off, and Margaret slipped an arm around Morgan's waist, resting her head against his chest.

"Young love can be so painful," she remarked, remembering her own first experience, the ugly way it had turned out. How well she knew the hurt.

"She's quite a fine lady," Morgan commented. "Hard to believe, considering who her father is. Do you think he sent her here just to see what's happening with Zeke?"

Margaret turned to watch Georgeanne disappear on the horizon. "No. The way she reacted to what she learned was too genuine. I think she truly didn't know what her father did to Zeke. She loves him, Morgan. How sad."

He sighed, kissing her hair. "Sad for both of them. But they'll get over it somehow. Like you said, time can heal a lot of things."

Twelve

It was a hot August night, and Abbie left the windows open, thinking how much cooler it would be higher in the mountains. The reservation was on the open eastern plains of Montana. Far be it from the government to give the Indians land that was truly beautiful and worth something.

She could not sleep, mostly because she knew Swift Arrow also could not sleep. He never had liked a real bed, and when it was warm he preferred to sleep outside under the stars. She had asked him to lie beside her tonight, but she knew he was wide awake. "Do you think I should be the one to go back with the deed instead of Jeremy?" she asked him.

He sighed and sat up. "You're awake, too, I see."

"I am very restless tonight. So many thoughts are passing through my mind. I told Margaret I'd bring back the deed myself, but if there is any hope of Wolf's Blood coming here, I don't want to be gone. He needs supplies by now, Swift Arrow, a tent, clothes, winter garb, a good horse."

"I know. I know." He sat on the edge of the bed, looking out the window. "There is no reason for you to go all the way back. You have been through so much, with Zeke and Wolf's Blood, helping console the children. In a few days they will be ready to go to Denver with Jeremy, and the last of the horses will be

sold, except for what Hawk wants to keep." He rubbed
at his eyes. "It hurts my heart so, Abbie. I think about
the days Wolf's Blood and I were so close, when he
was young and happy and eager. Even here, with his
ranch, the children, Jennifer, he was as happy as he
could be, considering he had to live on a reservation
and go on without his father. I will miss the children
so much when they leave. I know you will, too. With
Dan and Rebecca also choosing to move to Denver
with Emily, only Jason will remain here. It will be
lonely, and yet I could never live anyplace else than
here with my people." He turned to look at her in the
dim moonlight. "I am sorry, Abbie. I know you would
prefer to go to Denver and be with the children, or
perhaps move back to the old ranch."

Abbie sat up and moved beside him. "My children
are all grown and have their own lives now, Swift Arrow. They know I am here for them if they need me.
Now I only want to be with you for as long as we have
together. I had my reunion, and I know we'll never all
be together like that again, but I've learned to accept
what has to be. Zeke would want me to stay here with
you and continue teaching the children. And he'd
want me to be here for . . ."

He put up a hand to silence her and rose, going to
the window. Abbie watched curiously, then heard it, a
soft trill, like a birdcall. She'd lived among Indians too
many years not to recognize the sound as a signal. Her
heart beat faster in anticipation. Who else but Wolf's
Blood would be signaling them?

"It is he!" Swift Arrow whispered. "I am sure of it!"
He quickly pulled on a pair of denim pants he'd left
hanging over the back of a chair, and Abbie got up
and picked up her robe, putting it on as she followed
him out. "Do not light any lamps," Swift Arrow told
her softly. He opened the door and left it that way,

then stood back. He gave out a birdcall of his own, and moments later a figure loomed in the doorway.

"Wolf's Blood!" Abbie whispered.

He moved toward her, and Swift Arrow closed the door. Wolf's Blood swept his mother into his arms, and she thought for a moment how Zeke had done this so many times, returning to her at times when she feared she would never see him again. She burst into tears of joy to know he was alive, that he had made it here without being caught.

"Do not cry, Mother," he said softly. "We must not draw any kind of attention. Soldiers lurk everywhere, watching my ranch and this place."

He turned from her and embraced his uncle, and Abbie thought how few men could manage to get here through so many obstacles and watchful eyes without being captured. Her son still had the cunning of a wolf, the ability to move about without being seen.

"We were just talking about you," Swift Arrow told him. "Your mother has been praying you would come, so that you could see Hawk and Iris before they go to Denver."

"Come into the bedroom," Abbie told him, taking his hand and struggling against a need to weep openly. "It's darker. Someone might see our shadows moving about."

He laid his blanket on the table and followed her into the bedroom of the small log cabin she shared with Swift Arrow, and all three of them sat down on the bed.

"How are you, son? Are you injured? You must be so hungry."

"My only injuries are to the heart," he answered, "and the wounds I inflicted upon myself in mourning."

Abbie well knew what that meant, and it sickened

her to think of his lonely suffering. "Are you healing all right?"

"I am. My clothes are badly worn, though. I need you to go to the ranch house, get some clothes, winter jackets and moccasins, blankets and—"

"You don't need to tell me. I've been through this too many times. I know what to pack. And you'll want two or three good horses. I'll let Swift Arrow pick them out for you."

"I also want to see my son and my daughter. You said they are going to Denver?"

"Yes," Abbie answered. "Jeremy said that was what you wanted them to do if anything happened to you. He's here."

"Jeremy? He came all the way up here to the reservation?"

"He thought he should stay with the children and take them back himself. He'll take the deed with him, get everything legalized and take it to Margaret. I'll stay here with Swift Arrow."

Wolf's Blood sighed, kissing her cheek. "It will be lonely for you without us here. I am sorry for all of this, but I could not stop myself, nor do I regret killing those men."

"You know many men search for you," Swift Arrow told him.

"Oh, yes, I know. I lost one company of soldiers somewhere in the mountains in Wyoming. I knew more would be watching for me to come back here. I have been waiting for days to find the right moment to come. I left the horse I had been using many miles south of here, and earlier I threw the saddle into a deep ravine where it might never be found. It had that man's name on it. I did not want it to be found on the horse. I have been on foot ever since. My boots are badly worn, and yes, I am very hungry. I have been eating raw meat and berries. I miss your biscuits and gravy, Mother."

The words tore at her heart. She would have him for a day or two, then lose him again, perhaps for years. She would not have the pleasure of cooking for him and his family on Sundays, making things they'd always enjoyed. "I'll make some just for you. You can hide right here in the bedroom for the next day or two, see the children. We'll find a way to get the things you need over here without drawing a lot of attention."

He grasped their hands. "Once I leave again, I am afraid it must be for a long time. I will go to Canada."

Oh, the pain of it. Abbie had once thought a mother stopped worrying about her children and wanting to take care of them when they were grown, but that was not so. She would always feel this way, always look at her children as young and vulnerable and in need of her care, although Wolf's Blood had been one child who had never seemed to need her. Even when very small, he had always been wild and free and restless.

"Hawk is beside himself," she told him. "He loves you so, Wolf's Blood. This has been hardest on him."

He let go and rested his head in his hands. "I knew that it would be so."

"Lie down on our bed, son," Swift Arrow told him. "You must be so tired, and for a long time you have been sleeping on the cold ground with only that one blanket. I will sleep outside under the stars, and your mother can sleep on a couch in the other room. No one will know you are here. We will wait until the children come over tomorrow to tell them. If we go and get them now, it will draw too much attention."

"I am glad Jeremy is here. It shows that he cares about my children." Wolf's Blood suddenly was very weary. He'd left his wolf pet in the mountains. The animal seemed to understand it could not come with him, but he would go back for the wolf before be headed for Canada. The young wolf was his only friend now, his only companion.

Abbie rose and urged him to lie down, happy that for a short while she could bring her son some kind of comfort. "You'll be safe here," she told him. "We'll warn the children to be careful how they behave. They come over every day to talk, so no one will think anything of their coming tomorrow."

Wolf's Blood settled onto the bed, and exhaustion quickly set in once he realized he was safe. He had spent many nights on the cold ground . . . except the night the wolves came to comfort him. Now he was so tired he didn't even want to get back up to undress. He was aware that Swift Arrow pulled off his boots, aware his mother was covering him.

"My God, he's already falling asleep," he heard Abbie say. "He must be completely worn out."

"I worry the same will happen to you," Swift Arrow answered her.

Wolf's Blood managed to capture her hand and hold it tight. "Please do not worry, Mother," he said, his words slightly slurred from his being so close to sleep. "I am Wolf's Blood. I have lived this way before. Once I know Hawk and Iris will be all right, then *I* will be all right. You stay strong . . . for them. They will need you."

"And who will there be for you, son?" she asked, leaning down and kissing his cheek.

"The wolves. They came . . . slept with me . . . kept me warm. A young one stayed. He . . . waits for me in the mountains."

The last word was barely audible.

Hawk felt like crying at having to single out only three horses to keep. He'd been attached to all of them in one way or another, and he knew how precious they were to his father. He pulled Lone Eagle aside, picked out a black Thoroughbred gelding and another Appaloosa, a mare. "We'd better keep the pinto for Iris," he told Jeremy and Swift Arrow. "She likes that one."

"That's fine. I'll pay to board all four of them on the train once we reach Cheyenne," Jeremy told him. "Since Mary isn't with me we'll just ride there, using the horses. We won't need a wagon."

"I'll take care of the sale of the rest of them and send you the money," Swift Arrow told Hawk. "You have Jeremy set it aside for you, so that you can pay for some of your own things and help pay for an education. I will sell all your father's tools and the household belongings. That will bring you even more money."

Hawk wondered if he would ever get over this sick loneliness. "I want you to give some of them away to any of the Indians who need things—clothes and blankets and things like that. Father would want it so. I think Jennifer would have, too."

Swift Arrow smiled lovingly and nodded. "That is a wise decision, Hawk."

The boy felt a little better. "I want to stay here with the other horses for a little while. Then I'll come to Grandma's for lunch like always."

Swift Arrow nodded, looking at Jeremy. "You come now, Jeremy. I have something to show you."

Jeremy frowned curiously and left with him, and Hawk moved among the horses, petting each one, talking to them. Moments later he noticed Arianne watching him from the barn, and he realized he had not thought about her at all since he'd learned about the incident with Jennifer and his father. She had aroused a strange curiosity in him that day before he left for the reunion, but after a while he had forgotten about it. Now here she was again, watching him with those big, blue eyes. She wore a blue calico dress that matched her eyes and had ruffles at the shoulders and around the neck. It was quite pretty, and he suspected she'd worn it just to come and see him, which for some reason irritated him. Girls didn't dress like that on normal days on a dusty ranch. She looked ready to go to a party.

"Hi, Hawk." She stepped a little closer. "I'm . . . glad you're back, but I'm real sorry . . . About your father and mother. My brother told me about it. It must be terrible for you—for your whole family. I thought you'd come home all happy about the reunion. I was going to ask you about it, but I know you must be so sad inside . . . and you probably don't want to tell me about it."

"That's right." He walked past her into the barn to get a grooming brush for the horses. Arianne followed him inside.

"I'm so sorry," she repeated, "about your stepmother. And your father, if he gets caught—"

"He *won't* get caught! Nobody catches the great warrior Wolf's Blood if he does not want to be found! They want to hang him! He will *never* let that happen! Not my father!"

His eyes teared on the last words, and Arianne wished she knew what to do or say to make him feel better. "I . . . I hope you're right, Hawk, I really do. I don't want anything to happen to him either."

He picked up the brush and charged past her, back into the corral to brush down Lone Eagle. "Why don't you just go away?" he said, vigorously yanking the brush through the horse's mane.

This was not how Arianne had pictured his homecoming. She had wanted him to come back before she herself had to leave, and she thought perhaps they could deepen their friendship. She also wanted him

to promise again to write to her. Did he have any idea
how the sight of him flustered her, made her feel warm
all over, made her stomach flip? She wanted to touch
him, feel him kiss her again. She had not forgotten
that first warm kiss.

"I only came over here to tell you how sorry I am
about what happened. I waited a few days to give you
time alone. I'm sorry if I made you mad, Hawk."

He quickly wiped at unwanted tears, but remained
turned away from her. "Quit being sorry for everything," he answered. "None of it is your fault. Just go
back home. You shouldn't even be here. Your brother
wouldn't like it."

She shrugged. "I don't care. I like you, Hawk. I
wanted you to know you have a friend, and I still want
to write to you—"

"Don't be silly!" he interrupted. He turned, anger
and bitterness in his dark eyes. "Do you want to end
up like my stepmother?"

She frowned, her heart pounding with dread that
she had made him angry. He surely hated her, the way
he was looking at her. "What?"

"She was a white woman married to an Indian! And
now she's *dead!* My cousin, Zeke, down in Colorado,
he was beaten up and dragged behind a horse because
he liked a *white* girl! My grandma Abbie told me. It
happened after we left the reunion. Does that tell you
something, Arianne? You shouldn't want to be friends
with me, because I am *Indian.* I am *proud* to be Indian,
but most folks from your world look at us differently."

He stepped closer, and Arianne's eyes widened. She
wondered if he was going to hit her. For a moment
she saw the wildness in him, and she thought about
his father. He'd killed three men, even scalped two of
them!

Hawk pointed the brush at her as he spoke. "We're

not different!" he growled, his eyes red with tears. "We're just as smart and can do just as well in the white man's world as the best of them, and I'm going to prove it! I'm going to Denver, Arianne, to study law! I might even go all the way to Harvard or Yale. Uncle Jeremy is going to send me. And when I'm through, I'll fight for the rights of my people. I'll even be able to defend men like my father! He saw his wife shot down as she stood right next to him, with a bullet meant for *him!* How could he *not* be angry enough to kill! It isn't fair he should have to hang for it, but your white man's courts would see that he does if he ever gets caught."

"Don't . . . don't say *my* white man's courts. This isn't my fault, Hawk. I'm not like those others." Now her own tears started to come.

"It doesn't matter. What matters is, you shouldn't be here. I don't *want* to be friends with any white girl, understand? And I'm not going to write to you because once I leave here we'll probably never see each other again, so just go away, Arianne!"

She stood there shivering, hating him, loving him. "Is Iris . . . going to Denver, too?"

"My sister and I stay together. Yes, she will go."

"Will you tell her I was here? Tell her to come to my house and see me before you leave?"

He hated being mean to her, but he also hated her, because she reminded him of all the reasons why his father was in trouble. "I will tell her." He turned back around and began brushing Lone Eagle again.

"I will miss you, Hawk, and I will never forget you."

He kept brushing the horse and did not reply, until finally he began to feel bad about the way he had spoken to her. He turned around to apologize, but she was gone. "Damn!" he muttered. He walked back into the barn and threw down the brush. It was time to get over to his grandma Abbie's for lunch. He walked back

outside, and noticed Arianne walking up the dirt path
that led back to the main reservation area, where she
lived in a neat, frame house with her brother. He
turned again. To hell with Drake Wilder and his stupid
little sister! Maybe she hated him now. That was good.
That was best. She wouldn't bother trying to write him,
and he wouldn't have to hurt her by not writing back.

He tossed his long, shiny-black hair behind his shoulders and walked the half mile to his grandma's cabin,
noticing, when he reached the porch, his uncle, Jeremy,
had an odd grin on his face. "Did you eat yet?" he
asked.

"Lunch isn't quite ready," Jeremy answered. "Go on
inside, though. There's something your grandmother
wants you to see."

Hawk frowned, going through the doorway. It was
then he heard his sister crying in the bedroom. "What
is wrong?" he asked Abbie.

"You'd better go and see," Abbie answered with a
wry smile.

Hawk hurried through the curtained doorway to see
Iris sitting on the bed, crying against the shoulder of
their father. Hawk stood frozen, hardly able to believe
his eyes. A myriad of emotions swept through him—
gladness his father had somehow made it here unde-
tected, fear that now he would be caught. His father's
eyes lit up with great love when his son walked in, and
he slowly rose, patting Iris's shoulder and letting go of
her. "Hawk," he said, his eyes quickly tearing.

"Father!"

In the next moment Wolf's Blood's strong arms were
around him.

It was decided. When Jeremy left with Hawk and Iris
to go back to Denver, they would take two extra horses

besides those Hawk had chosen. Those two would be packed with all the items Wolf's Blood would need, and since the children were moving to Denver, no one would think anything of the extra horses and gear. It would be explained that they were simply things the children wanted to take with them from home. As they headed south, Wolf's Blood would follow, keeping himself hidden, until he found the opportunity to meet up with them and take the horses and gear before they reached Cheyenne and boarded the train. Dan and Rebecca would soon follow. Once Dan got things in order and packed a wagon, they would move to Denver with Emily.

Abbie's heart was torn. Morgan had sent a wire from Pueblo that Zeke had decided to leave the ranch. No one knew for certain where he had gone. Now one precious grandson was out there somewhere alone, trying to find the direction he should take in life, trying to forget the woman he loved. Her beloved firstborn son would soon be on the run again, also alone . . . so alone. Two more grandchildren were leaving her, entering what was a whole new world for them, having to say good-bye to their father, perhaps forever. Dan and Rebecca would take Emily to Denver, and Morgan's wire had said that Ellen and Hal would soon be moving to Pueblo.

Scattered, all scattered, this big, wonderful family she and Zeke had made. Abbie's only consolation was knowing Zeke was watching, somehow guiding his grandsons . . . and his precious son. She would stay here and teach, as long as Swift Arrow was alive and needed to be here among his people. And she would have Jason with her.

This was a day she would remember for the rest of her life, for this might be the last time she saw her son. Tonight he would leave, and within two weeks he would be living in the wilds of Canada. The time had come for more good-byes; she wondered how much hurt one woman could bear. She walked into the bedroom, where everyone was gathered, the window shuttered so no one could see inside.

"Jeremy and the children have to get back to the ranch soon, or someone might wonder," she told them. She looked at Hawk and Iris. "Children, you must behave normally and act as though nothing has changed. Sometimes, when it comes to good-byes, it is best to just get them done with and go on from there. Your grandfather would say that was the practical thing to do." She reached out her hands. "I think we should pray, for Hawk and his education, for the future of the children and certainly for Wolf's Blood."

She took hold of Wolf's Blood's hand on one side, Swift Arrow's on the other. The rest of them—Jeremy, Hawk, Iris, Jason—all held hands while Abbie prayed. Dan had been summoned earlier, had been able to see his nephew once more. Emily had wept bitterly in her stepfather's arms before leaving with Dan.

Wolf's Blood, now wearing clean clothes and new boots, moved around the circle, embracing each of them—his brother, Jason; his uncle, Swift Arrow; his brother, Jeremy. "I put my trust in you to raise my son and my daughter to be proud and successful. There was a time when I would not have given them into your care, nor would I have ever turned to you for help. Now I am honored to call you brother."

They gripped hands tightly. "And I am honored to call *you* brother. The *Rocky Mountain News* has already splattered the society column with the news that the wild Indian who killed three men in Cheyenne is brother to Jeremy Monroe, vice president of the Denver & Rio Grande, stockholder and board member of the Kansas-Pacific. The whole city is in a buzz, and poor Mary is there, handling all the questions. It's the most excitement we've had in years." He forced a smile, trying not to let the pain of this parting hurt any worse than it already did.

Wolf's Blood smiled through his own tears. "See? It is not so bad being Indian, my brother. Now you will be famous in Denver. They will want to write books about you."

Jeremy laughed lightly. "You're the one a book should be written about. Joshua has already started one about Mother and Father. He and LeeAnn are also moving to Denver, you know. Joshua has landed a high position with the *Rocky Mountain News,* so I know that regardless of how many stories come out about me and my family, they will at least be fair."

Wolf's Blood nodded. "That is good. I am glad LeeAnn will also be there with you and with my children. Hawk and Iris will have their cousins with them." Their eyes held, full of emotion, these two brothers who had taken years to find each other and had had such a short time to make up for it all.

"Father will be with you, Wolf's Blood," Jeremy told him, his voice breaking as he spoke. "We all . . . know that. And all of us . . . we'll be with you in spirit. You won't really be alone."

Wolf's Blood reluctantly let go of Jeremy's hand and turned to his mother, watching her lovingly, hating the agony he saw in her eyes and wondering how the woman had managed to keep going over the years. "I wonder if you know, Mother, that you have always been the real strength of this family. You always said it was Father, and in certain ways it was. But you . . ." He placed his hands on either side of her face. "You, Abigail Trent Monroe, were the true rock. Even Father could not have survived without that strength. He told me that many times. To this day the family turns to you.

We manage to face what we must because of the courage you have shown as an example through the years. I know that whenever my children need you, you will be there for them."

Abbie studied him, wanting to remember every feature, every line on his face. She grasped his wrists and kissed the palms of his hands. "I will be with you, wherever you go, son. You must try to find a way to let me know you are all right once you reach Canada, tell me where I can write to you and let you know how Hawk and Iris are doing."

Wolf's Blood nodded. "I will find a way."

Abbie shivered. "I love you, Wolf's Blood. And Jeremy . . . was right. Your father will be with you."

"One day I will see you and Father both," he answered, "in a place far better than what this earth has become since the white man came. We will all be in a land where the grass is always green and thick, and the buffalo roam in the millions, where the water is so clear you can see through it like glass. Father is there now, waiting for us." He embraced her, letting her weep against his chest. "I will be all right, Mother. I know that I am loved, and that is all anyone needs in this life." After a moment he gently pushed her away. "It is best I do this quickly," he told her, kissing her forehead.

Reluctantly he let go of her, turning to Hawk and Iris, who both hugged him as he put an arm around each of them. "Make me proud," he told them. "Do not ever deny your Indian blood. Learn the Cheyenne way and remember it, and show the world a Cheyenne is as good as any man or woman. If you can, have your uncle take you to the Apache reservation. It is right that you should also remember your Apache blood, visit with them, learn more about their ways and beliefs. By this you will honor your mother's people also."

He turned full attention to Hawk. "Get a good education, and use it for *all* Indians when necessary, my son. From here on they will have to fight for their rights in many ways, fight to keep their customs, to worship their own way, even to speak their own tongue. More land will be stolen from them. You can help stop it from happening." He looked at Iris, leaned down and kissed her hair. "My beautiful daughter, always be proud, never ashamed. Remain honorable in all ways. Let Grandma Abbie, your aunts—Margaret and LeeAnn— and Jeremy's wife, Mary, help guide you in the ways of a woman and the ways of love. Do not ever let a man abuse you or hurt you just because you are Indian. And do not ever marry a man of whom your brother and your uncle Jeremy do not approve. Promise me that."

Iris nodded her head. "I promise, Father." She sniffled. "I love you so much. I'll be afraid without you."

Wolf's Blood shook his head. "You have Hawk. He will be like a father to you now. He is a fine, strong young man who will look after you just as I would have. And you have Jeremy. *I* will always be with you in spirit. But remember you are not just part Apache and Cheyenne. You are also a Monroe, and over the years the Monroes have survived many things. You will survive this, Iris Monroe, and you will be a stronger woman for it."

Wolf's Blood drew a deep breath. "Go now, and do not let others see your tears, or they might suspect. Be strong, my children. I will see you for one last embrace when I meet you along the trail and pick up my horses and supplies. After that we'll go our separate ways, yet we will always be together." He stepped back from them. "Go. You must. There is no way to avoid it." He wondered how he managed to make his legs move as he turned away. "Go, all of you, and know that my love goes with you."

Their tears ripped through his heart like a knife.

Quietly and reluctantly they all left, Jason the last to go.

"I love you, Wolf's Blood," he said. "You'll always be my most special brother. You were always"—his voice broke on a sob he could not control—"always a hero to me. And men like you and Swift Arrow and our father . . . will be remembered—in the history books. And I want you to know I've met a young Cheyenne woman I'm in love with. I'm going to marry her, so there will damn well be plenty more Cheyenne Monroes."

Wolf's Blood turned to meet his eyes. Both men held their chins high in pride, and Wolf's Blood managed a smile and a nod. *"Wagh, Eo-ve-ano.* At heart you are still Yellow Hawk. You could take what you have learned and go to a big city and make much money, but you choose to stay here and doctor our own people. I am sure the white man's government does not pay you much for this, but you stay anyway. Who is the woman? Is it that pretty young thing you brought to the powwow last fall?"

Jason nodded, glancing at his mother. He had not even told her how serious he was about Louellen. He could see she was happy for him. "Her name is Louellen," he told Wolf's Blood. "Louellen Dancing Cloud. She is Cheyenne."

Wolf's Blood nodded. "I am glad for you."

Their eyes held a moment longer, and with tears on his cheeks, Jason turned and left. Darkness was already falling as Wolf's Blood walked over and sat down in the stuffed chair kept in the bedroom next to the reading table where Abbie sat every night to read her Bible before going to bed. "Come here, Mother. Let me hold you until I have to go."

Abbie suddenly felt very old, realizing this son of hers was almost forty himself. She walked over and sat down on his lap, aware that she was small and frail compared to him. He held her for over an hour, until there was nothing left to do but to go. He stood up, picking her up in his arms and carrying her to the bed.

"Stay here," he said softly. "Rest. Promise me."

Her only reply was to squeeze his hand. She could not speak for the ache in her throat. She turned away and pulled a blanket over herself. Wolf's Blood turned to his uncle, Swift Arrow. "You are not my uncle," he said. "You are my father."

It was the greatest compliment he could have given the man. Swift Arrow embraced him. "And you are my son." They held each other for several long seconds before Wolf's Blood turned and picked up a gunnysack that held one change of clothes and some food, as well as some ammunition for the rifle he would take. Two handguns and another rifle were packed into the gear he would pick up later. Without another word he opened the window and slipped out into the night.

Thirteen

1890 . . .

Abbie held up her new grandson for Swift Arrow to see. "Jonathan Morgan Monroe," she said with a happy smile. "A fine, healthy son for Jason and Louellen. Jason delivered him himself."

Swift Arrow nodded, touching the baby's cheek lightly. "Another little piece of Zeke Monroe."

Abbie felt the little pain in her chest that always came at the thought of Zeke. "He knows about this baby," she answered. "Let's take Jonathan outside. Jason is still tending to Louellen, and trying to get over the shock of having his own son!" She laughed lightly and wrapped a blanket around the baby, carrying him outside, glad for Jason and Louellen, who seemed so happy.

This new baby reminded Abbie that life went on, helped replace the loneliness she'd known over the past three years since Wolf's Blood left and everyone else moved to Denver. Hawk had completed three years of high school and would next attend the University of Colorado in Boulder to begin his study of law. He hoped to go on from there to Harvard. Never had she been more proud than when he passed the exams required to enter the university. How proud Wolf's Blood would be to know how far his son had already come! Her letters from Hawk told of a young man astounded at the kind of life people led in Denver, at what he'd learned about the government, what he already knew about law.

He was surrounded by a much different way of life, a different class of people, and he was learning how to deal with them, a valuable lesson that would help him fight for Indian rights when he got his degree.

Father always told me you have to gauge your enemy, he'd written in one letter. *He always wanted me to learn the warrior way, and I am doing just that, but in a way far different than what he meant. Father used to say he learned how to sneak up on the enemy, how to fool him, wage counter attacks, when to attack and when to hold back. I also am learning those things. I will one day use them in a courtroom.*

She would see both Hawk and Iris soon, for she planned a visit to Denver. Iris was sixteen now, and she had met a young man who was apparently an excellent carpenter and was making a good amount of money in a fast-growing city. What was interesting about the situation was that the young man was Mexican. Abbie could not help smiling every time she thought of it. If they should marry, could any family claim the blood of more different races than the Monroes? What made it even more humorous was the fact that Iris was half Apache, and the Mexicans and Apaches had warred for centuries, bitter enemies.

"I am so anxious to meet Raphael," she told Swift Arrow as she sat down on a porch swing. Jason and Louellen lived in a pleasant little four-room, frame house on the reservation, just a short walk away from the building that served as the doctor's office and the small hospital. "And you must be anxious to see Hawk and Iris again."

Swift Arrow sat down beside her, saying nothing for a moment as they rocked gently. He stared out at the horizon, and Abbie frowned, studying him closely. He had aged considerably over the last couple of years, and she knew the sedate life he led on the reservation was slowly killing him.

"My dear husband, did you hear anything I just said?"

"Hmmm?" He looked at her, love in his eyes, a rather sad smile on his lips. "I heard."

Abbie cuddled the baby close and bounced him lightly when he began to fuss. "Let me guess," she said. "You are wishing you were up in the wilds of Canada with Wolf's Blood."

He nodded. "I wish it sometimes, but that is not what I am thinking about now. I am thinking about all this talk concerning the Sioux and what is happening in the Black Hills, this new religion they have taken to heart."

Abbie knew a prickle of alarm. "The Ghost Dance religion." She sighed deeply. "It is supposedly harmless. They preach peace, nonviolence."

Swift Arrow rose. "They believe if they dance and sing long enough, old loved ones will rise and rejoin them. They will become strong again. The white man will give up and go away, and the buffalo will return. They wear ghost shirts that they believe bullets cannot penetrate. The scouts say they dance and sing all day and night, taking turns so that the singing and drumming never stop."

Abbie's alarm moved deeper, turning into dread. "Do you believe all that? That the dead will return? The buffalo will return? That a simple cotton shirt can stop a bullet?"

He stared into the horizon for a very long time before answering. "I would like to believe it. I would like to go there and see what this religion is all about. If nothing else, it is bringing hope to the Sioux. Great hope. Even joy. It would be good to dance with them, sing the old songs, listen to the drumming, feel truly Indian again."

Abbie rocked the baby quietly, awakened to the reality that her husband was a full-blood Cheyenne, that he needed to experience the old ways in order to feel alive. He was Indian enough to actually believe in this new religion. She had never been able to fully Christianize him. "I have talked to Agent Wilder about what's going on there, and he says it isn't good, Swift Arrow. The white settlers are very much alarmed. They think all the drumming and dancing means the Sioux are preparing to break loose and go to war again. More soldiers have been sent in, and there is bound to be trouble if they keep this up." She closed her eyes and sighed. "I suppose, like your brother, you intend to be right there in the middle of things. You want to go, don't you?"

He turned to face her, apology in his eyes. "I thought perhaps I would when you go to Denver. You know I would be unhappy in a place like Denver. I do not wish to go there, but it is right that you should go and see your children and grandchildren."

Abbie felt sudden tears wanting to come. "If you go to the Black Hills, Swift Arrow, you won't come back. You won't ever come back."

"You do not know that."

"Oh, yes I do!" She stood up and gently laid the baby into the swing, then turned to face her husband squarely. "I know it as sure as I am standing here. There is going to be trouble, and you damn well know it! You intend to be right there in the middle of all the action. If there is one tiny bit of hope that you can be a warrior one more time, that you can fight like the Dog Soldier you are, that you can let out one more war cry and wield a weapon just once more, you

will take it. And if you can *die* that way, you will welcome it!"

Their eyes held in a strange challenge, and for a
brief moment she saw it there in his own dark eyes—
the Indian, the proud, demanding man who would tell
his woman to stay out of his affairs . . . the Swift Arrow
who taken a small whip to her when she'd lived among
the Cheyenne and had dared to sneak a look at the
sacred arrows. He was angry, but the squint to his eyes
from that anger suddenly softened, and a hint of a
smile moved across his mouth. That was when Abbie
realized he knew what she was really telling him.

"It would be a good way to die, don't you think?"
he said. "Zeke also chose a good way to die."

Abbie stiffened. She had known since she married
this man that this day would come. "I would not stop
you."

He gently brushed away the tear that slipped down
her cheek. "I always knew I have only been here to get
you through the worst of it, my Abbie. First there was
the awful sorrow of losing Zeke. You needed someone
to fill the emptiness, someone who reminded you of
the only man you have ever truly loved. I did that for
you, and I loved you as dearly as Zeke did. But I am
even more Indian than he was, and all these changes
are more than I can bear. I do not know if this is the
answer, but at least if I go there, I can be Indian again.
I can dance, sing, pray to my own god, feel the spirits
of the animals and grandmother earth creep into my
very bones." His eyes teared. "You are among the few
with white blood who can understand what I am telling
you. Your children, all except Wolf's Blood, belong to
a new world, as do the grandchildren. I have done my
part here in teaching the young ones about the old
ways. I miss those old ways. I wish to return to them, if
but for a little while."

Abbie nodded. "I will stay here another month or so with the new baby and help Louellen. Will you stay that long?"

He nodded. "I will stay."

"When I go to Denver, perhaps I'll stay through the winter. It's been a long time since I've seen Jeremy and LeeAnn, the children. I'd like to spend time with them, maybe even go to the ranch again for a while."

Both knew the truth. Once they parted, it could be forever. "You are the only woman I have ever truly loved, Abigail Monroe. You—a white woman. You were my only weakness."

"We have had good years together," she answered. "But I know your place is here, among your people, or in the Black Hills, where you lived and rode with the Sioux for so many years. I suppose it is right that we go our separate ways. We will always . . . be together in spirit, Swift Arrow, just as we feel Zeke with us, and Wolf's Blood and all those who have left us over the years through death and change."

The baby began to fuss, and Abbie looked down at him, smiling through her tears at his dark red skin and the shock of straight, black hair that surrounded his round little face. "Maybe it will be easier for the tiny ones who never knew the old ways." She looked back at her husband. *"Ne-mehotatse,* Swift Arrow. You brought me strength and love when I needed it most."

He drew her into his arms. "And you did the same for me."

"Hey, you two, where's that son of mine? It sounds to me as though he needs some nourishment, and his mother is anxious to give it to him." Jason stepped outside, a proud grin on his face. It faded when he saw the tears in the eyes of his mother and uncle. "What's wrong?"

Abbie put on a smile. "Nothing. We're just happy

about having another son in the family." She took the baby from the bench and handed him to Jason, thinking what a grand mixture this youngest son of hers was, with his dark skin and high cheekbones, mixed in with sandy hair and blue eyes. "Raise him up to be a proud Cheyenne man, Jason."

He took the baby into his arms, grinning again. "You know I will. Come inside. Maybe you can cook up some soup or something for Louellen. She's doing great, already says she's hungry."

He went back in with the squalling baby, and Abbie leaned against Swift Arrow. He moved his arms around her from behind and kissed the top of her head. "And so life goes on," he told her. "It is good. For every sorrow there is something also to celebrate. Wolf's Blood is free in Canada, we have heard from Zeke and know that he is working at a sawmill in the mountains of Colorado, learning a new way of life. I will go to the Black Hills, and I will be who I must be—Swift Arrow, a Cheyenne Dog Soldier. I will sing and dance again, feel the power of the spirits, be the Indian that I am. It is all for the best, Abigail. From here on we can only accept what comes to us and be glad for what we have had."

She turned, and he kissed her tenderly. "Thank you for being the understanding woman that you are."

She ran her hands over his shoulders, still so strong for his age. "I never tried to stop Zeke, and I won't try to stop you." She leaned up and kissed him again, then went inside, needing to make herself busy so she would not break into tears she'd be unable to stop.

Swift Arrow sighed deeply, turning again to look across the horizon to the east, feeling drawn by the new religion and by old customs. It was as though wild things were calling him, ghosts from the past. He could hear the singing, feel the drumming, and he knew that he must go.

Haydon Seger studied the map spread out on a huge stump, gauging the best area to be clear-cut next. With Denver and the surrounding area growing so fast, there seemed to be an endless demand for lumber, and a man who knew how to log the trees could make a fortune, which was exactly what he was doing. A few people were beginning to protest that he shouldn't strip this mountain clean, but the United States government and those in charge of this state, as well as those who wanted cheap lumber, found nothing wrong with cutting every tree in sight. After all, more would grow back.

He tried to determine exactly where he was now and which area he should have his men start on next. A new flume would have to be built, or some kind of chute, depending on the water supply on the mountain. He mapped out another section while the loggers changed shifts, looking up when a shadow loomed over the map as someone came closer and blocked out the sunlight. He squinted, recognizing Zeke Brown, who stood in front of him holding an axe over one shoulder. "Afternoon, Zeke. Something I can help you with?"

Zeke nodded. "Yes, sir, at least I think so." Zeke liked Haydon Seger well enough—he was a fair man with his laborers—but Zeke didn't care for the man's attitude toward clear-cutting. It sickened him to see whole forests stripped away, and he felt even worse for being among the crew of loggers who did the dirty work. But it was good, hard work, something that kept him busy and tired. He'd gotten into it to keep his mind off of Georgeanne, had stayed in it because it was building him up physically and spiritually. He'd grown a little taller and was well muscled now, and working in the mountain forests had made him feel closer to nature. He liked the smells, the sounds, even liked the danger of the work. Most of all he liked the fact that land which had been clear-cut could be bought cheap. "I need your advice, sir."

Seger leaned back in a wooden chair, setting a rock on the map so it couldn't blow away. His big belly pushed at the buttons of his flannel shirt and hid the front of his leather belt; his chubby face sported a stubble of a beard. Zeke could tell the man had once been tough and well muscled, but he'd let himself go now that he was a boss instead of a worker. "Fire away, boy."

Zeke lowered the axe, leaning on its handle. "I've been doing this long enough to know most of this is government land, and sometimes it can be bought cheap once it's been forested. Is that true?"

Seger took a pipe from one shirt pocket and a tin of tobacco from the other "For the most part." He opened the lid of the tin and tapped some tobacco into the pipe bowl. "Some of it is private land already," he added, packing the tobacco tighter before adding more. "But most of it is government land."

"How would I go about buying some?"

Seger replaced the tobacco tin and flicked a match, lighting the pipe.

"Well, you just go to the nearest land office, which in this case would be down in Fort Collins, and they can tell you what's available. Remember that in most of these mountains water is hard to come by, except for winter runoff, and once the land has been clear-cut, it's not worth much. You can't farm it, and you're stuck with hundreds, maybe thousands of stumps, depending on how many acres you want."

"I'm not worried about that. I happen to think all

this land is going to be worth a lot someday, the more the area is settled. Even if that doesn't happen, I just want something to call my own. I don't have much, but I do have a bit of money saved, enough to buy some cheap government land."

Seger looked him over, thinking what a strapping young man he was. Few of his crew were built quite like Zeke Brown, pure brawny power, yet he was a quiet, rather humble man who didn't go around bragging about his muscle like some of the others. He kept to himself, didn't drink, hadn't even visited the camp whores more than once or twice in the three years he'd been here. He was one of Seger's hardest working men. "I hate to see you leave us, Zeke. I'd have to hire two or three more men to make up for you."

Zeke grinned bashfully. "I didn't say I'd quit right away. I'd just like some time off to look into it. In a couple of years I'd have enough money saved to get something going, raise horses maybe. I'm not sure yet."

Seger puffed on the pipe for a moment. "Well, if anybody can make something out of land that's been clear-cut, I have a feeling you could. Go ahead and take a few days. Just be sure to try to get a little flatland along with it. For the next few years it's the farmland that's going to be worth something; then later, land with a good view of the mountains will be in demand, you mark my words. There are already folks who come out here from the East for their summer vacations just to look. They've been going to Yellowstone up in Wyoming for a long time now, and every year more come, searching for new sights to see. There's plenty of rich folks back East willing to pay just to look at a mountain."

Zeke nodded. "I'll remember that. Thank you, sir. I'll leave tomorrow, if you don't mind."

"Do what you have to do. Say, how old are you anyway?"

"Twenty-one, sir."

Seger looked him over again, thinking how very dark he was. Maybe he was a descendant of some foreigner, Italian or Irish. He'd seen some Irishmen who were very dark. "You got family hereabouts, boy?"

Zeke nodded. "East of Pueblo—my parents and two brothers run a ranch there."

Seger's eyebrows arched in surprise. No ignorant immigrants from another country would already be running a ranch in Colorado. "They Mexican or Indian or something like that?"

Zeke grew wary. "Maybe. Does it matter?"

Seger shrugged. "I guess not, long as you got white blood in you, anybody can see that you do. I'm not being insulting, boy. Just trying to help. You go to Fort Collins, ask for Wayne Bishop. I know him. You tell him I sent you and said you're okay. I'll even give you a letter. The other land agent is Scott Taylor, and he can be a bastard sometimes. He might ask questions, might sell you a piece of shit land if he suspects you're part of some race he doesn't like—or he might find a way to keep you from buying any land at all. Bishop won't do that."

Zeke nodded. "I appreciate that, sir."

Seger kept the pipe between his teeth. "You come back in a little while and I'll have a letter for you. Me, I don't own much land. I prefer to just log it out. But if you want to settle on a place of your own, that's your affair. I like you, Zeke. You're not a braggart and a drinker and a gambler like the rest of these men."

"Thank you, sir. I just try to do my job and mind my own business." Zeke picked up the axe, feeling a little guilty that he had not actually come out and admitted he had both Negro and Indian blood. He felt no shame for it, but he had learned enough to know a man was better off keeping his mouth shut at certain times. He suspected this was one of them. If keeping quiet meant he could have some land of his own, then he'd keep quiet. There was a right time for all things, and one of the things he would find the right time for was squaring off with Carson Temple . . . somehow . . . someday—after he'd made something of himself. There were all kinds of ways to pay a man back; he didn't necessarily have to hurt the man physically. There were other ways to do it.

He wondered too what had ever happened to Georgeanne . . . or if he'd ever stop loving her.

Fourteen

Abbie stayed in Denver through Christmas, clinging to her family at a time when she knew she must. Swift Arrow was still with the Sioux, who had worked themselves into such a zealous frenzy over their new religion that an entire nation was on alert. No one seemed to care that the Indians continued to preach nonviolence with their new religion, that all the dancing and singing and drumming was simply to welcome their ancestors, who they truly believed would soon come back from the grave. It was even rumored that some of the Christianized Indians believed Christ himself would come to them soon.

But ten days ago the worst had happened, and Abbie knew disaster lay ahead. Sitting Bull had been shot and killed by the reservation's own Indian police. General Nelson Miles had wanted the man arrested, blaming the entire Ghost Dance situation on the infamous leader. Because of his job with the *Rocky Mountain News,* Joshua kept in touch by wire with everything that was happening at the reservation. The news about Sitting Bull had been devastating, and now hundreds of Indians were on the run, frightened and confused. They had fled the Standing Rock reservation, and the army was sure they were headed for Pine Ridge, where the once-great chief, Red Cloud, now lived. According to what Joshua had learned yesterday, they had joined up

with a Ghost Dance leader called Big Foot, who was
now the center of army attention, wanted by the War
Department as a "fomenter of disturbances."

Abbie had to struggle now to keep her mind on her
family and not go crazy worrying about Swift Arrow,
who she knew would be right in the middle of whatever
was happening. She had chosen to stay in Denver with
Jeremy and Mary, Hawk and Iris for several months,
wanting to spend Christmas with them. Hawk had been
living in Boulder while he went to school, but he was
home for the holidays, and this Christmas Day Iris's
new love also spent the day with them. Raphael was a
stocky, good-looking young man, with the husky shoulders of a construction worker. He was soft-spoken and
mannerly, and he and Hawk got along well. Hawk fully
approved of his sister's suitor, who was making a name
for himself in Denver for his carpentry work and, apparently a frugal man, had some savings.

Abbie could not help smiling at the reason he was
building his worth. It was evident Raphael Hidalgo intended to ask Iris to marry him, and he wanted to be
able to give her a good life. From the way Iris looked
at the young man, there was no doubt in Abbie's mind
that the young woman's answer would be yes.

Margaret and Morgan had left the ranch in the
hands of dependable hired hands and had come to
join them for Christmas, as had Ellen and Hal. Since
Zeke had left, and with proven title to Monroe land,
they had thus far had no more problems with Carson
Temple. Abbie suspected her children understood
what she was going through with worrying over Swift
Arrow, and they had dropped their own busy schedules
to come and make this a family holiday, which it most
certainly was, with Joshua and LeeAnn and their children also here at Jeremy's house Christmas morning.

Mary had her cook serve a breakfast fit for kings,

and although Jeremy's house was huge and ostenta-
tious, Mary brought a warmth to every room, not just
with her decorating but her personality. She had grown
very close to Iris, who was blossoming into a beautiful
young woman able to hold a candle to any of Denver's
loveliest debutantes. Now a gracious and graceful
young lady well taught by a woman accustomed to the
finer life, Iris had not lost her sweet personality. And
on a dresser in her bedroom upstairs sat a picture . . .
of a young Indian girl sitting on a fence at a ranch
where she'd once lived on a reservation in Montana,
and next to her stood a handsome Indian man . . .
her father, Wolf's Blood. There had been no word
from him in over three years, but Iris Monroe had not
forgotten her father.

Nor had Hawk. The first thing the young man asked
about when he came home for Christmas was his father,
wanting to know if there was any word. The loneliness
was still there in his eyes, but he was already excelling
in school, determined to make good enough grades to
go to Harvard after two years at the University of Colorado.

With full stomachs, the whole family marched into
the parlor, where a ten-foot tree took up half the room,
presents scattered beneath it. Eight-year-old Lance was
beside himself with excitement, and his laughter was
joined with screeches and more laughter from Ellen's
seven-year-old son Daniel, and eleven-year-old Lillian.
Dan and Rebecca were also here with Emily, now ten.
The room grew even more crowded when LeeAnn and
her brood left the table and joined the festivities with
little four-year-old Abbie and six-year-old Lonnie. Abbie
could see that Matthew, at twelve, was trying to act
grown-up, but his eyes glittered with a desire to tear
into the presents with the other children.

"Grandma, look at this!" Lonnie exclaimed, holding

up a toy metal train engine with wheels that really rolled and other moving parts that were made to scale.

Paper flew everywhere, children squealed, and Mary and Jeremy laughed with delight, happy to be able to fill the house with children, happy to have a family at last. It was obvious Jeremy had splurged sinfully on every one of them, but Abbie knew he'd wanted to do it.

She watched all the excitement, but her thoughts were in the Black Hills, with her Indian husband, who had apparently fallen under the spell of the Ghost Dance religion. He'd been gone six months, and every letter from him told of the joy he'd found in being part of such hope, how he felt truly at home, believing that soon the army and most whites would disappear from the face of the earth, that soon the land would be virgin again, lush with green grass on which millions of buffalo would graze.

There had been no promises of returning to Montana, and Abbie had not expected them. A young Indian man who could read and write prepared the letters for Swift Arrow, as Swift Arrow himself had never learned either skill. He was truly one with the old, old ways; years of living with her had not taken any of the "Indian" out of him. He had easily been caught up in the fervor for the new religion that brought hope to a people who until now had been without any.

Joshua had written several articles in the *Rocky Mountain News,* trying to explain that the Ghost Dance religion was not dangerous, but few whites believed that. Joshua feared that something disastrous was going to come of this. Abbie sorrowfully agreed, and she prayed daily for Swift Arrow.

Tension was mounting quickly now, and Abbie wanted to know about every action that took place.

The more Joshua learned, the more she wanted to go to Pine Ridge herself and try to find Swift Arrow. She wanted to be there if trouble broke out and he was hurt, but Joshua and Jeremy refused to let her go. Joshua was certain Swift Arrow did not want her there, and she knew deep down that was so. And Jeremy had said that if Zeke were alive, he would not want her to expose herself to the danger.

She could do nothing now but sit and wait for every bit of news. As soon as the opening of gifts was done, Joshua had promised he would go to his office and see if there were any new developments before coming back for the royal Christmas feast Mary had planned for them all. She wished Jason and Louellen and the new baby could be with them, but they had not wanted to travel this far in the winter cold with such a small child. She thought how she should go back to Montana soon, but the weather might not allow it. January was not a time to be traveling through the wilds of Wyoming into Montana. Jason would understand if she waited until spring.

And even if she went back, how could she stay in that little cabin alone, without Swift Arrow? Perhaps she could never go back to stay. She felt restless now; a woman without a true home; for her home had once been in the arms of Zeke Monroe, then his brother Swift Arrow. If something happened to him, the closest thing to home would be the ranch. Perhaps she would return there with Margaret and Morgan to spend the winter.

Winter. There were few places in the country where winter could be as cold and cruel as the Dakotas. Now Big Foot and his followers were a frightened, desperate people, fleeing to Pine Ridge in that terrible cold, probably thinking Red Cloud could somehow protect them from the growing numbers of soldiers. She had no doubt many of them still feared that the army was looking for revenge for Custer's massacre fourteen years ago. Some of those with Big Foot might even have been there.

Swift Arrow had. He must be so cold now. She wished she could hold him, warm him under a blanket.

She looked around the room full of children and grandchildren—all dressed like any white man or woman. The tree was decorated with lovely, expensive, handmade trinkets, and a fire glowed in the marble fireplace. The children sat on a richly carpeted floor, the adults on expensive, velvet-covered furniture. Velvet drapes hung at tall windows, and plants sat about in expensive vases.

No, Swift Arrow would not have been happy coming here with her. He was where he belonged.

Wolf's Blood carried in an armload of wood, dumping it beside the stone fireplace in the one-room cabin he now called home. "Hey, *Sotaju,*" he said to his pet wolf, "you are lazy today, huh?"

The animal looked up at him with yellow eyes, remaining sprawled in front of the fire, his head between his paws. His only other movement was a slight wag of his tail.

Wolf's Blood pulled his bearskin coat closer around his neck as he fed a few more logs onto the blaze. "I do not blame you for staying right here," he told *Sotaju,* whose name meant Smoke in the Sioux language. "It is so cold outside that it is a wonder my eyelids do not freeze to my eyeballs when I walk out the door." Even inside he could see his breath, and he thought how nice it would be to have an iron heating stove that would radiate the heat inside rather than suck it up through a chimney. The only way to keep relatively warm was to sit directly in front of the fire, over which hung a black pot full of a venison stew he'd made himself with the last of the deer meat he had stored in a smokehouse outside. He needed to do more hunting, but it was too cold to stay out for long. He prayed his horses were all right. They were in stalls in a large shed, with several other horses owned by old Joe Bear Paw, a Cree Indian who lived with his granddaughter, Sweet Bird, whose Christian name was Elizabeth Bear Paw, in a small village not far away.

He had found a bit of peace among the Cree, a tribe of Canadian Indians who had long ago stopped trying to save their land, like most Indians in the United States. They were left with this little bit of land, and were watched by the red-coated Canadian mounties. Unlike most tribes in the United States, these people did not get any help from the government that had forced them into this life. Though left to fend for themselves, there were few places where they were allowed to hunt. As a result, the tribe's numbers were dwindling, old ones dying from broken hearts and malnutrition, younger ones also dying from malnutrition and from the diseases that often swept through the camps, brought to them by white traders. There were a few of those, bringing mostly whiskey rather than the goods that were truly needed. Even the traders seldom came anymore, for the Cree had nothing left to trade. What animal skins they did manage to procure through hunting were needed for their own clothing and blankets.

Wolf's Blood stirred the stew, which besides the deer meat consisted of the last of his potatoes and onions. He'd spent most of the money he had on food, not just for himself but for the rest of the Cree, and he'd gone to the closest trading post two months ago to buy a wagonload of oats for the horses. Now those were running low, although the tribe had managed to farm some hay and alfalfa. If winter did not last too long into spring, the horses would survive . . . unless they all froze to death.

He decided it might be safe now to write to Hawk and Iris, and to his mother. He had faithfully carried pen and ink and paper in his supplies these three years, always meaning to write but afraid if he wrote too soon, authorities would discover the letter and his whereabouts. He had decided it was best to remain completely silent for all this time. Maybe by now the authorities didn't care anymore, or were too preoccupied with the new trouble in the Dakotas. He'd heard about the Ghost Dance religion through gossip at the trading post. He longed to go there himself and take part in the dancing and drumming, but it was more important to stay alive for his children, to live as long as he could bear the pain of his arthritis, long enough to know Hawk had graduated from law school, to know Iris was perhaps happily married.

No one up here knew he was a wanted man, and it was not uncommon to see Sioux and Cheyenne Indians up here, where Sitting Bull himself had once fled. The thought pierced his heart, for he had only recently heard that Sitting Bull had been killed. What sickened him most was that it was the tribe's own Indian police that had shot him down. This was something Sitting Bull had once predicted would happen—that he would be killed by his own people.

He gritted his teeth in anger. The U.S. government had done a good job destroying the Indians by keeping them divided, bribing the weak ones to their side, pitting tribes against each other. What had happened to Sitting Bull would probably cause internal strife among the Sioux for generations.

He leaned closer and tasted the stew, pleased with

himself for the good cook he'd become out of necessity. There was a time when, as a warrior, he would not think of doing such womanly things, but he had no choice now. He turned away to rummage through his supplies, and found the pen and the bottle of ink, as well as an envelope and a few sheets of paper that were now wrinkled and turning yellow. His family would not care what condition the paper was in, or that he misspelled words and his penmanship was not the best. That was his fault. He'd begun refusing his mother's lessons at an early age, preferring to be outside riding a horse and learning the Cheyenne way.

He sat down in a homemade wooden chair and set pen and paper on the storage crate he used for a table. He would send the letter to Jeremy in Denver, the one person in his family he knew would still be in the same place. He'd kept his brother's address with him all this time, knowing he would want to get a letter to his children and let them know he was all right. Jeremy could get word to everyone else. Abbie could be anywhere—at the reservation, in Denver, at the ranch. The thought of her and the children brought on a painful loneliness he knew would never go away. Hawk was almost eighteen now, Iris sixteen. If he'd figured the time right, it must be Christmas, or a little after. He hoped they had all had a nice holiday.

He was starting to uncap the ink when there came a tap at the door. He frowned, rising and walking to open it. Someone bundled in a wolfskin coat and leggings darted inside and went to stand by the fire, and Wolf's Blood knew it had to be someone familiar, since *Sotaju* remained still and did not growl. He closed the door. "You might have asked if it was all right to come in," he said in irritation. "Would you mind introducing yourself?"

The figure turned, pulling a heavy fur hood away

from her face and hair. It was Sweet Bird. She smiled, her black hair flattened to her head by the heavy hood. "I was worried about you, wondered if you were warm and had food."

He wanted to be angry with her for coming unannounced and uninvited, yet her presence was pleasing. "I have been taking care of myself since I was a young boy. You need not worry about Wolf's Blood, Sweet Bird, and you should not have been out walking in this terrible weather. This is becoming a blizzard, and it is nearly a mile to your village. You could have gotten lost."

"Would you have cared?"

He watched her warily. "Of course I would. You are the granddaughter of my good friend, Joe Bear Paw."

"Is that the only reason?"

He sighed, folding his arms in front of him. "Of course it is. What other reason would I have?" He could see that she was blushing slightly, in spite of her dark skin . . . beautiful skin . . . smooth and without blemish.

"Perhaps for the same reason I care about you as more than just my grandfather's friend. I have decided you should no longer be up here alone, Wolf's Blood. A man should have a woman to cook for him, clean and prepare the animals he brings back from the hunt . . . keep him warm in the night."

He waved her off, going back to sit down to his letter. "I am about forty-three summers. You could be my daughter. Do not be giving yourself to a man my age, Sweet Bird. Go and make eyes at the young men."

She sobered, stepping closer. "There are no young men left."

The words cut deep, filling him with sadness. How right she was. There were few young men for a maiden to choose from. He rose, looking down at her, studying her big, brown eyes and seeing desire there, youthful, eager love. "I have already loved three women, Sweet Bird. The first was when I was very young, and so was she. She was Cheyenne, and she was killed by soldiers at Sand Creek twenty-six years ago, before we ever had the chance to marry. The second was an Apache woman, whom I made my wife. She, too, was killed by soldiers. My third wife was a white woman, and *she* was killed by a drunken white man. Now I am a wanted man in the States, and for all I know someone might come here looking for me. I will not love another woman and watch her die. Soldiers and drunken white men have destroyed my life. I have little love left to give even if I would consider taking you for a wife."

"I do not care. Life is hard here. There is little hope for us, just as you have little hope. Why not enjoy what we can have for the moment? I want to be your woman. I want children. You cannot turn me back out there in the cold because the wind is growing worse and I could not make it back. I must stay here now until the storm is over, and I do not think you will be able to keep me here without taking me to your bed. Once you do, we will be man and wife, and that will be that. Grandfather would be happy about it."

A trace of a smile passed over his lips in spite of his anger with her. "Does Joe know you are here?"

She smiled seductively. "He thought it was a good idea. He is getting old and is afraid of what will happen to me if he dies. He wants me to have a man to take care of me. You are still strong, and a good hunter."

Wolf's Blood looked down at his hands. The extreme cold had brought pain to his joints. "I have a disease that will one day cripple me."

She removed her coat, and although she wore fur leggings and thick moccasins, she had deliberately left herself naked from the waist up. "You are not crippled yet," she answered, her heart pounding at her own daring. She hoped he liked the size of her breasts. Apparently he did, for she saw first surprise and then desire in his dark eyes. She did not care about his age. Wolf's Blood was a tall, strong, handsome man, and she knew from stories he'd told her grandfather that he was once considered a mighty warrior. He still would be, if the Cheyenne could still make war.

Wolf's Blood was stunned by her boldness. Her firm, full breasts were indeed enticing, and the cold made their nipples come alive. It was more than a man in his situation could resist. He swallowed, struggling against an urge to ravish her. He must remember she was a virgin. He did not want to bring her pain or make her cry after such a sweet offering. He tore his gaze from her breasts to meet her eyes. "If I take you now, it would not be out of love. I am a lonely man who has been long without a woman, and those I have known will remain alive in my heart forever. I still mourn my last wife."

"I understand. You will learn to love me. Take me to your bed now before I grow too cold to feel your touch."

Wolf's Blood suddenly felt like a much younger man. He reached out and cupped one breast in his hand, ran his thumb over a nipple, relishing the feel of it. He leaned down and met her mouth, pulled her into his arms, fiery passion gripping him as the kiss grew hotter, more demanding. She was eager, hot for him in her own youthful anxiousness to please. He left her lips, bent down and yanked off her leggings. She stepped out of them and the moccasins and stood naked before him, her skin covered in goose bumps. He remained on his knees, kissing her legs, her thighs, her secret lovenest. She gasped with the pleasure of it.

He picked her up and carried her to his bed of robes

near the fireplace. She watched in wide-eyed wonder as he, too, undressed, and her eyes widened with pleasure at his magnificent build. This man might be old enough to be her father, but he was as virile as any younger man. She knew a hint of fear at the sight of his man part, swollen like a stallion's, but she told herself she would get over the pain and after a while would take great pleasure in this man, giving him pleasure in return, keeping him warm, loving him as he needed to be loved. She knew he had a family somewhere that he loved very much. She would help relieve his loneliness.

He moved beside her, smothering her with kisses, moving down to suckle at her breasts like a babe. The sensations caused by his intimate touches made her cry out in ecstasy as his fingers explored hitherto untouched territory.

"It will not hurt so much after the first time," he told her, moving between her legs, which she parted willingly for him.

The next few hours were filled with a kind of pleasure Wolf's Blood had thought he would never know again. The paper and ink sat untouched while he gloried in the ecstasy of knowing a woman again, having a companion, someone to love him and ease the loneliness. Now when he wrote his letter, he could tell his mother and children he had a new wife and was not so alone.

Abbie looked up from her Bible when Joshua came into the parlor. For the last three days he had been in almost constant contact with authorities in Cheyenne, and the offices there had, in turn, kept in contact with officials at Pine Ridge. "Do you know anything about Swift Arrow?" she asked.

He breathed deeply before coming into the room, followed by LeeAnn, Mary and Jeremy. She knew then the news was even worse than she'd thought. Margaret and Ellen had already headed home, but she thanked God she at least had one son and daughter with her. She turned away to stare at the fire in the hearth near which she sat. "I want every detail."

Joshua cleared his throat, sitting down on a loveseat across from her. "They caught up with Big Foot, yesterday morning in fact. I didn't want to tell you until I had more details."

Abbie nodded. "Go on."

Joshua looked at LeeAnn and Jeremy, not wanting to continue but knowing he must. He turned sorrowful eyes back to his mother-in-law, this woman who had once almost died to protect him. "Major Whiteside was in charge. Word has it Big Foot was nearly dead from pneumonia by then. At any rate, it's most likely the Indians were skittish and afraid because Whiteside apparently ringed soldiers all around their encampment. They were told they should gather in the center of the camp and give up all weapons, not that they had many to begin with. Nor did they intend to use them, I'm sure, but they were ordered to give them up. Some say the Sioux were afraid they would not be sent to Pine Ridge as promised. They were afraid of being sent far away from their sacred Black Hills, which only added to the tension. Someone fired a shot. No one knows who, or why."

Abbie blinked back tears. "And then all hell broke loose."

"That's a pretty apt description. Soldiers began firing into the circle of Indians. Big Foot was one of the first to go down. I guess there were several one-on-one skirmishes, more Indians tried to flee. The soldiers opened up their Hotchkiss guns on them."

Abbie shivered. She remembered the sound of those big guns, the shattering boom, the flying shrapnel that tore apart tipis. She'd been at Blue Water Creek . . . so many, many years ago . . . another Sioux camp that had been attacked by soldiers. "How many dead?" she asked.

Joshua sighed. "They figure around three hundred, more than half of them women and children. A blizzard has set in, and they haven't been able to find the bodies or bury them. A few babies survived, found under the frozen bodies of their mothers who'd fallen on them to protect them from the bullets."

Abbie covered her face. "My God," she muttered.

LeeAnn rushed over to kneel in front of her. "Mother, you have us. We're here for you. Stay here now, will you? Stay right here in Denver."

She brushed at her tears and looked at Joshua. "Swift Arrow?"

He closed his eyes and quietly nodded. "It took a lot of wires and waiting, but I finally found someone who knew who he was. He's . . . dead, Abbie. They figure the only way to bury them once the snow lets up is in a mass grave."

"Of course," she said quietly, "like animals." She looked up at a painting of an eagle that hung above the fireplace. Jeremy had had it specially done by an artist who'd been staying in Denver to paint the mountain scenery. "They're together again at last, Swift Arrow and Zeke." She looked at LeeAnn then. "Don't worry. I won't act the way I did after Zeke died and try to deny Swift Arrow's gone. Your uncle and I said our good-byes last summer when we first parted. We knew then what would happen, just like Zeke knew the last time he left me. It was something that had to be." A tear spilled down her cheek. "All of you, please leave me alone for a little while."

"Are you sure you'll be all right, Mother?"

Abbie nodded. "Just go," she whispered.

LeeAnn turned worried eyes to her husband and brother. "Just for a few minutes," she answered.

They all left the room. Abbie looked down at her Bible, some of its pages bearing tear stains from other years. Now new ones dripped onto the thin, worn paper.

Fifteen

August, 1893 . . .

Zeke ran behind a cluster of boulders and ducked down, waiting for another stump to blow. The dynamite rumbled and the ground shook. At the same time the stump jerked sideways, but only half dislodged.

"Damn," Zeke grumbled. Some came out easy, others seemed determined to stay put. He wiped sweat from his brow and walked several yards to the crate of explosives he'd left in the shade of a cottonwood tree, where he'd also left food and a blanket, since he intended to stay in this section all day and blow out more stumps.

He took two more sticks of dynamite from the crate and carefully carried them back to the partially dislodged stump. He had paid a man to teach him how to do this, and over the last three years, since quitting his logging job and settling here, he'd managed to clear thirty of his hundred acres, determined to turn most of the land into a working ranch and farm so that, under an agreement with the land agent and the government, he would not have to pay anything for the land. The Homestead Act was a wondrous thing, one of the few good ideas the United States government had come up with, except that it had caused the loss of even more Indian lands. He did not feel guilty claiming property under that act since he was part Indian himself, something the government men didn't know. This was a small, personal victory for him.

He placed the dynamite sticks strategically. He did not trust the government of the United States or of Colorado. Someone could still come along and tell him he must pay for the land after all, and he intended to be ready. Already he was building a fine horse herd and was earning money training horses for other ranchers, as well as building a business in horseshoeing and the repair of saddles and other gear. He had quite a bit set aside, and he hoped to build himself a better home eventually. Right now he still lived in the little one-room cabin he'd built when first settling here. He had never built anything like that on his own before, so the cabin sagged here and there, but it was all he needed.

He lit the dynamite and ran for cover. When it blew, he peered above the rock to see that the stump had come clear this time. "Gotcha!" he said with a grin. He stood up and took a cold pipe from his shirt pocket, a small cloth bag of tobacco from a pocket in his denim pants. He stuffed the bowl and lit the tobacco with a match, sucking on the pipe and enjoying the sweet smell of the smoke. Striking out on his own was the best decision he'd ever made, in spite of the painful parting with his family and the lingering ache he still felt for Georgeanne. He had deliberately never written her, had no idea what had become of her; it was best that way. Carson Temple had apparently given his parents no more problems, and they had kept their promise that if they heard from Georgeanne they would not disclose his whereabouts. Apparently, though, they had not heard from her since the one visit she'd paid them shortly after he had left.

He scanned the land he owned. A little bit of forest still remained on a distant section, the rest was mostly flat, but eighty acres of it ran right up against a moun-

tain and inclined up it several hundred feet. He called
his ranch Cheyenne Hills, and he had a legal deed to
all of it. Things were working out pretty damn good,
except for his great-uncle, Swift Arrow, dying at
Wounded Knee three years ago. His grandmother had
been living with Jeremy since then. She had managed
to deal with her grief by turning her attentions to Denver's poor, a class that was growing even more quickly
now that Denver was suffering a financial panic. The
bottom had dropped out of silver prices, and some
owners of silver mines, only a short time ago million-
aires, had found themselves bankrupt. There had been
a few suicides, and jobless miners were now added to
the unemployed immigrants who had been brought in
to help build railroads and mines, but who were no
longer needed for that.

Zeke smiled fondly as he walked to the stump. Leave
it to his grandmother to be concerned about people
who needed help. For years she had given her attention to the Cheyenne up in Montana; now she was
turning it to immigrant orphans and the street people
of Denver. She apparently kept Jeremy busy trying to
convince his wealthy friends that something needed to
be done, and she kept Joshua busy writing newspaper
articles about the plight of Denver's poor. She had convinced Jeremy to build an orphanage, and Mary had
gladly volunteered to help there, since she loved children and had never had her own. Jeremy and Mary
had lost a few of their "elite" friends because of their
work for the poor, but they didn't seem to mind.

Hawk was at Harvard now, would graduate in another year or so; and Iris had married Raphael Hidalgo, converting to his Catholic religion. Already they
had a son, Miguel, and another baby on the way.
Raphael was doing quite well in his carpentry business,

and they were living comfortably in one of Denver's
middle-class neighborhoods.

The family had finally heard from Wolf's Blood, who
was living in Canada with a Cree woman he'd married.
Iris and Hawk had a little half brother now, named
Little Eagle in Cheyenne, Joseph for government rolls.
Grandma Abbie was comforted to know her eldest son
had found some little bit of love and happiness, but
she still worried about him. He did not write often,
and the authorities had no idea anyone had heard
from him. Their own letters were sent to his wife,
Sweet Bird, at a trading post near which Wolf's Blood
lived. Wolf's Blood's name was never written on the
envelopes.

Zeke walked up and kicked at the stump, sighing
over the thought of the hard work ahead of him. Once
enough stumps were blown out, then came the task of
piling them together, waiting for them to dry out for
another year or so before he could try burning them.
He'd bought three sturdy plow horses for the task of
dragging the stumps to one place for burning. He then
used brute force to shove and roll them into the pile,
and some days his back and shoulders ached fiercely;
but he had built his muscle power over the years, was
proud of his physique and strength.

The only thing this place would need eventually was
a woman. He'd found one in a tavern in Fort Collins
who had made it very clear she'd like to show him a
few things, and show him she had. He'd obliged her
out of a natural manly need to be with a woman, but
in spite of the physical pleasures of his little fling with
the barmaid, he'd been left feeling even more needful
of a woman he could really love, a woman he wanted
to claim for himself, one he could call his wife and
who would give him children.

The thought made him kick the stump again. He

was twenty-four now, certainly old enough to marry and start a family. But he'd been too busy to find time for courting, and he wasn't sure what type of woman he should look for. He had decided he would just keep doing what he was about, and if God meant for him to be with someone, he'd meet her one way or another. The trouble was, his own brother Nathan, two years younger, was already married, to the daughter of a ranch hand Morgan had hired. They had built themselves a cabin at the ranch, where Nathan intended to stay and continue helping his father.

"My little brother—married," he muttered, "and here I am still alone."

He blamed Carson Temple for that, and still harbored a strong need for revenge. The only way he knew how to get it without going back home and killing the man was to make something of himself and to be sure Temple knew about it. He still carried a faint white scar on one cheek and several scars on his chest, arms and back where the skin had been ripped away so deeply on that day years ago.

He set the pipe carefully aside on a flat rock, then walked back to the crate to take out two more sticks of dynamite. He would blow out one more stump before taking a break for lunch; then he'd go and get the work horses and start a new pile of stumps for burning. This would be a lot easier if he could afford to hire help, but he didn't want to spend the money if he could help it. He'd rather work extra hours himself and build his savings. He carried the dynamite and a shovel to yet another stump, digging two small holes in places where he felt the dynamite would do the most good and then placing the sticks in them. He lit the fuses and ran for cover, barely making it back to the rocks before the dynamite blew. This time the stump flew several feet upward, then landed a good ten feet away.

Zeke grinned with pleasure. He walked back to his supplies, picking up the pipe and quickly drawing on it to rekindle the smoldering embers in the bowl. It was then he noticed the fancy buggy coming up the road from the east. The road wound past his place, stemming from Fort Collins and meandering on down to a place called Masonville and then on to Loveland. What he saw looked like a buggy full of tourists, three men in suits and a woman. He could tell there was a woman by the different kind of hat she wore, and the cascade of auburn-colored curls that fell from under it onto her shoulders.

The woman pointed toward him and said something, and the driver of the buggy turned the horses to leave the road and come up the hill toward where Zeke stood. He puffed on the pipe, watching curiously and thinking he was in no condition to be meeting men in fancy suits and a proper lady, whatever their reason for coming here. He'd been working all morning, and it was a hot day. His hands and shirt were dirty from shoving around a stump earlier, and he was perspiring.

The carriage came closer, and suddenly he could not take his eyes off the woman, logic arguing it could not possibly be who this looked like.

"Zeke! It *is* you!" she called.

Georgeanne? He simply stood and stared as the carriage finally slowed to a halt in front of him. The woman opened a door and stepped out, smiling, her eyes brimming with tears. She walked up to him and grasped his hands.

"It's me, Zeke! Georgeanne! I never dreamed I'd see you again! When the land agent told us who owned this section—"

"Georgeanne?" He interrupted her, wondering if

he'd fallen asleep under the cottonwood tree and was dreaming.

"Yes!" She laughed. "When he said your name, I thought to myself, how many Zeke Browns can there be? And when they said you raised horses and all—"

"They? Who is they?" He looked past her at the three men who had disembarked from the buggy and were looking around. "What is this all about? Why are you here with these men?" It began to sink in that this was really happening. He looked into her eyes, those warm, brown eyes that had once shone with such love for him. And it was still in them. "Georgeanne!" he repeated, this time with great affection. "I . . . you look wonderful!" She was beautiful. She would be twenty-five now. Maybe she was married. He drew his hands away and ran one of them through his dark hair. "Excuse my appearance. I've been working all morning. You've caught me by surprise."

"You look as wonderful to me as you think I look, Zeke Brown, dirt and sweat and all!" She stepped back, admiring his appearance. "Look at you! They said you worked for several years as a logger. That's certainly easy to tell. How are you, Zeke? Are you . . . ?" Her smile faded. "Have you . . . married?"

He glanced at the three men again, not caring for the way they looked around his property. "Hell, no. I haven't had time to think about things like that." He met her gaze again. "How about you?"

Their eyes held in mutual understanding.

"No," she answered. "I went back to school, up in Michigan. All your talk back when we knew each other before, about Indians and ancient customs and all, how they consider the land sacred—I decided to study geology. And with all the gold mines here in Colorado, I thought there would be some use for my services. I work for Taylor Mines now. We explore new areas, trying to determine the potential for more gold finds. I was on my way with these men to Masonville. Someone actually found fish skeletons up in the mountains there. Can you believe it? They believe the Rocky Mountains were once entirely under water millions of years ago, when glaciers moved through this land and formed canyons and lakes. Oh, it's a long story, but that's the kind of thing I enjoy studying. Taylor Mines isn't interested just in gold. Mr. Taylor himself is also interested in building a museum that teaches people how this area was formed, tells them of the ancient history of Colorado. I thought perhaps you or your mother or grandmother could help me with Cheyenne history and customs. We could include that in the museum. Mr. Taylor is using his own money—"

"Wait! Slow down!" Zeke threw up his hands. "What has all this got to do with me? And why are those men looking around my property?"

Georgeanne laughed. "They're geologists, too!" She turned and called the others over to meet Zeke. "A geologist is *always* interested in the land, wherever he is. Don't worry. We aren't here to start digging on your land. We were studying a map of the entire area because of the fish skeleton find, and I saw your name as the owner of this section. I thought as long as we would pass by this way, I'd stop and see if this Zeke Brown was the same one I knew back at the ranch." Her smile faded again as she remembered the thing her father had done to him, the reason he'd left. Her eyes suddenly teared. "Zeke, I'm so sorry about what happened. I wanted desperately to talk to you . . ." She said nothing more for the moment as the other three came closer. Each man shook Zeke's hand as she introduced him.

"This is Robert Higgins. He works with me for Taylor Mines."

Zeke guessed Higgins to be no more than thirty, and he could see the man had an eye for Georgeanne. There was an extra firm grip to his handshake, as though to warn Zeke about something. Zeke gripped back, thinking how easily he could break this slender, fancy man in half. Higgins was good looking, and his pale complexion was ruddy from the Colorado sun. His blue eyes showed a slight cockiness. "Georgeanne says she knew you when she was younger and lived on a ranch in southeast Colorado," he said. "Her father's ranch neighbored yours."

"Yes," Zeke answered, glancing at Georgeanne again. What memories! He still remembered the taste of her kiss, the softness of her breast. She blushed, and he knew she was remembering the same things. He looked back at Higgins. "We were childhood friends," he added, trying to allay any thoughts that there had been something more between them. He had no idea how these men might feel about such a thing, or if Georgeanne wanted them to know the whole truth.

She then introduced him to the other two, James Dillingham and Albert Moser, both older men who were apparently married, as they wore wedding bands. Dillingham was a professor at the University of Michigan, and Moser worked as a consultant for various mining companies.

"You have a fine piece of property here, Mr. Brown," Dillingham told Zeke. "I can see it's been a lot of work for you, getting rid of all the stumps."

"That was the only way I could afford it. The government figures a lot of people don't want land after all the trees have been logged out of it, considering the work that leaves for someone else. In some areas I've left the regrowth alone. I want the pines to come back on the hillsides to prevent erosion. Personally, I disagree with cutting down every tree in one big area like this. I think it's a sin against nature to completely strip a forest." He told himself to be careful. He was tempted to call it a "white man's folly," but it might be best if these men didn't know he was part Indian. Haydon Seger had warned him to be careful about that if he wanted to own land. He'd made sure he talked to the right land agent, but that man had been replaced, so Zeke now kept a low profile with his neighbors and the new land agent.

"I think it's a shame, too," Dillingham answered.

Zeke liked the concern in the man's blue eyes. He was very distinguished, with gray hair and mustache, his suit a fine cut.

"We're working with Washington, trying to get laws passed to prevent forest stripping," Dillingham continued, "but you know how it is. When there's a dollar to be made, nothing else seems to matter. I swear we could all learn some lessons from the Indians if we'd stop to listen to them, but people think I'm crazy when I talk like that. The Indians believed in preserving the trees and the animals and such. I don't understand it all, but I figured out enough to know that savage as they were, they certainly did love Mother Earth."

Zeke glanced at Georgeanne, and Robert Higgins did not miss the odd look he gave her. "Yes, they did," he answered, turning to Dillingham again. "I'm glad to know someone agrees with me."

"Well, good luck with developing your ranch here," Dillingham answered, shaking his hand once more. "Miss Temple insisted we stop by so she could see if you were the same person she knew a while back. How long ago was that?"

Zeke looked at Georgeanne. "About ten years, I think," he lied. It had been only six. If they knew that, these men would realize they were not "childhood" friends, and they might make something more of their acquaintance. "Isn't that right?"

He saw the quick confusion in Georgeanne's eyes before she understood what he was doing. "More like twelve," she answered. "I wasn't sure I'd recognize you, Zeke."

He smiled. God, she was beautiful! If they were alone, he was sure she'd allow his embrace. There was so much to tell her, so much to apologize for, so much to explain. He wanted to know everything she'd done these past six years, where she'd been . . . if there was a man in her life. He could hardly believe that on seeing her again, those six years were instantly wiped away. He felt he could just take up where they'd left off. He wanted to tell her he still loved her, that no one had been able to fill that void in his life.

"We'd best get going," Higgins said. "We're expected in Masonville."

Zeke experienced a sudden panic. She couldn't leave like this. "Where do you live now, Georgeanne?"

"In Colorado Springs, at a rooming house there. I came up here for a seminar in Fort Collins. We'll be at Masonville for a while, and it isn't far. Perhaps you could come there if you can find the time. I don't work on Sundays." She waved her arm. "Look at us! Zeke, we don't dress this way when we work. We wear very different clothes for that, and we get very dirty! I love the work. Do come and see what we do! Just check at the Masonville Inn first. Not many women are allowed to have any kind of career in this country, you know, but out here women have much more freedom than they do back East. At first the university's dean didn't want to let me study geology, but I was not about to take no for an answer. So, here I am! Will you come to Masonville?"

He nodded. "I'll try." He could tell she felt the same

as he—so much to talk about—and he needed to feel his arms around her again.

"We'll be there for about six weeks," she said, climbing back into the carriage. "I'm so glad I found you, Zeke, and so glad you have a piece of land for yourself."

"Let's be off," Higgins told the driver, obviously anxious to get her away from Zeke, who watched them leave, feeling stunned and slightly bewildered. Georgeanne had blown back into his life like a sudden spring wind. It was incredible, wonderful. Still, although she didn't really seem any different, she had surely changed after having attended a university and getting a degree, meeting important people, having a career. Somehow it did not surprise him to see her stubbornly going against what society normally expected of a properly bred young woman.

He grinned. Always a little rebellious and extraordinary. That was Georgeanne Temple. She waved as the carriage rolled away, and he waved back, watching until the equipage was out of sight. He sat down on a rock, shaking his head.

"I'll be damned," he muttered. "A geologist." Would he be crazy to go to Masonville and see her again? Risk a return of all those old feelings? Hell, they'd already come back. He told himself to be careful. He *had* to see her again, simply out of friendship, and because so much had been left unsaid. It sure wasn't likely, after what she'd accomplished these last six years, that she would still be interested in him, not in a struggling rancher with little to offer. He would have to put aside the old longings and just see her as a friend. The trouble was, she was more beautiful even than he'd remembered.

* * *

Jeremy stood up in front of the gathering of Denver's high society, men and women who had paid fifty dollars a plate to attend the fund-raiser for another orphanage Abbie wanted built for the growing number of children who lived on the streets of Denver. The dinner was held in the banquet room of the Queen City Hotel, owned by Jeremy himself.

Jeremy had never felt so fulfilled. The frustration and guilt over the years he'd abandoned his family and denied his Indian heritage had finally left him. Iris was happy with her husband and family, and in spite of looking Indian and being married to a Mexican, she had been accepted by many of those in the sea of faces before him. She was here tonight, sitting at the head table.

Denver's elite were determined to prove their city was as advanced and civilized and modern as any city back East, with theaters and parks and a gold-domed capitol building. Most did not like to admit Denver had problems with the poor, the bulk of whom were now immigrants out of work. They did not care to own up to the fact that their city was not perfect, and it was easier to ignore those in need than face reality and help them.

Abigail Monroe was also determined, determined to change the policy of "looking the other way." She had begun an effort to open people's eyes. Leave it to her, a woman who knew no fear, to not be intimidated by Denver's most prestigious. Abigail Monroe was a woman who had faced Crow Indians with a rifle, who had suffered an arrow wound, watched her whole family die on the trail West. She was a true founder of Colorado, made of much more courage and grit than any of the other women present. He was proud of her efforts, in spite of some of the whispers about his mother being married to a half-breed man, then to a full-blood Cheyenne. He no longer cared that others knew he had Indian blood, or that he and Mary had lost a few friends because of it. Nor did he doubt that some of those who remained friends did so only because of his own wealth and his status with the railroad.

He'd come too far to let such things bother him. What was important was that he'd been able to help Wolf's Blood by raising his son and daughter. Hawk would graduate from Harvard next year, and he planned to return to Denver to practice law. Joshua had started his novel about Abbie's life. The excerpts in the *Rocky Mountain News* had brought a few more of Denver's "finest" around to Abbie's side, mostly out of curiosity over this fiercely determined and bold pioneer woman. He could not help smiling at what Zeke Monroe would think of his Abbie-girl right now, dressed elegantly tonight, looking as though she truly belonged with this circle of rich folk . . . a woman who had lived among the Indians for years, then in a simple log cabin on the Colorado plains. She had raised a great deal of money for the orphanage, opened a lot of eyes to Denver's worst problems. He supposed if his mother could conquer a man like Cheyenne Zeke at fifteen years of age, she could certainly have her way with these soft-handed people at sixty-three; twice widowed but still fighting for what she believed was right.

"I am now proud to introduce to you a true Colorado pioneer," he said aloud. "This woman came West from Tennessee close to fifty years ago and lost her entire family on the way. She ended up marrying the scout for the wagon train, a man who was half Cheyenne. His name was Lone Eagle, his white name, Zeke Monroe . . . and he was—" He stopped and swallowed, suddenly overwhelmed with how much he missed his father, how dearly he would like to be able to embrace him once more. "He was my father. And so I introduce to you my mother, Abigail Monroe, who is the reason for this benefit. She has worked diligently to have another orphanage built for Denver's homeless children, and I hope all of you realize we have to work together to create programs to help our poor." He turned to Abbie. "Mother, please say a few words to these people."

He put out his hand, and Abbie took it, looking at him proudly. She rose, and everyone in the room applauded her, some of them rising in her honor. It was an amazing moment for Abbie; so many memories flashed through her mind. If Zeke could see her now, wouldn't he have a big grin on his face? She could almost see him standing at the back of the room, in buckskins, his big knife in its sheath at his waist, ready to set straight anyone who might think to insult her.

She set her notes in front of her, as another man came to mind. He was buried in a mass grave at Wounded Knee, never to hold her again. Such a shameful way for such a man to be buried. He should be high on a scaffold in the mountains . . . with his half brother, Zeke. Pushing aside the memories, she began her speech about some of the sorry conditions she had personally witnessed in the poorer districts of Denver, and she warned that those in power must do something about problems that would not go away by ignoring them, or, as some had tried to do, by giving the poor a change of clothes and a ticket out of town.

"It took great courage to settle this land," she told them, "and now it will take courage to face the problems we have created with that settlement. This is a land that has grown too fast for its own good, a settlement that has destroyed one class of people, our Native Americans, and yet created another class of people that still cannot cope with this sudden growth. Settlers ignored the Indians, killed them, pushed them off the land into little corners of the country to be forgotten—and still there is a great problem with the Indian situation." She thought about Wolf's Blood, her precious son, gone so long now. "Just as that problem has not gone away, neither will this new one with the poor of our city, men—and their women—who came here to help build the railroads and to work in the mines, enterprises which made many of you wealthy. Now they are jobless, and we try to sweep them under a rug and pretend they are not here. But they *are* and we must do what we can, as Christians and as those who run this city, to help others not as fortunate as we are."

Jeremy watched her lovingly. Her thick, auburn hair had turned mostly gray since Swift Arrow was killed, but she was still a tiny woman, and the hint of the beauty she'd been for so many years was still there. Sometimes, when her eyes twinkled just so, he could imagine how she'd looked at fifteen when she'd chased after Zeke Monroe. How one woman could survive what she had was beyond imagination, and he realized now that in spite of how strong and wild and skilled Zeke Monroe had been, his real strength had come from this small woman who still carried the family on her shoulders.

He could see people were enraptured by her talk. When she finished she received a standing ovation . . . his pioneer mother who had lived such a simple, rugged life, standing before Denver's elite, fully accepted in a society totally foreign to her. But then Abigail Monroe had a way of adapting to any situation, if it meant helping her family or helping someone she considered less fortunate than she.

She deserved this acclamation. He glanced down the table at Joshua, who well knew what it was like to be the recipient of this woman's love. She had suffered and nearly died at the hands of a man who wanted to find and kill Joshua when he was a boy. He was not

even her own son, yet she had refused to tell where
he was. Joshua, too, stood and applauded, tears in his
eyes. Denver's society had a long way to go to match
the courage of those who had come before them. He
wished the whole family could be here, but all of them
were carrying on their lives with just as much bravery
as the mother and grandmother who had helped them
get this far.

Sixteen

Zeke headed Indian up the slope toward the spot where an old prospector had told him "them fancy-nosed geologists" were exploring the side of a mountain. He dismounted, worried that Indian, getting old for a horse, would become too winded from such a steep climb. It had taken three hours to get this far, along a winding switchback trail that snaked its way nearly to the treeline of the mountain, where the prospector had also said there was, "a good fishin' lake."

He had to grin at the memory of the conversation, the prospector a stark contrast to today's miners with their modern methods. He'd thought about doing some prospecting himself, but he'd been too busy with more practical things, and he didn't have the money to properly mine a find even if he did discover gold. He knew most prospectors, like the one he'd met in Masonville, were long broke, having sold their claims for far less than their worth to mining companies who then came in and made millions.

Zeke reached the lake, where the water was a deep blue and the entire perimeter was surrounded by boulders and pine trees. It was a peaceful, pristine scene that invigorated him. Everything up here was clean and clear and seemingly untouched. An old man sat on a rock with a cane pole, quietly fishing, and Zeke asked him where the geologists were digging. The man

pointed to the side of a mountain that rose straight
up, just to the west of the lake. "Through those trees
there and past that first big hill of rocks. They're on
the other side."

Zeke thanked him and led Indian along a pathway
around the edge of the lake to the huge mound of
piled boulders. He tied Indian, then hesitated. Was he
crazy to be doing this? He walked around the boulders
to see five men and a woman working along the base
of a mountain that jutted upward hundreds of feet
higher than he had just climbed. Its face was much
too steep for anyone to scale, but it sloped just enough
at the bottom for Georgeanne and the others to dig
into it.

Zeke did not recognize two of the men, and guessed
they were only there as guides. "No public allowed
here, mister," one of them told him.

"I'm not public. I'm just here to see one of the geologists," Zeke answered.

Higgins spotted Zeke when he heard the voices. He
left his dig and approached him. "Mr. Brown." He
nodded, irritation obvious in his eyes. "If you're here
to see Georgeanne, she is very busy right now. She's—"

"Zeke!" Georgeanne spotted him then. "Come over
here!"

Zeke couldn't help giving Robert Higgins a wry grin.
"I guess she's not too busy to see an old friend." He
watched the jealousy flare in Higgins's eyes. "A *friend*,"
he repeated, leaning a little closer when he said it. He
couldn't help enjoying the fact that he towered over
Higgins and was half again as wide in the shoulders.
He walked past him to where Georgeanne was working, wanting to laugh at seeing the dirt on her cheek
and the rumpled, wide-brimmed canvas hat she wore.
The knees of her split skirt were filthy, her leather
boots were badly scuffed. She wore a pair of scraped-up

leather gloves, and her hair was pulled straight back and tied with a ribbon at her nape. She wore no makeup of any kind, and he was struck by how pretty she was even when she was as plain as could be.

"You came!" she exclaimed. "I'm so glad! Did you have any trouble finding us?"

"Not really. Why isn't the public allowed?"

"Oh, they might step on something wrong or walk around and inadvertently destroy objects we've already dug up. You have to be very careful with things like this. Old skeletons can fall apart from being suddenly exposed or handled wrong, things like that." She looked him over. "Well, I guess it's the reverse today. You're the one looking clean and handsome, and I'm the one who's a mess."

"I figured I'd catch you hard at work—like you caught me last week," he teased. Why *was* he here? He knew damn well it wouldn't take much to want her again, get involved again. He should have stayed at the ranch and gotten his own work done.

She laughed, looking down at herself. "Well, now you've seen me at my worst."

You could never be anything but beautiful, he thought. "So show me what you're doing," he said aloud.

My God, you are absolutely the most handsome man who ever walked. She wanted to tell him so. The years had only enhanced his dark good looks and virile physique. Why had she invited him here? She knew good and well it only took the sight of him to bring back all the old desires, but there was so much to talk about, so much to explain. "That gentleman over there, the one you spoke to coming in, he's the one who found the fish skeleton. We've found more. See?" She knelt down, pointing to a neat, square dig. On one side of it he could see a fish skeleton beginning to appear. She gently brushed away some dirt, exposing more of it. "You have to be very, very careful at these digs. Sometimes we spend days or even weeks or months exposing an animal's bones, because it has to be done so gently, with brushes and such, so that nothing gets broken or mixed up. You can't go into things like this with a shovel, or you'd destroy something valuable."

Zeke knelt closer, studying the skeleton. "I'll be dammed."

"It's wonderful, fascinating work, Zeke. I love it. Finding things like this makes me feel so small. It makes me realize that one human's lifetime is like a breath of wind, so short compared to the millions of years this earth has been forming, and makes me aware of how foolish we are to waste what little time we have."

He met her eyes, their faces close. "I suppose," he answered.

"I'm going back to town tonight for the weekend. Men will stay here and guard the dig. Robert and the others decided to camp here. Will you come back down to Masonville? Stay the weekend there so we can talk?"

How could he refuse? "I'd planned on it, if it worked out all right for you. In fact, I'll watch the dig today and take you back down myself."

She smiled. "I'd like that."

He was sorely tempted to lean closer and kiss her. "You look pretty this way."

She blushed. "I look terrible!"

"I don't think that's possible," he told her. "But I do hope you'll wear a decent dress tonight when I take you to dinner."

She laughed again. "I'll try not to embarrass you."

He grinned, loving the sincerity in her brown eyes, eyes that reminded him of Grandma Abbie's. Everything she was feeling was written right there to see.

He lowered his voice then for his next remark. "What about Higgins? He seems a little possessive of you. Are you two . . . you know . . . seeing each other? Is this going to cause trouble?"

She scowled. "No. He'd like to *think* there is something between us, but there isn't. We're close friends with a mutual love for our work, and we've had to work closely the last year or so. He's taken me out to eat a few times, but that's all there is to it. He has voiced an interest in more, but I have never given him reason to believe there could be. As a matter of fact, I've told him on several occasions I have no interest in any man right now—just in my work." She saw a hint of disappointment and questioning in his eyes. "You aren't just any man, Zeke. You're different."

He sighed. "And I'm probably crazy."

She smiled again. "Probably." She sat down next to her dig. "Do you realize that we've dug up dinosaurs in Nebraska?"

"Dinosaurs? I don't know much about things like that, except that they were huge creatures; some ate plants and others ate meat."

"There are many different kinds, Zeke. I have a book about them I'll show you. And yes, they were gigantic monsters compared to the biggest buffalo or even to an elephant. They were here long before any of your Indian ancestors, and no one knows why they're extinct now, what it was that killed them off. It might have been a tremendous volcanic eruption that spread ash over the entire western half of the continent; or it might have been an earthquake, or a sudden change in climate. Now the winters in the Dakotas are bitterly cold, but we believe at one time this whole area, including Montana, was tropical. Then the glaciers came down from the north, scraping out canyons and rivers, leaving lakes in the low spots when they finally melted away again. The earth is ever changing, Zeke. It will change even more. Nothing is guaranteed. This work has made me realize how important each hour of each day is."

He nodded. "You sound like my grandmother."

She smiled. "I have to get busy right now. You can watch all of us, and if you get bored, you can walk around the lake. It's beautiful, so peaceful and quiet up here, isn't it?"

He stood up. "It sure is. I think I'll take that walk first and then come back here and watch for a while. When will you leave?"

"By three o'clock. Otherwise we won't get back down to Masonville before dark."

He tipped his hat. "Whatever you say, Miss Temple."

She kept her smile, but her eyes suddenly brimmed with tears. "I'm so glad you came, so glad we'll get the chance to talk. You've been on my mind ever since finding you a week ago." She sobered, standing up to face him. "Zeke, I never knew the truth of what my father did to you. He lied to me. I didn't know until I went to see your parents, but you had already left home. I'm so sorry for what happened. I cried for a week after I found out. I told my father exactly what I thought of him, and then I left. I went to my grandparents in Pennsylvania, my mother's parents. Father kept sending money, begging me to come back, telling me he needed me, that he was lonely; but I've never gone back. I used his money to go to the University of Michigan, and I told him the reason I wasn't coming back was because of school. I still haven't been back to see him. I can't stand the thought of what he did to you. He has no idea I've found you again, and I don't intend to tell him. Has he left your parents alone?"

He nodded. "He has, so far. They have a deed to

the land documented by an attorney in Denver. And my uncle, Jeremy, sent him a threatening letter, telling him if my folks had any more trouble he'd send a Federal Marshal. Ever since I left your father has minded his own business, other than buying up everything he can all around our place. I only know all that through letters from my mother. I've never been back myself."

She sighed. "I'm sorry. I know you were close to your family. They must miss you." She studied him closer, seeing the faint scar on his right cheek. "Is that scar from . . . ?"

He nodded. "I've got more on my chest and back, some on my arms."

She blinked back tears.

"Don't worry about it. Although I haven't gotten over a need for revenge, which is part of the reason I stay away. If I ever see your father's face, I'm afraid of what I might do to him, so I just stay away altogether. It's actually been good for me. I have something of my own now." He touched her arm. "Don't be blaming yourself. Finish your work here and we'll talk more tonight."

She nodded, quickly wiping at her eyes. "Thank you."

Zeke left her, stopping near Higgins on the way. The man had been staring at him and Georgeanne the whole time they talked. "I'll take her back to Masonville myself this afternoon," he told Higgins. "That way your guides can stay here and protect the place at night."

Higgins looked him over. "Fine. I trust you will be a gentleman."

Zeke couldn't help a snicker. "I'll try to control myself."

Higgins stiffened. "I am only looking out for her well-being. I have come to admire and respect Georgeanne a great deal."

Zeke grasped his shoulder, giving it a squeeze to remind the man that even if he were to bring Georgeanne harm, Higgins could do little about it. "I also admire and respect her. And I've known her a hell of a lot longer than you have. I told you she was a friend, so quit worrying. She'll be fine."

Higgins held his chin high, clearing his throat and trying to appear unimpressed. "I hope so. I suppose I should thank you for taking her back for us."

"I suppose you should." Zeke tipped his hat and left them. Already the old fire was creeping through his blood at the thought of being alone with Georgeanne that night, and this time free of the worry of being found out by his parents or her father. Never had they had such freedom to just be with each other. But then, it had been six years. He still could not be positive she felt the same way about him. She'd said she wanted to talk. Maybe that was all she wanted, but he already wanted much more.

Zeke felt awkward in a suit, but he wanted to look his best for this woman he'd loved since he was eighteen, this woman who had never seen him in anything but denim pants and dusty boots. There really was no place fancy to eat in Masonville, so they'd had to settle for the only restaurant in town, a small place where food was served on plain white plates by a woman with stains on the front of her dress.

"I wish I could do better by you," Zeke told Georgeanne, a little nervous for the first time since he'd picked her up at the rooming house where she stayed. "There isn't a place to take a real lady in this little town."

Georgeanne looked him over, realizing why he'd worn the suit. He looked wonderful in it. "It doesn't matter. All that matters is we're together at last. I enjoyed being able to talk on our trip down the mountain, learn about your dreams. I'm glad your family is well."

Her brown eyes were accented with a little color on the lids, her rosy cheeks a bit pinker with rouge, her full lips kissable and glowing with lip color. He liked the way she had of dressing and wearing cosmetics in such a subtle way that they only made her more beautiful, not cheap looking like some women. Her yellow checkered dress fit her perfectly, falling straight in front in apronlike layers, full at the back. Against the chilly mountain night air she'd worn a soft, yellow, knitted shawl, and a yellow ribbon was wound through the long auburn tresses piled on top of her head with combs. It struck him again how educated and refined Georgeanne Temple was, well traveled, working at a job unusual for a woman but daring enough and intelligent enough to do so anyway.

Was he worthy of such a woman? He had no higher learning, nothing to offer her but a struggling ranch with a dilapidated one-room cabin. "I bought this suit in Fort Collins, figured I'd need it. I didn't stop to think what a small mountain town Masonville was. The way I live, by the time I need another suit, this one will be outdated."

He smiled nervously, and Georgeanne reached out to cover one of his hands with her own. "It's a very handsome suit, Zeke. You made a good choice. But you didn't need to wear it just for me. You know me better than that."

He watched her eyes. "I couldn't be sure—not after six years and all that college education you have."

She smiled. "Education is just that—an education. It doesn't have to change a person. I'm the same Georgeanne you knew six years ago, only more mature, more sure of what I want, just as I'm certain you are. You

have so many admirable traits, Zeke, such strength and
determination. Education isn't everything."

She let go of his hand when the waitress brought
them plates of steak and potatoes, little bowls of corn
and hot coffee.

"Enjoy," the woman said, turning away.

Georgeanne looked down at the food and giggled.
"Mine looks ready to get up off the plate and kick
me." She glanced at his steak. "Yours is cooked more.
Would you rather have it a bit rarer?"

"Sure would."

They traded plates, but Georgeanne ate only a couple
of bites before putting down her fork. "Zeke, I can't
eat. Every time I think of what father did to you—"

"That's not your fault, I told you. It happened, and
it's over."

"It's his fault we lost so many years." She met his
eyes. "Surely after six years you've met some woman
you're interested in. That's all right. I'll understand.
You can tell me, Zeke."

"Why? Because *you've* met someone else? Are you
more serious about Higgins than you let on?"

"No! I've been courted by three different men, Zeke,
but none of them lasted, and not one of them made
me feel"—she blushed and looked down at her plate—
"like you used to make me feel."

"Used to?"

"You know what I mean." She closed her eyes and
sighed. "You still make me feel that way. And you
haven't answered my first question."

"About a woman?" He cut into his steak. "No.
There's no woman. First, I just had to find my own
way; then I worked hard for a logger. Oh, there were
women who followed the logging camps—the kind a
man stays away from if he has any common sense."
He put the steak into his mouth, watching her blush,

and enjoying the hint of jealousy in her eyes. "I had common sense," he added.

She grinned then, still blushing but looking relieved.

He chewed and swallowed the steak. "But I lost it in a tavern in Fort Collins a couple of times."

She frowned. "Lost what?"

"My common sense."

Her eyes widened then, and the jealousy returned. "I see." She looked back down at her plate.

"A man can take only so much neglect, Georgie." He found it so easy to use her nickname again. "It was just a woman who didn't mind being there for lonely men like me, and it only happened a couple of times. I haven't even been back there for a year." He cut another piece of steak. "I don't even know why it matters, unless . . ." He stopped cutting. "Look at me, Georgie."

She met his eyes, looking confused and ready to cry.

"Are you saying you think we can pick up where we left off six years ago?"

She studied his dark eyes, his handsomeness. He was so much more mature now, so sure. "I was hoping—"

"So was I. Why do you think I asked you about seeing other men?"

She took a deep breath, as though greatly relieved. "I don't feel any different, Zeke. I wanted so badly to find you again, to be able to talk to you this way, apologize for what my father did, tell you I . . . I never stopped loving you. Is that terribly bold, after not seeing you for six years?"

He put down his fork. "Not if it's true. I feel the same way."

She smiled again. "I'm glad." She drank some coffee. "Tell me about your family. How is your grandmother?"

"She's fine—living in Denver with my uncle Jeremy.

My aunt, LeeAnn, lives there, too, with her husband. He's a reporter for the *Rocky Mountain News*. Did you hear about my uncle? Wolf's Blood?"

"No. I left home not long after I spoke with your parents."

"After the reunion, on his way home with his white wife, some men caused some trouble up in Cheyenne. There was an accidental shooting, and Jennifer was killed. My uncle, well, he's mostly Indian, in the old sense. He reverted to his old ways without thinking—turned and killed the man who shot his wife, then killed two other men with him."

Georgeanne gasped. "That's terrible! Is he in trouble? Was he arrested?"

"He managed to get away, but he's a wanted man now, lives somewhere in Canada. His kids, my cousins, Iris and Hawk, went to live with my uncle Jeremy. Iris is married now, and Hawk is in law school, so we're going to have a lawyer in the family."

She leaned back in her chair. "I'm glad. And I'm glad your uncle got away. That must have been terrible for your grandmother, and for his children."

Zeke nodded. "Grandma is handling it okay now. On top of that, her second husband, my great-uncle, Swift Arrow, was killed at Wounded Knee."

"I *did* hear about Wounded Knee. The whole country heard about it."

A deep bitterness came into his eyes. "They thought it was a great battle, I suppose, a wonderful victory for the army. Most people don't know the real truth, but we'll talk about that another time. No more talk of sad things. My brother—Nathan—is married. I haven't met his wife yet, but I'm happy for him. And my little brother, Lance, he's eleven years old already. Oh, and my grandma is working to raise funds to build another orphanage in Denver. There's a lot of unemployment there now, what with the silver crash. A lot of needy families, and most of them are immigrants with no relatives here. If something happens to the parents, the kids turn to the streets."

"Yes, I stayed in Denver for a while. I read articles in the paper about that. If I had known your grandmother was there, I would have gone to see her. I always wanted to meet her."

He pushed his plate aside. No more hungry for the greasy steak than she was, he rested his arms on the table and leaned forward. "Well, maybe you'll get that chance, if we don't lose track of each other again."

She shivered with joy and relief at having found him again. "I don't intend to ever lose track of you again, Zeke Brown. God surely meant for this to happen. And out here, my father will never know we're together. He doesn't need to know. If God helped us find each other, then there must be a way we can work out that part of it."

"What about your work? Looks to me like it takes you all over the country."

"I'd give it up if I had to."

"You love it."

"I also love you."

The words momentarily stunned him. It seemed incredible they could so quickly fall back into those old feelings. "Think about what you're saying, Georgie."

"I've thought about it for six years, dreamed about being able to tell you in person."

He slowly nodded. "I love you, too." He stood up. "Let's get out of here. He walked over and paid a surprised waitress for the uneaten food, took Georgeanne's arm and led her out. "If you get hungry later, you tell me. We'll come back."

She did not reply. She only knew what had to be. As soon as they were out the door he pulled her into an alley and swept her into his arms, crushing her against his powerful chest, his lips meeting hers in a fiery kiss that left her breathless. She threw her arms around his neck, returning the kiss with equal hunger. How wonderful it tasted! How glorious it felt to be held in these strong arms again, to feel his hard body pressing urgently against her, to be with her Zeke again!

"I'm camped outside of town," he groaned. "All I have is a tent."

"That's good enough for me." They continued kissing hungrily throughout the conversation.

"You deserve better, a fancy hotel room or something."

"It doesn't matter." She gasped. "I've waited six years for this. I've never taken another man, Zeke."

Those were the only words he needed to hear.

Seventeen

There was no stopping what had to be. Georgeanne had not one doubt that what she was doing was right. She soon found herself inside Zeke's tent, and without question or conversation, deep kisses led to a tumble against a thick bed of blankets. Georgeanne, her clothes coming off, enjoyed the ecstasy of Zeke's big hands touching the part of her revealed as each item was removed.

How many nights had she tried to imagine what it would have been like if they could have stayed together? He cupped her breasts so gently, tasted of their fruits, and she gladly offered herself to satisfy that hunger, straining against him eagerly.

She was hardly aware he'd taken off his own clothes until he moved his powerful, naked body against her own, hot skin against hot skin. There was a power about him that made her weak, made her want to give herself to him without reservation; and when his fingers trailed over her flat belly to that private place no man had ever touched, she almost wept from the joy of it.

His fingers explored, moving in little circles, touching her magically, making her ache to have a man inside her. He smothered her with kisses while he caressed secret places until she felt the most wonderful sensation throughout her entire body, a deep pulsating that made her cry out his name and press against him for something more, something to satisfy this terrible hunger to be a woman.

Zeke seemed to be everywhere at once, her lips, her throat, her breasts, her belly; kissing her lovenest so that her desire was almost painful. In the next moment his magnificent body hovered over hers, and he used his knees to push her legs apart. She knew then what would happen, and she welcomed it. How long had she wanted only this man to make a woman of her?

"It's going to hurt," he whispered. "That's what I've always heard. Don't be afraid, Georgie."

"I'm not . . . as long as it's you."

She gasped when he filled her with his hard shaft. The tearing pain was almost unbearable at first, but still she had no doubts. She had waited . . . for this one man. This was right, and she had no doubt the act of love could be quite delightful once the initial pain of it was done. How could it not be wonderful with a man like Zeke?

She became lost in him then, and he in her. He moved in quick rhythm, groaning in his own pleasure. She leaned up and kissed his chest, dug her fingers into the hard muscles of his upper arms, gasping for breath from both ecstasy and pain. She felt the surge then, knew it was his life pouring into her. She didn't even care if that life took hold. Zeke Brown would never leave her now. They would marry. It was understood. And she would live in whatever way was necessary in order to be with him. Her father needn't know for now. But someday . . . someday he would discover his cruel efforts at keeping her from Zeke had failed. Zeke Brown was ten times the man her blustery, braggart of a father thought him. And he would never treat her as her mother had been treated.

Zeke let out a deep gasp with one last thrust, then relaxed on top of her.

"I can't breathe," she whispered.

Zeke moved off her chest, but kept her in his arms. It was dark inside the tent, as he had not wanted to cast shadows with a lantern. "I wish I could see you better," he told her.

"This is enough for now," she said softly.

He kissed her hair, now atumble. "Did I hurt you bad?"

"I'm not even sure."

"I'll get us a pan of water and we can wash. Will you sleep here with me tonight?"

"I was hoping you'd ask."

"I'm sorry this is all so crude."

"I told you it doesn't matter."

He rolled her against him, running a big hand over her bare bottom. "God, I love you, Georgie. I can't believe this."

"I feel the same way. We might as well find a preacher."

"Might as well. What will Higgins think of this, and the other men you work with?"

"I don't care what they think."

"What about the dig?"

"We have all weekend. We can get married and be together like this until Monday. I'll go back up to the dig then and finish with the skeleton I'm working on, and you can go back to your ranch. I know you need to be there. I'll be finished within a week or so. Then I will announce I have to quit for the time being because we are married."

"Georgie, you love that work. I'm afraid you won't be happy on the ranch."

"We'll take one thing at a time. As long as we're together, it doesn't matter."

"You're sure?"

She laughed lightly. "I just gave myself to you in the most intimate way a woman can show a man she loves him. What more proof do you need?"

He found her mouth again, kissed her deeply. "I don't know," he finally answered. "I just find this all so hard to believe. What about your father?"

"What he doesn't know won't hurt him for now. We probably shouldn't even tell your parents. We'll figure all that out eventually. All I know is I love you, and I want to wake up to you in the morning, make love again. Sometime tomorrow I'll get dressed, and go to my boarding house and clean up and change. Then we'll find a preacher. There's a little church in this town, so there must be a preacher."

He sighed. "You're used to a pretty fancy life, Georgie, with rich, educated friends."

"And I've been around people like that long enough to know how shallow they can be. You're far above them, Zeke. Stop judging yourself by your heritage and how much money you have. And stop judging *me* by the same standards." She kissed his cheek, realizing that in the darkness she could not see the scars left by her brutal father's act of violence. "And just think . . . just think, Zeke. Someday, if we handle this right—if father doesn't know I've married you—I will inherit all that he has . . . all that land. Just think about it. Maybe I can talk him into giving me a good share of it before he dies. What better vengeance than for him to discover that you, Zeke Brown, own most of the Temple ranch by way of marriage to me?"

He remained quiet for a moment. "I never even thought about that."

She smiled. "That's what I love about you. You just love me, not my money or what you might gain."

He sighed. "No matter. When your father discovers the truth, he'll disinherit you anyway."

"Let's just think about you and me for now. This is the first chance we've had to do that. In another week or so I'll come by the ranch on the way back and I'll stay there, as Mrs. Zeke Brown."

He kissed her again. "I love you, Georgeanne Temple. I am a happy man again."

She nestled against him. "I'm happy, too, Zeke. This is all I've really wanted since we lay together in that grove of pines before my father came and tore me away from you. Nothing is ever again going to separate us. God means for us to be together, or He never would have let me find you again."

He kissed her hair, her eyes, her mouth. Neither of them wanted to think any more about an unknown future. This was the present, and she was here in his arms. She would stay until sunrise, and they'd damn well find a way to share *all* their sunrises.

"I can't believe she's done this!" Robert Higgins fumed. "Gone and left the dig! Gone off with that . . . that man she hasn't seen in years and married him—just like that! It's preposterous!"

"He seems like a nice enough fellow, a hard worker," James Dillingham said as he brushed dirt from his pants. "There was never anything serious between you and Miss Temple that I noticed. She's a grown woman who has made a choice to marry and settle. What's so unusual about that?"

"She's born to better things than a dirt-poor rancher who owns land that will be worthless for some time to come!"

Dillingham chuckled. "You're just jealous, Higgins. She's in love and she got married. Personally, I liked her very much, but it bothered me a little, working with a woman. She's where she belongs now."

Higgins waved him off. "Georgeanne isn't like other women, and you know it. She won't be happy with that man in the long run. She'll miss her work, and she'll miss the luxury she's accustomed to. She mentioned to me once that she has a trust fund she can draw money from, in Denver. That's probably why he married her, for her money! He probably figures he'll get her father's ranch one day. Well, he'll find out he won't!"

Dillingham frowned. "How is that? You don't even know her father."

"Well, I intend to *get* to know him! I know where his ranch is—somewhere east of Pueblo. I intend to find the man and let him know what has happened! Maybe *he* can find a way to put a stop to this before the woman ends up pregnant and poor!"

"You'd best stay out of it," Albert Moser put in. "The whole thing is none of your business. They are adults, and Miss Temple, or rather, Mrs. Brown, seemed very happy when she left here. Why try to mess things up for her?"

"Because she's lost her mind!" Higgins answered. "And I don't like his looks!"

"His *looks?*" Dillingham laughed. "He's one of the best-looking young men I've ever seen."

"He's too dark! He's got Indian blood or something like that, maybe Mexican."

"So what? Half the people out West have Indian or Mexican blood. It's a different country out here," Moser told the man. "People live by different standards. Even the women do. Seems like out here the women are more independent, stronger. I've heard tell some single women have come West and settled under the Homestead Act. I've grown to like it out here myself, thinking of bringing out the wife."

Higgins waved him off in irritation. "The fact remains Georgeanne Temple has done a foolish thing, something she's going to regret one day, mark my words. And I believe her father would want to know about this. She's been estranged from him for a long time, but she never told me why. I'm beginning to think it had something to do with Zeke Brown. I intend to find the man and learn for myself what the trouble was, find out what he thinks about his daughter getting married behind his back!"

"If you really care about her, you'd leave it alone," Moser warned.

"I care about her enough *not* to leave it alone!"

Moser sighed, looking at Dillingham. "All I care about is finishing this dig. That's going to take a few more weeks." He looked back at Higgins. "Will you at least finish this with us before you go gallivanting off to find her father?"

"It might be too late to do anything about it then."

"You'll finish this dig with us, or I'll report you to Taylor Mining and get you fired! Taylor is paying you well for this, that I know. We've lost Georgeanne, so we need you here with us! Are you willing to give up your job and the money over this?"

Robert sighed, turning away to think for a moment. "I'll stay," he said, kicking at a rock.

"Good!" Moser replied.

"Just as I thought," Dillingham muttered. He liked Georgeanne. He hoped that after the passage of a little time Robert would forget about all this and stay out of her business.

Georgeanne took a stagecoach back down from Masonville, since the other men would need the company carriage. She had more belongings at a rooming house in Fort Collins, but she would get those later. All she cared about now was seeing Zeke again.

She looked down at the plain gold wedding band on her hand. It was all they had been able to find in Masonville. Zeke had promised a much nicer ring as soon as he was able to afford one. He'd refused her offer to use some funds from her trust account in a Denver bank, too proud to "live off" his wife. That was part of what she loved about him, that he truly had not even considered inheriting her father's ranch. As far as the trust money went, she decided that she would eventually be able to convince him there was nothing wrong with using it to help build the ranch.

Things would be hard for a while, but she was prepared. She had waited for this man for six years, and she would do whatever was necessary to keep him. Recognizing his stump-filled land then, she put her head out the window and shouted to the driver. "Stop here!" The coach came to a halt, and she climbed out. As the driver handed down her three carpetbags, already she could see Zeke riding toward her. He must have been waiting all day, watching for her to come!

"Thank you!" she told the driver.

"Good luck with your new marriage, ma'am," the man replied with a grin. He snapped the reins and the coach clattered away in a cloud of dust.

Georgeanne turned, smiling, then laughing when Zeke rode closer and dismounted before his horse even came to a halt. He swept her into his arms in a tight embrace.

"Part of me was afraid you wouldn't come after all," he told her.

"Zeke Brown! You are my husband."

He kissed her cheek, her mouth. "I was afraid I'd dreamed all of it," he told her then, grinning.

She leaned back, noticing he was clean shaven and

wearing a clean shirt, his dark hair neatly combed back in soft waves. "Did you let your work go all day just so you'd stay clean for my arrival?"

"Something like that."

He smiled, his teeth even and white, his dark eyes dancing with love.

"I love you so much, Zeke."

He shook his head. "I'm not sure why, but I'm certainly glad. I just wish I had more to offer you, Georgie. I'll start on a bigger cabin right away. I hate making you live in that sorry shack. In fact, maybe you should go on down to Fort Collins and stay at a hotel until I can have something better for you to live in. A couple of my logger friends who are out of work right now came by, and they said they'd help me build a place. They're at Fort Collins, but they'll be back."

"I am not letting you out of my sight, Zeke. This last week has been awful, wanting you so, worrying that for some reason you'd change your mind."

"You worried about that, too?"

Her arms went around him. "Don't make me go to Fort Collins. I can adapt, Zeke, I promise. I just want to be with you."

He kissed her again, a lingering kiss that turned from a welcome to an I want you. "Come on then," he said when he pulled away. He turned and picked up all three of her bags. "Lead my horse, would you?" He nodded to a small building in the distance. "That's it. Just one room and a sagging roof."

She looked at him with a gleam in her eye. "Does it have a bed?" His eyes raked over her in a way that made her eager to get to the cabin. He grinned and laughed as he started walking.

"Yeah, it's got a bed—a homemade one with rope springs, but a damn good feather mattress that's new, and I washed all the blankets and pillow cases. I cleaned up as best I could, swept the floor. It's just rough pine. You need to wear slippers or you might get a splinter in your foot. You can use the top of the heating stove to cook. That's all there is right now, but I think I have enough money to buy a real cookstove once we have a bigger place." He stopped walking. "You *do* know how to cook, don't you?"

She scowled at the remark. "Of course I can cook! I've been doing it for myself for six years now."

"I'll bet you had a cook and a maid most of your life, and at school or working for the mining company, you probably mostly ate food cooked by the lady who ran the boarding house where you stayed—or ate out at restaurants. Admit it, Georgeanne Temple Brown. You don't know a whole lot about cooking."

She sighed. "Does that disappoint you?"

He broke into a grin again. "Hell, no. I'll do the cooking myself if I have to, as long as I've got you with me."

"I'll learn. I promise."

"Yeah, you probably will. If you can learn how to be a geologist, I guess you ought to be able to learn how to cook an egg." He laughed. "You've got guts, Georgie, coming here like this. And if you want to work at what you do, it's okay with me. There are mines and assay offices around here, and there's a college in Fort Collins. Maybe you could teach geology there part-time or something. I don't want to keep you from what you love."

"I love *you*. For now I only want to be with you and to know this is real."

They walked another half mile to the sorry little cabin, and Georgeanne told herself to be brave. He'd promised to build her something better; she had no doubt he would do just that. Zeke Brown was a man of his word.

"Welcome home," he told her, setting down her bags.

She tied the horse to a hitching post and turned to him. "I want to see that new feather mattress."

They both laughed as he picked her up and carried her inside. She screamed when he threw her onto the mattress, then sank into the thick down. She sat up and pulled off her hat. Tossing it to the floor, she began undoing her high-button shoes. Zeke pulled off his boots and his shirt, and again Georgeanne was reminded of her father's cruelty when she saw his scars. She'd seen them when they'd made love again at Masonville after marrying, and it tore at her heart to think what he'd suffered for loving her. She held out her arms. "Come here, Mr. Brown."

He removed the rest of his clothes and climbed onto the bed. "I am at your command, Mrs. Brown."

They had been apart a whole week, an eternity for two people so full of passion. This time they needed no preliminaries. He had to be inside of her, and that was that. He pushed up her dress and yanked down her drawers, and quickly she welcomed his manhood inside her. It was just as she'd hoped and dreamed it would be—pure pleasure. As far as she was concerned, Zeke Brown was more man than any other male in Colorado.

Eighteen

June, 1894 . . .

Hawk headed his horse down the hill, following the trader he'd hired in Williston, North Dakota, who, he'd discovered, was headed for a little town called Moose Jaw in Saskatchewan. Letters from his grandmother had told him his father was living somewhere near Moose Jaw, with a small village of Cree Indians. He had married a Cree woman and had a son by her. He was glad his father had found companionship, and that he had a little half brother. He wanted to laugh at the thought of it: here he was twenty-one years old and he had a baby brother. Apparently some young Cree girl had caught his father's eye . . . or perhaps she had deliberately seduced him. After all, in spite of being forty-six years old now, Wolf's Blood was still a handsome man, Hawk had no doubt.

His heart pounded with anticipation. His father would be very surprised to see him. Hawk had not even been sure he could find him, but he had not seen the man in seven years, and he was determined not to go home to Denver to an apprenticeship with a law firm until he did see his father again. Once he got involved with a job, maybe one day opening his own law firm, it could be several more years before he could take the time to see Wolf's Blood—maybe never.

He was certain the man would never come back to the States.

The trader, who was driving a huge freight wagon loaded with supplies, reined in and waited for Hawk to come up to him on horseback. He pointed to a small building down the dirt road. "That's the post where the Indians trade," he said. "Moose Jaw is about a mile up ahead. It's most likely somebody at that post would know whoever it is you're lookin' for. Why can't you tell me his name?"

"Personal reasons. Thanks for helping me." Hawk tipped his hat to the man and rode off. The trader shrugged in curiosity and went on into town.

It felt good to Hawk to be riding again. He'd taken a steamboat from Omaha up the Mississippi as far north into North Dakota as he could go, then had purchased this black gelding from a rancher there, along with a saddle. The horse wasn't the quality of those his father used to raise, but it was sturdy enough. He had left a box of books as well as a trunk of clothes stored in Omaha, bringing along only the supplies he'd need for a journey into the wilds of Saskatchewan.

He would be forever grateful for the financial support Jeremy had continued to provide him, and he intended to one day pay back every penny of it. For now, he had to see his father before he started working, and he had decided not to tell the rest of the family what he was doing. They didn't even know for sure he was on his way home. This had been a last-minute decision once he'd reached Omaha.

Today he wore only cotton pants and shirt, the sleeves of the shirt rolled up against the summer heat. He reached the little clapboard building and dismounted, noticing an old Indian sitting on the porch of the trading post with a bottle of whiskey in hand. It had sickened him to see the hopelessness of those on the Sioux reservations on his way here, and apparently things were even worse for Canadian Indians, who got no government help whatsoever. His father had been right. The only way to beat the white man was to beat him at his own game—in the courtrooms, and through Congress.

He stepped inside the little building, and the rich scent of tobacco filled his nostrils. A very pretty young Indian woman stood in a corner eyeing some colorful ribbons. A little Indian boy he guessed to be about three stood beside her. The boy looked up at Hawk when he came in, his almost-black eyes staring in curiosity. Suddenly he smiled, showing dimples, and Hawk thought what a fetching child he was. He nodded to the lad, then couldn't help noticing the mother again. There was a dark, exotic beauty about her, and he thought how easy it would be to take an interest in a pretty Indian girl. He'd made up his mind that was the kind of girl he'd end up marrying one day, but for now he had to concentrate on his career.

He turned to the bearded white man behind the counter. "Can you tell me where I might find a Cree village around here? Maybe you know if there is a Cheyenne man living there named Wolf's Blood?"

"Wolf's Blood?" The man scratched at his beard. "Sure." He pointed to the woman in the corner. "That there squaw can tell you where to find him. She's married to him."

Hawk cringed at the word squaw, but decided not to make an issue of it. He turned to look at the woman again. She was already staring at him curiously, a defensive look in her eyes. "Who are you?" she asked.

Hawk grinned. So, this was the pretty thing who had given his father a reason to live. "Are you Sweet Bird?" He stepped closer. "I'm Hawk, Wolf's Blood's son."

She gasped, joy filling her dark eyes, then tears.

"Hawk! Your father talks about you all the time." She looked him over. "He says you went far away to the white man's land in the East, to one of those fancy schools, to be a man of law. He says one day you will be in Congress, perhaps!"

Hawk laughed lightly. "He says that, does he?" He looked at the little boy. "Is this Little Eagle? My brother?"

"Yes!" She put her hands on the little boy's shoulders, saying something to him in the Cree tongue. "Hawk," she said, pushing him lightly toward Hawk. The boy turned away shyly, grasping his mother's skirts.

Hawk noticed Sweet Bird wore a white woman's dress, probably a hand-me-down someone had traded in at the post. It was a little too big for her, but that did not hide her shapely figure or detract from her beautiful face.

"I cannot believe you are here!" she exclaimed. "Wolf's Blood's son! He has never dreamed anyone would come all the way up here . . ." Her eyes teared more. "How did you know where to come?"

"Grandmother Abbie told me."

"Oh, of course! He talks often of his mother. I wish I could know your whole family, but it is not safe for my husband to go home."

"I know. That's why I've come here. I'll be settling in Denver soon, and I was afraid I'd not get another chance to see him. Is he well?"

Her smile faded. "Some days are better than others. In the summer, he is not so bad. But in winter . . ." Pain filled her eyes.

"The arthritis?"

She nodded. "He could barely walk last winter, and my brother had to come and chop and stack wood for us because your father could not do it. Sometimes he takes laudanum for the pain."

"Damn," Hawk whispered.

"It is so hard for him. He is a proud man, you know."

Hawk smiled. "Oh, yes, I know."

She stepped closer. "It worries me. He does not want to die a crippled old man. He often talks about . . . about how he could perhaps die a more honorable way."

Hawk took a deep breath against the sorrow the words created. "I'm not surprised, but we won't worry about that now. This is today, and today you say he's feeling pretty good. His son has come to visit. That will make him feel better."

"Yes, it will!" She bent down and picked Little Eagle up in her arms. "I will take you to our cabin. I left him sitting on the porch smoking a pipe. He likes pipes."

"Oh, then, wait a minute." Hawk looked around, buying the finest pipe at the post, as well as a supply of their best tobacco. "And you pick out whatever ribbons you want," he told Sweet Bird. She tried to protest, but he insisted, and he bought her six ribbons of different colors, also a tin box of wooden blocks for Little Eagle. The man who ran the post wrapped everything in brown paper, and Hawk carried the packages out and packed them into his saddlebags.

"The village is about a half mile into the woods," Sweet Bird told him. "Our cabin is another half mile beyond that."

"Well, climb up then. We'll ride back." He mounted up, and she handed up Little Eagle. He took his foot from the stirrup so Sweet Bird could mount, straddling the horse's rump behind the saddle. Hawk kept Little Eagle in front of him, wrapping an arm around the boy, and Sweet Bird untied the blanket at the back of the saddle and draped it demurely over her legs.

Hawk shook his head at the idea of his father marrying this woman who appeared no older than he himself was, but he could not help being stirred by her beauty. He headed up the pathway Sweet Bird had indicated, and minutes later they rode through a small, sorry-looking Indian village that seemed to consist mostly of old people. His heart beat harder when they rode on and the little cabin came into sight. A man sat on the porch. He rose when he saw a horse approaching, and Hawk could not help calling out to him.

"Father!"

He noticed the man gripped the support post tighter, half stumbled down the two short steps to the ground. Oh, he was still tall and fine looking, but the muscles of his arms were not quite as hard and defined as they once had been, and as he came closer, Hawk could see that one of his elbows looked slightly distorted. The disbelief and utter joy Wolf's Blood's eyes showed were all the satisfaction Hawk needed.

Sweet Bird slid down and took Little Eagle; then Hawk dismounted, stepping closer to his father. "I was on my way home from law school, and I decided . . . I had to see you again, Father. It's been seven, long, lonely years."

Wolf's Blood just stood there staring, tears streaming from his eyes. "My . . . son!" he said, looking him over. "So tall and . . . strong and handsome you are! You are really here! You came to see me!" He shook his head. "My son!" he repeated.

"I missed you so much, Father." Hawk embraced him, and they both wept.

"For a long time I was not sure I should write, for fear white men would come and try to take me back if they should discover where I am." Wolf's Blood drew on the sweet tobacco in his new pipe.

"You should know the family would never let you be found."

Wolf's Blood looked at him again, unable to get enough of the sight of his precious son. "So, look at you, my son, an educated man. Harvard! Only the best go there, so I am told. I was never able to sit through my mother's simple lessons, never had any schooling past ten years old. I was happier out riding the wind."

"You don't think I'd be happier doing that?"

Wolf's Blood took the pipe from his mouth. "You are unhappy?"

Hawk smiled sadly. "No. But freedom and a bit of wildness are still in my blood, too. But I understand life can't be that way anymore."

"What is it like, Hawk, in the East? How did those rich white boys treat you?"

Hawk shrugged. "Not very nicely, most of them, but I didn't let it bother me. I wasn't there to please them. And I showed the ones who doubted I could make it, who figured just because I looked Indian I must be stupid. I graduated second highest in my class, and by then many of those boys were my friends. I did all right but it's good to be back home. The East is . . . so different . . . such big cities. Much bigger than Denver, if you can imagine it. Tall, brick buildings. Telephones. There is even something new, horseless carriages they are called. They'll be showing up out here soon, I'm sure."

"Horseless carriages? A wagon that moves without horses?"

Hawk nodded. "They use gasoline engines. They aren't very advanced yet, but knowing the white man and his inventiveness, he will improve on them."

Wolf's Blood shook his head. "Horseless carriages," he muttered. "And what is this . . . what did you call it? A telephone?"

Hawk grinned more, thinking what a wild and rugged life his father had lived. Wolf's Blood sat there in worn denim pants and a blue calico shirt, his long, black hair hanging straight and streaked with gray. "You pick it up, and through wires you can talk to someone miles away. They have them in Denver now, Grandmother Abbie says. A person in Cheyenne can talk to someone in Denver, or a call can be made from Denver to Pueblo. You actually hear their voices. And Denver has electric lights now. You simply turn on a light with a switch, as long as it is plugged into wires that lead outside to the street to poles that hold wire that goes to a place where the electricity is made. It's too complicated to try to explain. I can only say there are lights now that do not need oil, and they are much brighter than any oil lamp."

Wolf's Blood's eyes showed his astonishment. "Is there no end to what the white man can do?"

Hawk nodded. "He can't be Indian. Most of them have no true spirit, no connection with the earth and the animals. For all their riches and inventiveness, Father, most of them reveal a loneliness, and it is that loneliness that keeps them searching for greater things, exploring new lands, making new inventions, building big cities, wanting to own more and more land. Many worry little about honor and truth. Money and power seem to be their only goals."

"Don't get caught up in all that, Hawk. Your grandmother never was, and she *is* white."

Hawk rested his elbows on his knees, twirling his hat in his hands. "The real power is in Washington, with Congress; and in their laws and those who enforce those laws—in the men who interpret those laws. By being a lawyer, I can have the power without riches, and I can use it in the right way. I could never be like them, Father."

Wolf's Blood studied him quietly. "No. You could not. Tell me what you know about the family, Hawk. I have not written my mother or heard from her in over a year. I had told her not to write for a while in case someone had noticed the letters to Sweet Bird and would figure out where I am."

Hawk leaned back in his chair again. "I don't know much more than you. I stayed in school year-round so that I could finish quicker, so I have not been home in two years. I know from Grandma's letters that Iris is happy with Raphael. They have two sons now, Miguel and Julio. Nathan is married, but they have no children yet. And did you know Zeke is married?"

"No! Who did my nephew marry?"

Hawk shook his head. "According to Grandmother's letter, he married the very same girl who got him in so much trouble down at the ranch. I think you knew about that. Grandma told you when you snuck onto the reservation to see us. That girl found him somehow, and they were still in love. She must be something, a rich girl like that marrying Zeke. And she's a geologist! Do you know what that is?"

Wolf's Blood shook his head. "I have never heard of such a thing."

"They study the earth, dig into it to figure out how it was formed. Sometimes they find the bones of animals, creatures that died hundreds, thousands of years ago. At other times they have discovered whole cities where people once dwelled before they all died out."

Their eyes held on that comment. Is that what would happen to the Indian one day?

"Zeke owns some land of his own northwest of Denver, near the mountains," Hawk said, not wanting to dwell on the thought. "The girl he married, her father does not know about the marriage. They are not sure what will happen when he finds out."

"Hmmm. What is it about the Monroe men and white women?"

Hawk laughed lightly. "I have no white woman, nor do I have any interest in them. I have been so busy studying, I have not seen *any* women. And after what happened to Zeke . . ." He was surprised to realize he suddenly remembered someone, a young girl named Arianne. He wondered what had ever happened to her, remembered how rude he'd been to her that last day he saw her. Poor Arianne. She was only trying to be friendly. "I figured it was best to stay away from white women," he finished. "There sure aren't any Indian women back East, and there won't be many in Denver. Maybe I should stop at the reservations on the way home and find me a woman, huh?"

Wolf's Blood grinned. "Maybe."

Sweet Bird came outside then with Little Eagle, and Wolf's Blood smiled broadly, holding out his arms. Little Eagle went to his father, and the sight warmed Hawk's heart, although he worried at how swollen his father's knuckles were. Yes, the disease was beginning to take its toll. He hadn't asked, suspecting his father did not want to talk about it. For the next few minutes the man played and talked with his son, the affection between them obvious. For all his wildness, Wolf's Blood was a wonderful father, and from the way he talked about his own father, Hawk did not doubt Zeke Monroe had also been a good father.

How sad that Little Eagle would probably be allowed to know his father for only a few years. Hawk felt it in his bones. The question was, how would Wolf's Blood die? It wouldn't be from the arthritis. He would never allow that. And what would happen to Sweet Bird once he was gone? She seemed a devoted wife who truly loved her husband. She sat on the steps now, watching Wolf's Blood and Little Eagle talk, with love in her eyes. Hawk loved her for giving his father some love and peace in these lonely years away from his family. She had even given him a new family.

"I miss my Iris," Wolf's Blood said, setting down Little Eagle. The boy ran to his mother, then climbed down the steps to chase a butterfly. Wolf's Blood's pet, an ageing wolf, got up from where he lay curled next to his master and trotted down the steps after the boy.

"*Sotaju* watches over him. He could tear that little boy apart, but he guards him fiercely. The trouble is, the wolf is getting old, like me."

"You are not so old, my husband," Sweet Bird teased. "You sometimes act very young."

Wolf's Blood laughed. "You keep me young, woman."

She looked away bashfully and walked off to chase after Little Eagle.

"She is a good woman," Wolf's Blood commented. "She is the granddaughter of Joe Bear Paw, a good friend. She came to me one night, and she never left."

"I am glad for you, Father."

Wolf's Blood nodded, meeting his eyes. "I know that you are." He sighed. "You tell your sister I am happy for her and that I love her. This Raphael takes good care of her?"

"Yes, Father. He is a very kind man, and he does well with his carpentry work. There is always something to be built in Denver."

Wolf's Blood nodded. "I suppose." He sighed. "I wish I could see my grandsons, and the children you will have someday."

"Maybe you will."

Wolf's Blood leaned back, puffing the pipe again for a moment. "This is a fine pipe you bought me," he said. Hawk suspected it was his way of changing the subject. Both of them knew the man would never live to see any children of Hawk's. The thought brought a fierce pain to Hawk's chest. "I am glad that you like it." He met his father's eyes, saw tears in them.

"How long can you stay, son?"

"As long as you want me to remain."

Wolf's Blood smiled sadly, shaking his head. "No. That would be forever, and I know you cannot do that. A week, maybe? I would like that."

"I can stay two."

Wolf's Blood nodded. "Good. Now, tell me more about the university, what it is like there, the things you studied."

Hawk tried to explain some of what he had learned and how he might use it, but Wolf's Blood did not really hear it all. He could think only about the fact that he and his own father had had almost no schooling, that they had lived the old way, killed when it was necessary, warred when they must, ridden free on the plains. He would never forget holding the man in his arms when he died, never forget that was the way Zeke had wanted it. Now he faced the same fate. He had only to decide how to end his life honorably.

At least he would go knowing his children had a good life, a magnificent future ahead of them in a new world made for the young. But there was Sweet Bird and his new son. Someone would one day have to take care of them. It seemed only right that it should be Hawk, who was Little Eagle's brother. There was much to be considered, but for now he would enjoy having his precious firstborn with him for this little time they could have together.

Zeke and Georgeanne ducked behind a stack of logs, Georgeanne covering her ears. The earth exploded, and another stump flew up out of the ground.

"Got her!" Zeke said proudly. "That was one hell of a big stump." He moved out from behind the logs to inspect the hole that had been left.

Georgeanne followed, always finding this exciting. He had built her the bigger cabin, and she was learning to be quite a good cook, proud of herself for adapting to this new, rather rugged way of life. She didn't really mind, although at times she longed for the luxuries of running water and a real bathroom. But they would have those things someday, she was sure.

Never able to sit inside and knit or bake, she had helped her husband continue to clear his land, determined to help him realize his dreams. She decided she could always go back to geology or teach. For now she preferred to spend this first year of their marriage together, no matter what hardships that brought. She had not met Zeke's family in Denver yet, but he'd promised they could go there before the summer was over.

"Georgie, come here!" he shouted then, interrupting her thoughts. She walked faster, wondering why he was staring so closely at the roots of the stump they'd just blown. When she herself took in the sight, her mouth fell open.

"My God!" She looked up the side of the mountain where they'd been clearing the stumps, then back down at the stump, which was on the edge of a stream that flowed from a runoff higher up. Something glittered in the dirt around the roots and in the hole the stump had left. She knelt down, taking some dirt in her hand and fingering through it. "Zeke, this is gold!"

He knelt beside her. "I don't believe it. You sure it isn't pyrite?"

"I'm a geologist, remember? And I worked for a mining company. I know gold when I see it, even when it's in little flakes like this." She looked up the mountain again. "There has to be a source up there." She met his eyes. "Maybe on your own property!"

Their eyes held in mutual understanding of what that could mean, but Zeke did not want to get carried away with false hopes. "It's probably nothing. Supposedly, they checked this out before they sold it to me. The government wouldn't sell it if they knew it had gold on it."

She grinned. "Maybe they didn't know. Maybe they were careless. But this *is* gold, and I'm going to try to trace it up the mountain. I know how to do it, Zeke, and I know a man in Fort Collins who will assay this without saying a word to anyone. We have to keep this quiet for the time being until we know what's up there and what it will take to mine it . . . if it's even ours to mine."

Zeke blinked in disbelief. He fingered some of the dirt. "Sweet Jesus," he muttered. "Gold." He told himself to remain calm. This might not mean a thing.

Nineteen

"This is hard, Father." Hawk reluctantly finished tying his carpetbag onto his horse. "I hate leaving you like this. Maybe I should just stay here."

Wolf's Blood touched his arm. "The best thing you can do is go to Denver. Do not let all these years of learning and all the money my brother spent helping you be for nothing. Someday you will use your education to help our people, but first there will be more learning for you. You must practice what you have learned until you are the best you can be."

Hawk looked down at the hand on his arm, the distorted knuckles. "Father, you might be needing me."

Wolf's Blood shook his head. "When that time comes, you will know it. And I will come to you, not you to me."

"But how? You're a wanted man in the States."

"I will find a way. I have a new family who will need help. When a man is looking out for his family, he does whatever must be done and takes whatever risks that requires. For now you go do what you must do, and I will stay here and enjoy my wife and child as long as possible. Perhaps one day I will ask you to look out for them. Would you do this?"

"You know I would, Father."

Wolf's Blood felt a stab of guilt, thinking how much better suited Sweet Bird was for a younger, healthier man like Hawk than for someone of his age who was in too much pain some of the time to even cut enough wood for her. Still, it did not seem to matter to her, and he loved her all the more for it. Maybe someday, when he was gone . . .

He would not bring up such a thing to his son now. Hawk would not understand. "Take my love to Iris and embrace her for me," he told Hawk. "And do not go thinking you will never see me again. I will not leave this world without seeing my oldest son and my daughter once more. This is a promise."

Hawk knew the sting of tears wanting to come. He embraced his father, thinking how well Wolf's Blood fit the world that once was, but how out of place he was in this time. He could never survive in a place like Denver. "I don't ever want your wife or Little Eagle—or any other children you might have—to stay here and maybe starve to death, Father. If for some reason you can't find a way to come to us, at least send your family to Jason at the Cheyenne reservation. Promise me you'll do that."

"You know that I will, son. I will never let my new family suffer."

Hawk pulled away, quickly wiping at tears. "I'm afraid for you, Father. I hate seeing you in pain."

"Do not fret. I told you that when the time is right I will come to you. We will have important decisions to make then, but I will not burden you with them now. Go to Denver and show the white men what a Harvard-educated Cheyenne Indian can do!"

Hawk grinned through his tears, embracing the man once more. "I will, Father." He turned to Sweet Bird, who stood nearby with Little Eagle. She handed Hawk a cloth sack closed with a string. "Fry bread. I put a lot of sugar on it."

Hawk took it gratefully. "You make the best fry bread

I've ever tasted. Grandma Abbie will be jealous when I tell her."

Sweet Bird smiled. "I hope to one day meet Wolf's Blood's mother."

Hawk glanced at Wolf's Blood. "You probably will, someday." He reached out and embraced Sweet Bird for a quick moment. "Thank you for loving and caring for my father." He turned and picked up Little Eagle, telling him to be a good boy for his mother.

The child wrapped chubby arms around Hawk. "Love you, Hawk," he said with innocent sincerity.

Hawk felt a tug at his heart. "I love you, too, little brother. I will see you again."

He handed the child to his mother and tied the sack of fry bread onto his horse, then looked at his father once more, always feeling the presence of a certain power he could not name when they were together. *It is my own father, Zeke, that you feel.* Wolf's Blood had told him that once when he'd mentioned it. Perhaps it was. "Good-bye, Father."

He was afraid that if he hugged the man again, he would not be able to leave, so he quickly mounted his horse.

"Good-bye, my son. *Maheo* be with you and keep the wind at your back."

Hawk nodded. "I wish the same for you." He turned the horse and rode away from the little cabin, his heart aching so much it caused him physical pain.

Wolf's Blood turned to Sweet Bird. "He is a fine young man, is he not?" He smiled inwardly at the way she was watching his son.

"Yes, he is," she answered.

"I told you, I know what I am doing, Zeke Brown," Georgeanne repeated for what seemed the hundredth time. She hacked away at the cavelike hole Zeke had blasted out of the side of the mountain with dynamite. For weeks they had dug and picked and dynamited their way farther into the mountain, Zeke using brute strength to haul out rocks and dirt, and to shore up their cave with timbers. Nearly every day they argued over whether all this work was worth the effort, and Zeke worried about her doing too much. "It can take one heck of a long time to get rich just panning for the flakes," she added. "The real money lies in finding where those flakes are washing down from." Sweat stained her cotton shirt, and her shoes were soaked. She wore the same shoes every day, so they never had time to dry out.

They had traced the creek up the mountain to the place where it was fed by a runoff from a cluster of rocks on the side of the mountain. That was where Georgeanne had asked Zeke to start his blasting. Ever since then they had worked with their feet in water or mud, as the runoff from somewhere even deeper in the mountain kept the floor of the cave wet.

"When you see light through a crack in boards," she said, yanking out her pickaxe, "you know the source is something much bigger—the sun. We're going to find *our* light source, and it will be just as big and bright and yellow as the sun!" She smiled, facing him.

A weary Zeke hunched his shoulder to wipe at his perspiration with a shirtsleeve. "Georgie, we've been at this for weeks. I haven't been blasting any more stumps or tending my ranch like I should. Everything is going to hell, and I'm about out of money."

She turned and hacked away at more soft stone. "Money is the least of our problems. We can use my trust money. I can take a couple of days off, go to Fort

Collins and have the bank there wire my bank in Denver. We'll be fine."

"I don't *want* to use your money."

Georgeanne sighed in exasperation and dropped her pickaxe again. "Zeke, under normal circumstances, I would understand. But this is, well, this is extraordinary! Just think what it could mean to us if we find a vein of gold on your property! It would be the answer to everything. You would be a rich man in your own right. You keep saying you wish you could make a better life for me. It doesn't matter that much to me, Zeke, but just think of it! You, Zeke Brown, a wealthy mine owner! If we can find the gold, we can use my money to hire a mining company to dig it up the right way, and you, my darling husband, can have as big a ranch as you want. We could go together to my father and not only tell him we're married, but that we could buy him out if we wanted. Wouldn't *that* be a sweet revenge!"

Zeke studied her, shaking his head at how she looked, her hair twisted and pinned on top of her head but falling in strands around her dirty face, her clothes dirty and sweat stained. Wealthy and pampered as she'd been, she had not once complained about the simple life they lived here, and she'd worked like a horse helping him dig into this mountain. "I'm worried you'll make yourself sick."

"I'm fine." She stepped closer, sobering. "I hope you understand, Zeke, that the reason I'm so determined to find more gold is for you, not for me. I don't need a life any better than what we have now, because I have you; but I know what this could mean for you, how right it is that someone like you should strike it rich. You deserve it, and I'm going to help you."

He folded his hands over the end of his shovel handle and rested his chin upon them. "And what if we don't find the mother lode? The source could be clear on the other side of this mountain and might belong to someone else."

"You have to be more optimistic, my love. If we're lucky, the apex of any vein of gold we might find will be on your half of this mountain, which means you'll own the whole vein for as far as it runs, even if some of it is on someone else's land. That's the law. If we don't discover anything"—she shrugged—"then we build a sluice down by the creek and pan as many of the flakes that wash down as we can. We'll take turns so we can take care of the ranch at the same time. There's no sense wasting good gold now, is there?"

He chuckled. "Is there such a thing as *bad* gold?"

"Only the kind that turns a man's head and causes him to forget his roots, makes him all cocky and thinking he'd like to dally with all the fancy women who'd be hanging on his arm." She shivered when his dark eyes flashed with love and possessiveness.

"Is that what you think would happen to me?"

She sauntered closer. "It better not. But I must say, with your build and that handsome face, if you end up a rich man to boot, women will find you irresistible. You'll be fighting them off."

He straightened, shaking his head. "You're all the woman I'll ever need. And let's not forget how you look when you're all gussied up and strutting fine, let alone the fact that you know all about running in those circles. I don't. In fact, I don't *want* to run in those circles. All I'll ever want is for you to live just as good and fancy as you want, to have everything you need. As for me, I love horses and ranching, love owning my own land. That's all that matters."

She looked down at herself. "Speaking of being gussied up, I'm a far cry from a fancy woman today. Now that I think of it, I haven't been very fancy for a long time."

He pulled her into his arms. "I don't need fancy. I know what's under all that dirt and those dirty clothes." He kissed her forehead. "You're a hell of a woman, Georgeanne Brown. I—"

"Georgeanne!"

They both lost their smiles when they heard her name shouted from somewhere close by.

"Who in the hell is that?"

A chill ran through Georgeanne at recognizing the familiar ring to the booming voice.

"I know you're here somewhere, Georgeanne Temple! Show yourself!"

Their gazes held in mutual realization, and Georgeanne saw the bitter hatred that began to emerge in her husband's dark eyes. "My God, it's your father," Zeke said. He turned and reached for his rifle, which he always kept with him. There was always the danger of a bear or of wolves in this kind of country, and sometimes jobless men from Denver skulked around looking for money or food to steal.

"Not the rifle!" Georgeanne pleaded. "If he sees you with it, he could use that as an excuse to shoot at you!"

"I'll kill him before I let him do to me what he did once or before he takes you away from here! He's on *my* land now! *My* land! I have a right to order anyone off this property when I so choose!" He left her, charging out the cave entrance to see Carson Temple and three other men sitting on horses about twenty yards down the hill.

Georgeanne hurried out behind Zeke, her heart pounding with dread. How on earth had her father found them? Zeke's own family certainly would not have told him where they were, or that they were married. And no one else who knew of their marriage was

acquainted with her father. She nearly ran to keep up
with Zeke, who strode right down to stand in front of
the men. It was then she noticed one of them was
Robert Higgins.

"You're trespassing, Temple!" Zeke told the men,
holding his rifle in a position to fire.

Carson Temple straightened in his saddle, as though
to accent his size. He was dressed in denim pants, a
red checkered shirt and a leather vest. In his wide-
brimmed hat, he looked rough and rugged, and he
was well armed. He looked around. "Trespassing? On
your measly two hundred sixty acres of stumps? I've
already seen that excuse of a house you have, the piles
of stumps all over the place. You really expect to make
a ranch out of this dump?"

"Father! What are you doing here! You've no right
to insult my husband's hard work!"

Temple's face turned beet red, and he glared at his
daughter as he slowly dismounted. "So, it's true! You
did marry this half-nigger, half-Indian bastard! I was
hoping Robert Higgins was mistaken!"

"Don't you come one step closer!" Zeke warned,
raising his rifle more. "You might have a lot of men
with you, but I guarantee that if they start shooting,
you'll go down, Temple, first thing, father-in-law or
not!"

Temple sneered. "Father-in-law!" He spat, then
shifted his cold blue eyes back to Georgeanne. "Look
at you! My beautiful, refined, educated daughter. You're
a mess! You *look* like a poor rancher's wife! What the
hell are you doing up on that mountain!"

"If you want the truth—"

"We're looking for the source of some water that's
been springing from up there," Zeke interrupted, as
he cast Georgeanne a warning look. "I want to make

sure the creek that runs through my place won't dry up on me."

Temple looked at Zeke as though he were garbage. "That creek won't do much to make anything out of this place," he warned. "What kind of a ranch can you build on two hundred and sixty acres?"

"We'll make do," Zeke answered, still holding the rifle at a warning level.

Temple stepped a little closer in spite of it, giving Zeke another once-over, realizing he was a much bigger man than when he'd been dragged off seven years ago. And he had a more determined look to him, the look of a man who knew what he wanted and meant what he said. Temple usually liked that kind of man. Too bad this one had the wrong blood in him and had dared to marry his daughter behind his back. "You'll never survive," he warned Zeke. "And if you figured on using my daughter's money to build this pitiful homestead into something profitable, forget it! I stopped in Denver on the way here and put a halt to her trust fund. As of a few days ago there *is* no trust fund!"

Georgeanne's heart sank. She had counted on using that money to help Zeke, to invest in the proper mining equipment and to hire professionals if they found the gold was theirs. "Why can't you understand that I love Zeke Brown?" she asked her father, tears of anger forming in her eyes. "He's a man, Father, a good man who works hard and has dreams and is willing to make sacrifices to realize those dreams! I've never given a thought to his mixed blood. I don't *care!* I only know that I love him, and as my father, you should honor that! Even so, if you *had* come here to make amends, I'm not sure I could truly love you again! You *lied* to me! You hit me and dragged me away from the man I loved, and then you lied about not hurting him any more! I told you before why I left home, and why I never wanted to come back! We have not been a part of each other's lives for years now, so why don't you just go back to the ranch and leave us alone!"

Temple sighed, his jaw flexing in anger. "I came here because you're my daughter, and I won't have you living in squalor with a man who can only bring you shame and poverty! I came to tell you that anytime you want to come home, you can. Just make sure you get your marriage annulled and get rid of the sonofabitch you married first! You're going to wake up one day, girl, and realize what a mistake you've made."

"My only mistake was trusting you to keep your word." She raised her chin a little higher. "And it would be impossible for me to back out of this marriage now, considering the fact that I am carrying Zeke Brown's child!"

Zeke turned to look at her, in shock. "Georgie! Are you sure?"

She kept her gaze fixed on her father.

Zeke struggled to keep his emotions in check. She'd never said a word before now. If she had told him, he'd never have let her work so hard in the mine. She damn well knew it, but apparently was so determined to help that she'd kept the pregnancy a secret. A baby! That was all the more reason he had to make a go of it here. He'd have a family to take care of. "I've got work to do, Temple," he told Georgeanne's father. "Get off my land. After what you did to me, I've got every reason to put lead into you. If you weren't Georgeanne's father, I'd do just that!"

"Is that so?" Temple undid his gunbelt. "Just how brave are you without a rifle in your hand, kid?" He dropped the gunbelt.

"Father! You can't fight a young man like Zeke!"

"Can't I?" Temple kept his eyes on Zeke. "I can

fight anybody if I hate him enough. I won't shoot your *husband,*" he sneered, "but I can, by God, show you who's the *real* man, who has the *real* power!"

Zeke laid his rifle aside. "There's no need for this," he warned, noting the fury in Temple's eyes. "A *real* man, as you put it, doesn't behave the way you're behaving now. What the hell do you think you can prove here?"

Temple's hands moved into fists. "I *need* to do this! I need to hit you, you bastard! To see you lying bloodied on the ground!" He took a sudden swing at Zeke, but Zeke jerked back, and Temple's fist whirled through the air. The man stumbled and nearly fell, off balance from the missed blow.

"Your daughter's a grown woman, and I'm a grown man," Zeke told him, as both of them moved in a circle. "We're two adults who love each other and who decided to get married. Georgeanne is going to have my baby. You'll just have to learn to accept that, Mr. Temple."

"I don't have to accept *any* of it!" Temple lunged into Zeke, and they both fell to the ground. With powerful arms Zeke managed to shove the older man off him and deftly got to his feet, while Temple grunted and got to his knees and then slowly rose.

Zeke decided to put an end to this farce. Perhaps Carson Temple could intimidate others with his size, but he'd met far more than his match today. He grabbed Temple's arm before the man had his bearings and jerked him around, then landed a fist in his face, sending him sprawling. Georgeanne let out a little scream and covered her mouth with her hand.

Temple lay on his back, stunned. Zeke bent over him, grasping the front of his shirt. "I've had fist fights with loggers, Temple! Men who could break you in half! *I* could break you in half if I really tried! I went easy on you because of Georgeanne, but after what you did to me, I'd dearly love to beat you until no one could recognize you. So I suggest you get back on your horse and get the hell off my land!"

He hauled Temple up, forcing him to his feet and shoving him toward his mount, then walked to where Robert Higgins sat on his own horse. Before Higgins realized what was happening, Zeke yanked the much smaller man off his mount, throwing him to the ground.

"That's for interfering in my personal affairs," he said.

Higgins stared at him in wide-eyed fear, literally shaking. He slowly rose and brushed himself off. "Georgeanne's father had a right to know the foolish thing his daughter was doing," he told Zeke. "I only did what I thought was best for her."

"Sure you did." Zeke yanked him closer, then buried a fist in his middle. "And best for *you*, you little snake!" He picked Higgins up and slung him over his saddle facedown as though he were a mere rag doll. He then turned to see Temple climb up on his horse, wincing and grunting, blood dripping from his nose and trickling out of a cut under his left eye that was fast being surrounded by an ugly bruise. The man slung his gunbelt over his saddle horn, then straightened and looked down at Zeke.

"You've done me dirty, boy," he growled. "And you broke a promise to stay away from my daughter. That means I don't need to keep any promises I made about your family and their ranch."

"I kept my promise for six years," Zeke reminded him, "and I didn't go looking for your daughter. We met again by accident. You use this against my folks, and I *will* kill you! They're innocent of all of this! They've built their spread even bigger now, and they've always worked hard. They deserve some peace. If they don't get it, I'll have you arrested! I have an uncle who can see that it happens. He's got connections in high places, so you'd better stay away from the Monroe ranch. It doesn't just belong to Morgan Brown. It belongs to my grandmother, and to Dan Monroe and Jeremy Monroe. You do something against my parents, and you won't get away with it!"

"Father, it doesn't have to be this way," Georgeanne pleaded. "Zeke and I are happy. I don't want to be estranged from you forever, but that's how it will be if you can't learn to accept Zeke as my husband."

Temple took out a handkerchief and pressed it to his nose for a moment. "That will never happen," he answered. "And the sorry-looking woman I see standing before me right now is no daughter of mine! You'll regret this one day, Georgeanne Temple! *Temple!* That's how I'll always think of you. And when you discover what life is like without a trust fund to dip into whenever you like, you'll come back home soon enough!"

He turned his horse and rode off. The others followed, Higgins having managed to right himself and sit on his saddle. Zeke watched them until he was sure they would stay gone; then he turned to face Georgeanne, who looked forlorn, tears running down her dirty face. "I'll never let you be sorry you married me, Georgeanne. I promise that."

She wiped at her tears, smearing the dirt. "I'm only sorry for the terrible things he said—for not being able to help you now, with my money. What if . . . if we find the gold? We won't have the funds to mine it right."

His heart ached for her, and he walked up and drew her into his arms. "Don't worry about it. We'll find a way. Maybe my uncle Jeremy can help. I don't like going to anybody for help, but if we find that gold . . ."

He pulled back, keeping hold of her arms. "Georgie, is it true? You're carrying?"

She nodded. "I was going to surprise you, maybe celebrate when we found the gold."

He frowned. "Well, one thing is sure, you'll not be working yourself into a sweat with a pickaxe again. You shouldn't have been doing that. You could have hurt yourself, maybe lost the baby. From now on you give me instructions and I do *all* the digging, understand? And we *will* find that gold!"

He had no idea if it would happen, or how he was going to dig for gold and keep the ranch going at the same time—or where he'd get more money once his had run out. But he didn't want to worry her. He had to think positively now, for his Georgie. He had to believe he'd be able to provide a decent living, not just for her, but for a family.

He hugged her close. The episode with Temple had been a rude reminder of old hatreds, and now he realized how right she'd been about the satisfaction they could get if they found gold, not in being rich but in being able to wield a new power over her father. "We'll find that gold," he repeated.

Abbie answered the door herself, having never gotten used to letting servants do things for her. Jeremy had often teased her, saying that since she'd come to live with him, he might as well get rid of his cook and housemaid because Abbie insisted on doing those chores herself half the time. *I've worked hard most of my life,* she thought as she approached the door. *Why hire someone to do something as simple as cook meals and dust furniture?* She liked being busy, wanted to stay busy. It helped her not to dwell on memories of lost loved ones, not to worry so much about Wolf's Blood and

his arthritis or about Zeke's being married to a woman
who could bring him a good deal of trouble . . . or
about Dan, Zeke's precious, devoted brother who had
been such an important part of their lives and then
her own after Zeke died. Dan was ailing—cancer, they
called it. Poor Emily was only fourteen and had lost
her mother so violently at seven, had lost her real father to death at a much younger age, then had barely
gotten to know and love Wolf's Blood before he had
to leave her. Now she would lose her grandfather. She
at least had Rebecca, who was much younger than Dan.
Rebecca loved Emily as if she were her own daughter
and would take good care of her. And Jeremy would
see they got financial help if necessary.

Dear Jeremy, the son she thought she'd lost forever,
the son she'd once thought must be so selfish, how
would most of them have managed without him these
past years? He had done a wonderful job with Hawk
and Iris. Iris was so happy now, and thanks to Jeremy's
connections, Hawk was working at a law firm in the
city. He was a promising attorney, already more than
proving himself. How wonderful that he had gone to
find his father before coming back to Denver. It
warmed her heart so to hear what a good, loving wife
Wolf's Blood had, and to learn of his beautiful son. If
only she could see Little Eagle, the only grandchild
she'd never seen.

"I've got it, Jenny," she told the maid. The woman
was rushing down the wide staircase that led to the
marble-floored entranceway in answer to the knock at
the huge oak front door to Jeremy's home.

"Mrs. Monroe, you're supposed to let me do these
things."

"You have enough to do. I've always thought it silly
that one should have to hire someone to answer the
door for them."

Jenny laughed lightly and hurried back up the stairs, and Abbie opened the door, gasping in surprise and pleasure to see Zeke standing there. "Hello, Grandma." He greeted her with a big smile. A woman was with him, and Abbie realized she had to be Zeke's wife. At last she would get to meet Georgeanne Temple.

"Come in out of the cold!" she said, stepping aside. In spite of being bundled into a heavy, fur-lined, velvet cape, it was obvious that Georgeanne was pregnant. She wore a matching velvet hat, and Abbie was struck by the contrast of the woman's elegant clothing and Zeke's garb. He wore weathered boots and denim pants, a worn leather hat on his head and a wolfskin coat around his big shoulders that looked as though it had seen many winters. "My goodness! What brings you here after all these months away?" she asked as Zeke embraced her. "I would think you would have waited another month—until Christmas at the least—but . . ." She stepped back, opening her arms to Georgeanne. "You must be Georgeanne. And you're carrying! What are you doing traveling in this bitter cold and snow in your condition?"

"We had to come," Georgeanne answered. "We've so much to tell you." She pulled away, warmed by how readily Abbie had embraced her. As she removed her hat, she realized Zeke had been right about his grandmother. The woman was indeed beautiful for her age. Georgie had learned so much about Abbie that she felt honored to be in her presence. She immediately sensed a wonderful grace and strength about her, this woman who was dressed quite simply for someone who lived with a son who could give her anything she wanted.

"Oh, you poor children, come and sit by the fire in the parlor. And where are your bags?"

"They're still outside," Zeke answered. "I'll get

them. You take Georgeanne in by the fire, and get her something hot to drink, will you?"

"Oh, of course!" Abbie hung Georgeanne's cape and hat on a rack near the door and led her down a carpeted hallway to double sliding doors that opened to a cozy room decorated with paintings and plants, a fire crackling in the marble fireplace. She encouraged Georgeanne to sit on a chair beside the hearth, already seeing why a young Zeke had so easily fallen in love with her. Still, she could not imagine that anyone fathered by Carson Temple could be as wonderful as Zeke had always claimed Georgeanne was. "I am so glad to finally meet you, Georgeanne. Needless to say, we were all surprised and concerned when we got Zeke's letter over a year ago, telling us he'd found you again and you had married! We haven't been sure what to think since then. You didn't come for Christmas, and we've heard nothing from you. Apparently your father still doesn't even know you've married Zeke. Margaret writes that there have been no problems at home, and—"

"Please, wait!" Georgeanne put up her hand, laughing. "First, let me tell you, Mrs. Monroe, that I am honored to finally meet the grandmother Zeke has told me so much about. What an incredible life you've led! There is so much I want to talk to you about, but . . . I hope Zeke's parents told you I visited them after—" She lost her smile. "After my father did that terrible thing to Zeke, forcing him to leave home. I hope you know I didn't even realize what father had done until Zeke's parents told me. I do love Zeke so, Mrs. Monroe. We found each other quite by accident after six years apart, but I never stopped loving him and thinking about him that whole time. As soon as we saw each other again, we knew we had to be together, no matter what the danger."

Abbie smiled, kneeling in front of her. "Yes, there it is, in your eyes. The love, the genuine kindness. This is why I have wanted for months—for years, actually—to meet you, to see for myself that you truly were the kind of woman deserving of my grandson." She sighed, losing her smile. "That you truly were nothing like your father. I'm sorry to have to say that—"

"Don't be. I fully understand why you would have your doubts."

Zeke came in then, followed by Jeremy, who had come out of his study to discover who was at the door. Jeremy sent for Mary and rang for the maid to bring a tray of hot tea and biscuits, and the next several minutes they spent catching up on family matters. Zeke learned that Hawk had visited Wolf's Blood and Wolf's Blood was a father again; learned about Hawk's new position with a law firm. He told them about his ranch, and the fact that Georgeanne was six months pregnant. Abbie could see Zeke was concerned, and when he talked about the living conditions Georgeanne had learned to accept, she knew he felt guilty over not being able to provide better for her. Still, there was a wonderful glow about both of them, as though they were hiding some marvelous secret.

"You must stay here the next three months," Abbie ordered Georgeanne. "You don't want to be having your first child out there in near wilderness with no good doctors close by. Here in Denver you can get the best of care, and another woman who loves you will be with you to comfort you. That's so important. I know your mother died tragically when you were very young. I also lost my mother at a young age. That is hard, and so is having babies with no woman to help."

Georgeanne's eyes suddenly teared. "You said 'another woman who loves you.' Does that mean . . . ? Are you saying you love me?"

Abbie was touched by the hunger in Georgeanne's eyes. "Of course! I love anyone who my children or grandchildren love. You are my granddaughter now by marriage, and you are carrying my great-grandchild. Why wouldn't I love you?"

"I guess I thought it would take time, considering the kind of man my father is, and what he did to Zeke."

"You'll find no woman who has more love to give than my mother," Jeremy told her. "No tears now. We're glad you came here, but we're all very curious as to *why* you're here at this particular time." He looked at Zeke. "You having problems of some kind? Has Georgeanne's father found out about the marriage?"

Zeke got up from his chair. "Yes," he answered. He walked to the fireplace. "But that isn't why we're here. I did write Mother to warn them there could be trouble. I told her to let you know right away and you'd send out a marshal. You haven't heard from her?"

"Nothing. Things are all right, as far as I know."

"Good," Zeke nodded. He went on to explain about the incident with Temple. "I'm not worried about Carson Temple anymore," he finished. "I *am* a little worried about Georgeanne having a baby out there, and I brought her here so she'd be close to a doctor. But there's one other reason we're here, and it's the main reason I no longer worry about her father's power and money. With your help, Uncle Jeremy, Georgeanne and I will have more money than Temple ever dreamed of. I'll be able to buy him out if I want to."

Abbie, Jeremy and Mary stared at him in surprise. "What?" Jeremy asked.

Zeke grinned. "It's called gold, Uncle Jeremy, and there's a vein of it on the side of the mountain that is part of my property. Thanks to Georgeanne's training in geology and her work for a mining company, she helped me find the mother lode. I was dynamiting stumps to clear my land, when lo and behold, one of them—near a creek—turned out to have a little sparkle on the roots, flakes of gold washed down from someplace higher up. Georgie and I hacked and shoveled and dynamited our way into the mountain, and, by God, she found a vein that's assayed out to be almost pure."

"Dear Lord!" Abbie whispered.

"Damn!" Jeremy exclaimed. "Zeke, that's the best news I've heard in years!" He looked to his mother. "Just think of it! Gold in the Monroe family! Gold! My God, what would father have thought of this!"

Abbie was speechless. Never in his wildest dreams would Zeke Monroe have thought he'd have a son as rich as Jeremy, a grandson who was a lawyer in Denver, another grandson who just might turn out to be among the richest men in Colorado! What a glorious satisfaction this would have been for Zeke Monroe.

"Our only problem," Zeke was saying, "is that after Georgie's father found out about the marriage, he cut off her trust fund. We were going to use that money to buy the proper mining equipment, hire men who know what they're doing. It's one thing finding the gold, something else getting it out of the mountain."

"Say no more," Jeremy told him. "Did you really doubt I would back you? How could I go wrong, if the vein is as rich as you say it is?"

"It is. I brought verification from an assayer, should you want to see it." He dug into his pants pocket and took out a nugget, holding it out. "Go ahead and bite into it if you want. That's no pyrite."

Jeremy took the nugget, grinning. He studied it closely, rolling it between his fingers. "I'll be damned." He handed it to Abbie, while Mary stood watching with her hand over her mouth, not knowing whether to laugh or cry.

"We'll all be rich," Zeke told them. "It's a legitimate claim. I intend to build my folks a real nice place, the kind of house Mother never dreamed she could have. And I'll build a beautiful home for Georgie and my family, maybe right here in Denver. She deserves to live better than I've been able to manage so far."

"Zeke, I would not have minded if things didn't change."

"I know that." Zeke walked behind Georgeanne, putting his hands on her shoulders. "You put up with a big change in your way of life to be married to me, Georgie, and you never once complained. You've got grit, like my grandma." He smiled at Abbie, seeing the tears in her eyes. "Georgie is the kind of woman who belongs in this family," he told her. "I told you she was nothing like her father. Now you can all see I was right. If Georgie hadn't come along, I'd still be alone out there. And I sure as hell never would have known that gold was in my mountain!"

"Congratulations, nephew!" Jeremy said. "We'll go into town tomorrow and find a mining contractor. I'll set you up with whatever you need. From the looks of that nugget, I'd risk everything I owned if that was what it took."

Zeke walked over to Abbie. "Can you believe it, Grandma?"

Abbie studied the nugget she still held, stunned by the news. "No," she said quietly. "This is surely a godsend." She looked up at him, handing back the nugget. "Make good use of it, Zeke. Never let it change you."

He shook his head. "It won't." His gaze went to Georgeanne. "Your father doesn't know it, but what he did turned out to be the best thing that ever happened to me. It made me leave home to find a life for myself, led me to that land, the gold. Your father has made us rich, Georgie. And won't that be a hard pill for him to swallow!"

He snickered, and Georgeanne smiled through her tears. "I've found my gold right here, Zeke, with your family. I don't need the other kind."

A great warmth filled Abbie's heart. Her grandson was already a rich man. Someone was indeed watching over this family . . . someone . . .

Twenty

"Well, who would have thought?" Abbie said to herself. Abigail Trent Monroe, attending a governor's ball in Denver, Colorado. Here it was eighteen ninety-six, fifty-one years since that fifteen-year-old orphaned girl married a half-breed scout and went off with him to live among the Cheyenne. Seventeen years since that most precious man of her life died. It was the children who had kept her going after that, and Swift Arrow.

Now, because of her work for the City of Denver, she was somewhat renowned, and thus had been invited, along with Joshua and LeeAnn, as well as Jeremy and Mary, to the governor's mansion for a party honoring her. If Zeke was watching her now, he must be smiling at how far his family had come! Because they were her grandchildren, and were successful themselves, Zeke and Hawk were also in attendance.

Georgeanne looked ravishing, a young woman who knew how to fit in with a crowd like this. Since giving birth fifteen months ago to a fine, healthy son, she had regained her shape, and her brown eyes sparkled with love and pride as she walked around the room on Zeke's arm. Her husband was a rich man now, and he'd dressed for the part tonight, although money had not changed him. He clung to his first love, ranching, and he owned a good deal of prime ranch land east of Denver. Now he talked of nothing but building a home for his mother, while Abbie looked forward to going back to the old ranch soon, to living in the old cabin once Margaret and Morgan moved out. She was not getting any younger, and she did not intend to die in a place like Denver. She wanted to go home.

She held her chin proudly, aware that Zeke and Hawk were by far the most handsome men at the gathering, so handsome that many of the women stole glances at them and the unwed ones even made a point of talking to Hawk. It irked Abbie that many of these people were biased against Indians, but if an Indian man was educated, well dressed and was making a lot of money, they would then ignore their prejudices. At twenty-three Hawk was fast establishing himself as a good attorney, having already won the first few cases assigned to him by Webster, Dillon and Jacoby, the law firm with whom his uncle had helped him find employment. His superiors were very impressed with his work. Eventually, Hawk intended to work for the government, handling cases involving Indian affairs. For now, he wanted to learn all he could as an apprentice at one of Denver's finest firms.

Abbie's grandsons each took an arm and escorted her to Governor Albert McIntire, who beamed, taking her hand in both of his and squeezing it lightly. "Mrs. Monroe! One of Colorado's founding women. I am honored to finally meet you. I am aware of the work you have done to bring Denver's citizens together in the effort to help those who are destitute, and I thank you for it. I know there are many who feel such work is not necessary, but crime in the streets is growing, and it is only through helping to find jobs and homes for these people, and through getting orphans off the streets, that we can hope to have a law-abiding city which is clean and safe. I do thank you for your hard work—and for having the courage to speak out."

"Thank you, Governor McIntire," Abbie replied with a gentle smile, recalling that at one time a man like this had ordered Colonel John Chivington and his Colorado Volunteers to clean all Indians out of Colorado, an order that led to the horrifying slaughter of hundreds of Cheyenne women and children at a place called Sand Creek. She could not blame that on this governor. The days of the proud, warring Cheyenne were over. None were left in Colorado, only their descendants like Zeke and Hawk, even Jeremy, men who had proved themselves just as adept and honorable as any of the white men who'd come here to get rich.

Abbie felt out of place in the fancy evening dress Jeremy and Mary had insisted she wear. Mary had had her seamstress make the gown, a mauve silk with a bell skirt gathered in accordion pleats at the back. The gown fit Abbie's still-slender frame tightly, its bodice coming to a point in front and making her appear even smaller than she really was. White lace revers accented the bodice in wide splashes and the dress was cut low, nearly off the shoulders. Zeke had presented her with a gold necklace that held a diamond pendant, and Jeremy had given her diamond earrings. Her hair, mostly gray now, was swept up into fancy curls and decorated with a diamond comb, a gift from Mary.

Abbie smiled as people stared, wondering if she really was shrinking as her grandsons teasingly claimed, for they all towered over her. She was sixty-six now, could hardly believe it herself. God had blessed her with relatively good health in her ageing years, although she had her aches and pains. When the orchestra struck up a waltz, Zeke and Georgeanne danced, Georgeanne looking elegant and happy. Jeremy danced with Mary, who seemed equally happy and quite beautiful in her ivory lace dress, as she was led around the ballroom of the governor's mansion.

The governor himself asked Abbie to dance with him, and she accepted. It felt strange to be socializing with people who understood nothing about her true feelings, what she had been through in her life. She looked up into the governor's face as he talked about city doings, but she hardly heard him. She was wishing he were taller, darker; wishing he were someone else.

From the side of a banquet table laden with spiked punch and fancy finger foods, Hawk watched his grandmother, proud of her. He was also happy for his cousin Zeke's new wealth, and he realized what a long way he himself had come from the young Indian boy who helped his father with ranching chores on a reservation in Montana. He felt a tug at his heart when he thought of Wolf's Blood. According to the last letter they'd received, Sweet Bird had given birth to another child just two months ago, a little girl named Laughing Turtle, her Christian name Sarah. He grinned at the thought that his father's arthritis apparently had not kept him from enjoying his young wife.

"Hawk? Is it really you?"

The words, spoken by a woman, interrupted Hawk's thoughts. He turned to see a lovely young lady standing at his left, her honey blond hair, swept to one side of her head and falling in a cascade of curls over one bare shoulder. Her blue eyes were alight with joy . . . and something else. He didn't know her name, but she did look familiar. "If you're looking for Hawk Monroe, yes, that's me. I'm sorry, but I don't—"

"Arianne! Arianne Wilder, only it's Arianne Ralston now." Her smile faded a little. "I am married to Dr. Edward Ralston."

Hawk blinked in surprise. The Arianne he remembered had been a skinny, nosey young girl who had more often than not made him mad when she came around his home on the reservation. In fact, he re-

membered being mean to her the last time he'd seen
her, sending her off practically in tears.

"Arianne!" He could not help noticing her beauty,
how her bosom filled out her low-cut gown. "I can't
believe it, after all these years! What's it—"

"Nine. Nine years." Arianne drank in every inch of
him, knowing it was wrong to allow the thoughts that
raged through her mind at this moment. Hawk! He
was a hundred times better looking now than he'd
been back at the reservation, and he still wore his hair
long, except it was neatly pulled back and tied with a
strip of leather. The suit he wore was black silk and
obviously expensive, perfectly cut for his muscular
frame. His dark eyes flashed with pleasure at seeing
her again, and Arianne experienced a sinful tingle
when his gaze fell to her bosom for a moment before
meeting her eyes again.

"I thought it was you all along, but I was afraid to
come up and ask," she told him. "When the governor
introduced you as Hawk Monroe, of course, I knew.
But he introduced you as *Attorney* Hawk Monroe! Is it
true? You really did go to school and become a lawyer?"

He beamed proudly. "Harvard—top of my class."

"Oh, Hawk, that's wonderful!"

Their gazes held for a silent, awkward moment,
thoughts rushing through their minds, questions, desires neither would have expected. Arianne felt almost
weak, remembering the youthful passion she'd held
for this man.

"How on earth did you end up here in Denver?"
he was asking. "And at a governor's ball? You said
you're married. Your husband is a doctor?"

"Yes. Edward Ralston. In fact he was just called away.
Someone had an emergency. He told me to stay and
he'd come back for me. We're here as guests of Dr.

Henry Mead—he's the personal physician of Governor McIntire. Edward will be taking over when Mead retires, so he has to get to know the governor. I met Edward in Illinois when my brother sent me back there to a finishing school. He was a little worried about me being on the reservation after all the trouble with the Sioux at Standing Rock." Her smile faded. "Did you have any relatives involved at Wounded Knee?"

He nodded, sobering. "My great-uncle, Swift Arrow. He was married to my grandmother at the time, but she was here in Denver when it took place. A lot of things have happened to everybody in my family since I saw you last."

"I remember your grandmother and her husband. What about your father? Do you ever see him?"

He looked around, taking her arm then and leading her out onto a veranda. "Don't ask that in public. We try not to mention him to others. He's essentially been forgotten about, and we want to leave it that way. Yes, I've seen him, once, but I don't want to say where."

"I understand. I always felt so sorry for what happened, Hawk. That last day I came to see you, I truly just wanted to be your friend, maybe comfort you somehow. I hurt so much for you."

He nodded. "I know. I was angry and hurt myself. The last thing I wanted was some white girl coming around bothering me." He smiled sadly then. "I'm sorry for the way I sent you off."

She turned to look across a railing at the gaslights of the city below. "It doesn't matter anymore." *My God, he's still so beautiful,* she thought. Now that she was married, knew about men . . . Oh, this was so wrong, what she was picturing, her wondering what it would be like to be the wife of such a man! *God, forgive me.* She faced him again, trying to be casual, wishing she had her shawl with her so she could cover her breasts. "So,

have *you* taken a wife, Hawk? A handsome young attorney who is making good money must attract young
women like honey draws bees. I saw how some of the
unattached young ladies in there watched you."

Hawk grinned. "I haven't had time for women. I put
all my time into studying law and practicing it. Besides,
there aren't any Indian women in Denver, and that's
the only . . ." *Damn, she's beautiful!* In all these years
he'd resisted white women, but this one was special, a
sweet friend from the past, a white woman who knew
all about Indians and how they lived and thought, one
who had actually lived on a reservation for several
years. But she was married to someone else now. He
saw her face fall a little when he spoke of only marrying an Indian woman, but why should it matter to her?
She had a husband. "Well, anyway, there's no woman
in my life."

"That's too bad. Every man needs . . ." She stopped,
hoping the dim gaslights helped hide her blush. "I
mean, you're getting older now, and you must want a
family someday." Why was she saying these things! How
terribly bold!

"It will happen when the time is right. That's what
my grandmother always says. She's been living here in
Denver with my uncle. Iris and I lived with him for the
last several years, until Iris got married five years ago."

"She did! Who did she marry?"

"A Mexican man, Raphael Hidalgo. He's quite a successful builder here in Denver. They have two sons,
Miguel and Julio, and another child on the way."

"Oh, I'm glad for her! I would love to see her. You
must give me her address. Edward and I have been here
for six months, and in all this time I never knew you
and Iris were right here in Denver. When Edward said
we were invited tonight, and that it was a special ball
to honor Abigail Monroe, I hoped it was for the Abigail

I knew and that maybe, just maybe, you would be here. I'm so glad to see you again, and I can't wait to visit with Iris. I haven't made many women friends yet. It's hard to just go out and try to join the social circles."

"Well, my grandma and my uncle's wife, Mary, would be glad to have you visit, so would Iris. Let's go back inside and I'll introduce you to them. I'll bet Grandma will remember you." As he took her arm, she shivered. They walked back into the ballroom to see Abbie dancing with Dr. Mead. "How about a dance first?" Hawk asked.

"Well, I guess it would be all right. After all, we do know each other. I'll introduce you to Edward as soon as he comes back." Hawk put a hand to her waist, and she placed her gloved right hand in his raised hand. Lifting her skirt slightly, she moved gracefully around the ballroom floor. Meeting his eyes, she was unable to stop looking at him as they danced, so many thoughts and emotions rushing through her. There was so much to say, so much that had to be left unsaid. She could see it in his eyes. He wished she did not belong to another. And for a few moments *she* wished she did not. "Edward is thirty," she told him. "He's been doctoring for seven years now. He's Dr. Mead's nephew, and that's how he got to take Dr. Mead's place. We love it here in Denver. Do you?"

I want to embrace you. "It's fine. I won't always work here, though. I intend to look into working as an attorney who represents American Indians in Congress. There are still a lot of problems with the whole government's involvement with Indians. The Indians need someone on their side, someone who understands them."

She smiled. "Years ago you said you'd find a way to help them. I'm sure you will. I always admired the way you were so sure of yourself and of what you wanted.

I'm so proud of you, Hawk. Please don't think me too bold when I tell you I thought about you many times over the years, wondered what you had done, wondered about your father. I truly never thought, though, that I would ever see you again. This is such a pleasant surprise."

"It is for me, too." His gaze dropped to her bosom again just for a moment. "Little Arianne." He met her eyes again. "You were a skinny, bashful girl back then, and I was ornery as hell, always telling you to go away." They both laughed. "It's nice seeing you again."

Did you ever realize how in love I was back then? she wondered. How easy it could be to feel that way again, but she had Edward now, and he was a good man, loving and gentle.

"You mentioned I should have a family," Hawk was saying. "How about you? Any children?"

She blushed deeply. "I . . . no. We aren't sure what the problem is. Edward says there is nothing wrong . . ." *Good Lord,* she thought, *such an intimate subject!* How could she explain it? She'd never conceived, and it worried and upset her that she'd been unable to have children, but such subjects just weren't discussed with casual friends.

"I'm sorry," Hawk said. "I didn't mean to bring up something that upsets you. I didn't know."

"It's all right." The waltz ended, and she put on a smile. "Let's go meet your grandmother."

Hawk took hold of her hand, squeezing it as though to tell her not to be embarrassed. The old friendship was still there, and although it made her feel a little guilty, she felt better for it.

Abbie sat beside Dan's bed, holding his hand, Rebecca on the other side, holding the other one. What hurt most was that he no longer recognized them; the once so robust and handsome Daniel Monroe had wasted away to a mere skeleton. The end was near, and seventeen-year-old Emily sat in a chair nearby, quietly crying.

Dan had managed to hang on three years longer than expected; Abbie was grateful for Emily's sake. Now she actually prayed he would die soon, for he had been in unbearable pain this last week. It seemed such a hideous way for a man like Dan to die, and Abbie felt part of her was dying with him, bits and pieces of her heart gone with her loved ones.

This was the last remaining white brother of Zeke Monroe, and the one to whom Zeke had been closest. It was Zeke who had saved Dan from death during the Civil War, and while in the army, Dan had done the same for Wolf's Blood more than once, risking his own career to keep her warrior son from being arrested and shot. There was a time when she and Dan had been very close, after Dan's second wife, Bonnie, died. Later he'd married Rebecca. At least he'd been happy these past years.

Dan had been so very handsome in his prime, with his blond hair and blue eyes, the opposite of Zeke in looks and personality but very close in build.

Another good-bye. Another loved one to look forward to seeing when it was her turn to go. Somehow she had learned to accept death. It had not been easy, and she would never quite get over losing Zeke. But she had accepted these losses as facts of life. She was grateful for Arianne's husband, Dr. Edward Ralston. The governor had sent the man to tend to Dan, and Ralston had been able to provide some relief for Dan's pain. However, nothing could be done to stop the inevitable.

Outside in the hallway the rest of the family waited,

LeeAnn and Joshua, Jeremy and Mary, Zeke and Georgeanne. Even Ellen and Hal had come from Pueblo, but
Margaret and Morgan had stayed at the ranch. Several
pregnant mares were due at any time, and oats had to
be harvested. Besides that, their new home was under
construction, at Zeke's direction and expense. Soon the
old cabin would be empty again; Abbie looked forward
to going there to spend her last days. She wished Jason
could be here, but his own doctoring duties at the reservation kept him very busy, and it was a long trip to
Denver. He and Louellen had three children now,
Jonathan, Marian and James, seven, three and one.

It was the children and grandchildren who kept
hope alive in time of death. The old moved on, the
young took over.

Edward came in to look at Dan again, and he could
only shake his head. He was a nice man, very caring.
Arianne had chosen well, but Abbie could tell by the
inflection in her voice and the look in her eyes whenever she visited and asked about Hawk that Arianne
had never lost her infatuation with him. She did not
come often, always stayed away when she knew Hawk
might be visiting. Abbie wondered if Edward knew how
Arianne had once felt about Hawk. She also wondered
if Arianne was pregnant. She had looked heavier in
the waist and stomach when she'd visited two months
ago, but Abbie hadn't wanted to ask, afraid she would
embarrass the woman if there was no pregnancy.

She watched the doctor leave the room, saw Hawk
approach him and put out his hand.

"Thanks for your help," Hawk told the doctor.

Edward shook his hand firmly. "I know Dan Monroe
is important to your grandmother, and your grandmother is important to the governor. I'm glad to be
of whatever help I can."

Abbie turned away, glad it was Hawk who had made a point of thanking him.

"And how is Arianne?" Hawk asked Edward in the hallway. "I haven't seen her at all since the governor's ball six months ago. I was hoping I could visit with her once more, talk about old times."

Edward eyed him closely, certainly not oblivious to Hawk's dark good looks. When his wife had first told him about her life on the reservation in Montana, he had not missed the look of longing in her eyes. Arianne had had a childhood crush on this man; yet now she seemed to deliberately avoid him. There could only be one reason, but he told himself that was not Hawk's fault. Feelings were feelings, and that was that. This was simply a case of nostalgia. He loved Arianne, and he knew she loved him.

"Arianne is carrying," he told Hawk. "It took us quite a while to make that happen, and she wants to be sure she hangs on to this baby, so she's been staying home to rest." He liked being able to tell Hawk that. In his mind the pregnancy cemented his marriage. He told himself he was a fool to think of Hawk as competition. The man had not done one thing to show an interest in Arianne, had made no advances; and Arianne had remained devoted and loving. Neither of them had done anything to elicit the feelings of jealousy Edward sometimes experienced. Perhaps it was simply that he knew Hawk was bigger and more handsome than he, and shared a past with Arianne that he could never share.

"Well, I'm glad for you both," Hawk said, sincerity in his eyes. "I hope she has no problems." He could not quash the little pangs of jealousy, the silent wish that Arianne was still unattached. He thought himself a fool for caring. He told himself he was truly happy for her. He'd recently been seeing a young Mexican woman, although he had no true romantic interest in her. All this time he'd managed to keep his schooling and career his primary concern, deciding women would only get in the way. It was not until he'd seen Arianne again that his needs had begun to plague him. "Please give her my regards. Perhaps when this is over you can both join us here at Jeremy's for a family dinner. My grandmother would enjoy seeing her again."

Edward nodded. "Maybe we'll do that. It depends on whether Arianne feels up to it."

Their eyes held in unspoken understanding, and although Hawk only knew this man slightly, he could tell there was a hint of jealousy in Edward's gray eyes. The doctor was not a big man, but he had a good build. Rather plain-featured, he had brown hair, fair skin, a thin mustache. "Arianne is a fine woman. I only knew her when we were kids, and that's how I still picture her. We were actually just friends. My last words to her before leaving the reservation were quite cruel. I always felt bad about that. I'm glad she found such a fine man for a husband and is happy. I truly wish you the best with the child. At least she's in good hands."

Edward breathed a little easier. "I like to think so." He grinned then. "Although when the time comes, I believe I'll let Dr. Mead take over. I'm not sure I could stay calm enough to deliver my own child."

Hawk laughed lightly. "I can understand that."

"Dr. Ralston," Rebecca called.

Everyone sobered as Edward hurried back into Dan's room. The rest of the family gathered outside as Edward bent over Dan, listening for a heartbeat but hearing nothing. "He's passed on," the doctor told Dan's wife.

Rebecca began to sob, putting her head down against the back of Dan's hand. Hawk watched his grandmother, who leaned down and kissed Dan's other hand, then rose so that Emily could come and sit by him. She looked at Hawk, and he saw the agony in her eyes, knew she was nearing the point where she would not mind leaving this world herself. The only thing that kept her going now was Wolf's Blood, and the hope she might see her eldest son once more before she died.

A quick pain stabbed his heart at suddenly realizing what an empty place this world would be without his grandmother in it.

Twenty-one

1898 . . .

Abbie stared at the new home built for Margaret and Morgan, who stood beside her with big grins on their faces. Zeke and Georgeanne were also there, with their three-year-old Peter and the new baby in Georgeanne's arms, another son, named Jason, after Zeke's uncle Jason.

"My, oh my," Abbie exclaimed.

"It's wonderful!" Ellen added. She and Hal had come from Pueblo to the ranch with Abbie, wanting to see the finished house Zeke had built for his parents. It had taken nearly two years to complete.

Lillian and Daniel, now nineteen and fifteen, were with Ellen and Hal, Lillian itching to get back to Pueblo and the young man there who had been courting her.

"There are two separate apartments upstairs. Susan and I live in one of them," Zeke's brother Nathan told them. He held his son, Joseph in his arms. The boy was four years old now, and Susan's stomach was heavy with a second child who would be born anytime. That would bring the number of Abbie's great-grandchildren to seven, all born after the family reunion eleven years ago.

"If only Zeke could see this," Abbie commented, tears welling in her eyes. "Such a home on the Monroe ranch." The three-story structure was completely surrounded by a wide veranda, providing a wonderful place to sit in the afternoons and watch the sun set behind the mountains to the west. The second floor also had a veranda, as well as two turrets, and four wide, brick chimneys rose from the rooftop, vents for the eight stone fireplaces inside.

"It's Queen Anne style," Zeke told them. "The ground floor is brick, and the second two floors are sided with shingles. I wanted it plenty big, as Georgie and I plan to spend a lot of time here and we'll want our own private apartment. That's what the second apartment upstairs is for. There are several rooms at the back of the house where Lance lives, a big enough area for him to live there with a wife when he gets married." He glanced at his little brother, not so little anymore. Lance was sixteen now, and he grinned bashfully at the mention of taking a wife. "I wanted a place where the whole family can be together. You're welcome to live there, Grandma, now that you're back home."

Abbie turned her gaze to the simple log cabin Zeke Monroe had built for her nearly fifty years ago. It had been altered some since then, Morgan having added on to it because of the need for more room, but the basic cabin was still there. "No, thank you, Zeke." *Oh, the memories in that little cabin!* Zeke's mandolin still sat in the corner, and her faithful old mantel clock, a gift from him, still worked, ticking away . . . waiting for her to come home. "It's a beautiful home, and Margaret and Morgan deserve such luxury; but home for me is that cabin. That's where I want to live out the rest of my days. I'll be quite happy there, and if the children need me, I'm nearby."

Margaret, her dark hair splashed with even more gray now, shook her head. "If the *children* need *you*? Don't you think it's getting to the point of being the other way around? I think it's our turn to be there for you, Mother. You've been our strength for too many years. It's time you leaned on us a little."

"Oh, I wouldn't want to be a burden to any of you. I'll just live quietly in my little cabin and enjoy my memories. I'll live in the past." She turned to face them. "The rest of you belong to the future." She looked at the house again. "Maybe this Christmas, instead of all of us going to Denver, LeeAnn and Jeremy and the grandchildren can all come here for Christmas. That would be nice. Hawk and Iris should come, too, and see this wonderful house. And I hope this time Jason and Louellen can come down for the holidays. It's been so long since any of us have seen your little brother, Margaret. You've never seen his children, and even I haven't seen little Marian and James. They're already four and two, and Jonathan is eight already."

"Well, let's go inside and look around," Zeke told her, taking her arm. "I'll take you over to the cabin and unload your things later. The house doesn't have much furniture yet. I've ordered some from New York City. Nothing but the best for my mother and father."

"I think we should send my father a personal invitation to come and visit," Georgeanne said to her husband. "Wouldn't this house make him eat some of his words?"

Zeke still hated the man. His trips back here this year had been the first since he'd originally left in '87. It felt good to be home, but at first he'd been plagued with bad dreams prompted by memories of his last days spent here in pain. His gold discovery, the fact that he had two million dollars in a bank in Denver, that he'd been able to buy more land and build this home for his parents, were all forms of sweet revenge. They made him glad to be here again, although from now on the elegant ranch home outside of Denver would be his and Georgeanne's true home.

"I think we *should* pay your father a visit," he answered. "Maybe seeing his grandchildren will bring him around a little."

Georgeanne wanted to think that was so; still, she had her doubts. Little Jason was a sweet, good baby, but it was already obvious that he was going to look very Indian. He had a shock of straight, black hair on his tiny head, and his skin was dark brown. Peter, who now walked with his great-grandmother, was a handsome little boy with curly, dark brown hair and beautiful brown eyes surrounded by long lashes. His skin was a very soft brown, and like his father's, his face had no distinctive features to say just what blood he carried. Georgeanne loved her children, did not want them hurt. "I don't know if we should. He might say something to upset the boys. I never want them insulted, certainly not by their own grandfather. They would never understand that."

"Well, either way they've got to be told the truth eventually, about their heritage and about their grandfather, that he does exist. We'll have to find a way to explain to them why they never get to see him."

"We'll find a way. Right now let's just enjoy your parents' new home and bask in the satisfaction of having paid for it ourselves, Mr. Brown."

He smiled, and they all went inside for a grand tour of the library, the study, the game room, parlor, dining room, living room, the huge kitchen, and the big apartments on the second floor. There were laundry chutes, and oil lamps of every size and style were placed throughout the house. "Before you know it they'll be bringing electricity all the way out to places like this," Zeke suggested.

"That will never happen!" Margaret insisted. "Not clear out here."

"You should see the progress in Denver," Abbie told her. "I wouldn't be surprised at all if electric lines came out this way someday. I have ceased to be amazed at what man can do when he sets his mind to it. When I first came out here, there were no roads, no railroads— there wasn't even a Denver yet. We'd been living out here twelve years before gold was discovered along Cherry Creek and Denver was born. Now look at the size of it." She shook her head. "I swear, I can't keep up with how fast things are growing and changing. I know it's hard for the Cheyenne, too . . . all the Indian tribes." Quickly pain stabbed her at the thought of Wolf's Blood, and she walked out onto the second-floor veranda to look across the plains toward the north.

Margaret walked up beside her and put an arm around her waist. "You're thinking of my brother."

"Yes."

"He knows you'd want to see him once more, Mother. If we have to, we'll take you up to Canada ourselves. Maybe Hawk can find some free time to show us where he is."

Abbie sighed. It would be such a long, long trip. She wasn't sure she was up to it anymore, much as she hated to admit it. She became tired much more easily these days. The least little effort sometimes left her breathless, as though her heart just couldn't quite keep up. She hadn't seen a doctor, for she believed in letting nature take its course. She did not doubt the only trouble with her heart was that it had been broken too many times. She welcomed the walk along *Ekutsihimmiyo* someday, for she knew who would be waiting for her at the end of the Hanging Road to heaven.

"We'll see," she answered Margaret. "If God means for me to see my son once more, He'll find a way for it to happen." She turned to Zeke. "I'd like to go to the cabin now."

He smiled lovingly. "All right, if that's what you want."

"The old brass bed is still in the main bedroom, Mother," Margaret told her. "I put clean sheets and quilts on it, and a new feather mattress."

Abbie nodded. "Thank you." Memories came of glorious, fulfilling nights spent in that bed with Zeke Monroe. And she and Swift Arrow had made love in that same bed. She had not lain with a man now for eight years, the last time being that beautiful month she had spent at the reservation with Swift Arrow before he'd left to join the Sioux in their Ghost Dance religion.

She breathed deeply against the ache of memories and followed Zeke outside, climbed into the wagon and rode to the old cabin. Nathan had come along to help carry in her things. She opened the door, thinking how much better she liked this little place than that big house Zeke had built for his parents, but she would never tell him so.

Home. She was home. She walked to the ancient rocker that still sat in front of the old, stone fireplace, where she'd sat so many nights over the years with her Bible in her lap, praying for one of the children or for Zeke. She sat down in it and closed her eyes while Zeke and Nathan brought in her baggage.

"Grandma? You all right?" Zeke asked, leaning close to her.

She smiled, looking into his handsome, dark eyes. She could see a little bit of Zeke in every one of her children and grandchildren. "I'm fine. I'm home."

He smiled, kissing her cheek. "I'm going back to the main house. We'll come get you for supper."

"Never mind. I'll walk over. A woman my age needs to keep exercising, or I'll end up sitting down and never getting up again. I'm not that feeble yet, Zeke Brown."

He laughed lightly. "All right. Come over about six." He kissed her again, and Nathan did the same before they both left.

Abbie rocked, listening to the ticking of the mantel clock. Years. That clock had ticked away so many years.

"Damn!" Hawk read the headlines again. DR. EDWARD RALSTON, PERSONAL PHYSICIAN TO GOVERNOR MURDERED! "Sweet Jesus," he muttered, sitting down behind his desk. He could hardly believe what he was reading. Dr. Ralston had died from several blows to the head, delivered by thugs apparently bent on stealing whatever money he had on him. Crime was on the rise in Denver, due in part to many jobless people, but also to the fact that many of those in power, and the city's wealthy, continued to ignore the problems of a city that had grown too fast too soon. The governor had been trying to do something about the situation, but he couldn't do much alone.

" 'Dr. Ralston leaves behind a widow and seventeen-month-old daughter,' " Hawk read. He noticed the article in the *Rocky Mountain News* was by Joshua, and he wondered if Joshua knew anything about who had committed the crime.

He threw the newspaper down and walked to a window, three floors up. He was in one of the newer brick buildings, ten stories high, and one of the city's finest. He watched the busy street below, paved with brick; fancy carriages and coaches moving up and down it; two city cleanup men walking around and scooping up horse dung. Living in the busy, central part of the city, dealing mostly with the rich, it was difficult to realize what was really going on out there, how many desperate people lurked in the city's back streets.

Poor Arianne, a baby to care for and no husband. How would she get by without her husband's income? "The city's government is to blame for this," he said aloud. *There must be more law and order, more programs to help the poor and jobless. Those in power have to wake up to the facts.* He thought about that for several minutes, and the idea that this death was the city administration's fault kept eating at him. Maybe he could do something about it, and at the same time do something to help Arianne. She would need money, especially with a baby to care for and no parents to run home to.

He let the thought brew, feeling suddenly restless. He should go and see Arianne, express his condolences. But surely he could do something more. He paced, thinking, feeling sick about the murder. After seeing the honest concern in Edward's eyes in those few days the man had doctored his great-uncle, he'd come away liking him immensely. No man of Edward's age and ability should die as he had.

He threw the paper aside, thinking how awful this must be for Arianne. There had to be a way to help her through this.

Arianne placed little Joanna in her small bed, glad she had her little girl to help soothe her shattered nerves. If only she and Edward could both have been there for their daughter during her growing-up years. Now the child would have no memory of her father when she was older.

She fought new tears, wondering if they would ever stop coming, if she would ever get over this. If Edward had not died so violently, perhaps it would have been easier to bear the loss. The thought of those cruel men beating him over the head sickened her, and she wondered what the world was coming to. She also wondered what she should do now. She couldn't live with Dr. Mead forever. Her brother was now an agent on a Sioux Indian reservation in North Dakota, but in his last letter she'd learned he wasn't well. He'd sent his condolences and had asked her to come live with him again, but she really did not care to take Joanna to such a remote place.

She supposed she would have to find work of some kind, although there were few jobs for women, and what would she do with her baby? Without a father, Joanna would need her mother even more than the normal child. Arianne felt so helpless. She'd been in a quandary for six weeks now, and still she had no answer to her dilemma. She had always counted on Edward being there, hadn't realized how much she loved and depended on him until now. Such a vital young man with such a wonderful future ahead of him, cut down in the prime of life! It was sickeningly cruel. The men who had committed the murder had never been caught, and the citizens of Denver were in an uproar, demanding more law and order.

She heard a knock at the door then, and moments later Henrietta Mead came to her room to tell her a man had come to see her. "It's that young attorney we met at the governor's ball, the Indian one with the strange name of Hawk. I believe you said you knew him when you lived on a reservation with your brother years ago."

Arianne could not suppress the rush of joy she felt. A true friend from the past, Hawk represented something stable in her life. "Yes!" She wiped at her eyes. "I'll go down to the parlor. Would it be all right if I had the maid bring something? Tea perhaps?"

"Of course, dear." Henrietta pressed her arm. "You don't need to ask permission for such a thing."

"I know, but I feel as though I'm putting you out. With Edward gone, I just couldn't afford the house. It took every ounce of our savings to make the down payment. I guess we just thought with the wonderful new job Edward had, money would always be there."

Henrietta, a plump, ageing woman with a kind heart, led her out of the room. "Arianne, you need not keep explaining. Dr. Mead was very fond of Edward. That's why he brought him to Denver. He'll take care of you as long as necessary." She sighed. "He's so upset over this. I worry about him, Arianne, at his age. He feels so guilty for what happened, for bringing Edward to Denver."

"My goodness, he shouldn't." Arianne suddenly realized how old Dr. Mead was. He could die, and then where would she be? Even Henrietta might be in trouble then. She followed the woman down the wide staircase and into the parlor, where Hawk turned from the fireplace to greet her with a sad smile.

Henrietta left them to give the maid some orders, and Arianne suddenly realized she hadn't even taken a look at herself in the mirror first. She hadn't worn any makeup since Edward's death, mostly because she didn't care about how she looked, also because she cried so much it was useless to powder or rouge her cheeks. Her hair was drawn back into a plain bun, strands of it falling around her face, and her eyes were puffy from crying. "Hawk! I'm so glad you came."

He stepped closer, aching at seeing the drawn look to her, the circles under her eyes. He noticed she'd lost weight. "I thought I'd wait a few weeks before I came to talk to you. I'm so damn sorry, Arianne. This is a terrible waste of life, and you with a little girl to raise. It must be hard for you."

She nodded. "I appreciate the flowers you sent to the funeral home." She turned away. "I'm sure I look terrible. I'm afraid I'm not in shape for a visit." As a firm hand came to rest on her shoulder, a strange warmth moved through her, a kind of peace, as though she suddenly had nothing to worry about.

"How you look is the least of my concerns, and this isn't just a friendly visit to express my sympathy. I want to talk to you about something."

She turned to meet his gaze, moved by his handsomeness and the true concern in his dark eyes. She remembered how intense and caring he'd been as a young man, seemingly one in spirit with his horses. "What is it?"

He urged her to sit down. "I might have a way of awarding you some money. You must be having a hard time of it, and I'm sure it's a bit awkward having to live here with the Meads."

When the maid brought a tray of tea and cookies, Hawk waited until she left before continuing. He sat down beside Arianne on the loveseat, and she poured each of them a cup of tea while she spoke. "How strange that you should come here concerned about money. I was just worrying about that very thing upstairs, as I put Joanna to bed for her nap. I have to find a way to support myself now." She handed his cup to him. "I won't take handouts from people. I hope you haven't come here to give me money, because I won't take it. I might be a woman with a child and no means of support, but I'll manage."

He smiled as he took the cup. "I didn't come to give you money. But I figured things would be hard, and Dr. Mead is getting old himself. If something happens to him . . ."

She shook her head. "It must be the Indian in you."

"What?" He frowned, curious.

"Oh, that spiritualism or whatever it is your people have—that way of reading other people's minds or something. Maybe because of our past we're spiritually connected or something. All I know is I was just thinking about the very things you're talking about, and suddenly you're at the door." She drank some of her tea. "What on earth are you planning, Hawk Monroe? Are you going to offer me a secretarial job? I probably wouldn't be very good at it. I've never done anything like that, and I have a new baby to care for."

"I'm not here to offer you a job." He set his cup down and took her hand. "But I do think I can help you in another way, if you're willing, and if you're strong enough to go over this whole crime in public, relive the nightmare of it."

She frowned. "I don't understand."

He squeezed her hand. "I want to sue the city."

Her eyebrows arched in surprise. "What!"

"Sue the City of Denver, for not doing a good enough job of aiding the needy, finding jobs for them, seeing that they're housed and fed, bringing more law and order. As far as I'm concerned, this is partly the city's fault. I think you're owed some kind of recompense. I want to file a lawsuit on your behalf against Denver. I'm not sure it's ever been done before, but many people are furious about what happened, and we'd have them on our side. The lawsuit could put enough pressure on the authorities to force them to give you something for your loss, to help support you. At the same time, maybe we'd get some laws and programs that would help clean up this town. What do you think?"

She was flabbergasted at the suggestion. She rose, pacing for a moment. "I don't know. People in high places might hate me for doing such a thing."

"I don't think so. Everyone, rich and poor alike, is

upset by this. People are afraid to walk the streets, even in wealthier neighborhoods. We can do this, Arianne, I'm sure. It isn't the money that counts, it's the principle of the thing, but the money would certainly help you."

She folded her arms, facing him. "How much are you talking about?"

He grinned, rising. "I intend to make a strong point, make this a memorable case. My aunt's husband, Joshua Lewis, is a top man at the *Rocky Mountain News*. I know he'll help by publishing some positive articles about the matter, and all the newspapers are already full of headlines about changes the city needs to make. I think we should try it, Arianne. You being a woman with a young child wins you even more sympathy. I'm going to ask for a hundred thousand dollars."

"A hundred thousand!" Arianne gasped. She threw up her hands. "That's ridiculous!"

He stepped closer. "You always ask for a lot more than you expect to get. That's how the system works. You might only end up with twenty, maybe forty thousand. God knows this city can afford it. It used those poor people to bring gold and silver out of its mines, the gold and silver that built this city. It owes them some help, and it owes *you* some. I'm going to get some cash for you."

She shook her head, pacing and thinking. "I can't believe you'd do this! I mean, you must have friends in high places who will be upset by such a suit. And you being part Indian . . ." She sighed. "I mean, you know what I mean. You could make enemies."

He grinned. "I'm not worried about that. I don't intend to stay here forever anyway. And my law firm is behind me. I already discussed it with them. I don't think this will work against us, Arianne. I think people are for this. And as for enemies, my family has been facing and conquering enemies since my grandfather first married my grandmother. There isn't much we're afraid of."

Old feelings began to touch her heart again. Hawk. Her Hawk. That was how she had always thought of him. So brave. So caring. She stepped closer. "All right. I'm willing."

He grasped her hands. "Good!" He leaned down and kissed her cheek. "I won't fail you, Arianne. I owe you a little something myself, for the way I treated you just before I left the reservation."

She shook her head. "That was a long, long time ago."

Their eyes held, both realizing there could have been something between them if not for the tragedy that had taken Hawk away from the reservation.

I loved you, Hawk Monroe. I still do, in spite of how I loved Edward.

I think I could love you, Arianne.

It was there, in the eyes, but this was not the time to speak of such things. Now was the time for mourning, a time to respect the dead and a time for daring to go after the City of Denver. "We'll win this," Hawk told her.

Her eyes brimmed with tears. "Knowing you, I have no doubt, Attorney Monroe."

Twenty-two

Wolf's Blood watched his young wife, her head thrown back in ecstasy, her long, black hair hanging to her bare hips, her full breasts a pleasure to touch and behold as she sat over him, a wild, beautiful thing, rocking rhythmically. It had come to the point where most of the time this was the only way he could make love to her. The pain in his joints was worse again, and constant. It was simply too difficult to bed his wife the traditional way, and that hurt his pride. He knew instinctively that this time the pain was not going to get better again. One more winter. That was all he could give her.

She leaned back again, grasping his forearms as he grasped hers in return, hanging on while she moved in a gentle rocking, taking him inside her moist love-nest. He loved her, hated the thought of leaving her, especially now that they had two children. Little Eagle was nearly eight, and his beautiful little girl, Laughing Turtle, was four. There had been another child, a son who had died two years ago from a coughing sickness.

The infant's death had affected Sweet Bird so deeply that it had been many months before she could make love again. Wolf's Blood understood. He also understood that if they did not live in this remote Indian village in a land where there was no help for people like themselves, perhaps the child would have had the proper medical help and would have lived. This new family of his deserved better, and it was getting close to the time for him to die, before this arthritis killed him the slow way. Who would take care of his wife and children then?

He studied her naked beauty. Bearing three babies had not changed her exotic radiance. Her skin was still flawless, her dark eyes full of passion, her full lips as fetching as ever. He never wanted her to be lonely or destitute, nor did he want such things for his children.

He released his life flow, groaning with his own pleasure when he could no longer hold back. Sweet Bird let out a long sigh, leaning down to rest her head beside his on the pillow. Slowly Wolf's Blood pulled out of her, but they remained lying close. "In the spring I will take you to my mother," he told her.

Sweet Bird lay silent for several long seconds. "So soon?"

Wolf's Blood kissed her hair. "I have already given you more years than I had thought possible. You have always known this time would come. I do not want to wait until I cannot even be a man to you this way. You are still young and beautiful, but with your father dead now, and the village dwindling away, I cannot leave you here. In this place, not even the government will help you. My family has money now, thanks to my nephew Zeke, and my brother Jeremy. But if you would rather live on a reservation, my brother Jason can probably help you be accepted at one. I hope that one day you will find a good man to love you"—he began to choke up and hesitated for a moment—"as I have loved you."

Sweet Bird shivered on a sob. "There will never be another like you, a grand warrior from the days of freedom. I have learned much from you."

He stroked her hair, breathing deeply to stay in control of his own emotions. "Our young men have to learn other ways of being a warrior, like my son, Hawk. What do you think of him, Sweet Bird?"

She sniffed. "I . . . I am not sure what you mean."

He sighed. "You are sure. He is most handsome, don't you think?"

She wiped at her eyes. "How could he not be? He is your son."

"And he is the same age as you. He is a successful lawyer, all Indian; yet he knows how to live in the white man's world. He will be able to take good care of a wife and children. I wonder if he has found a woman yet."

Sweet Bird scooted back a little, frowning at him. "Are you saying I should go to Hawk? I hardly know him! It is you I love, not your son."

Wolf's Blood studied her beautiful face. "I am only saying that I will ask him to care for you and our children until the day comes that you belong to another. Perhaps after a while . . ." He smiled softly, kissing her. "It is only wishful thinking. If my son were to fall in love with you, it would be almost the same for me as still being with you. I would like that. But at first I will take you to my mother, on the ranch where it is quiet. It would be hard for you to go directly to a place like Denver. We have lived here, far from nowhere, for a very long time. The children will have much adjusting to do. The ranch will be better for them in the beginning, but eventually it is their big brother, Hawk, who should guide them in the right pathways." He touched her cheek, hating the sight of his swollen knuckles. "Hawk told me once he felt he should marry Indian, but that in his circle there are no Indian women, so he has not taken a woman to his side. And you, my love, being Indian, our children being Indian, you, too, should marry Indian."

"I do not want to think about any man but you." Sweet Bird nestled against his chest, causing tears to drip onto his skin. "I do not want to talk about your going away, or what I should do with my life after that." She kissed his chest.

Wolf's Blood sighed. "Just tell me one thing, woman. When first you set eyes on my son, before you realized who he was, what was your very first thought? Do not lie to me."

Sweet Bird smiled through her tears. "You are teasing me."

He smiled wryly. "I will tell you what you thought. You wondered, for one brief moment, what it must be like to be married to someone young and strong like Hawk. His handsomeness took your breath away for one quick second. You were attracted to him. True?"

She lay there quietly, knowing he would sense it if she lied. "Only for a moment."

He chuckled, moving a hand over her bare back and hips. "You would not have been a natural woman if you had not noticed him that way. When he visited us, I saw how he looked at you sometimes, and I did not mind. I was proud to call someone so young and beautiful my wife, and he knew that. The way he looked at you, it made me think he could see you as more than his father's wife. Promise me you will leave that pathway open to him."

"He may not want to walk down that pathway. Perhaps he has already taken a woman. Perhaps he has lived in the white world so long that now he is not so against taking a white woman, if she will have him."

Wolf's Blood stared at the pole beams that supported the cabin's ceiling. "I have been down that pathway, and so have many of his relatives. His white stepmother was killed because of white men's hatred of the Indian. He knows the troubles his relatives have gone through by marrying into the white world, knows of the long struggle my mother went through being married to my father. I do not think he will want that for the woman he chooses to love, or for his children to be torn between two worlds. I know that struggle all too well. Hawk is really more Indian by blood than I am, because his mother was a full-blood Apache. In his heart he knows what must be." He hugged her closer. "I love you, my wife. I will love you to the end of my days and beyond. Please understand what I must do . . . and why I must do it . . . and why I speak to you this way about my son."

She shook with more sobs. "I understand."

"Zeke, look at this!" Georgeanne carried the latest edition of the *Rocky Mountain News* into her husband's study, where the air hung rich with the smell of pipe tobacco. The many petticoats of her taffeta day dress rustled as she approached the desk where Zeke sat studying the latest figures pertaining to his gold mine and the many investments he'd made at Jeremy's advice. She handed him the paper, pointing to an ad.

Zeke looked up at his wife, taking great satisfaction in being able to give her the life she deserved. Their children played in a nursery, where a nanny watched them. The ranch was flourishing, and their home was one of the finest in the Fort Collins area. Its varnished wood floors shone from daily dusting by a cleaning woman, beautifully setting off the bright Oriental rugs that decorated them. He thought how perfectly Georgeanne fit into this home he'd had built for her, and he wished her father could see her now.

"What's this? More news about my cousin's case against Denver?"

"Not this time. It's an ad—land for sale. Read it." Georgeanne shivered with excitement, sitting down on the leather chair near his desk, waiting.

Zeke did so.

> *Prime land for sale in eastern Colorado. One hundred thousand acres of rich land for ranching and/or farming, or can be divided into parcels for settlement. Includes a twelve-room mansion with ballroom, built by English royalty. Don't miss this opportunity to own a valuable Colorado commodity—land! Contact Land Agent Cory Randell, Pueblo, Colorado, or Carson Temple, owner, Temple Ranch and Horse Farms, eastern Colorado.*

Zeke rubbed at his chin, setting the paper aside. "Well, well, well. So, your father has decided to give it up."

"He always talked about how much he missed Georgia. Maybe he's thinking of going back there. It's been over thirty years. He has a brother there. Now that he knows I'll never return to him, he's apparently decided to leave Colorado." Georgeanne rose from the chair. "Zeke, this is our chance! *We* have to buy that land! Just think of it, after what my father did to you. All his land could end up belonging to you, legally! Not by inheritance. All you need to do is send someone there to act as a buyer. Only when that land belongs to you will I go to my father, just to see the look on his face when he learns the truth! We have the money. We can do it!"

Zeke turned to study her. "I'm sorry you've never been able to have any kind of relationship with him, Georgie. It isn't right."

Her smile faded. "And it isn't your fault. It's his. Not even the fact that you are now a rich man has made any difference to him. He still refuses to accept you or to be a grandfather to our children." She turned and walked to a window. "I'm sure it irks him to know you struck gold on that pitiful piece of land he made fun of, and it must infuriate him to see the fine home you built for your parents back at the ranch. This would be the final insult, Zeke, to buy up all his land!" She faced her husband again. "Let's do it!"

He grinned and nodded. "I'll call Jeremy and talk to him about it, see what he thinks it's worth." He thought how handy the new telephone service was, all the way to Denver. It was amazing that a piece of wire stretched on poles could carry a man's voice that far. His next goal was to get a telephone installed at his parents' ranch.

Georgeanne came closer. "I was hoping my father would try to sell that land before he dies. He still has a lot of years ahead of him. I want him to spend them realizing the man he nearly killed—to keep him away from me—bought him out, lock, stock and barrel."

Zeke frowned in a rather chastising look, rising and grasping her shoulders. "I swear, woman, you want revenge worse than I do."

Georgeanne reached up and touched his face. "He took away six years of our lives. I'll never forgive him for that, nor for putting those scars on your chest and back and nearly killing you. I am ashamed to call him my father."

Zeke pulled her close, crushing her against his chest. "Well, I am very proud to call his daughter my wife." He leaned down and met her mouth in a kiss of love that led to one of celebration as the reality of it all began to sink into him . . . he could buy up all the Temple land—own it! What more perfect revenge could there be, other than having the pleasure of killing the man? That was what his grandfather Zeke would have done, but the days of a man taking his own course with another man were over. He would defeat Carson Temple the legal way, by buying his land and home right out from under his nose! He picked

up Georgeanne and carried her to the door, kicked it
closed, then locked it.

"Zeke, what are you doing?"

He carried her to the leather couch and settled her
on it, then pushed her skirts and petticoats up to her
waist. "I am celebrating with my woman."

"Zeke! Here? Someone might come!"

"The door is locked." He pulled her drawers down
over her high-button shoes and moved between her
legs.

"Zeke Brown! We can't do this!" She teasingly
pushed at him as he unbuckled his belt and unbuttoned
his pants.

"Oh, we've done this hundreds of times."

"Zeke!"

He smothered her protests with a kiss. Grasping her
bare bottom and pressing himself against her teasingly,
he invaded her mouth with his tongue, drawing
breathless desire from deep within her. When he broke
off the kiss, her face was flushed, her eyes liquid with
passion. "You still protesting?"

"Don't tease me one second longer," she whispered.

Zeke grinned, reaching down and guiding himself
into her. She closed her eyes and drew a deep breath,
arching up to greet him, glad she had dared to marry
this man who gave her so much pleasure, both physically and emotionally, this man who had given her a
life far beyond their wildest dreams, and with whom
she had produced two beautiful sons. This was one of
the things she loved about him, his spontaneity, the
way he had of making her feel so desirable, the man-
liness that made her want him so easily.

What a wonderful way to celebrate, by mating with
this man whose love her father tried to destroy! Nothing could destroy true love. Zeke's grandmother had
told her that once, and she'd been right.

* * *

Outside the winter winds howled, yet the courtroom was packed. The case of *Mrs. Edward Ralston* v. *the City of Denver* had dragged for months, the City Council stalling for one reason and another, determined they should not be responsible for paying one dime to Mrs. Ralston "for whom we have the deepest sympathy," as they had publicly stated. "But we cannot be responsible for every crime committed in our city; no city is free of crime."

"That is not the point," Hawk Monroe had argued in the courts and in the newspapers. "The point is that Denver has too long ignored its poor and desperate, people with no work who have children to feed and who often turn to crime. We cannot allow Dr. Ralston's death be in vain by not devising ways to help the poor, nor can we allow his wife and child to become as destitute as those very people."

The case had been the topic of discussion and political moves since the trial had begun, and today, in spite of bad weather, people had turned out in too great numbers for all of them to fit into the courtroom. Today a Supreme Court judge for the State of Colorado would hand down his decision in the matter.

Hawk waited with a pounding heart, as did the attorneys for the law firm for which he worked, who to his relief continued to back him in this matter. Jeremy and Mary were here, as were Iris and Raphael, Joshua and LeeAnn. LeeAnn's son Matthew was with them, twenty-one now, home from college in Illinois. Hawk knew his grandmother would dearly love to be here, if it were not that the winter weather compelled her to stay at the ranch. Still, she was with him in spirit, as was his grandfather Zeke. This city held some bad memories for his grandparents, and a victory today would in a sense be a victory for them also, their grandson going against Denver's most powerful and winning!

Power. That was what his father had told him he could attain with his education, and the man was right. He had handled this case like a true warrior. This was the new way of fighting battles his father had told him about, and there was not one person he wanted here more than Wolf's Blood. But that could not be.

He moved through the general summary statements, listening first to the attorney for the City, then once more presenting his own plea. Through it all he kept glancing at Arianne whenever he referred to her plight, realizing he loved her but not so sure anymore how she felt about him. They had grown close throughout this lawsuit, but she seemed still to be lost in mourning and was giving most of her attention to her daughter. She was rather aloof and distant to him most of the time, in spite of being grateful for what he was doing. The initial warmth and desire he'd sensed when first they'd seen each other again, when he'd come to her house to talk about suing the city, did not seem to be there now, and he was puzzled.

He sat down, and the courtroom quieted as people in the back and in the balcony above strained to hear Judge Henry Worth speak.

"I have weighed this case heavily for many weeks," the man finally said, glancing at Hawk over the top of his spectacles, then at the opposing counsel. "Both sides have presented their case well, which only makes more of a dilemma for the judge."

A few people snickered, and the city attorney grinned, a smug look on his face. "I agree that no city can be responsible for every crime committed within its boundaries."

Hawk's hopes began to sink.

"However . . ."

The city attorney lost his smile, and Hawk's hopes rose.

"In this situation, I have come to the conclusion that the City of Denver has too long put off facing its problems with jobless and homeless citizens. It could take a lesson from programs already in place in New York, Chicago and other Eastern cities, and it could also learn a lesson from some of the women of this city who have taken it upon themselves to do something for the poor."

Hawk wished his grandmother were present to hear the judge's words. The man had obviously done his homework, studying programs in other cities, learning what had already been done in Denver.

"Considering how vigorously the City has fought this case, it only tells me that if they should win it, they will simply continue to put off programs for the poor and will continue trying to ride their unwanted citizens out of town with a suit of clothes and a ticket to nowhere. Such tactics must be stopped, and the only way to do that is to begin making the City pay for its failure to give as much attention to such matters as it gives to new water and sewer projects. I therefore have decided in favor of Mrs. Ralston in the amount of thirty thousand dollars, to be deposited in a bank of Mrs. Ralston's choice no later than seven days from today. The City will also be responsible for attorney's fees." He banged his gavel. "Case closed!"

Cheers went up from the indigents seated at the back of the room. They jumped up and down, hugging each other, and instantly Joshua and Jeremy and LeeAnn and Hawk's other relatives who were present were hugging him and shaking his hand. Hawk felt as though he were in a daze, hardly realizing whose hand he was shaking, who was congratulating him next. His fellow attorneys beamed, slapping him on the back. Even those in the courtroom from Denver's upper class cheered, wanting better laws and programs to protect their persons and property. Joshua scribbled frantically in his notebook, excusing himself quickly to go and get the story ready for the front page of the next day's *Rocky Mountain News.*

"You've got the charm, Hawk Monroe, to get yourself into Congress!" Jeremy was telling him. "You just plain outtalked your opponents!"

Through it all Hawk could think only of his father and of the grandfather he barely remembered. If only they could be here! No one here understood the real reason this victory meant so much. He'd mastered the game of law, and now he could use it to be like the warriors his father and grandfather had been—in a new way—to help the Sioux and Cheyenne. Fame and fortune and city life were not for him, not ultimately. He knew now he could use his knowledge at the U.S. Supreme Court level to fight for Indian rights. It was time to begin thinking about using his services as an attorney for Indian tribes. The best way to do that was to move to one of the Sioux reservations or perhaps to Indian Territory. It would mean a great cut in pay compared to working for a Denver law firm, but he would be pursuing his ultimate goal.

No one among those who surrounded him now truly understood what he wanted to do with his education. But Wolf's Blood would understand. He had to talk to his father again before he made his final decision. In the meantime, he would bask in victory. He stood still for a picture. The powder flashed, then Arianne was hugging him, thanking him.

Arianne. That was another matter that had to be settled. He'd left it alone while the case was tried, not wanting to become personally involved with his client; but his heart already was hers. Now they were free to talk about such things. He escorted her out of the court-

room, followed by a throng of people who continued
to congratulate him and ask questions. Jeremy called
for a public carriage for Arianne, who wanted only to
go home to her little girl, to get away from the crowd.
One of those surrounding her rudely asked if there was
something more between her and her attorney than a
lawsuit.

"Of course not!" she answered, a little too quickly,
Hawk thought. He helped her into the carriage, and
she looked at him with tears in her eyes. "What can I
say, Hawk? How can I ever thank you?"

"My thanks is winning," he answered. "I'll come by
tomorrow and we'll talk about where you want the
money deposited. We have other things to talk about,
too."

She nodded. "I know."

Their eyes held in mutual understanding, and hers
seemed to be telling him she was sorry about something, but there was no time to discuss that. The driver
whisked her away, shouting at people to get out of the
way, and Hawk was left to answer hundreds of questions. Jeremy managed to get his own carriage driver
to maneuver through the crowd to the front of the
courthouse, and he and Hawk, LeeAnn and Mary
climbed inside. Matthew had hurried off to the newspaper office with Joshua.

In the enclosed carriage, Hawk leaned back and
closed his eyes, breathing deeply with relief as the
driver managed to pull away from the crowd. "I didn't
even sign any final papers," he told Jeremy.

"I'm sure the judge understands. It will all be there
for you later. Some of the other men in your law firm
will see to that, I'm sure. Let's just go home and celebrate." He put out his hand. "You're a hell of a lawyer,
Hawk Monroe. Your father couldn't have more reason

to be proud of his son. I'd love to see the look on his face when he hears about this."

Hawk grinned, but his eyes teared. "So would I."

Twenty-three

Arianne walked into the parlor to greet Hawk, holding out her hands to take hold of his. "I'm afraid I didn't show enough gratitude yesterday," she told him. "I was so shocked and overwhelmed, and all those people . . . I just wanted to get out of there."

Hawk took her hands, squeezing them gently. "I know. So did I. I went back this morning and took care of the paperwork. I've brought a few things for you to sign, and I need to know where you want the money deposited." She appeared radiant, relieved, free of doubt. Now she could survive on her own.

And she was beautiful in her burgundy-and-white-striped taffeta day dress, which she filled out with her nicely curved shape. Her light hair was drawn up at the sides, and her eyes seemed bluer, perhaps with happiness. What bothered Hawk was the strange, almost apologetic look that came into them when he asked where to deposit the money the city owed her. Again he felt the change in her attitude toward him, a very subtle change that had continued for several months. She pulled her hands away.

"Sit down, Hawk. We need to talk."

He laid his hat and briefcase on a coffee table and settled himself on a rose-colored velvet loveseat, putting an arm across the back of it and facing her as she sat down beside him. He noticed her cheeks were slightly crimson, and she suddenly looked ready to cry. "What is it, Arianne? You've seemed bothered by something for a long time now, something more than this lawsuit or even your husband's death."

She met his gaze. "We both know . . . what we feel is more than friendship, Hawk. Please stop me right now if I'm wrong so that I don't make a fool of myself."

He grinned. "I don't need to stop you. I've been falling in love with you all these months."

She closed her eyes and turned away as though in sudden pain. "It's been the same for me, but I've been doing quite a bit of thinking."

Hawk lost his smile. "Say it, Arianne."

She sighed deeply, looking down at her lap and toying with one of the little embroidered flowers on the ruffled trim of the apron skirt. "I can't begin to tell you what winning this settlement means to me. You risked your reputation as a lawyer on this case, and with your being part Indian, you had much more to prove than most. Well, you did it, and I'm happier for you than for me in many ways." She met his eyes again. "I've sensed how you felt, and I've cared deeply for you since I was a young girl. Back then I would not have given a second thought to loving an Indian, even though my brother would have been against it. I still don't really think there is anything wrong with it."

Hawk began to feel some of the bitterness toward those who looked at him differently just because he was Indian. He'd managed to handle the hurt all through college, and in dealing with fellow attorneys when he came to Denver, most of whom had come to fully accept him. Still, he knew damn well none of his colleagues would allow their daughters to date him. There had been that Mexican girl, but nothing had come of it. After meeting Arianne again, he'd begun to change his mind about not being able to love and marry a white woman. "If you don't personally think there is anything wrong with it, then why are you suddenly so hesitant?"

Her eyes began to tear more, and she had to look away again. "Through all of this, I've heard remarks, been asked crude questions. Other women have given me what they consider sage advice; that I shouldn't turn to the first man who comes along because of my loneliness, that I must be very careful about my heart at this time, things like that."

Hawk's anger was rising. "And that you shouldn't stoop so low as to marry an Indian?" He stood up. He had to get away from her. He was too tempted to grab her and have his way with her, make her understand it didn't matter what other people thought.

"Essentially, yes," she answered. She looked up at him. "Hawk, please understand. I love you." A tear slipped down her cheek. "But I have to think of my little Joanna. I don't want her to grow up being teased about her mother. And when I think of what happened to your stepmother in Cheyenne, all the stories I've heard about the things your own grandparents went through . . . When I hear some of the remarks people make, I just think it's unfair of me to make my daughter suffer for the sake of my own happiness. And realizing the courage it takes to face the prejudice"—she looked away again—"I just don't think I'm strong enough for it, Hawk. If Joanna should be hurt by all of it, I could never forgive myself, and I'd end up resenting you." She shivered, crying quietly for a moment. "Then there is the problem of . . . our own children. They would have to go through all the trauma and confusion of wondering to which world they belong, who they should marry." She looked at him again. "The same struggle *you* have always had! I don't want that for my children. I'd like to think I am strong enough for all of that, but I have to admit that I'm not. That's why I think it's best if I just leave Denver, go back East. Before they died, my parents had some very good friends back in Ohio. I know they would help me settle there. I have enough money now . . ."

The look on his face stabbed through her. "My God, Hawk, you must know how grateful I am for what you've done! How hard this is for me!"

His jaw flexed in repressed anger. He simply had not expected such attitudes from her. "I stuck my neck out on this one, Arianne! I even received threats from the Klan! I don't doubt a few of our fine city councilmen *belong* to the Klan! I could have been murdered over this mess, but I stayed with it, for *you!* Not just because you damn well deserved the money, but because I *loved* you!"

She covered her face and turned away. "They threatened me, too," she answered. "They hinted how hard life could be for me and Joanna if it was discovered there was more than business between me and my attorney." Her shoulders shook in a sob. "I can't live with that kind of prejudice, Hawk. Your family is . . . so strong. Somehow they manage to rise above the talk and ignore it. And the white women they marry . . . have to be very strong and sure." She took a handkerchief from the sash tied at her waist and blew her nose. "I'm just not like that. When I first saw you again, I thought how easy it would be to love you as a woman, rather than in the childish way I once did. But the woman in me is so much wiser than that young girl. And this woman has a daughter of her own to think about. I just . . ." She threw back her head and took a deep breath. "Now that the hearing is over and we've won, I've decided it's best I leave Denver and we go

on with our separate lives. I'm not just thinking about
me, Hawk. I'm thinking about you. I love you enough
to want what's best for you. God knows you'll have
enough problems in life."

She turned to face him, her cheeks streaked from
salty tears. "You've told me many times your real
dream is to go back to a reservation and act as an
attorney for the Indians." She shook her head. "I've
lived on a reservation, Hawk, and I don't want to go
back to one. I don't want Joanna to grow up on one;
maybe fall in love with an Indian man and go through
all the hurt and confusion of what to do about that
love, as I have. I don't want her to marry an Indian
and have half-breed children. I'm sorry, but I just
couldn't live that way. I want to live in places like this,
where Joanna can meet men of her own color, where
she'll have the opportunity to blossom into an educated, refined young lady, where there are bricked
streets and theaters and . . ."

She felt sickened by the hurt in his dark eyes, such
handsome eyes, such an utterly beautiful man. She
wanted him so she could hardly stand it, but she had
to face reality. "You know you should marry Indian,
Hawk. You know it in your heart. Your own father
would tell you to marry Indian. You told me yourself
that was how you wanted it. Someday you'll be working
on a reservation. You'll need a wife who understands
and can put up with that life. Only an Indian woman
can do that, and only an Indian woman can truly understand the heart of an Indian man. I can never do
that, Hawk. I could never be a proper wife for you."
She stepped closer. "I am so sorry, Hawk! Don't think
this doesn't pain me. It's the"—more tears came—
"hardest thing I've ever had to do!"

She covered her face and wept again. Hawk just
watched her, wanting to cry himself but too angry to

do it. He had taken too much for granted. Many times while growing up he'd been subtly rejected because of his Indian blood, but never had it been done so openly by someone for whom he truly cared.

"The hardest things *I've* ever done were face up to how I feel about you," he answered, "then risk my neck suing the City of Denver on your behalf." He turned and picked up his hat. "The papers on the table there are self-explanatory. Read and sign them. I will have someone else from my firm come and pick them up. You fill out where you want the money deposited, somewhere in Ohio, I suppose. I hope you find new happiness there, Arianne, and a *white* man to love and support you."

"Hawk, don't be this way!" She wiped at tears, facing him again. "Tell me you understand why I'm doing this. It's because I love you. I love you enough to give you up!"

More sobs came. He ached for her, but he did not want to admit it. It was easier right now to hate her. The reasons his own father once went on the warpath suddenly became very clear to him. He thought about his stepmother, a bullet hole in her forehead. No, he wouldn't want that to happen to Arianne just because she'd loved an Indian. She was right, and he damn well knew it; he also damn well hated her for it. Nothing had changed from the days of the Indian wars. They were simply fought a different way now. White was still white. Indian was still Indian. His own power lay not in the lance or the tomahawk or the gun. It lay in his education, in knowing how to use the white man's law to get what the Indian wanted. But there was one thing neither the law nor his education could get for him, and she stood right here in front of his eyes.

"I understand," he told her. "I understand many things more clearly now. But you should have told me long ago, Arianne, when you first allowed others to make you so afraid. Did you think I would have dropped the lawsuit if you had revealed your decision? Did you fear you would lose your chance to win all that money?"

She stiffened. "I . . . I wasn't sure."

He closed his eyes, his hands clenching. "And so you led me on, waiting until it was all over, using me—"

"No, Hawk! Not in the way you think! I knew you had so much on your mind. I didn't want to make it even more of a burden for you. And yes, I *did* want the money, but not for greed! I wanted it because I knew I had to leave Denver and start out on my own in someplace new. I'm doing this for *you,* Hawk, whether you want to believe that or not!"

He studied her, shaking his head. "I am sure you want to believe that, but it doesn't matter. You're right, in the long run. You *aren't* strong enough to be married to a Monroe. And you *wouldn't* make a good wife for me." He put on his hat. "I hope you find happiness, Arianne."

"I want the same for you. Please believe that. I'm just facing reality, Hawk. You have your own reality to face. You are an Indian, and that's something to be proud of. Your father, your grandfather and your granduncle were warriors, part of a proud people. You yourself come from *two* Indian bloods, Cheyenne and Apache. That is your world. It is where you belong in your law career, and where you belong in a marriage. Your grandmother would understand what I am doing. She would say it's a good decision. She knew she was strong enough to marry your grandfather; I know I am *not* strong enough to marry you. She faced her own reality, and I am facing mine, painful as it is. I never loved Edward as I loved you, and no man in my future will ever take your place in my heart."

He drew in his breath, his lips set tight, an obvious

emotional struggle going on behind his dark eyes. He only nodded. "Good-bye, Arianne." He turned and left. Arianne ran to the door, watched through the glass as he disappeared into a windswept snowfall.

"Good-bye, Hawk Monroe," she whispered. She stood there weeping for several minutes, then forced back the tears and marched to the parlor. It was a few minutes before she was able to read the papers he'd left behind. Hawk's signature was on most of them, his handwriting flowing and beautiful. She signed them all, then came to the form signifying where the money should be sent. She would have to wire the family friends in Cleveland first, find out their banking recommendations. The money would then be sent, and she would pack her things as quickly as possible and get out of Denver, away from all the ugliness she'd known here, away from a situation in which her courage did not match her love.

"Thirty thousand dollars," she muttered. For the rest of her life she would have Hawk Monroe to thank for this. She hated hurting him, but she also knew she would end up hurting him much worse later on if she married him for all the wrong reasons. She simply could not be the wife he needed, and she would not subject Joanna to life on a reservation or to ridicule for having an Indian stepfather. That was the hell of it—he was so handsome, so intelligent and educated . . . but so Indian.

Spring, 1899 . . .

Carson Temple opened one of the double front doors to his stone mansion to see his daughter standing before him and holding a little boy perhaps one year old. The child beamed a bright smile, dimples showing in his cheeks, his nearly black eyes sparkling innocently. Behind Georgeanne stood a tall, powerful-looking Zeke Brown, holding another boy who looked three or four years old. The child was as handsome as his father, his straight black hair hanging to his shoulders, his eyes lighter than the younger boy's but still brown.

"What the hell are you doing here?" Temple asked, looking at Zeke.

Georgeanne marched inside, shoving her way past her father. "We came to see the house, decide what we'll do with it. I never did like this place, Father. It's much too big and drafty, never seemed homey to me. Perhaps I'll make some kind of museum out of it—you know, have people come and see the kind of home the English used to come West and build, something like that. What do you think?"

Temple blinked in confusion, stiffening when Zeke also walked inside. "I think you've lost your mind. For one thing, if I still owned this place, I would never will it to you and this half-Indian, half-nigger man you married, but as it is, I don't own it anymore, so what happens to it is up to the buyer, a Mr. Evan Dillon. He's an attorney out of Denver, who apparently also has his hands in a gold mine. Wherever he got his money, it's well spent. You've been out of my life so long now you probably didn't even know I've sold the ranch and the one hundred thousand acres that go with it."

Georgeanne faced him, amazed he could hate so deeply that he would not even be happy to see his own daughter after the years apart, that he would not be thrilled to see his grandchildren. "Well, hello to you, too, Father. It's nice to know you've missed your only flesh and blood so much—that you're excited to see your grandchildren, the only grandchildren you will ever have."

The man glanced at the children again, then at

Zeke, his eyes blazing. "I can't tell if they look like niggers or Indians. Either way, I don't want them in my house, especially not their father."

Zeke slowly set four-year-old Peter on his feet. "I won't have the term nigger used in my house."

"What?" Temple looked at Georgeanne again, thinking reluctantly that she was more beautiful than ever. She was radiant in a stunning day dress of blue velvet with a matching cape. He watched her set the baby down on his rump. The child immediately turned onto his knees and began crawling away to go exploring. "Your mine run out already?" Temple asked Georgeanne. "You two here for a handout, maybe think you're going to live with me? Well, you're sadly mistaken. I never thought that gold you wrote and told me you'd discovered on that worthless piece of property up by Fort Collins would prove out. I see you blew what money you made building a castle for Zeke's folks at the Monroe ranch. That was a stupid thing to do. People like that don't appreciate fine things."

Zeke started to speak up, but Georgeanne put up her hand, realizing how quick he could be to anger. She stepped closer to her father. "Oh, they appreciate fine things, all right, Father. That's why they wanted some of this fine property of yours. And that's why we bought it for them." She threw out her hands and turned in a circle. "There's enough land here for *all* the Monroes to live on if they wish; each one of them could still have plenty of acres. Of course Zeke's uncle, Jeremy, he'd stay in Denver. He has quite a mansion there, you know. He's a successful railroad man. And Zeke's cousin, Hawk, he's a very respected attorney in Denver, in spite of being three-quarters Indian. Zeke's aunt, LeeAnn, also part Indian, is married to a successful newspaper man, and his uncle Jason is a doctor on an Indian reservation. Let's see." She put a finger to her chin.

"Zeke's aunt Ellen and her husband, they're doing quite well in a supply business in Pueblo. Zeke's cousin Iris is married to a man with a successful construction business, a Mexican, no less, Raphael Hidalgo. And Zeke himself . . ." She put her hands on her hips. "He hit the mother lode, you might say. Zeke has invested in Raphael's construction business, in the Union Pacific and the Denver & Rio Grande railroads; he owns stock in a couple of banks in Denver and a huge ranch northeast of that city, where we live in a house as grand as this one. We're planning a trip to Europe as soon as little Jason there is two—that's your grandson's name, by the way. The four-year-old is Peter." She shrugged. "Well, anyway, we have so much money we can't find enough ways to spend it, so we bought more land and built that house for Zeke's folks, and then we decided that as fast as Colorado is growing, we might as well buy even more land. That's where the real value will be someday, you know. Once the gold runs out, land is going to be man's best commodity. Don't you think so? That's why we decided to buy the Temple Ranch and everything that goes with it. The ad you ran in the Denver newspapers was simply too inviting."

Georgeanne watched her father's face begin to redden. "I told you I sold this place to an attorney from Denver, Evan Dillon."

"Oh, we know. Mr. Dillon owns shares in Zeke's gold mine. So does Zeke's cousin, Hawk Monroe, the attorney. He works for the law firm of Webster, Dillon, Jacoby & Monroe. *Monroe.* Do you understand what I'm saying? What you don't know is, actually the entire law firm bought your land, Father, with the specific, contracted intention of turning right around and selling it to Zeke and me, which has already been done. Zeke Brown now owns everything that once was yours, and the best part is, we still haven't come close to spending all our money. Isn't it a shame? A man with Negro and Indian blood owns half the eastern section of Colorado. And just think, some of his ancestors were slaves to men like you. What's even better is a lot of this land used to belong to the Cheyenne, more of Zeke's ancestors. Now some of *their* descendants will own this land again, fair and square."

Temple simply stared at her, dumbfounded. Zeke hurried after little Jason, who was rapidly making his way on hands and knees out the door. He picked him up and came back to stand in front of Temple with the boy in his arms. "The Cheyenne believe life is one great circle," he told the man. "And I suppose it is. This only proves it. My Indian ancestors were chased off this land, robbed of everything that was rightfully theirs. Now I and my children will own some of it again. My Indian cousin, Hawk, will also own some of it, as will any of my other relatives who wish to live here. I believe you have sixty days to vacate the premises, Mr. Temple. It might be easier on all of us if you left sooner than that, but you may have the sixty days. Take whatever you want. I don't need the house. The land is all I care about."

Temple literally trembled. "You bastard!"

"Watch your language in front of my sons." Zeke handed Jason to Georgeanne. "In spite of everything you've done to us, in spite of what you did to me, Temple, Georgeanne and I are willing to let you be a part of your grandchildren's lives, if you decide you would like to be. The door will always be open, but not if you are going to say things hurtful to my sons! The decision is yours."

Temple glanced at the boys again, unable to deny they were beautiful. But when he thought of the kind of blood that ran in their veins . . . He looked at Georgeanne, his beautiful daughter. He'd been so proud of her strength and courage. She was so different from her weak, whimpering mother, but he never thought she'd use that strength to defy her own father. "You honestly own my ranch?"

She faced him squarely. "Every inch of it. We have the deeds to prove it. You can take the money and go back to Georgia, Father. I know that's what you've always wanted to do. There you can enjoy your empty, lonely life, or you can think about the gentle wife you killed— my *mother!*—think about how you let your hatred ruin your daughter's love for you. You will grow old and die without your daughter near you, without ever having known your grandsons and any of the children Zeke and I will yet have. It's your decision, Father. I've never wanted any of this. If you can't see Zeke as just a man, a very intelligent, successful, hardworking man who loves his family and provides well for them, then go back to Georgia and don't let me hear from you again."

For a brief moment Temple saw himself through his daughter's eyes. She had his grit, his strength. That was what he'd loved about her. Now he hated it. "You had no right doing this behind my back."

"You had no right promising me you wouldn't hurt Zeke that day you found us together, then nearly killing him and never telling me about it. You stole six years from us, Father. If I hadn't found Zeke when I did, you would have stolen a *lifetime* of happiness from me. I *am* happy now, and I want you to be happy *for* me. If you can't be, then this will be our last meeting. I just wanted to be sure you knew who owns this place now!"

The man slowly nodded. "You've always hated me because of your mother, haven't you?"

Georgeanne's eyes suddenly teared. "Part of me has. Another part of me has always wanted to be close to you, Father. But you don't know how to be close to anyone. You only know how to rule and manipulate, to use people. I don't want you to die a lonely old man, but that is how it's going to be for you. Oh, you'll die rich, I'm sure, probably on some new plantation in Georgia. But money can't love you, Father. I know if Zeke and I lost everything today, we'd still have each other and our little boys, and Zeke's loving family. We'd be all right. I'm sorry for you, Father. You've missed out on all that's important in life."

She turned with Jason in her arms and walked out, ordering little Peter to come with her. Zeke stood alone with Temple in the foyer for several seconds, studying the man, realizing the real victory lay in seeing the look on Temple's face at this moment, not in killing him. Briefly, sorrow showed in Temple's steely, blue eyes, but just as quickly hatred replaced the sorrow as he looked back at Zeke.

"She doesn't know it, but a slave raped and killed my own mother!" he growled. "How can I *not* hate them—*any* people of color!"

Zeke stepped closer, his gaze never leaving Temple's. "*White* men raped and killed some of my Indian ancestors. The Indians raped and killed in return. Negroes have been brutalized by men like you for a hundred years! It's all part of the great circle I told you about, Temple, and it's up to each man not to let the hatred and vengeance go on and on from one generation to the next. We can choose to stop the hatred and put an *end* to the violence! The Indian people have learned they can no longer fight for what once was theirs. They have resigned themselves to being on reservations, but some, like my cousin, Hawk, have learned to live a new way, to fight a new way. The Negroes now also have that opportunity, and most of them only want peace, the right to live a good life. It all has to stop somewhere, Temple. As for my part, it's going to stop with me and my sons. When—and if— you stop being part of a cycle of hatred and vengeance

is up to you. Life is too damn short to spend in loneliness. You have a beautiful daughter who would like
to feel free to love her own father, two handsome
grandsons who would like to know their grandfather.
I can't beat you into doing what's right, although part
of me wants to do just that. It has to come from you,
from the *heart!*"

Zeke turned and walked out. Then Temple walked
over and slumped down onto the winding stairway that
led to the empty rooms on the second level. The house
was pervaded by loneliness. He listened to the rattle
of the carriage outside as Georgeanne left with Zeke
and her children . . . his grandchildren. The first time
he'd seen little Peter, something had tugged at his
heart. Now there was a second grandson. A little part
of him felt like crying, but he refused to allow it.

Never! He'd never allow himself a relationship with,
or acknowledgment of, grandsons with Negro and Indian blood! He rose, feeling an odd pain in his chest
but ignoring it. Rage filled him at the thought of Zeke
Brown owning his land! Well, the man could damn
well have it! But, by God, he'd not enjoy this beautiful
home or the use of any of the outbuildings! Everything
would be burned to the ground!

Twenty-four

Abbie hoed a row of vegetables behind the old cabin, grateful for the return of warm weather. This was one of her most pleasant tasks, planting seeds and watching vegetables grow, storing carrots and potatoes in the cellar Zeke had dug under the cabin for that purpose . . . so many, many years ago. She canned other vegetables, still had several jars of peppers and tomatoes left from last year.

She smiled at Margaret's teasing that she still lived as though she had a big family to feed. *Mother, you don't need to store so much food anymore. Why do you go to all this work?*

"Because I need to," she muttered now, reaching down and pulling out a stubborn weed. "I need to keep busy, and I need to pretend I do still have a family to feed." That family was grown and scattered. This was July, 1899, and Jeremy was forty-six now. Wolf's Blood was fifty-one, his new son by Sweet Bird eight, their daughter four . . . grandchildren she had still never seen.

Dan's granddaughter, Emily, had married and moved to Nebraska; and Dan's widow, Rebecca, had moved back East. Young Zeke was thirty, not so young anymore. He and Georgeanne were among the richest people of Colorado and owned more land now than just about anyone in the state.

She straightened, leaning on the hoe and shaking her head. Wouldn't Zeke love to know about his namesake's new wealth? And wouldn't he be proud of all his grandchildren? Zeke and Georgeanne's Peter was four, little Jason one year old. Zeke's brother, Nathan, was twenty-eight, and he and Susan had two little girls. Lance was seventeen, a fine, strapping young man who worked hard on the old ranch, helping his father as much as he could. Morgan was beginning to feel the aches and pains of growing older. One day soon Nathan and Lance would take over most of the ranch work.

Ellen and Hal's Lillian was engaged to be married. Daniel was sixteen, and he was fast learning the merchant business from his father. LeeAnn was forty-seven, Joshua forty-five. Matthew, twenty-one, was in college in Michigan. It seemed impossible that her youngest son, Jason, turned forty this year. It had been so many years since she'd seen him. His and Louellen's oldest son Jonathan was nine, their daughter Marian five. And just a year ago Louellen had given birth to another son, James.

Fifteen grandchildren and seven great-grandchildren! She was sixty-nine herself now! Sixty-nine! Wasn't it only a few years ago she was fifteen and headed West on a wagon train? How could time possibly go so fast? How could it be twenty years since Zeke was killed by soldiers at Fort Robinson? Nine years since Swift Arrow died at Wounded Knee? It was all so incredibly impossible, yet all too real. This cabin Zeke had built for her was fifty years old and beginning to sag. Margaret had begged her to come and live at the big house with her but the old cabin was enough for Abigail Monroe. It was where her memories lay. It was wonderful that Zeke had been able to buy all of his father-in-law's land, but the old, original ranch was all she cared about. It was protected now, thanks to Margaret and Morgan's early years of struggle to hang on to it, and to Zeke's buying up so much land around it.

Carson Temple had died of a heart attack before he'd gotten back to Georgia. His death had been difficult for Georgeanne, who had hoped the man would reconcile with her and his grandchildren before his death. He had not, and Abbie had to wonder if God would accept such a man into heaven. Temple was buried on the land he'd been so determined his daughter and Zeke would never get their hands on; now they owned all of it. Some of his help had said Temple had threatened to burn down the beautiful Tynes mansion, but had died before he could do so.

Somehow, almost miraculously, her family had survived many obstacles, rising above all of them. Her children were successful men and women, her grandchildren enjoyed the same success. She was especially proud of Zeke and Hawk for their wonderful accomplishments, but she felt sorry for Hawk. He had allowed himself to fall in love with Arianne, who had left Denver and gone back to Ohio. He had tried to hide the truth when he'd come to the ranch to visit at Easter, boasting only about winning the case against Denver. But Abbie had seen the hurt in his eyes, and she'd gotten the truth out of her grandson.

Perhaps it was for the best. She had told him so. It was hard enough surviving a mixed marriage, let alone having Arianne going into it unsure her love was strong enough to withstand the problems that would arise. She knew Hawk's hurt was not so much over losing Arianne as over the basic *reason* for losing her. Her spurning him because he was Indian had rudely awakened him to the fundamental hostility that still pervaded the minds of many whites. Abbie's relief came in seeing the stubborn pride in Hawk's eyes. He had not let what happened make him ashamed to be

Indian. It had only made him more determined to continue proving himself as good as the next man.

Her thoughts were interrupted when she heard
horses and wagons approaching. She set her hoe
against the back of the cabin and walked around the
front to see Daniel driving a wagon, Ellen beside him
in the seat. In the back was what looked like an Indian
woman and three small children. Behind her wagon
came another, both wagons stamped H. D. SUPPLIES;
the wagons belonged to Ellen's husband, Hal Daniels.
The second wagon was driven by someone she did not
even recognize at first, but she did know the man beside
him, or at least she hoped so. The years rolled away as
the wagons came closer, and her heart pounded harder.

Wolf's Blood! He was dressed like a white man, but
his long, black hair hung loose, and he still looked so
much like his father! In the back of the wagon was
another Indian woman with two more young children.
Abbie drew in her breath, putting her hands to her
mouth in surprise. Wolf's Blood had come, and surely
he had his family with him, the family she'd never
seen! It was Jason, her baby, Jason, who had brought
him. Her oldest and youngest sons, with their families!
She was too surprised and happy to care about how
and why Wolf's Blood had come here. All that mattered was that she would see these two sons she had
not seen in so very long, as well as the grandchildren
she'd never known.

Wolf's Blood began climbing down before the wagon
even came to a halt, and Abbie forgot all of her own
aches and pains and began running, throwing out her
arms. Moments later her eldest son was holding her,
oh, so much in the way Zeke used to greet her. She
burst into tears, clinging to him, knowing somewhere
in the back of her mind the real reason he was here.
She did not want to think about it. Not yet.

After several minutes she exchanged an embrace with Jason, who seemed bigger and stronger. Jason had always been the shorter, more slender son, but he was forty years old now and had filled out in the way of men who are happily married. She noticed he had let his hair grow long also. He had always kept it short. She supposed now he'd owned up to his own heritage and was fitting in better on the reservation. "Your hair!" she commented.

"I got tired of the Cheyenne looking at me as a white man. Some of them wouldn't let me doctor them because of that. I had to make them understand I am part Indian myself, and letting my hair grow seemed to impress them. More of them let me doctor them now."

She grasped both of them, unable to stop her own tears. "Oh, Jason! Wolf's Blood! I can hardly believe it! Margaret will be so happy! And Ellen, you've come, too!" She caught the sadness in Ellen's eyes in spite of her smile, and she knew her daughter probably was already aware of why Wolf's Blood had come.

"I wanted to see as much of my long-lost brothers as possible," Ellen answered. "Lillian stayed in town because she can't stand being away from her fiancé for five minutes!" she laughed. "And Hal had to take care of the store."

"Of course. Oh, Wolf's Blood, Jason, I want to see my grandchildren! And Wolf's Blood, I've never even met your wife! How did you get here? If anyone saw you—"

"I'll explain after you've had time to meet and visit with the families," he told her.

Jason went to help Louellen and his three children out of a wagon, and Daniel helped Sweet Bird down. Abbie turned to Wolf's Blood again, her eyes clearing of tears. Old! No, not her son. Not her young warrior! He should not have lines on his face! She looked down and grasped his hands, noticing the swollen knuckles . . . just like Zeke. Dear God! She met his dark eyes, and she knew what was to come.

"I could survive many more years in the wilderness," he told her, "if not for the crippling disease. I do not want Sweet Bird and my children to see me die that way, and I do not want to leave them alone in a land where no one takes care of the Indians now that they have been displaced. Sweet Bird has no one left. I must do what I must do, so I brought her here to you."

Abbie's eyes teared anew, and she nodded. "Of course."

He leaned down and kissed her cheek. "I knew my mother would understand." He squeezed her hands. "You are still beautiful, Mother. How do you do it?"

She smiled through her tears. "I only look beautiful because I am your mother and it's been so many years since you've seen me."

His own eyes were tear-filled. "I have missed you so much. I could not do what I must do without seeing you once more. And it has been many years since Jason was home. I went to him first. The agent there is a good man. He understands what I want to do, and he gave us a special pass, giving me a fake name so that I could get here without trouble. We took a train most of the way. When we came through Cheyenne"—he lost his smile—"I remembered why I had to leave, and why now it is time to end it all."

Abbie closed her eyes. Here was reason to hope. Here were her grandchildren! She turned away, introducing herself, learning who each one was, hugging Louellen, overwhelmed at how much Jonathan had grown! "He was just a baby when I left the reservation!" she exclaimed. "Oh, I wanted so badly to come back again, but old age is beginning to take its toll, and I didn't think I could handle such a long trip."

She turned to Sweet Bird as Wolf's Blood introduced her and Little Eagle and Laughing Turtle. Abbie took great pleasure in seeing what a beautiful and very young woman Wolf's Blood had won as a wife. She cast him a sly glance.

"You aren't one in spirit with the wolves, my son. You are one in spirit with the sly fox, wooing and capturing this lovely creature."

Wolf's Blood grinned proudly, keeping an arm around his wife's shoulders. "Is she not the most beautiful Indian woman you have ever seen? She is Cree, and she speaks good English. *She* captured *me*. You might say she tricked me into marrying her."

They all laughed, while Sweet Bird blushed and covered her face.

"And you were completely unwilling, I suppose," Abbie answered her son.

"Of course! I told her she was too young for me."

Abbie folded her arms as they all laughed again. "You forget how well I understand Indian men," she answered. "Most of the ones I remember had no problem taking young wives."

Abbie's heart pained her, so full of love and happiness was it, at the same time breaking from the knowledge of the real reason for her son's presence. They all climbed back into the wagons and headed to Margaret and Morgan's house, where screams of joy were mixed with tears and laughter as Margaret greeted her brothers and their families. Wolf's Blood was astounded at the home his nephew, Zeke, had built for his parents.

"For so long I have lived far from all civilization," he said, he and Sweet Bird gawking at the grand chandelier in the two-story entranceway, the polished floors and velvet rugs and furnishings. So, Zeke Brown truly was a very rich man! For some time they all sat and talked, and Wolf's Blood learned of what Zeke had been through with Georgeanne's father. Now he owned all the man's land. How fitting! It made Wolf's Blood proud. "If only my own father could see this!" he said, gazing around the lovely parlor.

"I think he knows everything and is watching," Morgan told him.

Wolf's Blood nodded, astounded at how his sister and Morgan had aged, both of them gray now. Still, Margaret had a lingering beauty that came not just from her looks and the way she carried herself straight and proud; it came from a strength that showed in her dark eyes.

So much to tell. They were joined by Nathan and Susan and their children, as well as Lance. The talk ran past suppertime. Finally Margaret left to prepare something to eat, and still they talked, filling Wolf's Blood in on the ages of all the grandchildren, what they were doing. Wolf's Blood's heart nearly burst with pride when he heard about the lawsuit Hawk had won against the city of Denver on behalf of Arianne Ralston.

"No one thought he'd do it," Ellen said, "but he did. He's quite the famous lawyer there now."

Wolf's Blood breathed deeply with pride. "I can hardly wait to see my son again." He looked at his mother. "I remember Arianne. She was just a young girl with a crush on Hawk the last time I saw her."

Abbie nodded. "She was married to Edward Ralston when they met again. Then Edward was murdered." She sobered. "You should know that the two of them fell in love over the several months it took for the lawsuit to be completed. But once it was over, Arianne left for Ohio. She felt it was wrong for her to live her life with an Indian, for her little girl to have to put up with the remarks that might be made. Hawk wants to live on an Indian reservation and act as an attorney for the Indians; Arianne didn't think she could live that way. It hurt Hawk deeply."

Wolf's Blood frowned, turning to look at Sweet Bird. "So, my son still has not taken a woman to his side," he said, looking back at his mother.

Abbie found the remark curious, considering the way he'd looked at Sweet Bird first. What did this son of hers have in mind? She knew the spirit of the Indian man well, and relatives were expected to care for each other. A brother often took the wife of a dead brother into his tipi to care for her and provide for her children. Had he brought Sweet Bird here to find a man to take care of her? His *son?* She smiled at how simple and right that would seem to Wolf's Blood . . . but certainly not to Hawk, who in these last years had lived in a world far different from his father's. Perhaps she was wrong in her suspicions, but either way, it was a matter to be settled between Wolf's Blood and Hawk.

They talked about everything but the real reason Wolf's Blood had come. Jason's and Ellen's laughter did not quite ring true, and Sweet Bird looked ready to cry. Abbie suspected it was from more than the fact that she was among strangers, far from the only home she had ever known. She was losing her husband, and she well knew it, just as Margaret and Jason and Ellen knew they were losing a brother.

They ate, talked more. Lance and Daniel went off to the stables together to bed down horses, and Susan went to her and Nathan's wing of the house to put their children to sleep. Wolf's Blood's and Jason's sleepy children were shown to rooms upstairs and put to bed. Sweet Bird stayed to sleep with Little Eagle and Laughing Turtle so they would not be afraid, and Wolf's Blood, Ellen, Margaret, Morgan, Jason, Louellen, Nathan, and Abbie retired to the parlor, where their smiles faded and the atmosphere grew more somber.

"Sweet Bird's Christian name is Elizabeth," Wolf's Blood told them, "and our children's Christian names are Joseph and Sarah. I myself have never taken the Christian religion, but Elizabeth has, just as you did, Mother, while Father continued to pray to the Great spirit *Maheo.*"

Abbie nodded. "You might as well tell us, son, why you are really here. You always said you would not die a crippled old man, as your father would not. You brought Elizabeth and your children here so they would always be cared for. I know in my heart you have decided to die a warrior's death. How do you plan to do this?"

The room was silent, and Margaret looked away, struggling not to weep openly. Her brother had been through so much sorrow in his life. It was Wolf's Blood who was with his own father when Zeke died, and who had lost the first girl he'd ever loved as well as two wives to white men's bullets. He had lived the warrior's life, yet he'd also seen the end of the Indian way.

As Wolf's Blood rose, everyone could see him wince with pain. He still looked strong and was handsome for his age, but he walked slowly to the marble fireplace. "I had Hal send for Hawk and Iris, and for Jeremy," he told them. "I want to meet Iris's husband and see by his eyes that he is a good man." He grinned slyly, glancing at his mother. "Hawk and Iris's mother was Apache, remember. Down there I learned much hatred for Mexicans. Often the Apache stole Mexican women, or sometimes the other way around. I find some humor in my daughter marrying a Mexican man, but I am sure he is a good man or Hawk would not have allowed it."

Abbie smiled. "He is a very good man, and he does well. Iris is living quite comfortably."

Wolf's Blood nodded. "Good." He sighed. "I also

need to talk to my brother and my son before I do what I must do. It is better you do not ask me what that is. I can only tell you now that I will give myself up in Denver. I will let Hawk take care of it. They will take me to Cheyenne, I suppose, for trial."

Abbie frowned. "Wolf's Blood, if you do that you could be hanged. That is the last way any Indian wants to die. I wouldn't allow it! I'd shoot you myself first!" she exclaimed.

Wolf's Blood saw the terror and pain in her eyes. "I will not let myself hang. I am giving myself up because in that way I can draw attention to the hatred and misunderstanding that surrounded Jennifer's death. Joshua can come with us to Cheyenne. He will print the truth. I want the whole story told—why I did what I did—the useless way Jennifer died. Once that is done, I will choose my time."

"But . . . Hawk might be able to have you acquitted," Ellen told him. "Then you would be free. No violence would be necessary."

Wolf's Blood shook his head. "My son is good at what he does, I am sure, but he is not that good. It has been twelve years since it happened, but there will be people who remember I went after two other men who had fired no shots. I not only killed them, I took their scalps."

Morgan frowned and shook his head in wonder.

"Few white men would get away with such a thing, let alone an Indian," Wolf's Blood continued. "And it was white men I killed. There is no doubt in my mind how a hearing would go. But at least I will have my say." He walked over to Ellen, showing her his half-crippled hands. "Do you see this? I have no desire to be set free, my sister. My freedom can come only in death. I am sorry it must be this way, but if you truly love me, you will understand and accept what I must do." He turned to the others. "There are certain things I must talk about with Hawk first. I will stay here until he comes, then spend a few more days with my family . . ." He looked at Abbie. "Then it will be done." He held his chin a little higher, breathing deeper. "Be happy for me, my brothers and sisters. The summer sun is warm, and when it is warm and dry, I am not in so much pain. This is a good time to die, is it not, with the sun shining upon me? And outside, out there somewhere, the eagle waits for me. It sings its death song, calling me. I will be with my father again, and with Swift Arrow, and we will ride free in a land where there are many buffalo, and all the loved ones who have gone before us will be with us again." He looked proudly at his mother. "You understand. You long to go there yourself."

Abbie ached with emotion. Wolf's Blood's dark eyes captured hers, and she slowly rose. "Yes," she answered quietly.

Wolf's Blood nodded. "Your children and grandchildren need you a little while longer. But someone else needs you also, and when you go to him, it will be the right time."

Abbie could not speak. Only Wolf's Blood fully understood just how deeply she had loved his father. She walked closer and embraced him, and he wrapped his arms tightly around her.

"Mother, my mother," he said softly. "So much sorrow you have known. You knew how it would be from that first day you saw my father, yet you took the chance. There is no other woman like Abigail Monroe."

Abbie clung to him, weeping. "Oh, there are many, son," she finally answered through tears. "Your sister Margaret. Georgeanne, the fine woman who married young Zeke." She pulled away. "Your own Sweet Bird.

Surely she knew when she married you that she would never grow old with you. It took great courage for her to do what she did." She wiped at her tears. "You should go to her. She must feel so alone and afraid. We will help her all we can, and we will love her."

Wolf's Blood blinked back his own tears. "I knew that you would. But it is possible she will not always have to stay here. You will understand when the time comes. For now I am very tired. I will do as you say and go to her." He looked at Margaret. "Which room is it?"

She sniffed and wiped at her eyes. "Go up the stairs, if it isn't too painful for you to climb them. It's the third door on the right." She rose and embraced him. "I love you, Wolf's Blood. I was always so proud of you."

"And I have always been proud of you, of all in my family, even Jeremy. He has done so much for my children."

"He's helped all of us in one way or another," Abbie said.

Wolf's Blood embraced each person in the room, then turned to all of them. "I go to my family now. All of you should also rest, and do not be sad. Not for me. Only be sad if I should die of this ugly disease instead of dying with honor."

He turned and left them, and they all stood there looking at each other, not a dry eye in the room. "He's really going to do it, isn't he?" Ellen asked her mother. "We can't let him, Mother. The authorities don't even know he's here. Why can't he just stay here? We can take care of him if he gets too crippled to walk. I'd come from Pueblo and help as often as I could."

Abbie smiled in spite of her tears. "I am sure you would, Ellen, but you know how it was for Zeke. Wolf's Blood is just like him. Can you really see him dying that way, all crippled up in a wheelchair or in bed? Don't you understand what that would do to his pride?"

Ellen brushed tears from her cheeks with a shaking hand. "I just keep hoping he'll change his mind."

"A Monroe? Change his mind once it's made up? Ellen, I thought you knew this family better than that." Oh, how she wanted to fall to the floor and weep. Her son! Her precious firstborn! But her children needed her to be strong now, and Wolf's' Blood needed her to understand. "He is right, Ellen. His only freedom will come with death. We have to sit back and let him do what he must, and be happy for him. He needs our understanding and support. We have him for a little while yet. Let's just enjoy that much and try not to think too far ahead. Hawk and Jeremy will come soon. We can at least have one more family reunion. It's been twelve years since the last one. Sweet Bird will meet the rest of the family." She thought again of Wolf's Blood's remark about Hawk, the way he had looked at Sweet Bird when he'd made it.

Hawk wearily stepped down from the carriage. He'd spent the last two days in court in Fort Collins, defending a Chinaman accused of theft. He'd managed to get the poor man acquitted, and he was glad; but the strain of the case and of having to travel back and forth had taken their toll. He was glad it was dark enough that no one would notice his wrinkled suit and the shirt open halfway down his chest because of the heat. He paid the driver of the buggy that had brought him from the railroad station and picked up his leather bag, then walked the hedge-lined sidewalk to the front porch of his small but elegant home. Only then did he realize someone was sitting in the swing on his front porch.

"Jeremy! What are you doing here at this hour!"

"Your office said you'd be home about now. How did it go?"

"I got the man off." Hawk frowned, noticing the strained look on his uncle's face. "What is it! Is it Grandma?"

Jeremy sighed and rose, shaking his head. "No. It's Wolf's Blood. Your father is home—at the ranch. He wants to see both of us. I don't like the sound of it, Hawk. Sweet Bird's letters have told us his arthritis is getting worse. You know how like your grandfather he is."

Hawk felt the remaining energy go out of him, and he set down his bag. "Damn!" he muttered. He'd wanted so badly to see his father once more, but not under these circumstances. There was only one reason Wolf's Blood would finally come back to the land where he was still a wanted man.

Twenty-five

The family was together again, but with many new faces, family members who were not present at the original reunion: Sweet Bird, Little Eagle, Laughing Turtle; Louellen, Jonathan, Marian, James; Lillian's fiancé, Matt Wilkerson, a boot- and saddle-maker; Nathan's wife Susan and their family; Raphael, Miguel, Julio and Eduardo; Georgeanne, with her and Zeke's two sons, Peter and Jason. New faces, grandchildren and great-grandchildren, new generations to take the place of the old.

Abbie thought how joyous the occasion could still be if not for the cloud hanging over Wolf's Blood's head. Still, being Monroes, everyone put up a good front, deciding that nothing should detract from their pleasure in having the family together again, and all could feel the spiritual presences of their uncles, Dan and Swift Arrow; the more powerful presence of Zeke Monroe. Abbie could see all her children and grandchildren had Zeke's stubborn strength, his smile, his courage. They were survivors.

Other than a tearful reunion between Hawk and his father, and between Jeremy and Wolf's Blood, nothing more had been said yet about why Wolf's Blood was here. For a few days he wanted only family togetherness, and Abbie suspected there was something else he wanted from Hawk besides taking him to Denver to

turn himself in. He seemed to constantly be finding
ways to bring Sweet Bird and Hawk together, making
them sit beside each other at the supper table, insisting
Hawk spend time with his new little brother and sister
and get to know Sweet Bird better, since he wanted
Hawk to help care for his family in case something
happened to him. Abbie suspected Wolf's Blood meant
more than monetary support and an older brother's
guidance for his children. Hawk did not seem to understand yet what his father was after, but there was
no doubt in Abbie's mind that her grandson did appreciate Sweet Bird's gracious beauty and gentle personality. He probably loved her simply because she
loved Wolf's Blood and had given his father some bit
of happiness in these last years.

This morning Wolf's Blood had insisted Hawk take
Sweet Bird and the children on a ride around the perimeter of the old, original ranch, even though Hawk
was not even sure himself of just what the boundaries
were. He had not been raised here as Wolf's Blood had,
but Wolf's Blood told him the landmarks to look for,
then asked him to tell Sweet Bird some stories about
the family, about his grandfather and grandmother.

The younger children played, the older boys helped
Morgan with chores, and the women were in the house
discussing what to prepare for lunch. Abbie watched
Wolf's Blood strain to lift his son onto a horse in front
of Hawk, his daughter onto a horse in front of Sweet
Bird, who today had decided to wear an Indian tunic
rather than a white woman's dress. The tunic pulled
up slightly when she straddled her horse, revealing her
tawny, slender thighs. Abbie almost laughed, guessing
Wolf's Blood had asked her to wear the tunic. He said
something more to Hawk, then smacked the horses
and sent them on their way. Abbie stood on the porch
and waited, noticing her son watched his wife and his

son for a very long time, until they disappeared over
a hill. When he turned and headed back to the house,
Abbie greeted him with folded arms.

"You should have gone with them," she suggested.
"You know more about this place than Hawk does."
She could see the hurt behind the twinkle in his dark
eyes.

"I have too many aches and pains now. Riding is
hard for me."

"Oh? You were always an even better rider than your
own father. I hardly think you would allow a few aches
and pains to keep you off a horse's back. *You* are the
one who should be off riding with your wife, considering that the two of you probably don't have much
time left together."

He watched her closely, then smiled sadly. "You have
always been too smart for me, Mother. Father could
never hide anything from you, and neither can I." As
he started inside, Abbie grasped his arm.

"You can't force love, Wolf's Blood."

He turned and looked to the hill over which his son
and wife had disappeared. "I know Sweet Bird. And I
know my son. I won't have to force anything. It will
happen naturally." He met her eyes. "Did you see how
he looked this morning, his hair hanging loose? He
feels very Indian today, I think. I remember when I was
like that, strong and sure and handsome. That is the
kind of husband my Sweet Bird should have, not a crippled old man." He sighed. "She is a good, good woman.
Hawk will see that." He put a hand over his mother's.
"When my father died, did you not marry his brother?"

Abbie reddened a little. "That was years later."

"You were older, and your children were mostly
grown. You did not need a man so much in the way
Sweet Bird will need one. But even so, be honest with
me, Mother. What was the main reason you married

Swift Arrow? Because he was lonely, and you were? Or was it perhaps because he reminded you so much of my father?"

She let go of his hand and turned away. "Now *you* are the one who is being too clever."

Wolf's Blood smiled, touching her shoulder. "Hawk *is* very much like me in looks and temperament, don't you think? He is his father's son."

He squeezed her shoulder and left her, and Abbie slowly sat down on a porch swing, memories flooding in on her . . . Swift Arrow . . . Zeke. Yes, Sweet Bird would be needing a man; right now she was full of fear and worry, a vulnerable woman. Hawk was still hurting from Arianne's scorn. "You're a devil, Wolf's Blood," she muttered, realizing his timing was perfect, and he damn well knew it.

The day turned blistering hot, and Hawk guided his horse to a swimming hole he remembered from when he was a little boy. He was pleased with the fine Appaloosa he was riding. His uncle, Morgan, had kept up with his grandfather Zeke's reputation of breeding and raising only the best horses, which were sold to buyers from all over Colorado and even into Kansas and Nebraska.

"I remember coming here when I was a little boy and lived here at the ranch for a while with my Apache mother while my father was away with Grandfather Zeke. This little pond is a breakoff from the river, so you can swim in it without worrying about getting caught in the current. I thought the kids might like to take off their clothes and get cooled off."

"Oh, they would love it!" Sweet Bird answered.

Hawk dismounted, lifting down Little Eagle. He walked over and took Laughing Turtle from Sweet Bird,

unable to avoid noticing her lovely legs as she slid down
from her horse. About halfway through their ride this
morning it had hit him what his father was up to. The
knowledge had left him confused and a little angry, not
just with Wolf's Blood, but with himself for being so
well educated and such a clever lawyer, yet allowing himself to be blind as to what was going on. Did Sweet Bird
understand it, or was she just being led along by Wolf's
Blood, too? *Damn him,* he thought. He loved the man
beyond description, but the decisions Wolf's Blood had
made in life often frustrated him. It was the Indian in
Wolf's Blood that made him do some of those things
he did. Some customs were born and bred into a man,
educated or not. It was simply the way.

The sweltering heat did nothing to ease Hawk's frustration, but he forced himself to give Sweet Bird the
benefit of the doubt and not blame her for any of this.
What irritated him most was that he had some of the
feelings his father wanted him to have. He already
loved Little Eagle and Laughing Turtle, and it was not
easy to ignore Sweet Bird's beauty, both in body and
spirit. He'd held a deep appreciation for both since
first meeting her five years ago.

Already Sweet Bird had removed Laughing Turtle's
simple cotton dress, her drawers and moccasins, and
the little girl screamed and laughed as she toddled to
the edge of the pond, sitting down in a shallow spot
and splashing water with her hands. Little Eagle took
off his own clothes and went farther in. Hawk laughed
at their excitement, thinking how good the cool water
must feel. "It's not deep anyplace, as I remember," he
told Sweet Bird.

She took off her own moccasins and waded in to
take Laughing Turtle farther in, holding the little girl's
hands while she wriggled and jumped on her chunky
little legs. Laughing Turtle's smile was infectious, set

off by the deep dimples in her cheeks and her big and bright eyes. Hawk felt a pain in his chest at the thought of how ignorant the children were of what could soon happen to their father. If only the whole world could be as innocent and accepting as children.

"The water feels wonderful," Sweet Bird told him. "I wish I could also cool off this way."

A picture of how she must look naked flashed into his mind, and he turned away, wanting to hit something. "Go ahead, if you want. I won't look."

Sweet Bird dipped Laughing Turtle, and the girl giggled and sputtered. Sweet Bird thought how nice it would be if Wolf's Blood could be here with them, but she understood why he was not. She could not help but feel a flush of attraction for Hawk. Few men were as handsome, and she suspected Wolf's Blood had been very much like his son at Hawk's age. "Are you sure it is all right? What about you? You must be very hot also."

"I'm all right."

Sweet Bird glanced over to see that Little Eagle was fine. He was in deeper water, but he was hanging onto a log and splashing his feet. She set Laughing Turtle in the shallow water again, then removed her tunic. "Do not look until I tell you it is all right." Most Indian women didn't wear anything under their tunics, but she had grown accustomed to wearing drawers. She removed those also, then picked up Laughing Turtle and carried her into deeper water. "Oh, it feels wonderful, Hawk!" She lowered herself to her neck, holding her wriggling daughter's chubby little body only halfway in the water and wincing when the child kicked water in her face. "You should come in, too! It is all right. We are related now, you know. I will not look if you want to come and get cool."

He walked closer to the edge, taking off his boots and shirt. "I'll just get my feet wet and splash some

water over my face and shoulders." He was growing an-
grier with his father by the minute. This was a damn
awkward situation, and he sure as hell was going to talk
to the man about it. He leaned down and relished the
feel of the cold water as he threw some over his face
and neck and shoulders. "It is cooling. We'd better get
back pretty soon, though. They'll have lunch ready."
He looked at Sweet Bird, instantly alarmed when he
saw her standing waist-high in the water, clinging to
Laughing Turtle and suddenly unconcerned about her
nakedness.

"Hawk! Hawk! I cannot see him! I cannot see him!"

Hawk knew she was referring to Little Eagle, who,
he now noticed, was no longer kicking and splashing
beside the log. The log itself was positioned differently.
It must have slipped a little. "What the hell?"

"Hawk, find him! Find him!"

Hawk ran into the pond, wading past Sweet Bird and
realizing this area was deeper now than it had been
years ago. A slight undercurrent told him the river was
taking more control over the pond, eating away at the
center and making it deeper and more dangerous. He
swam to the log, dived under it and felt around. The
water was so murky he could see nothing. He came up
for air, his heart pounding at Sweet Bird's screams of
terror. Wolf's Blood's situation was bad enough for her.
It would be terrible if she lost one of her children.

He dived down again, frantically grasping at everything he touched, finally sure he had hold of a child's
arm. He held on tight, feeling a little body, pulling the
boy up with him. He gasped and choked for air when
he came up the second time, half blaming himself for
this. It would be terrible for Wolf's Blood as well if his
precious little son died! And this was Hawk's little
brother, a part of his father that would go on forever.

"God save him! Save him!" Sweet Bird wept. She followed Hawk as he carried the boy's limp, naked body ashore and laid it in the grass beside the pond. "My son! My Little Eagle! How did this happen!" She knelt beside them, rocking a now-crying Laughing Turtle.

Hawk noticed a bloody cut on the boy's forehead. "The log somehow rolled. He must have slipped when it did, then gotten hit on the head." He cleared Little Eagle's airway, rolled the boy onto his stomach and pressed on his back. "Come on, Little Eagle! You weren't under that long! Spit the water out and start breathing!" He noticed some water gush out of the boy's mouth. Placing an arm under Little Eagle's stomach and raising him to his knees, he pounded on his back some more, until finally Little Eagle began coughing and sputtering and finally threw up. Hawk quickly carried the boy back to the water, helping him wash his face and rinse his mouth, talking soothingly to him. "You'll be all right, Little Eagle." He felt like crying himself, only then realizing just how much he loved these children who might soon lose their father. Someone had to be a father to them.

"Is he all right?" A still-crying Sweet Bird stood beside him, holding Laughing Turtle. She finally set the little girl down and pulled Little Eagle into her arms. "Dear God, thank you!" She wept. "I could not live without my babies!" She looked up at Hawk, then hugged him with one arm while grasping Little Eagle with the other. "You saved him!"

Hawk embraced her, trying to ignore the naked breasts pressed against his chest. "It's my own damn fault it happened," he answered. "I should have checked out the depth before I let any of you go in. It was different when I was little." He let go of her and stooped down to check a still-dazed Little Eagle. "How do you feel, little brother?"

The boy put a hand to his head. "I don't know. What happened?"

"You hit your head somehow and slipped under the water. You scared us, Little Eagle." He made the boy sit down. "Stay right there and rest a minute. Then we'll get dressed and go back to the ranch house."

The boy blinked, his eyes tearing. He kept hold of Hawk's hand. "Is something bad going to happen to my father? Mama is always sad."

Hawk glanced at Sweet Bird as she knelt down beside them, her waist-length hair hanging in wet strings over her shoulders and breasts. "It is a time for all of us to be very brave," she told her son. "Your father wishes to die like a proud warrior. He has explained this to you."

Little Eagle's lips puckered, and he looked back at Hawk. "Will you stay with us, my brother, if my father goes away? I don't want you to go away, too."

Hawk looked at Sweet Bird, his gaze falling to her full breasts, the nipples taut from the cold water. She seemed only then to realize she was still naked. She drew in her breath and hurried away to find her tunic. The man in Hawk could not help noticing how firm and slender her bottom and thighs were, her skin like soft brown velvet. He grimaced with awkwardness and guilt, then looked back at Little Eagle. "I won't leave you," he said.

The boy sniffed. "I like you. Father says I should be with you if anything ever happens to him."

Again the anger returned. "He did, did he?"

The boy nodded, then threw his arms around Hawk's neck. "Thank you for getting me out of the water."

Hawk hugged him tightly, watching Sweet Bird drop her tunic over her head and cover herself. "Everything will be all right," he told Little Eagle. He left the boy, kissing his hair before rising, and walked over to Sweet

Bird, grasping her arms. "I know what my father is up to," he told her. "And I don't like it. You are my father's *wife,* damn it!"

Her eyes teared, and she touched his chest. "Do not be angry with Wolf's Blood. It is the Indian way." She hung her head. "He wants only to be sure the children and I are cared for. He can think of no one else he would want to be a true father to them save you. As for me, you do not have to . . . It is not necessary that you love me . . . that way. I will not be a burden to you. You will always be free to marry whomever you choose, as long as she would love my Little Eagle and Laughing Turtle and be good to them. If you do not find me desirable, it is not necessary—"

"Desirable? Of *course* I find you desirable, damn it!"

He squeezed her arms until they began to hurt. She looked up at him, a little surprised, sure he did not want her that way. She felt the same confusion he did, the same guilt, the same love for Wolf's Blood. "It is not wrong. It would make him very happy. You talk to him, Hawk. You need to talk about it."

"You *bet* we're going to talk about it!"

"You will not have him long, Hawk. Do not be angry. It is not easy for him to do this. Surely you know that. It only shows how much he loves me and our children."

Hawk closed his eyes and sighed, pulling her into his arms. "I know." He felt her tremble, knew she could no longer hold back the tears.

"I love him so," she wept, "but I always knew . . . I would not grow old with him."

Hawk stroked her damp hair. "I'll be here for you, Sweet Bird. I don't know how it will all work out, but we'll just take one day at a time. This is all so awkward. I don't quite know what to do, how to feel. My own heart is hurting over someone else."

She looked up at him, tears on her cheeks. "We both

know what it is to love someone and lose them. My own people have all died off, and you have seen much loss in your own life. I admire your strength and courage, Hawk. You are very much like your father, also a warrior, but in a different way. You can teach his children a new way, but help them to still be proud to be Indian. That is all Wolf's Blood wants of you."

She felt good in his arms, and suddenly he could not stop himself from leaning down to kiss her full lips. She was so sad, so lonely, so beautiful. It was all there in an instant, perhaps from desperate fear, loneliness, uncertainty about what lay ahead. Both needed—wanted— something real and dependable in their lives, someone to hold and to love. She threw her arms around his neck, appreciating the feel of his strong arms around her, his virility. She already loved him because he was a part of Wolf's Blood; being with him was like being with her husband, as she imagined he'd been when he was younger.

He left her lips, still holding her close. "My God, Sweet Bird, this isn't right." He let go of her, gently pushing her away.

"It *is* right," she answered, capturing his gaze. "It is your father's greatest wish. But as long as he is alive, I will always belong to him. We both honor him and love him, and now we understand that perhaps we can honor him in the way he most hopes to be honored when he is gone. Until then, he is my husband, and your father, and it can be no other way. We have discovered something here today, and it is a wonderful thing. It is not wrong."

She turned away, walking over to pick up Laughing Turtle. She dressed the girl, saying nothing more. Little Eagle pulled on his clothes, still seeming a little dazed and confused. Hawk lifted the boy onto his own horse, helped his mother and sister onto theirs. When he climbed up behind Little Eagle, the boy turned so that he sat backward. That way he could put his arms around Hawk and hug him all the way home.

Twenty-six

"Will you come with us to Cheyenne if I am sent there?" Wolf's Blood sat in a wicker chair on the porch of Margaret's house. Because of the heat he wore only deerskin pants and a vest, a pair of old moccasins on his otherwise-bare feet. His hair, a streak of gray at one side, hung loose, a beaded hairpiece sporting an eagle feather tied into one side of it. He studied his brother Jeremy, who had put on a little weight but still seemed to be quite healthy.

Jeremy wore neatly pressed cotton pants with suspenders, and the sleeves of his starched white shirt were rolled to his elbows. He sat in the porch swing, looking at Wolf's Blood, feeling sick inside because of all the years they'd missed being together. "You know I will."

Wolf's Blood nodded. "I feel the same as you do. It is sad that for many years we never understood each other. It was good to talk to you when we had that reunion twelve years ago. But for what happened in Cheyenne, I would have liked to spend more time with you." He grinned. "I have never even seen your grand house in Denver."

Jeremy sighed. "That's not important. What was important was that we see more of each other, but those bastards who shot Jennifer cheated us out of that." He sighed. "I'm glad you found a halfway decent life up in Canada. Sweet Bird is beautiful, and her name fits her. She's very sweet, and slender and wispy as a bird."

Wolf's Blood grinned. "She and our children keep an old man like me very busy. I can no longer keep up with them."

Jeremy wiped at the sweat on his brow with the back of his hand. "Well, I'm hoping things work out when you go to Denver. But if . . ." He leaned forward, resting his elbows on his knees. "If something happens to you, you know I'll do my part in taking care of those children. Between me and Margaret—and mother and everybody—they'll want for nothing."

A gust of hot wind ruffled Wolf's Blood's hair, and Jeremy glanced at him curiously, sure he'd heard a distant drumming.

"I cannot tell you how grateful I am for what you did for Hawk and Iris," Wolf's Blood told him. "But my new family . . . I am hoping Hawk will take care of them. He always said he intends to one day work at a reservation, represent Indians in their cases against the government. On a reservation, Sweet Bird would feel more at home, and my children would grow up with their own kind, yet they would have Hawk showing them how to survive in the white man's world. Sweet Bird would not be happy in a place like Denver, and here at the ranch, in this part of Colorado, there are no Indians. She is *all* Indian, and she needs to be near her own kind."

Jeremy nodded. "You always needed to be near them, too." He met his brother's gaze. "Just as Zeke did."

"It was as natural for me as breathing, like going the way you chose was natural for you."

Jeremy stood up, walking over to lean on the porch railing and stare out at the rolling hills beyond the barns. "I feel I can never make up enough for hating you as I did, abandoning the family for so many years."

Wolf's Blood watched the hills himself . . . wondering. It was nearly lunchtime, and Hawk and Sweet Bird had not yet returned. "You have more than made up for that. I was not such a good brother myself. I blamed you for things I did not understand. That is long in the past now. Look at the way you have taken care of my children, helped Margaret over the years, helped Mother, young Zeke; you are a good man, Jeremy."

Jeremy shrugged, a little embarrassed. He straightened, folding his arms. "How about that Zeke? Hell, he's richer than I am, but investing in his gold mine has made me richer, too. Can you believe his stroke of luck? The best part is, the Browns and Monroes own one hundred thousand acres of land, most of it where the Cheyenne spent their winters when they were free to migrate."

"*Hinta Nagi,* the Ghost Timbers," Wolf's Blood replied with a grin. "I remember when our uncle, Swift Arrow, would come there with a whole tribe, and Mother and Father would join them. That was when Zeke's brothers, Red Eagle and Black Elk, were still alive. Those were good times! Good times!" His smile faded, and he held Jeremy's gaze. "I want you with me, Jeremy, whatever happens. I had a dream . . ." He rose, wincing at the pain in his knees. "I will not say what it was. I can only say it is important that you are with me. Will you be able to leave Denver if you have to?"

"Of course I can. I'm just glad as hell I've been able to see you again." Jeremy felt a little uneasy. What was the dream his brother had had? One thing he knew, dreams were very important to the Cheyenne. They could predict the future, and were often right. Before he managed to question his brother further, Margaret appeared at the door.

"Lunch is ready. Meals are beginning to be quite a chore around here, one big table in the kitchen for all the children, another big table in the dining room for all the adults. If it were not for Mother's help and that of my sisters-in-law and daughters-in-law, we could never keep all these mouths fed in one sitting. You two get in here now and eat." She put her hands on her hips. "By the way. Where are Hawk and Sweet Bird?"

"I think they're coming now," Jeremy answered, watching the hills again.

"Well, at least they are not lost," Wolf's Blood commented, a sly look in his eyes. He glanced at Margaret; he knew she suspected what he was up to. She gave him a chastising look and left the doorway. "I will wait for them," Wolf's Blood told Jeremy.

Jeremy turned and grasped his shoulder. "Don't take too long or there might not be any food left."

"The way my sister cooks? She probably made enough for fifty people."

Jeremy grinned. "The way this family is growing, that might not be such a stretch." He went inside, and Wolf's Blood watched the little group approach, noticing Hawk's pants looked wet, and Sweet Bird's hair had been wet and had dried in stringy, unbrushed layers. Little Eagle was riding facing Hawk, his arms and legs wrapped around his big brother.

Wolf's Blood frowned, walking down the steps to greet them when they rode up to the house.

"Father!" Little Eagle said, letting go of Hawk and reaching for Wolf's Blood. "I almost drowned! Hawk saved me!"

"Is that so?" Wolf's Blood lifted him down, ignoring the pain in his arms and shoulders. "Look at you! You have a cut on your head. How did this happen?"

"We went swimming," the boy answered, as his father set him on his feet. "It was hot, and Hawk took us to a place where he said he swam when he was little. Do you know where it is?"

Wolf's Blood grinned. "I know of it. I took Hawk there myself once. Hawk's mother liked to go there." He thought how most Indian women liked to swim naked, and he glanced at Sweet Bird. "I see you went swimming also."

She handed Laughing Turtle to Hawk, their gazes holding for a moment before she slipped down from her horse. "More of a dunk than a swim. It felt good to get wet," she told her husband. "Little Eagle was playing by a log, and it slipped. It cut his head and he went under. Hawk pulled him out. It was so terrible! I thought we had lost our son." She embraced Wolf's Blood. "Thank goodness Hawk found him quickly. The pond was deeper than he remembered." She turned and knelt in front of Little Eagle, stroking his hair. "Hawk got him to cough up most of the water, but I think he should rest this afternoon. Do not eat too much when you go inside, Little Eagle. It might not be good to fill your belly right now. Eat only a little, and then go upstairs and lie down."

"I will, Mama." The boy looked up at his father. "Mother and Hawk were glad I was okay. They were so happy, they kissed each other," he said innocently.

Wolf's Blood met Sweet Bird's eyes, and she quickly looked away. He glanced at Hawk, who turned from the hitching post to cast his father an angry look.

"You and I have to talk," he told Wolf's Blood boldly. "Right now! Forget about lunch."

Wolf's Blood's eyebrows arched, and he was inwardly amused at his son's obvious frustration. He struggled with his jealousy, yet secretly rejoiced to know there truly was an attraction between Sweet Bird and Hawk. "That is fine with me. We will go to the barn, where no one will hear us." He looked at Sweet Bird, touching her arm. "Do not look away from me. It is not necessary." She met his eyes, and he saw tears in hers.

"I love you more than my own life," she told him.

He leaned down and kissed her cheek. "I have no doubt of that. Take the children inside and tell the others Hawk and I will come later."

Sweet Bird turned away and chased after Laughing Turtle, picking her up and carrying her into the house, where Little Eagle had already gone to tell the others about his mishap. Wolf's Blood looked at his son, who still stood at a distance, watching him sullenly. "Untie the horses. We will take them to the barn with us."

Hawk obeyed, handing his father the reins to Sweet Bird's horse. It pained him to see how much slower Wolf's Blood walked now. He said nothing until they reached the barn; then his anger showed in the way he jerked the saddles and blankets off the horses. Wolf's Blood only watched silently as Hawk slapped the horses on their rumps and put each into a stall. "They need to be brushed down, but I'll have to do it later," he said. He turned then, facing Wolf's Blood and folding his arms. "What the hell are you up to? I am not *blind*, Father! You've been getting me and Sweet Bird together for a week! Sweet Bird is your *wife*, not a piece of property! I *respect* her as your wife, the woman who loves my father and gave him two children!"

"Of course you do. I would not want my wife to go with any man who did *not* honor her. And I honor *you* above all men." Wolf's Blood held his chin proudly. "I am Indian, and *you* are Indian. The Indian way is for a man's wife to be taken care of by a relative when he dies, usually a brother. I have no brothers Indian enough to take this duty upon themselves. Jeremy is too white in his thinking, and Jason also is, even though he is himself married to an Indian woman. Your own grandmother went to Zeke's brother Swift Arrow after Zeke died."

"That was years later, and it was of her own choosing!"

"And you do not think being with you would be of Sweet Bird's choosing? Do you think I would want her to go to you unwillingly?"

Hawk threw up his hands. "I don't know *what* you want! I saw the look in your eyes when Little Eagle told you we . . ." He hesitated, turning around and slamming shut a stall gate.

"Told me you kissed Sweet Bird?"

Hawk sighed, his back to him. "It just . . . happened. We were both relieved that Little Eagle was all right. She was crying, and I felt sorry for her."

"You wanted her. You even wanted her five years ago when you visited us in Canada. I *also* am not blind, Hawk."

Hawk shook his head. "I just thought she was very pretty and awfully sweet. I left thinking what a lovely woman she was. I cared about her because she cared about *you* and gave you happiness." He turned and faced his father. "Back in Denver, I met Arianne. After her husband died we fell in love. I always thought I'd marry Indian, Father, but Arianne changed all that."

Wolf's Blood nodded slowly. "And then she left you, because *you* were Indian! Some white women cannot rise above that, no matter how much they love a man. Did that hurt not tell you something? Some people simply belong with their own kind, and you are one of them. Whether it is Sweet Bird or not, you will marry Indian. When you go to a reservation, *that* is where you will find the woman you love. All I am asking of you is to take Sweet Bird and my children with you, where they can live among their own kind. But I want you to always remain an influence in their lives, to teach them how to survive in this new world. And I want you to watch over Sweet Bird. Make sure she marries a man who will be good to her, not a drunken Indian with no job and no hope! That is all I want, Hawk. I need to know my family will be taken care of and that Sweet Bird will be happy. My greatest wish is that *you* might be the man to bring her that happiness. With you she would always live well, and for her, being with you would be a little like being with me. She is still very young, still beautiful and pleasing in the night."

Hawk rolled his eyes and turned away at the remark.

"And she can bear more children. Not only do I want *her* to be happy, Hawk, I want *you* to be happy; and I know how happy Sweet Bird can make a man, what a good wife and mother she is. You are of an age at which it is time you took a wife and had sons and daughters of your own."

Hawk ran a hand through his hair. It felt damp from diving under the water to rescue Little Eagle. "I know that," he answered.

"Tell me you could not love Little Eagle and Laughing Turtle as if they were your own son and daughter."

Hawk remained turned away. "You know I could. I already do."

"And tell me it would not be easy to love Sweet Bird."

Hawk gritted his teeth, grasping the stall gate. "Damn it, Father, she's your *wife!*"

"Of course she is. Do you think I would want you sleeping with her while I am still alive? I am not asking you to do something so against your honor, son, nor would Sweet Bird ever consider such a thing. I only need to know that you both have feelings that might grow into something much more precious if something happens to me. I can see that this is so, and it pleases me greatly. For now I only need to know you would always look after my family."

Hawk hung his head, not replying right away. Finally

he faced his father. "I will always look after them. You
should know you don't need to ask it of me. As far as
the other . . . yes, I do have feelings for Sweet Bird.
Up to now I had attributed them to the fact that she
is the mother of my little brother and sister—and my
father's wife. I have looked at her more as a sister than
anything else. She's certainly too young to be called
my stepmother, wouldn't you say?"

Wolf's Blood studied him a moment, realizing his
son was beginning to joke with him. The idea of Hawk
calling Sweet Bird mother was indeed amusing. He
smiled. "It would seem very strange."

Hawk sighed in resignation, a hint of a smile on his
lips. His dark eyes drilled into his father's gaze lovingly.
"I would never, never dishonor you, Father."

Wolf's Blood stepped closer. "If I thought you would,
I would not have seen that you and my wife were often
alone. It is only that the Indian in me wishes to know
his wife and children will always be protected and pro-
vided for when he dies."

A look of determination came into Hawk's eyes.
"You aren't going to die. I'm going to get you off,
have the Monroe name cleared; and then we'll get the
best doctors in Denver to see what they can do for the
arthritis."

Wolf's Blood smiled sadly. "You will not get me cleared.
You can try, but I did what I did; that cannot be erased,
especially since I am Indian. I will at least get the truth
out, maybe make a few people understand *why* I did it.
And nothing can be done about arthritis, Hawk, except
perhaps to drink something for the pain; then, instead
of dying just a crippled old man, I would die a drunken
or drug-filled crippled old man. That would be even
worse. I have often thought of turning to whiskey to dull
the pain, but I do not want to go the way of so many

other Indian men. Stay away from the firewater, Hawk. Never lose your pride. Promise me that."

A lump rose in Hawk's throat. "I promise."

Wolf's Blood grasped his arm. "I do not know exactly what will happen, Hawk, but you will know when I choose the right time. I have asked Jeremy to be with us through all of it. Your uncle loves you as his own. He has been like a father to you, and that is good. You will still have him to turn to. You have not had me as a father for many years, but you have done just fine. I am proud of you, very proud."

Hawk drew a deep breath. "And I am proud of you. You have never been afraid to be the Indian that you are, and by Indian law everything you have done has been right. But you have suffered so much over the years, Father, losing three different women you loved to white man's bullets. I am glad you had your days of glory, your days of riding as a warrior with Swift Arrow." He paused and frowned. "It's grandfather, isn't it?"

Wolf's Blood's eyebrows arched, and he stepped back a little. "What do you mean?"

"You want to be with him. You want to be with Cheyenne Zeke, with Lone Eagle."

Wolf's Blood's eyes teared. "I miss him as much today as I did when I held his dying body in my arms at Fort Robinson. My father and I were one spirit, just as you and I are, Hawk. And as I know my father has always been with me, know that I will always be with you. When you hear the wolves howl, you will know that I am near, as I know my father is near when the eagle's shadow passes over me."

Hawk closed his eyes and swallowed. "Do you know what is really strange?" He looked at his father again, a tear slipping down his cheek. "All these years we've been apart, I haven't been able to talk to you, ask your advice, turn to you for anything; and yet I can hardly imagine life without you in it."

Wolf's Blood only nodded. He stepped closer, embracing his son, and they hugged tightly, both crying quietly.

"Does Grandma Abbie know?" Hawk asked.

"No one understands better than my mother."

"She thinks as much of you as she did of Zeke. It would kill her if something happened to you."

"No, son. It would kill her to see me die a crippled old man." Wolf's Blood pulled away. "Come. There is food waiting for us."

Hawk quickly wiped at his eyes, then put an arm around his father to help him walk back to the house, where they were greeted with stares of worry and wonder. "What's everybody looking at?" Hawk asked, irritated.

"Little Eagle told us how you rescued him," Abbie said with a grin. "It sounded like quite an adventure."

Hawk shook his head and took his chair. "It wasn't anything. I got to him quickly, so he was easy to find. It scared us to death at first, but he's all right."

Wolf's Blood looked at his mother, suspecting Little Eagle had told everyone that Hawk kissed Sweet Bird. He decided to change the subject. "I remember the story you told us once about rescuing a little Indian girl when you were first married to Father," he said.

Abbie smiled. "What a long time ago that was! I was only sixteen. Zeke's Indian stepfather gave me a knife and a blanket for saving the girl, and a warrior named Two Feathers gave me a coup feather to honor my bravery. I still have the knife and the coup feather in my trunk."

Wolf's Blood stood behind Hawk. He squeezed his shoulder as he spoke. "So my son gets some of his courage from his white grandmother."

Everyone smiled. "Sit down and eat, Wolf's Blood," Margaret told her brother. "Sweet Bird went upstairs to put the children to bed for naps. Little Eagle needs to rest this afternoon."

Wolf's Blood nodded. "I will go up and see him again first. I will say, Margaret, it is a good thing I did not have to live in a house like this. Climbing those stairs is not an easy task for me. I hate to admit that." He sighed, leaving Hawk and heading toward the double sliding doors to the dining room. "I must tell you all I have decided I will go to Denver in two days. It has been good seeing all my family again. The time is near now to do what must be done." He turned and left, and everyone sobered. Margaret looked at Hawk.

"What were you two talking about out there?"

Hawk reached for a biscuit, although his appetite had suddenly left him. "It's personal."

"You *can* get him off, can't you, Hawk?" LeeAnn asked.

Hawk just stared at the biscuit in his hand. "I don't know. It isn't likely, but I'll try."

"All we can do is pray the Lord's will be done," Abbie told them all. "Whatever happens, we all have each other, and we'll all be here for Sweet Bird and the children, and for Hawk."

Wolf's Blood could hear the conversation as he made his way to the stairs. Yes, this was a good, strong family. He would never have to worry about his wife and children. He painfully climbed the carpeted stairway to the room where Little Eagle and Laughing Turtle lay in a big bed together. Sweet Bird straightened from kissing them both. He watched her eyes as he came closer. Yes, she loved him. "It is all right," he told her.

She ran to him, breaking into tears. "He is a good man," she whispered.

"Of course he is. He is my son. Someday he will be your strength."

Twenty-seven

"No, Mother, you will not go. If I have to have Morgan tie you to a chair, I will do it." Wolf's Blood sat on the porch swing with Abbie, watching the family members who lived in Denver and Pueblo load their baggage. The adults had responsibilities to go back to, and no one knew how long the situation with Wolf's Blood would take to resolve. They would have to await the outcome. Wolf's Blood had asked that only Hawk and Jeremy go with him to Cheyenne.

"You are my son, and after so many years without you, I have to be with you through this, Wolf's Blood."

Wolf's Blood faced her, taking her hand, hating the agony in her eyes. "Father would not have wanted you at Fort Robinson, and I don't want you in Denver or Cheyenne. Trips are too hard for you now, and if something should go wrong, perhaps your heart could not bear it. Stay home, Mother. Do it for me, and for Sweet Bird. She will also stay here, with the children. I do not want them to go through this in public. Besides, a place like Denver would frighten them. If the news is bad, they will need you. Please promise me you will stay with them."

Abbie squeezed his hand, leaning forward and putting her head on his shoulder, unable to stop the tears. "My God, Wolf's Blood, you mean so much to me. I might never see you again, and I've had you such a short while. All my life I've only had you for a few days or months at a time, then you were gone again. You're like the wind, as Zeke was."

He put an arm around her and let her cry. "It was the only way we could be. You should not weep for me, Mother. This is what I want and if it ends badly, know that I am with my father. Nothing could make me happier."

"I know," she answered.

He gave her a squeeze. "I must tell you, there is no woman on earth who can compare to you in strength and courage. Father must have seen those things when he married you."

She sniffed as she let go of him and wiped at her eyes with a handkerchief she held wadded in her hand. "I never want to forget your face," she told him lovingly.

He touched her cheek with the back of his hand. "A mother never forgets."

"I'll go crazy wondering what is happening."

"Jeremy and Joshua can keep you informed by telephoning Ellen in Pueblo. She can send messages to you."

Abbie closed her eyes and kissed his hand. "Somehow I knew from the day you were born the course your life would take. From the first day you learned to walk, I could never catch you." She studied every line of his face, his dark eyes, his long, black hair, now streaked with gray. He was dressed all Indian for this journey, in buckskins, a hairpiece and feathers in his hair. He even wore stripes of war paint on his cheeks. He wanted to be fully Cheyenne when he entered Denver, that city where thirty-five years ago a Colonel Chivington and the Colorado Volunteers had paraded through the streets showing off their "bounty" after raiding a peaceful Cheyenne camp and slaughtering hundreds of women and children. One of those women was the young Indian girl Wolf's Blood had loved. It was Sand Creek that had made a warrior out of him, for his heart had been filled with hatred and bitterness ever since. That awful slaughter had been the beginning of many years of warring by the Cheyenne.

"I'm glad I at least managed to get you out of that prison in Florida," Abbie told him. "You had a few good years. I'm sorry you didn't have longer with Jennifer."

"Everything happens as the Great Spirit wills it. And now I must go, before the look in your eyes breaks my heart and makes me stay. I am doing the right thing, Mother." He leaned forward and kissed her cheek, and she drew in her breath in the pain of sorrow when he quickly rose and moved away from her. "Last night I said my good-byes to Sweet Bird and the children," he said. "It was very hard for her, but as I held her in my arms, so young and healthy and beautiful, I was even more certain she belongs with someone younger. Hawk has promised to care for her."

The others came out to pack things into wagons, Zeke and Georgeanne and their children, Iris and her family.

"God go with you, *mi amigo,*" Raphael told Wolf's Blood.

"*Gracias,*" Wolf's Blood answered. "Take good care of your *esposa,* or the ghosts of her Apache relatives will come for you."

Raphael grinned. He was rather awed by this father of his wife, a man who right now looked like a fierce warrior. "I will care for your daughter, as I have always done."

A crying Iris hugged her father tightly. "We will be in Denver, should you need us, Father."

He kissed her cheek and pulled away. "I want you to stay home with the children. Be there for them, Iris. Only Hawk and Jeremy should be with me. It is best."

There came a flurry of good-byes then, as Wolf's Blood walked off the porch to say farewell to the others, afraid to take too long saying good-bye to his closest loved ones, his sisters Ellen and Margaret. Ellen would stay here at the ranch a while longer with Abbie. Most of the others he would say good-bye to once they reached Denver.

"Look at him" Georgeanne commented to Zeke. "I can almost hear war drums and chanting when he looks like that."

"He was always the most Indian of all the children," Zeke answered, feeling sorry for his mother as she hugged her brother tightly and cried. Zeke put an arm around Georgeanne's waist. "You might as well round up the children and get them into our carriage. We'll make quite a caravan going back into Denver. It must be killing Grandma Abbie to stay here."

"I'm sure it's best she does." Georgeanne loved the closeness in the Monroe family, something she'd never had. It still hurt to think of her father buried without ever acknowledging his grandchildren, but Margaret and Morgan were wonderful grandparents. They had all shown her more love than she'd ever known since her mother had died.

Brothers and sisters, nieces and nephews, cousins, aunts and uncles, great-grandchildren—all climbed into various wagons, until those who had come from Denver were ready to leave. Wolf's Blood rode his own horse, as did Hawk. They would ride into Denver together, arriving later than the others, as they did not intend to take the train from Pueblo. Father and son would take their time, camp along the way.

All knew it was very difficult for Wolf's Blood to mount and ride now, but from here on he intended to be a warrior, and warriors did not travel in wagons or on trains. Morgan had given him his finest Appa-

loosa gelding for the journey, and the horse's rump
was painted, an eagle on one side, a wolf on the other.

Wolf's Blood turned his horse to look at an upstairs
window of the house, where Sweet Bird stood, holding
Laughing Turtle. Little Eagle was visible beside her,
waving to his father, his little face sober with fear.
Wolf's Blood felt as though his heart was being torn
from his chest at the sight of his young family. His only
solace came when Hawk also looked up at them, and
Little Eagle finally grinned when he waved at Hawk.
Wolf's Blood ached to hold his wife just once more,
but he had insisted she stay in the house when he left.
What was the use of one last hug and kiss? The pain
in their hearts was bad enough as it was.

He turned his horse and rode out ahead of the others, followed by Hawk. Margaret and Abbie clutched
each other and wept, and from a window above Sweet
Bird watched until her husband disappeared over a
rise. It was then she noticed an eagle, silently winging
its way in the same direction.

Even in the East there were newspaper stories about
the half-blood Cheyenne called Wolf's Blood who had
murdered three white men in Cheyenne, Wyoming,
scalping two of them right in front of a crowd of people; about how he had managed to escape and had
been in hiding in Canada until he'd turned himself
in to his son in Denver, Colorado. The stories varied
in accuracy, as did most tales about Indians in those
times, white men interpreting the truth as they saw it.

Nowhere were the headlines bigger than in the Denver papers. After all, the "wild Indian" called Wolf's
Blood was the father of the noted attorney Hawk Monroe, who had won the famous case of *Mrs. Edward Ralston* v. *the City of Denver.* And Wolf's Blood's own brother

was none other than Jeremy Monroe, one of Denver's wealthiest businessmen. His sister was LeeAnn Lewis, the wife of Joshua Lewis, a top man at the *Rocky Mountain News* and the author of numerous magazine articles about Indians and the West. It was said he was also working on a book about one of Colorado's pioneers, Abigail Monroe, LeeAnn's mother and the woman responsible for the establishment of one of Denver's first orphanages. Rumor had it that Abigail Monroe was living in seclusion now in an old cabin on her original homestead in southeast Colorado. Some wondered if she was even still alive.

Zeke Brown, one of Colorado's wealthiest men and biggest landowners was Wolf's Blood's nephew. Iris Hidalgo, wife of a successful Denver contractor, was Wolf's Blood's daughter. It seemed amazing to Denverites that such a notorious Indian, who had once ridden in war against whites, and whose own uncle, it was said, had fought at the Little Big Horn and at Wounded Knee, could have a son and brother and other relatives so successful in the white world. Most were convinced it had to be the white blood in these people that gave them the intelligence and the ability to get an education and to do so well. They believed no full-blood Indian could possibly accomplish so much. Indians just didn't have it "in them."

Wolf's Blood became quite an attraction. Crowds turned out to watch him be escorted from jail to the courthouse, all wanting to get a "last look" at a real warrior. Wolf's Blood had expected as much, and he had deliberately brought along full Indian garb to wear, white deerskin leggings and shirt, beads tied into some of the fringes at the sides of the leggings and sleeves, a sunburst pattern of beads on the front of the shirt. He wore a bone hairpipe necklace at his throat, a beaded belt around his waist, beaded mocca-

sins. He had painted his face in his prayer color of
white stripes leading vertically down the left side of his
face, over forehead, eye and cheek. The same three
lines were painted horizontally across his right cheek.
He wore his hair long and loose, beaded rawhide
wrapped into one narrow braid at one side, an eagle
feather was tied into his hair at the crown of his head.

On the way to the courthouse, Hawk and Jeremy
walked on either side of Wolf's Blood. Young Zeke followed behind, Georgeanne at his side. LeeAnn walked
with them, Jason accompanying her. Joshua was already
in the courthouse taking notes for the newspaper. The
courtroom was quickly filled to standing room only.
Not only were people interested in gawking at Wolf's
Blood, but after Hawk Monroe's famous case against
Denver, they were anxious to see what he was up to
now with his father. All rose when the Circuit judge
entered the room and called the court to order with
a pound of his gavel. As those present quieted, Judge
Gerald Hanson studied Wolf's Blood for a moment,
then looked at Hawk, asking him to rise and declare
the reason for this hearing.

"I am a busy man, Mr. Monroe, and I see no reason
why I should have anything to do with exonerating Mr.
Wolf's Blood here of a crime he committed in Wyoming."

Hawk rose, disappointed that he was not before the
judge he'd had in the case against Denver. He was well
aware that Hanson had been against that decision,
which could prejudice the man against him in this case.
"I am not asking that you exonerate him of any crimes,
Judge Hanson," he answered. "We are only asking for
sanctuary here. Wyoming authorities are demanding
my father be extradited to Cheyenne to stand trial, and
the public opinion there will be so against him he could
not possibly have a fair trial. He is not saying he is not

guilty, but his crime was a crime of passion, sir. One of
the men he killed had threatened him and his family
with a gun, then carelessly had shot his wife, my stepmother, killing her before my father's eyes. She was
white, not Indian, for the benefit of anyone who thinks
it's no great loss to kill an Indian woman. She was also
educated, the mother of a young daughter by her first
husband, a schoolteacher. She had taught right here in
Denver before going to the reservation to teach after
her husband died. The point is, her shooting was a hor-
rible act, and my father, having just seen the woman he
loved senselessly murdered, reacted in the way a lot of
men would, Indian *or* white!"

The judge rubbed at his chin a moment, studying
Wolf's Blood again. He sighed, leaning back in his
chair. "Mr. Monroe, I agree that a man might react by
attacking and killing the man who had just killed his
wife. However, I think I can safely say that such a man
would not go on from there and kill the shooter's
friends, let alone scalp them. That is what I am told
Mr. Wolf's Blood did. The Indian people have to learn
that they cannot commit such horrid mutilations. If
your father had simply killed the man who shot his
wife, this would be a much simpler decision."

"I understand that, Judge Hanson, but the white man
has never understood that Indian culture can't be
changed overnight. My father had been living on a reservation in Montana and was a law-abiding citizen. He
owned a horse ranch there and was doing quite well.
He had been in Colorado for a family reunion and was
on his way home when the shooting happened. He reacted in the only way he knew how to respond to such
a thing, with an inbred need to avenge his wife's death.
The other two men had taken part in the confrontation
that led to my stepmother's shooting, so in my father's
eyes, they, too, had to die. Scalping the enemy is a cus-

tom that just naturally came to surface again when my
father killed those men. I might add that scalping is
something that was encouraged for a time by white
men, mostly French and English. During their war they
paid *money* for enemy scalps—white or Indian."

A wave of whispers moved through the crowded
room, and the judge pounded his gavel again. "I don't
need or want a lesson on Indian history and culture
today, Mr. Monroe. Such things have no bearing in a
court of law. I am only interested in deciding this case,
and in the severity of the crime committed. Culture
or not, natural or not, it happened; and by today's
laws, no man has the right to deliberately murder another because of a crime committed against him or
his family. I am sorry for what happened to your stepmother, but your father should have allowed the law
to do something about those men, not taken it upon
himself to kill them. Be that as it may, it matters little
here in Colorado. The legal aspect of this case needs
to be decided in Wyoming. All I want from you is your
reasoning as to why we should give Mr. Wolf's Blood
sanctuary here in Colorado."

Hawk glanced back at his father, seeing the proud
look in the man's dark eyes. He thought what a contrast they were, his father sitting in full Indian dress,
having lived in the wilds the past several years while
his son had attended Harvard Law School and had
lived in luxury in Denver. Hawk stood before the judge
today in a fine silk suit and black bow tie. Suddenly
he wished he were dressed like his father. He wanted
to be and feel Indian, to ride like the wind and go
into the hills to feel close to the earth and the spirit
world, away from this so-called civilization.

He clasped his hands behind his back and faced the
judge, trying not to think about what the consequences
could be if he had to take Wolf's Blood to Cheyenne.

"Judge Hanson, my father is a legal citizen of Colorado.
He was born here, raised here. I ask for sanctuary for
that reason. He has a new wife and two young children
who need him. He wishes only to be able to be with
them a while longer; he would live peacefully at the
ranch where he originally grew up, east of Pueblo. It is
a quiet place, far removed from cities and crowds of
people. His mother is getting old and would like to have
her son with her until she dies. Out of respect for my
grandmother, Abigail Monroe, who has done much for
the City of Denver, I would ask that her son be returned
to the ranch with a promise he will never be extradited
to Wyoming, so he may live peacefully with his family
until his death, which, I might add, will be in not so
many years. My father is suffering from crippling arthritis. He is no threat to society. He is a devoted son, a
devoted brother and a devoted husband and father. The
wrongs he has done in this life he did out of Indian
pride and because of terrible losses of his own. The first
woman he loved, a Cheyenne girl, was murdered at
Sand Creek."

A few gasps and murmurs rippled through the
crowd.

"Everyone here now knows the hideous crimes that
were committed there by the Colorado Volunteers under John Chivington, *white* men. My father's first wife,
my Apache mother, was murdered by white soldiers.
My father's second wife, a white woman, was, as we
already know, also killed by white men. It is under-
standable that he reacted as he did. A man can only
take so much. But he is getting old now, and he is in
pain most of the time." He turned and looked at
Wolf's Blood. "I ask this Court to respect Wolf's
Blood's Colorado citizenship and to give him sanctuary
in this state and to let him go to his boyhood home
and live out his life in peace."

Wolf's Blood gave his son a proud but rather sad smile, as though to tell him he'd done his best but not to expect much. Hawk turned back to the judge. "I beg the court's mercy, Your Honor."

The crowded room was nearly silent while the judge leaned forward, studying Wolf's Blood again, then looking down and studying some papers, his lips pursed in thought. Hawk sat down beside his father, who reached over and squeezed his arm. "You may not win this, my son, but I can see you speak well for the Indian. You will help them a great deal when the day comes that you stand for their cause."

People began whispering, then mumbling, then talking in full voice, and after several minutes the judge finally pounded his gavel again. He asked Wolf's Blood to rise, and was obeyed, Hawk rising as well.

"Tell me, Mr. Wolf's Blood, why are you wearing war paint in this courtroom?" the judge asked him.

Wolf's Blood raised his chin proudly, still standing tall in spite of his arthritis. "This is not war paint. These are my prayer colors. My war colors are red and black, red for blood, and black for death."

The judge rubbed at his lips pensively. "And why did you choose to wear Indian garb instead of dressing in a civilized manner in a court of law?"

Wolf's Blood did not like this judge. "I *am* dressed in a civilized manner, for an Indian. And that is what I am."

"You are actually only about one-quarter Indian, if I figure it right."

Wolf's Blood felt like laughing. "I suppose that is how a white man would look at it. Indian blood is Indian blood, sir, and I chose to be Indian. With my looks, what white man would have treated me as just another white man? My own father raised me to be proud to be Indian, as I raised my son. My father was Lone Eagle, called Cheyenne Zeke by some. His white name was Zeke Monroe, and he did much to help settle this land. We all did our part in making Colorado what it is today, in spite of the fact that for many years I chose the Indian side. Sometimes white men were also ruthless. They murdered Indians for no good cause. We are all to blame for both the good and the bad, Judge Hanson. It was a time of change, and all of us learned many lessons."

The judge slowly nodded, his gaze moving to Hawk. "Now I understand why you are so good at arguing a case, Mr. Monroe. Your father is also very clever with words."

A few people laughed, but they quickly quieted.

"If you could go back to the moment your wife was killed," the judge continued, watching Wolf's Blood carefully, "knowing what you know now, if you could change your actions in order to have your freedom and live out your life on your ranch with your mother and family—if you could go back and do it over, would you still kill and scalp those men?"

Hawk felt as though his heart was rising into his throat, while Jeremy was thinking, *Answer no, Wolf's Blood! Answer no!* Somehow he knew what his very stubborn Indian brother would say.

"Yes," Wolf's Blood replied, his chin held proudly, his black eyes holding the judge's gaze. "They deserved to die."

This time the talking in the courtroom was difficult to control. The judge had to pound his gavel several times. Through it all Hawk's hopes were deserting him, though he knew, just as Jeremy did, why his father had answered as he had. Wolf's Blood had given Hawk a chance to free him, and he knew damn well Hawk might just have done so. His son was damn good at what he did, but Wolf's Blood did not want freedom. He wanted to go to Cheyenne, where he knew he would die.

He looked down at Jeremy seated beside him, while gasps and gossip continued to resonate through the crowd. Jeremy looked up at him, tears in his eyes. "*Why*, Wolf's Blood!"

Wolf's Blood had the look of stubborn pride on his face Jeremy had seen many times before. "You know why."

The judge finally managed to quiet the courtroom. He ran a hand through his hair and sighed, facing Wolf's Blood, who was still standing. "Sir, I have a feeling you know what your answer should have been. It would have made a big difference in my decision, since I feel Attorney Monroe here presented a damn good argument. I am sorry about your arthritis, sorry for what you've suffered in life, even a little sorry for what other Indians have suffered at the hands of white men. But the fact remains, many whites have suffered at the hands of Indians; and you apparently still have enough Indian in you to cause you to kill again, right or wrong, out of vengeance, if you or one of your family is threatened or hurt. If you had answered no to my question, I would have felt you perhaps regretted what you did and understood the magnitude of your crime. However, I see no remorse in your eyes, and your answer only verifies that. If I give you sanctuary here in Colorado for a crime committed someplace else, I could start a precedent that would cause problems for other states in the future, for Colorado as well. We might require similar cooperation from Wyoming on some other matter in the future. Because of that, I am ordering you extradited to Cheyenne, Wyoming, to stand trial for three counts of murder. Extradition will take place at eight A.M. tomorrow morning, when you will be put on a train under guard and taken to Cheyenne."

He pounded his gavel, and the courtroom exploded with noisy talk. Hawk slowly sat down and put his head in his hands. He felt his father's hand on his shoulder then.

"You did good, son. You had it won. That is all I needed to see. You had your will and your say, and I had my say. I have decided my own future. You bear no responsibility, except to come with me."

Hawk looked at him with tear-filled eyes. "I can't practice law in Wyoming."

"It does not matter. You can advise whoever is appointed to represent me. I only want you to be with me—you and Jeremy."

Hawk quickly wiped at his eyes. "You know I'll go. So will Jeremy."

Wolf's Blood nodded. "From here on, I want you to remember I do what I do out of Indian pride, that I will always believe killing those men was right, that everything that happens from now on is a matter of honor. Always be proud of your father, as I have always been proud of mine."

A tear slipped down Hawk's cheek. "You know I'll always be proud of you."

Wolf's Blood only smiled. "As your own children will be proud of you, my warrior son. This place, this courtroom, is *your* battlefield!"

As a Denver policeman came to take Wolf's Blood away, Hawk stood up to embrace him, unable to speak.

"Wagh!" Wolf's Blood told him, patting him on the back. "It is good."

The policeman led him away, and people crowded around to get another glimpse of the "murdering savage" called Wolf's Blood. Hawk looked at Jeremy.

"I learned a long time ago never to argue with your father," Jeremy told him, his own eyes misty. "He's made up his mind to something, so there is no one to blame but him."

Hawk shook his head. "They'll hang him, Uncle Jeremy. That's the worst way for an Indian to die. They believe if they're hung, the spirit is trapped inside the body and can never get out." Another tear slipped down his cheek. "He can't die that way, but I don't know how to stop it."

Jeremy grasped his hand. "Trust in God, Hawk, and in your father's wisdom."

Twenty-eight

Abbie sat in her rocker in front of the fireplace at the old cabin. The rocker was drying out from age, and she wasn't sure how much longer it would hold her without collapsing, but this was the only place where she found true comfort . . . and where precious memories became more vivid.

The fireplace was blackened from years of use. She'd cooked many a pot of stew over its hearth, before Zeke had bought her a cookstove. Even when there was not a fire burning, one could smell the coals and soot. She glanced at Zeke's mandolin, and she could almost see him sitting across from her, singing Tennessee mountain songs. The mantel clock still ticked above the fireplace . . . ticking away the time . . . weeks, months, years. So many years.

She could see the children running in and out of the house, hear their voices. Today she was thinking of one child in particular. They'd called their first son *Hohanino-o*, Little Rock, and somehow she'd always known he was one child whose spirit was free as the birds and wild as the wolves. From the moment of his birth, when she saw his big, dark eyes and that shock of straight, black hair, she'd known there would be hardly a hint of his white blood, and it had been the same with his spirit. He'd learned to ride a horse almost before he could walk.

No father and son could be closer than Little Rock and Cheyenne Zeke. As soon as the boy was old enough to choose, he had ignored his schooling and had preferred learning the Cheyenne way. He had insisted on enduring the Sun Dance ceremony, and he had almost died from the infection that followed. But he had survived, and because of a vision he'd had and a later encounter with wolves, he had changed his name to Wolf's Blood. Cheyenne men often changed their names when they grew older and knew the pathway they would choose in life.

The name had fit him. Most of his life Wolf's Blood had had wolves for pets. They had seemed to be drawn to him, and he to them, as though sharing the same spirit. She was even more sure of that last night after a rider had come from Pueblo, bringing the message from Jeremy that Hawk's request for sanctuary in Colorado had been denied and that Wolf's Blood had been taken to Cheyenne. Hawk had come very near to winning the case for his father, Jeremy's letter had explained, until Wolf's Blood was asked if he would kill those men all over again.

He had answered yes.

Abbie closed her eyes and sighed. Of course he had. It would be just like him to do that. They had deserved killing, so he'd done it. He saw nothing wrong with that. And he'd seen nothing wrong with raiding and killing as a warrior, because there was no other way for the Cheyenne and Sioux to try to stop white settlement. Men like Wolf's Blood did not understand the soft ways of the whites.

What pained her was that she knew good and well Wolf's Blood was baiting the authorities, that he *wanted* to be sent to Cheyenne. He'd given Hawk his chance, so that his son would always feel he had done all he could to protect his father. He didn't want Hawk to have any guilt over what might happen next. She knew in her soul what that would be, and so did Sweet Bird, who was probably still crying in her room at the big house this morning.

By now, Abbie was more worried about Hawk and Jeremy than Wolf's Blood. This was going to be a very trying time for both of them. In a way it could be even harder on Jeremy than Hawk, for Jeremy was the one who had suffered for abandoning his father for so many years and for denying that he was related to someone like Wolf's Blood. It was such a shame he and Wolf's Blood could not have had the last twelve years together after finally uniting again at that first reunion.

Waiting for more news was going to be hard, but she had no choice. Though she wanted to be with her son, he had asked her not to come, and she had respected his wishes. Besides, it seemed everything she did anymore made her tired. She hated feeling this way. It just wasn't like her. All her life she had had so much energy, except for a couple of times when Zeke had threatened to leave her just because he loved her so much and thought she'd have a better life without him. Whenever she was without her husband, the life simply went of her, and she still wondered sometimes how she had survived after his death.

It all came down to Zeke. In death she would be with him again. Of that she was sure, and she knew Wolf's Blood felt the same way. He was ready to be welcomed by his father's open arms. How it would happen, when it would happen, that was to be seen; but it *would* happen. She had prayed all she could, cried all she could. Now she could only tell herself to be prepared for the news, to accept the fact that this was what Wolf's Blood wanted. Death would be his peace, his release from pain, his chance to be with his father again.

She closed her eyes and rocked, seeing a little boy's

round, happy face, big, dark eyes and shining smile.
"God, be with him," she whispered. "Don't let him suffer."

Jeremy awoke to the sound of shouting in the streets
below. He frowned, throwing off the light sheet he'd
used, the night air hardly any cooler than the miserably hot breeze of the day. He walked to the hotel
window and looked down at the street to see men walking with torches in their hands.

"What the hell?"

He listened. They halted before a man who himself
stood on a buckboard's seat across the street, apparently the leader of the unruly mob. "The sonofabitch
don't deserve to be shot!" the man shouted. "Hangin'
is the only good punishment for an Injun! He *wants*
to be shot, think's it's a warrior's way to die. Piss on
that! He killed my brothers, and he's got to die with
a rope around his neck!"

Those crowded around him agreed, raising torches,
shouting their support. "Hang the Indian!" most of
them were shouting.

"Jesus!" Jeremy muttered. "Wolf's Blood!" He
turned away and grabbed his trousers from the foot of
the bed, just as he heard a pounding at the door.

"Jeremy! It's me, Hawk! They're out to hang Father!"

Jeremy quickly yanked on his trousers, buttoning his
pants as he hurried to the door and opened it. "I just
woke up myself and heard them!"

Hawk, himself only half dressed, ran to the window.
"For Christ's sake, they're headed for the jail!"

"Maybe the sheriff can hold them off," Jeremy told
him. He pulled his suspenders up over bare shoulders
and quickly drew on a shirt, leaving it unbuttoned as

he sat down to put shoes on his bare feet, not wanting to take the time to find his socks.

"That goddamn sheriff doesn't give a shit about Father!" Hawk answered. "You saw how he looked at Wolf's Blood when he locked him in that cell, heard him tell Father he's getting what he deserves. One of those men Father killed was his best friend. He testified to that! He'll hand Father over to those men without any argument!"

Jeremy stood up and faced him. "They're determined. Their leader is the brother of the other two Wolf's Blood killed and scalped. He was the most volatile one in the courtroom, the one who demanded Wolf's Blood be hanged, not shot."

"Let's go!"

Jeremy grabbed his nephew's arm. "What the hell can we do? They won't listen to us!"

"We've got to try! Do you have a gun?"

Jeremy was struck by the contrast between his life and his brother's—Wolf's Blood so violent, his so civilized. "The last time I held a gun in my hand, it was to put it to my own head. My wife stopped me from using it that day. I haven't picked one up since."

Hawk felt his pain. "Those days of guilt are long over, Uncle Jeremy. Father loves you, and we've got to help him somehow. The trouble is, there are so many of them, and I don't have a gun either. All I know is we have to go to him."

Their gazes held in the dim lamplight. "We can't let him hang," Jeremy told Hawk. He closed his eyes, letting out a strange groan. "My God." When he opened his eyes, they were wet with tears. "Let me take care of this, Hawk. I need to do this."

Hawk's mind raced with confusion as Jeremy walked past him and out the door. Then he quickly followed, somewhere deep in his mind suspecting what his uncle intended to do, yet unable to believe it. He raced along behind him as Jeremy, his shirt still hanging open, his hair askew from just getting out of bed, headed for the crowd of vigilantes. The poor excuse for a trial his father had had infuriated Hawk. It had lasted only a few minutes, with plenty of witnesses ready and willing to tell everyone what they'd seen that day, a savage stab three men to death, scalps taken right in front of women and children! Sure, the man's wife had been killed before his eyes, but that had been an accident, and he'd had no right to do what he did.

Two of the men killed were brothers of Stacy Barlow, who owned a big cattle ranch outside of Cheyenne. Barlow was rich, and belonged to the prestigious Cheyenne Club, a cattlemen's establishment whose members were the wealthiest ranchers. He wanted revenge, and he apparently "owned" the judge and the law in this town. Wolf's Blood had quickly been found guilty of three counts of murder and mutilation. The only mercy the judge had shown was to sentence Wolf's Blood to be shot rather than hanged, bowing to Hawk's plea that death would not be by the rope.

Now this. A mob led by Stacy Barlow was headed for the jail to drag Wolf's Blood out and hang him. A mob hanging, Hawk had always heard, was worse than a normal hanging, because it was seldom done right. In a proper hanging, a man's neck was snapped so that he died quickly. A mob usually just put a rope around a man's neck and slowly raised him up, causing death by slow strangulation. They would enjoy watching Wolf's Blood kick and gag and struggle for breath. He couldn't let his father die that way!

"What are you going to do?" he shouted to Jeremy. "Leave it to me!"

Hawk caught up with him. "Uncle Jeremy, I can't let them hang him that way! I'll shoot him myself first!"

Jeremy, his face red with rage and sorrow, grasped his arms, fury in his eyes. "He's your *father!* A son shouldn't have to live with that kind of a memory! And you're a lawyer now, Hawk! Don't do anything that might get you kicked off the bench! That's the last thing Wolf's Blood would want! Let me handle it."

He gave his nephew a mighty shove, and Hawk stumbled backward but did not fall. Hawk knew that if he wanted, he could easily lick Jeremy. Still, the man seemed determined, and he had already disappeared into the crowd of angry men, shoving some aside to get to the jailhouse steps, where already the door had been beaten in.

Several of the men pushed Jeremy aside, began beating him. Hawk hurried to his rescue, but by then everything was bedlam, and the sheriff was not lifting a hand to stop it.

"Get them!" he heard men shouting. "It's the Indian's brother, his son! They're Indian, too! Don't let them stop us!"

Everything became a blur for Hawk as more men beat on him, too many to do much in the way of fighting back. He swung his fists, sending two or three of them to the ground, but a rain of blows and kicks descended upon him until he felt gravel in his mouth and his whole body began to scream with pain.

Finally they left him. He struggled to his knees, his feet. Then he stumbled over to Jeremy, who was getting up, his face covered with cuts and blood. They looked at each other, neither saying a word. By then the mob was dragging Wolf's Blood out of the jail, some of them beating on him. The crowd opened up so that Jeremy and Hawk could watch. Men laughed and began tormenting Wolf's Blood, whose crippled condition made fighting difficult, although he surprised some of them with a few vicious kicks that put some men down.

"He's still a wild one!" some yelled.

"Bastard Indian!"

"He's a savage!"

Hawk felt helpless. His father had wanted to die fighting, so perhaps this was what he had to let him do, but it tore his heart out to see him struggle, knowing the kind of pain he was in, seeing the blood on his face. He was totally unaware that Jeremy had left him, unaware his uncle had run into the jail and grabbed a rifle. The sheriff was locked in a cell.

"I couldn't stop them!" he protested to Jeremy. "What the hell are you doing with that rifle! You go killin' men, you'll hang, too!"

"You *let* them put you in there without a struggle because you've agreed to this, you sonofabitch!" Jeremy yelled. "I'll have your badge for this, just as soon as I do what I have to do!"

He stormed out, hardly feeling the pain of his own injuries. He couldn't succumb to his bruised ribs, swollen lip and cracked cheekbone. He could not let anything stop him! Wolf's Blood had had a dream that had involved him, and now he understood what that dream was. He put away all other thoughts as he ran down a side street and cut through an alley to come out ahead of the mob, which now had hold of Hawk and was dragging him along with them so that he could watch his father hang. They were headed for the blacksmith's, where a signpost that jutted out from that building's rooftop was just the right height to sling a rope over and hoist a man up.

Jeremy moved out in front of them, shooting the rifle into the air. The loud noise put a halt to their march, and they all stood staring at him, most of them unarmed, as there was now a law against wearing guns in Cheyenne. They had figured they wouldn't need any-

thing more than fists and clubs, torches and a rope to
do what they had in mind.

The street was lit with gaslights, and Hawk stood staring at his uncle, who had a look on his face he'd never
seen there before . . . wild-eyed, determined . . . Indian. For once in his life Jeremy Monroe looked like
an Indian. It was how he stood there, not his physical
looks. He was beaten and bloody, his shirt ripped most
of the way off, one suspender hanging loose. His chest
and arms were scraped and bloody, yet he held the
rifle at the ready, waving it at the crowd.

"My brother is not going to hang!" he growled at
them.

Wolf's Blood, still wearing his Indian garb, although
it was now torn, and stained with dirt and blood,
yanked his arms loose and stood facing his brother,
holding his chin proudly in spite of what he'd suffered.
He remained silent, keeping his eyes on Jeremy.

"You gonna stop this whole crowd with that gun?"
one man shouted. "You might get one of us, mister,
but some of us have guns. You kill one man here, and
we'll shoot you down—you, your nephew and your
murderin' savage brother!"

Jeremy kept the rifle steady. "I won't have to shoot
any of you." He slowly aimed the rifle at Wolf's Blood
as he spoke.

The entire crowd calmed, staring in disbelief. Those
near and behind Wolf's Blood quickly moved away
from him. Jeremy remained steady, tears running
down his cheeks, mixing with the blood. Wolf's Blood
shook his hair behind his shoulders and raised one
arm high, making a fist. He faced his brother squarely
for several long, tense seconds. Then, strangely, he
smiled. "Aim well, my brother. I have fought like a
warrior this night. I will *die* like a warrior! It is a *good*
time to die, and tonight, for once, you are *Cheyenne!*

Our father thanks you!" He took a deep breath, then
let out a fierce war cry. Fire spit from the end of the
barrel of Jeremy's rifle, and Hawk gasped when a hole
opened in Wolf's Blood's chest. The man stumbled
backward, his fist still in the air, and he stared at
Jeremy a moment longer before finally collapsing.

For a moment there was only total silence.

"I'll be damned!" someone in the crowd muttered
then.

"He killed his own brother!" someone else exclaimed.

Hawk looked from his father to Jeremy, and to his
horror, Jeremy was slowly turning the rifle upward, po-
sitioning the end of the barrel under his chin, his arms
long enough so that he could get to the trigger with
his right hand.

"No, Uncle Jeremy!" Hawk lunged at him, pushing
the rifle away. He kicked at it until Jeremy had to let
go. Hawk embraced him, holding his uncle's arms
tightly to his sides so Jeremy could not try to pick up
the rifle again. "You did right!" Hawk reassured him.
"He *wanted* you to do it!" He began to sob, keeping
hold of his uncle, who had been as much a father to
him these past years as Wolf's Blood. "It's all right, Uncle Jeremy."

Hawk could feel him trembling then. Slowly Jeremy
bent his arms to grasp hold of Hawk. "I'm sorry," he
said, and he wept.

"Don't be. It had to be done. And you were right. I
couldn't have done it. He knew. He knew it would be
you."

Jeremy stood there weeping, while the crowd began
to drift away. "So many years . . . I wanted to kill
him . . . just because I hated him," Jeremy sobbed. "I
hated him because . . . he reminded me of what *I*
was . . . Indian. I didn't want to admit it. But all

along . . . he was everything I . . . wanted to be deep down . . . but didn't have the courage to be." He slowly let go of Hawk. "But this . . . I didn't do this . . . out of hate, Hawk. I did it out of love. You . . . believe that, don't you? I couldn't . . . let him die that way."

"I know, Uncle Jeremy." Hawk wiped at his own bloody tears. "Please don't blame yourself. My father was probably more proud of you . . . just before you pulled that trigger . . . than he's ever been. You've made up for it all, Uncle Jeremy. Don't feel bad about it."

Hawk kept an arm around his uncle as they both walked over to where Wolf's Blood lay in the dusty street. They went to their knees beside him. Only a few men remained from the original crowd of vigilantes, and among them was a newspaper man, who was scribbling wildly, anxious to get this story out as fast as possible. A sobbing Hawk felt his father's neck for a pulse. There was none. He quickly tore off his own shirt and laid it over his father's face. "I promised him . . . I'd bury him in the mountains," he told Jeremy. "Will you help me?"

Jeremy only nodded, putting a hand on Wolf's Blood's shoulder. "It's like . . . the end of something, Hawk. I can't even . . . find a word for it."

Hawk grasped his father's hand, still slightly warm, but already growing stiff. *"Tseke-heto,"* he groaned. "My father." He could not control his sobbing then as he lay down beside the man and wept. Jeremy remained kneeling beside them, his agony buffered by a strange warmth and a feeling of freedom. He could swear he felt a strong hand on his shoulder, but when he turned to look, no one was there. It was then he heard the cry of an eagle somewhere in the distant hills, something that was seldom, if ever, heard after dark.

Twenty-nine

Sweet Bird came to the doorway of the old cabin. It had been left open because of the heat. "They are coming!"

Abbie turned from where she'd been cleaning some green beans to be canned. Since hearing about Wolf's Blood's death and how it had happened, she'd had to keep busy, so as not to think about it too much. She had worked hard in the garden, picking vegetables, then washing and cooking and canning them, even cleaning the cabin—anything she could think of—so that by night she would be so weary it would be possible to fall asleep. She studied Sweet Bird, noticed that in only these two weeks she had grown thinner. There were dark circles under her eyes.

"I should have spent more time with you," she told her. "I'm sorry, Sweet Bird."

Sweet Bird shook her head. "I understand. You had to stay here, where you can live in the past and not think about the present."

Abbie set her paring knife aside and wiped her hands, coming closer to Sweet Bird. "You must be so lonely in a place so foreign to all you've ever known." She took hold of Sweet Bird's hands. "I know full well what it is like to be a stranger in a new land, Sweet Bird, surrounded by people you don't even know. When I first married Wolf's Blood's father and was brought to live with the Cheyenne, Zeke had to leave for several weeks, and I was alone with them. Back then his brother, Swift Arrow, disapproved of me. It was not an easy time for me. I felt abandoned. You must feel the same way."

Sweet Bird blinked back tears. "My husband did what he felt he must do. I knew even when I first went to him what would happen one day. I loved your son very much, Abbie. Sometimes I wonder what I will do without him, how I will go on; but at least I have the children."

Abbie embraced her. "Thank you for loving him and giving him a few more years of happiness."

"He was not so hard to love." Sweet Bird pulled away, wondering when she would get over this grief. "I think perhaps he was much harder to put up with when he was younger."

Abbie smiled. "Oh, yes. Even as a child he was difficult."

Sweet Bird shivered with a sob. "I am so sorry for you. To lose a son—"

"Wolf's Blood is where he wants to be now. He's with his father, and I don't suppose it will be so long before I join them. I belong to another time, Sweet Bird. My grandchildren, even some of my children, belong to this new way of life."

She walked with Sweet Bird to the doorway to see the wagons coming, the children and grandchildren returning from Denver, this time not for a joyful reunion. Now the family would grieve together. Apparently they all wanted to be closer, for they were packed into only two of Ellen and Hal's supply wagons. As they came nearer, Abbie and Sweet Bird walked out to greet them—Zeke and Georgeanne, who had apparently left their children at home; Iris and Raphael with their three sons; LeeAnn and Joshua with Lonnie and Abbie; Ellen and Hal with Lillian and Daniel; Hawk, Jeremy, Mary and Jason, who had left Louellen and the children at the ranch when he and the others followed Wolf's Blood to Denver and to Cheyenne.

Margaret and Morgan were approaching from the main house with Louellen. Nathan and Susan also hurried toward the wagons, their children as well as Jason's and Wolf's Blood's, all running or toddling behind, most of the little ones oblivious to what had happened, except for Little Eagle, who ran straight to Hawk, calling out his name and reaching up for him. Hawk jumped down and swept him up into his arms, walking away from the others to talk to the boy alone.

Abbie felt torn, realizing all the children needed her right now, and certainly poor Hawk. But she suspected it was Jeremy who needed her most.They were all relieved he had not been held on any charges. After all, Wolf's Blood had been sentenced to death. Jeremy Monroe had simply carried out the sentence.

She watched him closely. She knew from messages she'd received that he had gone into the mountains with Hawk to bury Wolf's Blood. She also knew by the circles under his eyes and the drawn look to his face what he had been through. He seemed hesitant to look at her, even when she called out his name as she walked up to where he still sat on a wagon seat. Abbie glanced at Mary, who looked at her pleadingly, as though to ask her to help Jeremy.

Abbie reached out and grasped Mary's hand. "He'll be all right." She looked at Jeremy again, noticing the remains of cuts and bruises on his face. Joshua had written that newspaper articles out of Cheyenne had mentioned that Hawk and Jeremy had been beaten by the mob. "Are you all right, Jeremy?"

He shrugged. "Just a few bruised ribs. My face did look a lot worse."

"Please come down from there, son."

He finally looked at her. "Do you know all of it?"

"Of course I know. You did what you had to do, Jeremy. I'm sure Hawk understands that."

He sighed wearily and climbed down, glancing at Sweet Bird. "I'm so damn sorry."

She faced him boldly. "You could not let him hang. You did the right thing."

Jeremy looked back at his mother. His own absence and denial had been as hard on her as losing a child to death. "He just . . . stood there looking at me. He said it was a good time to die. He *knew*, Mother! He told me before we even left that he'd had a dream about me, but he wouldn't tell me what it was. Later he told me I would know what to do. Now I realize what he meant."

Abbie took hold of his hands. "Then you also know it was right."

He took a deep breath, blinking back tears. "The fact remains I killed my own brother."

She squeezed his hands. "And God himself put that gun in your hands!" she told him firmly. "Don't you think of it any other way, Jeremy Monroe! God put the gun in your hands, and Zeke himself pulled the trigger. If Zeke were there and had no other choice, he'd have done the same thing. For once in your life you were fighting on *their* side, Jeremy, for your father, your brother, for the *Cheyenne!* You *were* Cheyenne in that moment! And there isn't a member of this family who does not understand that!"

A tear slipped down his cheek. "It must have been terrible for you when you found out."

Abbie reached up and touched his cheek. "My sorrow was more for you than Wolf's Blood. Hawk wrote that you started to turn the gun on yourself." She shook her head. "Jeremy, Jeremy. Don't you know that it is an honorable thing you did? Don't you understand that you should be proud, as I and the rest of the family are, of your courage? What a loving thing to do for Hawk. He could never have done it himself."

Jeremy sniffed and swallowed. "Then . . . no one blames me?"

Abbie smiled through tears, seeing a little boy before her. "No one blames you." She thought about the times he'd tried so hard to please his father, but just did not have it in him to be like Wolf's Blood. "You have no idea how proud your father was of you. You completely misinterpreted how much he loved you, Jeremy."

He let go of her and wiped at his eyes with his shirt-sleeve. "I have to tell you . . . when I knelt down be-side Wolf's Blood, I felt . . ." He closed his eyes and drew a deep breath. "I felt a strong hand on my shoul-der. I looked up, and no one was there, but then I heard an eagle's call." He jerked in a sob. "It was him, Mother. I know it was Zeke."

She embraced him. "Of course it was."

They were then surrounded by the rest of the family, all expressing their love to Jeremy, hugging him, giving him their support. Hawk returned with Little Eagle, who was sniffling. He walked up to Sweet Bird, seeing the terrible sorrow in her eyes. "I decided to explain it to him my own way. I hope it's all right."

Their eyes held in mutual sorrow. "He is old enough to understand," Sweet Bird said. "I had already told him, but he was waiting to hear it from you. He has been asking every day when you will come back. He was afraid something had also happened to you."

Little Eagle continued to cling to Hawk, his arms around his neck. "Stay right there," Hawk told Sweet Bird. "I want to walk with you." He went over to his sister, and she embraced him and Little Eagle, crying.

"I should have been there with you," Iris wept.

"He didn't want it that way. Your place was with your family. He understood that. He wouldn't have wanted you to see it."

"I was scared for you, Hawk. I was afraid some man would shoot you and Uncle Jeremy, or maybe hang both of you."

"Well, it didn't happen." He kissed her cheek. "Just thank God you have Raphael and your children. I have to go now. You know that, don't you? I have to go to one of the reservations. Probably to the Dakotas."

"I know." She wiped at her eyes as she pulled away from him. "Father would want it. And they're building more and more railroads. We can probably come and visit you fairly often, or you can come to Denver."

"I will. I probably won't go until spring. For now I'll stay at the ranch a couple of weeks with Grandma Abbie. I'll be taking Sweet Bird with me to the reservation. That's what Father wanted me to do. Until then I think she should stay here, so Grandma can have some time with Little Eagle and Laughing Turtle before I take them north."

The others began walking toward the big house, Margaret and Mary with their arms around Jeremy. Hawk kissed his sister again, then managed to pull Little Eagle away and set him on his feet. "You go with the others, and take care of your little sister," he told the boy. "Your mother and I will be coming soon."

Little Eagle sniffed and ran off to find Laughing Turtle. He took her hand and led her toward the house, as Hawk shook hands with Raphael. "I'm glad you could come, too, and be here for Iris."

"*Sí, amigo.*" Raphael squeezed his hand. "I am sorry about your *padre.* I only knew him for a little while, but a man who has two such fine children as you and my Iris has to be a good man. I felt much honor for him."

Raphael put a supportive arm around Iris and led her away. Hawk turned to his grandmother, who was waiting to give him a hug. He wrapped strong arms around her. "Are you okay, Grandma?"

"I'll be fine. All of you underestimate my strength."

"Oh, I don't think so." He gave her a squeeze. "You knew, didn't you?"

"I had no doubts, but I'm sorry it had to be Jeremy." Her voice broke on the words. "I thought perhaps . . . it would be one of the authorities."

Tears threatened to come again, and Hawk wondered if the hurt would ever go away. "I'll never forget it. It gave me more determination to help all of them, Grandma."

She nodded, pulling away but keeping her hands on his shoulders as she forced a smile. "And you will. I have no doubt you will do much for the Indian cause." She noticed that he, too, had lingering bruises on his face. "I'm sorry you were hurt. Are you all right?"

He nodded. "You should have seen Father fight them, in spite of his age and condition." He let go of her. "And Jeremy! I never knew my very civilized uncle could be such a scrapper!"

Abbie wiped at her tears. "*All* my children were scrappers, in one way or another."

"And so were you, I'll bet! You still are."

Abbie shook her head, smiling sadly. "Oh, my wonderful, handsome grandson. You look so much like your father and grandfather. And you are such a joy to me. I am glad you were with your father through it all. He was one of the last of a special breed. You will show the Indians a new way now."

He squeezed her hand. "I'll try, Grandma." He glanced at Sweet Bird and back to his grandmother. "I want to talk to Sweet Bird alone."

"Of course." Abbie leaned up and kissed his cheek.

"I'm glad she'll have you to talk to, to watch over her. She can stay here as long as necessary, until you know what you're going to do."

She turned to Zeke and Georgeanne, who were waiting to walk with her to the main house; and to break the sorrow of the moment, Zeke picked his grandmother up in his arms, exclaiming that she was shrinking and that he would carry her to the house. Abbie protested, saying she was perfectly capable of walking, but Zeke would have none of it. "You're as light as a kid," he told her.

Georgeanne laughed and walked with them, and Hawk turned to Sweet Bird. He put out his hand and she took it, letting him lead her away.

Abbie looked over young Zeke's shoulder to see her grandson and Sweet Bird heading toward the creek along which she and Hawk's grandfather Zeke used to sit and talk, in the place where purple irises bloomed most of the summer.

"My grandmother likes this place," Hawk told Sweet Bird. He led her to the creek, nearly dried up now from the summer heat and drought. Still, a few irises bloomed on both sides of the bank.

"I know. I walked here with her after you left with Wolf's Blood." Sweet Bird sat down in some thick but yellowed grass. "She told me many stories."

Hawk sat down beside her. "Grandma always says all her children and grandchildren get their strength from Grandpa Zeke; but we all know where it really comes from. It's from her. Aunt Margaret told me once that even Grandpa Zeke seemed to get his strength from her. He was stronger in a physical way, but she was stronger emotionally. Margaret says it was best that Grandpa Zeke died first, because she doesn't think he

could have gone on without her." He leaned down to
rest on one elbow, meeting Sweet Bird's gaze. "It would
have been that way for my father. You're young, Sweet
Bird, and you have Little Eagle and Laughing Turtle.
You'll be all right, and we'll all help you. We both know
what my father wanted, but this is a time for mourning;
your heart is heavy, as is mine. We'll let time take care
of the pain, and we'll let our hearts do the deciding. I
only brought you here to assure you that I'll look after
you as father wanted, and I'll be here for his children.
They will never want for anything."

Sweet Bird nodded, bending her knees and folding
her arms around them, watching the small trickle of
water that still meandered through the creek bottom.
"I thank you for that. What will you do now, Hawk?"

He sighed, breaking off a weed and twirling it between his fingers. "You know I want to go work on a
reservation, now more than ever. Father was railroaded
up in Cheyenne, and things like that happen to Indians
all the time. Right now there are a lot of land swindles,
citizens and the government finding ways to cheat all
the different tribes out of reservation land. The worst
problems are with the Sioux, so I'll probably go to the
Dakotas, but not right away. You and the kids have had
enough change and emotional upset for the time being.
I think this ranch is a good place to be for a while, give
yourselves time to recoup, time to build back your
strength. Besides, Grandma is not looking so well to
me. I think you should stay here for the winter and let
her see as much of Little Eagle and Laughing Turtle as
she can. Seeing Wolf's Blood's children gives her the
feeling that her son still lives. It's good for her, and it
will be good for them to get to know her well."

She turned and met his gaze again. "Will you stay,
too?"

Hawk sat up, crossing his legs and resting his elbows

on his knees. "For a couple of weeks. I have things to get back to in Denver. I'll clean up what's left of my court cases over the winter, sell my house, things like that. There are government agencies I need to get in touch with, the BIA, some people who represent the Sioux. In the spring I'll come back and get you and the children, and we'll head north."

Sweet Bird nodded. "We will try not to be a burden to you."

Hawk frowned. "A burden? My father loved you. Your children are his, my own brother and sister. Why do you think you would be a burden? You're family."

She shrugged. "I don't know. I just want to be sure you are doing this because it is what you want. You are a young, single man with big dreams and with places to go. Now you will be encumbered with the responsibility of feeding and looking out for three more people, playing father to two little ones."

Hawk turned to face her. "Sweet Bird, I have never— *would* never—think of that as a burden or encumbrance. After what I've just been through with my father, how could you think such a thing? What I am doing is in honor of his memory, but I also love Little Eagle and Laughing Turtle. I feel they belong to me now." He saw the quick question in her eyes, a hint of fear. "For God's sake, Sweet Bird, do you think I feel I own *you* now? That I can dictate what you will do with your life, or that . . ." He closed his eyes and sighed. "What is bothering you, Sweet Bird?"

She bent her head to rest it against her arms. "I am just feeling very confused. I want . . . I need you to hold me . . . but I do not want you to think I am turning to you in some other way. My heart longs for your father only. If you would want something else . . . now that he is gone . . . knowing what he wanted for us"—

she sniffed—"I don't know. I do not want you to think
bad of me . . . for wanting you to hold me."

She shivered with a sob, and Hawk's heart went out
to her. "Sweet Bird, I know you too well to ever think
bad of you. If you were not completely honorable, my
father would never have married you. Don't you think
I know how much you need to be held? How afraid
you are of the future? You've been torn from a quiet
life in the Canadian wilderness, brought to a new land,
are living among strangers; your husband, the only an-
chor in your life, killed. I know what it's like. I lost my
mother and stepmother. I had to tell my father good-
bye, knowing I might never see him again, leave the
reservation and go live in Denver with my uncle, a
place entirely different from anything I had ever
known! I attended Harvard, lived among total strangers who wanted nothing to do with an Indian. I know
exactly what you're feeling! What better person to hold
you than one who understands your loneliness?"

She looked at him, tears running down her face.
"I . . . was not sure . . . why you brought me here."

It struck him then just how Indian she was. Did she
really think he might choose to take some kind of hus-
bandly rights with her so soon? He wasn't sure he ever
would, even months from now. Perhaps they would go
separate ways, both find someone else after living for
a while on the reservation. He put a hand to her face.
"Sweet Bird, I brought you here only to explain what
I'd be doing next, to assure you I'll always take care
of you and my brother and sister, and to let you know
you don't have to pack up and leave here right away.
We'll take things slowly, including our feelings for each
other. You will always be free to choose what you want.
I hold no claim on you."

"It . . . it is not that I would not someday"—she
looked away—"perhaps think of you . . . that way. You

are a most honorable man . . . a man of courage, like your father. But for now . . . my heart is broken . . . and I can think of no one but Wolf's Blood."

"Of course you can't." Hawk reached out hesitantly, slipping an arm around her shoulders. "You said you needed to be held."

Her shoulders shook and she suddenly turned and flung her arms around him, weeping bitterly on his shoulder. Hawk lay down in the grass with her, holding her and letting her cry, his own tears joining hers. His father, her husband, was gone.

Thirty

"Abbie! Abbie-girl!"

Abbie sat straight up in bed, sure she'd heard some-one call to her. The voice had been so familiar. "Zeke?" It had seemed so real that she trembled slightly, realizing she had broken out in a cold sweat. She slowly rose, pulling on a robe. She touched a brass bedpost, remembering . . . So many years ago it had been when Zeke bought her this bed. And so many nights of glorious lovemaking they had shared in it.

She blinked, shaking her head. She had apparently dreamed the voice, yet when she first awoke she had almost expected to see Zeke standing there. So shaken was she by the incident, she knew she would not be able to go right back to sleep. She walked into the main room, where she turned up an oil lamp and added some wood to the cookstove so she could heat some water for tea. Hot coals remained, so she was able to start a fire quickly.

She set a kettle over the grate, realizing she could have more conveniences if she wanted them, gaslights and a gas cookstove, things Margaret wanted her to have; but she preferred it this way, the way she'd lived most of her years in this cabin. There was even talk now of bringing electricity to these rural areas, and Margaret finally had a telephone. Whenever there was the need, she could call Ellen in Pueblo, or even Jeremy in Denver.

Such contraptions! Yet what a wonderful thing the telephone would have been when Zeke used to go on scouting expeditions, or when he had to put himself in danger to help a loved one. So many changes. And here it was the turn of the century. Nineteen hundred! She had never once dreamed she would live to see this. Fifty-five years since she met Zeke Monroe on a wagon train West. Could she really be seventy? My, my. When she was fifteen few people lived to be seventy. She would have thought that very, very old. She looked down at her hands, wrinkled with age now. She'd managed to keep her skin nice far longer than some women, but there came a time when it was impossible to stop the inevitable. What would Zeke think of these hands?

She smiled. He would love them. He would not notice the wrinkles on them or on her face. She was almost glad he had not lived any longer than he had. He was always so tall and strong and handsome. She wouldn't want to see him grow into a shriveled old man. Not Zeke Monroe. He had died the way he should, and so had Swift Arrow and Wolf's Blood.

She sat down in her rocker and picked up her Bible, terribly worn now, practically falling apart. How many times over the years had she turned to the Good Book for comfort . . . sitting by this same stone fireplace, listening to the clock tick away the time? She read a few passages . . . *Intreat me not to leave thee, or to return from following after thee, for whither thou goest, I will go; and where thou lodgest, I will lodge; thy people shall be my people, and thy God my God; where thou diest, will I die, and there will I be buried . . . Ruth 1: 16-17.*

That was her favorite. It was the passage that best described how she'd felt when she first met Zeke Monroe and knew she wanted to be his wife, in spite of the hardships that would entail. Just like Ruth she had followed her man into a strange new land. Never once had she gone back to Tennessee in all these fifty-five years. She had always known she would never go back, that she belonged right here in this great big land that had once belonged to the Cheyenne.

The tea kettle began to whistle, and she set the Bible aside, rising to pour some hot water into a cup. She took some tea leaves from a little tin can and packed them into a little metal strainer basket, which she placed into the cup of water. She carried her tea back to the rocker, stopping for a moment when an odd little pain pierced her chest. She waited for it to subside, then sat down and sipped the tea.

"Abbie."

She nearly dropped the cup, setting it aside again at hearing someone calling her name. Zeke! That *was* Zeke's voice! She looked around the room. What was happening? Was she losing her mind in her old age?

"I've missed you, Abbie-girl. Come with me. You've done all you can do here."

"Zeke," she whispered. "Where are you?"

The pain in her chest grew worse and began to move down her left arm.

"Out here, Abbie. Come to the door."

She blinked, suddenly confused, torn between reality and this mystical happening over which she had no control. She tried to rise, but the pain was too great. She felt her breath leave her, and then suddenly the pain was gone and she felt wonderful! She rose easily, surprised there were no aches in her joints. She walked to the door, not sure she should open it. When she looked back, to her surprise she saw herself still sitting in the old rocker!

"What! What is this!"

"It's all right, Abbie. Open the door."

She looked down at herself, noticing her hands were smooth and young! Glancing into the small mirror that hung by the door, the one she used to take a last look at her hair or to see how her hat looked before she went out. The face that looked back at her was that of a woman of perhaps twenty! She knew then. She knew. And it was a wonderful, beautiful thing! She quickly opened the door and was nearly blinded at first by a bright light.

"Don't be afraid, Abbie. Walk through the light."

Yes, that was Zeke talking to her, and he would never tell her to do anything that would bring her harm. If he said not to be afraid, then she shouldn't be. She walked into the light, feeling a wonderful warmth as an indescribable love flowed over her. She took several more steps, moving into a mist. Beyond that she came out upon a hillside. It was daylight, and the weather was warm and beautiful. The land all around was covered with bright wildflowers, and in a valley below sat an Indian village, tipis everywhere, children running and playing, horses grazing, buffalo browsing on the hill beyond. The grass seemed an intense green, the sky a deeper blue than she had ever seen.

"Mother!" she heard another voice say.

She turned, and there stood Wolf's Blood, young and strong again. He was wearing white buckskins, and he smiled in welcome. "Son! My son!" She reached out for him, and they embraced. "Others wait below," he told her, "my little sister, Lillian, and our many Cheyenne friends and relatives, Gentle Woman, Deer Slayer, Red Eagle, all of them."

"Lillian! My Lillian?"

He nodded, pulling away and turning to another. "And my uncle." He put out his arm, and there stood Swift Arrow!

Abbie gasped, for he, too, was young and strong again! "My dear, darling Swift Arrow," she whispered.

He reached out and took her hands. "My beautiful Abigail. Here we can all be happy together. Wolf's Blood's first wives are here, Sonora and Jennifer. You will like it here." He leaned down and kissed her cheek. "I am glad for what we had, but there is another who is more glad you are finally here. Here there are no hard feelings, there is no jealousy, only love. Here we have total peace, never a worry. There is no hunger, no pain. And here we can be with whoever it is right to be with. We know who it is right for you to be with. He is waiting for you."

This time it was Swift Arrow who turned and put out his arm, and out of a mist he came, tall, strong, also young again. He, too, wore white buckskins, gloriously beaded. A wide sash around his waist held the infamous knife that he had used so viciously at times to protect her or someone else in his family. She knew instinctively it would never be used in a place like this. This was a place where Zeke Monroe would never have to fight again.

At first she stood staring, hardly able to believe her eyes. His long, black hair hung well past his shoulders. His smile was bright. There was no sign of the arthritis. He was whole and well and young again! "Zeke," she whispered.

"You're as beautiful as ever, Abbie-girl. I've been watching you for over twenty years. I'm proud of how you carried on, kept the family together, brought Jeremy and Wolf's Blood together, gave strength to all the children and grandchildren." He came closer. "That's quite a family we had, isn't it, Abbie? Who would have thought one of our own grandsons would end up owning all that land, or that another would attend a school like Harvard and become a lawyer? We sure started something all those years ago when we dared to marry, didn't we?"

Tears of joy ran down her cheeks. Was she dreaming? Or was death really this wonderful? "Zeke. My Zeke. I don't know how I did it without you."

"You did it because you're a damn strong woman, Abbie-girl. I always knew that. And you knew I was with you. I was always with you, just like I promised I would be."

Shivering with tears, she held out a shaking hand. "Do I dare touch you? You won't go away, will you? I won't wake up?"

He kept smiling that smile that had melted her as a young girl. "You won't wake up, not to that other world, anyway. You'll wake up to a whole new world, Abbie."

He reached out his own hand. Abbie stepped closer, touched his fingers, and in that moment she remembered that very first time their hands had touched, when she'd handed him a cup of coffee over her father's campfire. In the next moment his strong hand was folded around her own, and then she was in his arms . . . in Zeke Monroe's arms again! And she knew she would never leave this place. Why would she ever want to? Never had she experienced such a feeling of peace and love.

Abigail Trent Monroe was buried along the creek where the irises bloomed. She'd been found slumped in her old rocker, her Bible and a cup of cold tea beside her. Everyone in the family was there for her burial, and all agreed that the creek's side was the best place for her grave. Sweet Bird was sure enough tears were shed to make that creek overflow.

"She's with him, you know," Margaret spoke up, as

each took a turn at saying something about "Mother"
and "Grandma." "She's with Zeke."

"And Wolf's Blood," a sobbing Jeremy added.

"And Swift Arrow," Hawk said.

"And Lillian," Ellen put in.

"She's happier than she's ever been," LeeAnn wept.

"She's probably watching us right now," Jason said.

"I'll miss her so much," Nathan told them.

"So will we." Zeke put an arm around Georgeanne.

"I've never known anyone like her," Georgeanne
added. "She taught me so much about love and forgiveness."

It was spring, the year nineteen hundred and one.
Birds chirped, and wildflowers bloomed everywhere.
The family formed a huge circle around the grave,
some having to straddle the little creek, there were so
many of them. Jason and Louellen had come back for
the burial ceremony. Abbie had had to be buried before they could travel all the way from Montana, but
Margaret had delayed the ceremony until they arrived.

Hawk stood beside Sweet Bird, holding Laughing
Turtle in his arms. Nine-year-old Little Eagle stood between Hawk and his mother, his lips pursed in sorrow.
He didn't like this strange thing called death that took
people away, yet all these relatives of his had seemed
almost happy for Grandma Abbie. They said she was in
a better place, a happier place. He decided that someday he was going to go there and see her.

They all sang hymns taught them by Abigail Monroe,
songs they knew she'd like sung at her funeral—"In
the Sweet Bye and Bye," "Shall We Gather By the
River." They knew they wept for themselves, for the
void that would be in their lives now that their mother
was gone. None wept for Abbie, because they all knew
she was where she wanted to be. None could under-

stand quite how she had survived the hardships and heartache she'd faced in life, all envied her strength.

"We have that same strength," Jeremy told them. "And so do her grandchildren. Look what Hawk has already been through, and Zeke. I've discovered even I have more strength than I ever thought I possessed. Mother would want us to go on from here, stay together, keep bringing pride to the Monroe name, be there for each other whenever we're needed. We've had to part ways over the years, and we'll have to again. Some of us will go back to Denver, Hawk is going to the Dakotas with Sweet Bird, Jason will go back to Montana. But we'll be together in spirit, just like Mother always said, and she'll be with every one of us. She and"—he hesitated, always finding it difficult to talk about the father he'd abandoned and never seen again before his death, the father he wished he could hold once more and tell of his love for him—"she and Zeke both. Wolf's Blood is with us, too. I have often felt him near me."

They shared some memories, good memories. There was even a little laughter mixed with the tears. Then they all quieted, even the littlest ones, when a shadow moved over them, causing them to look up. An eagle floated above them on the wind, its wings spread grandly. It circled several times, then cried out and flew away.

"Look!" Zeke called then, pointing to the western rise. "It's a wolf, isn't it?"

"In the *day*time?" Nathan commented.

Hawk smiled through tears. "In the daytime." He put an arm around Sweet Bird. "We are not alone. Not today. Not ever."

The eagle disappeared over the rise, and then the wolf gave out one long howl before doing the same. Inside the old cabin the mantel clock stopped ticking.

No amount of winding or repair would ever make it work again.

The late-summer storm rumbled out of the Black Hills, moving over the Wounded Knee gravesite, illuminating the black sky with brilliant flashes of lightning that woke Hawk. A clap of thunder seemed to literally shake the simple frame house he shared with Sweet Bird and the children. Most of the Indians here still lived in tipis. There were few true "white man" homes, but those had all been occupied when he'd arrived. Only this very plain, four-room structure that had been used by a teacher had been left. He'd had little choice but to move into it, and because Little Eagle had refused to be anyplace but where Hawk was, Sweet Bird and the children had moved in with him. Neither the reservation agent nor anyone else seemed to think much of it, since the children were Hawk's brother and sister.

He sat up in bed, listening to the heavy rain let loose outside and hoping the house had no leaks. He intended to build something much nicer for his inherited family. Sweet Bird kept the place neat, and she was a good cook. While she'd lived at the ranch, his grandma Abbie and aunt Margaret had given her lessons in reading and writing, and she'd learned fast. Now Hawk was teaching her more, since she'd never had any schooling in Canada. She seemed determined to learn, and was self-conscious because of his education. He wished he could make her understand it didn't matter to him that she was still learning. But it embarrassed her that he knew so much and she so little.

She dressed as a white woman most of the time now, and she was beautiful. He'd bought her an entire wardrobe in Denver, hoping to make her feel better after so much loss, and with having to bring her to yet another strange place. The fact that she'd been Wolf's Blood's wife had kept both of them from talking about their real dilemma—each other. He wasn't positive how she felt about him, over a year after his father's death, but he knew how he felt about Sweet Bird . . . Elizabeth Monroe. That was the Christian name she'd given the reservation agent. He loved her. He'd probably loved her since he first met her. He simply could never allow himself to acknowledge it. It was all right now, and he knew his father would approve; but he just couldn't bring himself to tell her. Still, it was getting to the point where something had to be said, or when he got his own place built, he would have to leave her here. He could not tolerate living with her any longer, watching her, wanting her, knowing what a wonderful wife she would make.

Sweet Bird was well liked by the other Indian women, and she'd managed to encourage more of them to bring their children to the white doctor, even take them to school, quite an accomplishment on this reservation. The Sioux were suspicious, sullen, uncooperative—at least a lot of them were. Hawk intended to work with them, make them understand their rights, do what he could to keep them out of trouble and help those who did get in trouble. He still had a lot of studying to do regarding land ownership and what he could do to stop encroaching whites from claiming more Indian land.

He felt hot. He stripped off his sleeveless undershirt and left on only his knee-length, light cotton longjohns, but he thought about removing those, too. Another clap of thunder hit, followed by a knock at his bedroom door. He got up, walked over and opened it to see Sweet Bird and the children standing there.

"They are afraid," she told him. "They want to sleep in your bed. Do you mind?"

Hawk shook his head, grinning. "I don't mind. Come on, you two."

Little Eagle and Laughing Turtle ran to his bed, squealing as they climbed into it. Sweet Bird caught sight of Hawk in a flash of lightning, noticed he wore only his longjohns. She did not have to see him well to know how he was built, and she already knew how handsome he was. Lightning flashed again as he walked over to the bed, revealing his slender hips, his muscled back, his long hair hanging loose. Did he know she wanted him now? Did he understand how easy he was to love, just as his father had been? To be held by Hawk was like being held by Wolf's Blood. She ached for her husband, yet at the same time ached for Hawk. She loved him, but was afraid to tell him. Maybe he thought it was too soon for her to speak of such a thing. Nothing had been said between them about the situation, but to have to live so close to him day in and day out, to lie in bed at night knowing he was right in the next room, it was all getting too hard to deal with.

"Come on, Mama," Laughing Turtle told her. "You come sleep with us, too."

Sweet Bird stood unmoving, embarrassed. "It . . . is not right."

"Why, Mama? It's just us and Hawk," Little Eagle told her.

"Yeah, just me and the kids," Hawk said. She could not see his face, but knew there was probably a teasing grin on it. "Come on over here, Sweet Bird. It's all right. We'll keep the kids between us."

Her heart fell at little at the statement. It seemed to tell her he would not be at all bothered by her lying in his bed. She walked over and lay down carefully, clad in only a thin cotton nightgown. The children lay between them, but when lightning lit the room again, she could see Hawk's dark eyes watching her. They each put an arm around one of the children, their hands meeting in the middle of the bed, which was barely big enough for all four of them. When Hawk gently grasped her hand, a heat moved through her that had nothing to do with the weather.

Neither of them spoke. The storm finally subsided, and by then the children were asleep. Hawk got up, picking up Little Eagle. "Let's take them back to their own beds in your room," he said quietly.

Again Sweet Bird supposed he meant to leave her there also, that he had not been thinking what she'd hoped. She picked up Laughing Turtle and followed him into the other room, laying the girl down on a small cot. She covered her daughter and rose, preparing to go to her own bed, but she felt Hawk's hands on her shoulders then.

"Come back with me," he said, running his fingers under the wide straps of her gown and pulling them off her shoulders. Without even a kiss or anything else to see if she minded, he slid the gown down over her arms, her breasts, her waist, letting it drop to the floor. "We've avoided this long enough, Sweet Bird. There is no longer any need. We both know what my father wanted for us, and I know what *I* want for us." He remained behind her, putting his arms around her, pressing powerful forearms against her full breasts. "What do *you* want, Sweet Bird?"

She shivered, tears of both joy and sorrow wanting to come, her whole body crying out to be a woman again. She grasped his powerful biceps, leaning her head against his chest. "I want to be a woman again. I want to feel a man inside of me, and I want that man to be Hawk Monroe."

He needed no more urging. He scooped her up in his arms and carried her to his bed, realizing when he lay her down and heat lightning lit the room that she was completely naked. She'd worn nothing under the gown. He wondered how many nights she had slept that way, perhaps waiting for him to come to her. He removed his longjohns and climbed onto the bed, pulling her into his arms. His mouth found hers, and fire ripped through his veins when she parted her lips in a groaning kiss, her slender fingers moving over his arms and shoulders, into his hair.

He devoured her mouth in a hungry kiss, a man long without a woman. He'd taken little comfort in the few ladies of the night his money had bought him in Denver. A man had to find his pleasure somehow, but there had been no true comfort there. He'd found himself wishing they were Sweet Bird.

Eagerly he left her mouth, acting on all the desires he'd been ignoring too long. He tasted her neck, licked at her chest, moved to her breasts, enjoyed her gasps of ecstasy when his mouth found her swollen nipples. He tasted each breast with passion, cupping it high, pulling at the nipples so that she arched against him in an eagerness to give him more.

Sweet Bird was lost in him. She had wanted this longer than he knew, and at last he had decided it was time. She had been afraid he would never want her this way, but then there had been that kiss at the swimming pond over a year ago, a kiss that had told her his true feelings. Now here she was in Hawk's bed, and this beautiful specimen of a man was kissing and tasting her everywhere, his lips moving over her belly, his tongue flicking at the crevices of her thighs, his long hair tickling her belly and legs. She wondered if a woman could die from pure pleasure. If so, she had not long to live.

He moved between her legs, and she spread them willingly, her breathing coming in quick gasps now as she felt that most secret, wonderful part of man pressing against her thigh, probing her own private places. In the next instant he was inside her, burying his hot shaft deep in her. She cried out with the sheer joy of it, arching up to him to enjoy every inch of him. His rhythmic invasion quickly brought an exploding climax, for she had been too long without this herself, and the excitement was almost painful.

He groaned her name, raising to his knees and lifting her, moving in ways that sent her into ecstasy. She ran her fingers over his powerful arms, relishing the feel of hard muscles and a powerful chest. In the next moment his life poured into her, and he cried out with his own pleasure. He remained rigid for a moment, then breathed deeply, slowly letting his body wilt against her own as he lay down beside her. "I love you, Sweet Bird."

Her eyes teared as she pulled a sheet over herself. "And I love you, Hawk Monroe. It is a good thing we have done. It is right."

He leaned up on one elbow and kissed her tenderly. "We'll go see the preacher tomorrow."

"Is that your way of asking me to marry you?"

He kissed her again, fondling one breast, teasing a nipple. "I guess it is."

She reached up and ran her fingers into his hair again. "Tell me, Hawk. If we have a child, what will he be to your brother and sister?"

Hawk frowned, thinking a moment. "Well, I guess he'd be their nephew."

"And yet they would all have the same mother, so my children would be his aunt and uncle, but also his half brother and sister?"

Hawk thought again, then chuckled. "I guess you're

right." He moved on top of her again. "Us Monroes just like to keep things in the family I guess. How many people can call another both an uncle and a brother?"

Sweet Bird sighed, running her hands over his muscled arms and shoulders again. "I think just brother and sister is best. They will understand when they are older. And I hope you understand there will always be a special place in my heart for Wolf's Blood."

Hawk sobered. "Of course I do. But from now on I will love and cherish you, Sweet Bird. I'll take care of you, just as I promised, but not because my father wanted it that way. I'll do it because I truly love you and want you as a wife. I hope it is the same for you."

She leaned up and kissed his chest. "I would not lie with you because it is what someone else wants. I do it because it is what *I* want. I have seen how other young Indian women look at you. You are very pleasing to the eye, Hawk Monroe. You could have any one of them. I am honored that you have chosen me. I will help you in any way I can with your work here."

He stroked her face with his fingertips. "I have a lot to do. It's going to be a long fight, probably for years, maybe the rest of my lifetime. The Indian struggle is far from over, Sweet Bird."

"I am well aware of that. But you are a Monroe. Fighters, all of you. The government will not like going up against you."

He grinned. "You think so, do you?"

"I know so. You will be speaking for your ancestors. Through you, your grandfather, Zeke, will speak, and your grandmother, Abbie. Through you Swift Arrow will speak, and Wolf's Blood . . . all those who have gone before. You will be their voice."

He kissed her gently. "It makes me happy to think that."

He kissed her again, and her legs parted again, her

body still alive with the want of him. She could feel his magnificent manpart probing at her again, and she knew it was going to be a wonderful thing being the wife of Hawk Monroe.

Joshua walked into the kitchen of his Denver home, placing a stack of paper on the table. "There it is."

LeeAnn turned from trimming a cake. "The book?"

"I finally finished it. Your mother's death seemed to be a sign that I should get busy and get this thing published."

LeeAnn wiped her hands and walked over to touch the manuscript, studying her husband's handwriting. "So much work you've put into this over the years. It must feel good to finally finish."

"It does. Do you want to read it before I send it off?"

"Oh, yes!" She sat down, fingering through the several hundred pages of writing. "I wonder what Mother would think of this. She'd probably be embarrassed to see a whole book written about her life. She'd argue that she hadn't done enough or experienced enough to have a whole book written about her. She never truly understood what an exciting life she led, how important it is to tell others about it." She drew in her breath when he added the cover sheet to the manuscript, showing her the title. She picked it up, staring at it. "Oh, Joshua, how fitting."

He smiled, but his eyes were misty. "I'm glad you think so. I thought about what a savage land this was when she came here, and how she always said it was her destiny to meet Zeke and live here. That's what made me think of the title."

LeeAnn nodded, her own eyes tearing. It was good that many others would know the story of this remarkable woman, her own mother, the small woman with such big shoulders, the woman known to her father only as Abbie-girl.

"Savage Destiny," she read aloud, *"The Life of Abigail Trent Monroe, A True Pioneer."* Yes, it was truly a fitting title.

From the author . . .

I hope that through my SAVAGE DESTINY series you have felt as though you were a part of settling the American West. All my books are based on the excitement and romance of this era, and I hope this story has made you want to read more about this fascinating time in America's history. For more information about me and other books I have written, feel free to send a self-addressed, stamped envelope (letter size, #10, please) to me at 6013 North Coloma Road, Coloma, Michigan 49038-9309. I will send you a newsletter and bookmark. You can also reach me on the Internet at http://www.parrett.net/~bittner. Thank you!

Taylor-made Romance from Zebra Books

WHISPERED KISSES   (0-8217-5454-8, $5.99/$6.99)
Beautiful Texas heiress Laura Leigh Webster never imagined
that her biggest worry on her African safari would be the handsome Jace Elliot, her tour guide. Laura's guardian, Lord Chad-
wick Hamilton, warns her of Jace's dangerous past; she simply
cannot resist the lure of his strong arms and the passion of his
Whispered Kisses.

KISS OF THE NIGHT WIND   (0-8217-5279-0, $5.99/$6.99)
Carrie Sue Strover thought she was leaving trouble behind her
when she deserted her brother's outlaw gang to live her life as
schoolmarm Carolyn Starns. On her journey, her stagecoach
was attacked and she was rescued by handsome T.J. Rogue. T.J.
plots to have Carrie lead him to her brother's cohorts who murdered his family. T.J., however, soon succumbs to the beautiful
runaway's charms and loving caresses.

FORTUNE'S FLAMES   (0-8217-5450-5, $5.99/$6.99)
Impatient to begin her journey back home to New Orleans,
beautiful Maren James was furious when Captain Hawk delayed
the voyage by searching for stowaways. Impatience gave way
to uncontrollable desire once the handsome captain searched
her cabin. He was looking for illegal passengers; what he found
was wild passion with a woman he knew was unlike all those
he had known before!

PASSIONS WILD AND FREE   (0-8217-5275-8, $5.99/$6.99)
After seeing her family and home destroyed by the cruel and
hateful Epson gang, Randee Hollis swore revenge. She knew
she found the perfect man to help her—gunslinger Marsh
Logan. Not only strong and brave, Marsh had the ebony hair
and light blue eyes to make Randee forget her hate and seek
the love and passion that only he could give her.

*Available wherever paperbacks are sold, or order direct from the
Publisher. Send cover price plus 50¢ per copy for mailing and
handling to Penguin USA, P.O. Box 999, c/o Dept. 17109,
Bergenfield, NJ 07621. Residents of New York and Tennessee
must include sales tax. DO NOT SEND CASH.*